# BUTTER HONEY PIG BREAD

# BUTTER HONEY PIG BREAD

## FRANCESCA EKWUYASI

### A NOVEL

ARSENAL PULP PRESS
VANCOUVER

ARSENAL PULP PRESS
Suite 202 – 211 East Georgia St.
Vancouver, BC V6A 1Z6
Canada
*arsenalpulp.com*

The publisher gratefully acknowledges the support of the Canada Council for the Arts and the
British Columbia Arts Council for its publishing program, and the Government of Canada, and the
Government of British Columbia (through the Book Publishing Tax Credit Program), for
its publishing activities.

Arsenal Pulp Press acknowledges the xʷməθkʷəy̓əm (Musqueam), Sḵwx̱wú7mesh (Squamish),
and səl̓ilwətaʔɬ (Tsleil-Waututh) Nations, custodians of the traditional, ancestral, and unceded terri-
tories where our office is located. We pay respect to their histories, traditions, and continuous living
cultures and commit to accountability, respectful relations, and friendship.

This is a work of fiction. Any resemblance of characters to persons either living
or deceased is purely coincidental.

"Ships," words and music by Ikon Ekwuyasi, from the album *Hungry to Live: An Audio
Documentary*, copyright © 2018 Syndik8/Freespirit/Notjustok Distro, all rights reserved,
reprinted by permission of the artist

Cover art by Brianna McCarthy
Cover and text design by Jazmin Welch
Edited by Shirarose Wilensky
Copy edited by Doretta Lau
Proofread by Alison Strobel

Printed and bound in Canada

Library and Archives Canada Cataloguing in Publication:
Title: Butter honey pig bread : a novel / Francesca Ekwuyasi.
Names: Ekwuyasi, Francesca, 1990– author.
Identifiers: Canadiana (print) 2020020646X | Canadiana (ebook) 20200206478 |
    ISBN 9781551528236 (softcover) | ISBN 9781551528243 (HTML)
Classification: LCC PR9387.9.E355 B88 2020 | DDC 823/.92—dc23

*For my grandmother,*
*my brothers,*
*my family by blood and by choice.*

*Pain-eater fast today; starve yourself a while*

# Prologue

WE ARE KIN.

Here at the in-between place, we are one being, eternal, moving in rotation to the flesh realm only because we must. As sure as the tides, as sure as the sunrise, bound to the rhythm of its particular dominion—we must.

"I" is only a temporary and necessary aberration. "I," "Me,"— such a lonely journey! We separate, single out to "I"s and "Me"s, only when we traverse between realms, when we take breath and body. Only because we must.

But we always return to We, you see? Because we must.

We sing reminders to the "I"s. We sing them back home in time. We sing them to a doorway.

Death is only a doorway.

We are Ogbanje.

# 1

# *Butter*

# Kambirinachi

There was a spirit, a child, whose reluctance to be born, and subsequent boredom with life, caused her to come and go between realms as she pleased. Succumbing to the messy ordeal of being birthed, she would traverse to the flesh realm, only to carelessly, suddenly, let go of living like it was an inconvenient load. Death is only a doorway, and her dying was always a simple event; she would merely stop breathing. It was her nature. The dark tales of malevolent spirit children, Ọgbanjes, are twisted and untrue. It was never her intention to cause her mother misery; she was just restless. It was just the way.

The time before her final birth, in an attempt to make her stay, her mother marked her with a red-hot razor blade, just as the Babalawo instructed. Three deep lines at the nape of her neck, below the hairline, smeared with a pungent brown paste that burned and burned. All this so the Ọgbanje would stay bound to its body, and if not, at the very least, she would recognize it should the child choose to be born again.

The child died, of course.

She returned again. And maybe she took pity on the woman, or perhaps she was bored with the foreseeable rhythm of her existence, but this time she chose to stay. And the three horizontal welts on the back of her neck signified to the woman, her mother, that this was the same child. It might have been a coincidence; perhaps the woman's mother-in-law (she'd never liked the woman, found her haughty) marked the child in secret to torment her.

Nevertheless, for Kambirinachi, living was a tumultuous cascade between the unbearable misery of being in this alive body indefinitely and an utter intoxication with the substance, the very matter, of life. When there was peace, life was near blissful, but otherwise, Kambirinachi's childhood was nightmarish for her mother. Ikenna was an exhausted woman, a woman made hard by nearly two decades during which her body betrayed her. Or, as some might put it: almost two decades of being plagued by an Ọgbanje that caused her three late-term miscarriages, one stillbirth, two dead infants, and a dead toddler. She used to be much sweeter, softer, kinder, but it's impossible to go through that particular brand of hell and stay untouched. She couldn't help it; she hated the child a good portion of the time. And the child, too, must have hated her, after making her wait and suffer, only to wail the way she did—unprovoked, inconsolable, and seemingly interminable. To preserve her sanity and, frankly, the child's well-being, Ikenna retreated inside herself, saving all tenderness for her husband, and leaving only a barely concealed indifference for Kambirinachi.

KAMBIRINACHI WAS ELUSIVE. Even if she was sitting right before you, her absence would be palpable. As an eleven-year-old, her attention was always elsewhere.

"Where is Kambirinachi today?" her father often teased, childlike, a broad smile stretched across his bearded face to reveal crooked and tobacco-stained teeth.

Kambirinachi chose that smile to be her anchor when the songs calling her back home were most persistent. One doorway back home was the unfinished borehole in the backyard, covered in flimsy, rotted wooden boards, with an opening just wide enough to swallow her small body and water just deep enough to drown her. Really, anything that would kill her was a doorway. The songs and voices of her Kin were loud loud shouting; it shocked her that nobody else could hear them. They made her accident-prone. The unfortunate thing tripped on stones that weren't there and ended up with broken bones that couldn't entirely be explained. She would go to sleep healthfully robust but wake up with blistering fevers. So she learned to think of her father's smile and to sit still until the voices grew muffled and she could carry on with her adventure of the day.

Any thoughts of the future worked like a loosened tap that let the voices of her Kin rush out in a high-pressure stream, so she also learned not to think too far ahead. She thought of things she liked about being in her alive body: the smell of dust rising from the ground outside when heavy rain struck the earth, the burnt-sugar coconut taste of baba dudu. She thought of things she disliked: the sound of her mother's voice when it was hardened by anger—she was angry often—the fervour in the pastor's voice when he shouted on Sundays—he shouted often—about hellfire, Holy Ghost fire, and God smiting his enemies. She thought backward, about the in-between place before birth and after the hollowing of her body: her home—the place where she could become the things she loved most, where she would join the rays of sunlight and sing sing in sharp tones, high and joyful.

It struck in her a sadness, the pitying kind of sorrow, to know the things that alive bodies could never be.

There were lovely things about being alive, she had to remember, like the taste of guavas. Their existence filled her with so much joy that it burst out of her in gleeful laughter. This is how she ate them:

She found the sharpest knife in the kitchen, hiding it if her mother was near, the woman could shout, eh! She held the blade as far away from her body as her thin arms would allow—because images of her throat, tattered and bloody, flashed through her mind whenever she saw a knife (knives could also be doorways)—and sliced the bumpy emerald skin off, always trying and often failing to make a single long ribbon of the tart rind. After taking delicate bites of the soft pink flesh, shallow bites to leave the grainy seeds undisturbed, until the fruit became a knobby, slimy ball, she would pop the entire thing into her mouth, and spit out the fruit's tiny seeds, one by one, all sucked clean.

KAMBIRINACHI DIDN'T KNOW ABOUT ANY FUTURE—how could she? Even if she struggled past the voices, she couldn't have imagined a future that involved leaving Abeokuta, studying fine arts at a university in

Ife, meeting a person who would want to keep her, or becoming a mother, for that matter.

But before all that, how could she know, that day when she found herself in her father's decrepit Peugeot 504 pickup, that she was being taken to boarding school in Lagos? Queen's College in Yaba. She would be a QC girl. She couldn't dare imagine that far.

So you'll understand her confusion that day, dazed by the sweltering heat—for as long as they'd owned the truck, the A/C had never worked. Her mother sat in the driver's seat in a faded adire iro and buba, talking talking.

"Kambirinachi, you have to behave o! But don't worry, it's a good school. It's far, but not that far, we will visit every two two weeks. Don't cry, biko, it's okay."

But even as her mother said these words, her voice strained against the jagged emotions she attempted to mask by clearing her throat. Kambirinachi let tears fall freely down her face. She looked to her father leaning against the dusty truck window, his weathered face inches from hers, the smell of chewing tobacco on his breath.

"Kambi, my girl, be a big girl now, okay? Ebena akwa nwa m. Don't cry." He smiled despite his sadness.

"See you soon, Papa." Her small voice shook with a question mark. "In two weeks?"

"In two weeks, my darling," he reassured her. "If it weren't for this rubbish car with only two seats, me sef I would be coming with you."

Her mother started the car and a blast of heat filled the bottom of the pickup. Kambirinachi moved her legs to touch the Ghana must go shoved underneath the rusted metal of the passenger seat. Her father had filled it with tins of powdered milk, Milo, Golden Morn, and guavas—eight of them, tied tight in a black polyethylene bag. She watched him wave as the truck pulled out of the compound, watched him grow smaller and smaller as the distance expanded between them, waving all along. She waved back furiously, sobbing quietly.

It wasn't until he was entirely out of sight, until she thought about seeing him again, in two weeks, the future, that the voices started their song again. At first, a single voice, high-pitched and familiar. And then another. More and more, until they were an overlapping riot of noise. Hard and harsh, relentless waves.

*You won't see him again. He will die.*

She clutched her ears; they were inexplicably hot. She cried out through her tears, "No, no, please."

"Ewo, this girl, you've started again. It's okay!" her mother said.

Ikenna wanted to be firmer, but the tremor of the child's voice softened her. She felt warm wetness slide down her plump cheeks, found that she, too, was crying. She wiped her tears with the back of her hand, pretending they were only sweat.

# Taiye

TAIYE AWOKE TO A WARM SLICK OF DARK BLOOD sticking between her lean thighs. Menstrual fluid soaked through her green underwear and made a splotchy maroon map on the orange batik sheets of her bed. In recent mornings, since moving back home to Lagos, she awoke to thoughts of her bees; they lived in an olive-green hive underneath the dappled shade of the palm trees clustered in the backyard. Among the palms, lush bougainvillea cascading over the fence between the neighbour's compound dropped bright pink paper blooms like blessings upon the hive. Taiye had been romanced by the notion of keeping bees since she was a small girl, so the moment the dream was within reach, she seized it and clutched it tight. And learned hard lessons on loving the living.

On that particular morning, her first thoughts were of her sister, Kehinde.

Taiye stretched, breathing in deeply.

On the exhale, she whispered, "May I be safe," and hoped that her words would fall upon open ears. Kehinde was coming home with her husband. Taiye hadn't met him yet. She hadn't seen her sister in a long time.

"May I have peace."

She peeled off her damp underwear, pulled the stained sheets off the bed, and threw them in a pile at the corner of the bathroom. With a wet washcloth she wiped crusty streaks of drying blood from her thighs, and then inserted a silicone menstrual cup, discoloured to a light brown from many years of use, to catch her period as it left her body.

With her footsteps muffled by the plush emerald carpet of the hallway, she walked toward her mother's bedroom. The heavy wooden door squeaked in its tired frame when Taiye slowly pushed it open. Her mother, a soft lump underneath white sheets, was illuminated by slits of light escaping past heavy red curtains into the otherwise dark room. She listened for gentle snores and shut the door quietly behind her.

"May I have joy."

Early in the morning the house existed in a quiet hush, a spell destined to break moments after a power outage, when the generator would roar electronics back to life. Taiye liked quiet. She wondered if, and how much, it would change when Kehinde and Farouq arrived.

When she'd arrived almost a year ago with intentions to stay, she found the house in a sort of passive disarray. Thick cobwebs hung in dirty grey clusters in every corner. A layer of dust had settled in and covered all the surfaces. Really, the house seemed untouched, as if no one lived there. Hot rage shot through Taiye's travel-worn body at the sight of the place, because she'd paid a housekeeper to clean and cook for her mother. And when she saw her mother, saw how prominently the delicate bones of her clavicles pushed so taut against sallow skin, saw her sunken cheeks and the utter joy that brightened her face when Taiye appeared, she choked on the gasp that threatened to escape her throat. She'd embraced her mother, and then marched to the kitchen, where the plump housekeeper was eating a large portion of amala and chicken stew. Taiye said, "Please finish your food. I'll pay you for next month, but you have to leave today."

Afterward, before unpacking, Taiye had tasted egusi soup from a pot in the fridge and found it flavourless and void of feeling. She threw it out and made a tomato stew with azu eke, smoked mackerel. She served it with boiled yam to her mother, who devoured the whole thing and licked the plate clean.

Now, walking down the stairs, Taiye was careful not to step on the cat, Coca-Cola; the ancient and volatile black thing slept curled up in the corners where the spiral steps changed directions. The cat moved out of the way and trailed behind Taiye into the kitchen.

"May I be healthy."

Although it was still a soft whisper, Taiye's voice filled the high-ceilinged kitchen. She filled a fire-blackened stainless-steel kettle with tap water and placed it on the gas stove. As she sat by the window, she let the cat curl up in her lap, and they waited for the water to boil.

A shrill beep from her phone told her that an email awaited. Even before reading it, Taiye knew she wouldn't reply.

Subject: I'm Sorry
Banke Martins <b.martins@sau.edu>
April 23, 2017, 7:43 AM
To <t.adejide@qmail.com>

Taiye, I know it's been a while, but your phone is still disconnected, and you haven't answered any of my previous emails. I'm really sorry about the letters, can we please talk? I heard that you had to go home. Something about your mother. How is she? Please write back.

Banke

Taiye rolled her eyes and put her phone down. Banke was a former lover, a flash in the pan. A mistake. The heat of Taiye's anger had fizzled out, and in its place was utter disinterest.

As a detour from the undesirable path down which her mind wanted to wander, Taiye abruptly decided that she would make a cake to celebrate Kehinde's homecoming. And jollof rice with smoked fish, curried chicken, and soft-boiled eggs.

"A feast," Taiye said, and lifted Coca-Cola's soft body from her lap to the cold tiled floor.

She made a cup of Lipton tea with condensed milk and honey—the first offerings from her beloved hive. She fished a foil-wrapped block of butter out of the overstuffed freezer to let it thaw on the counter by the open window. Then, she listened for the low humming of her bees.

This is how you make a salted caramel chocolate cake for your twin sister whom you haven't seen in ... God, a long time. In hopes that you avoid talking about the things you haven't been talking about and just eat in silence. For the batter, you will need as much butter as you can manage without leaving your cake too dense and greasy. Taiye would die in pure bliss if she were to drown in a tub of good butter, so she used plenty. You should use a little over two cups of all-purpose flour, three quarters of a cup of unsweetened cocoa powder—preferably fair trade; no need to have the exploited labour of children on your hands just for chocolate—a teaspoon and a half of baking powder, a quarter teaspoon of baking soda, a half teaspoon of salt, and three large eggs. You may add a cup of sugar, but Taiye used a cup of honey instead. And finally, some vanilla extract.

In place of buttercream frosting, Taiye made honey caramel to pour over the cake.

She lit the gas oven and turned the dial to 325 degrees. Some minutes crept by before the pungent odour of burning fish drew Taiye out of a reverie. Like her mother, she was prone to daydreaming and had forgotten a newspaper-lined tray of smoked mackerel in the oven the previous night. In a rush to take it out, she burned her hands on the metal tray and dropped it with a loud clank on the floor tiles, startling Coca-Cola, who jumped and darted out of the kitchen in a blur of black fur. At the sink, she ran cold water over her burned fingers. It wasn't too bad. Smirking at the memory, she recalled a previous lover who had cooed and treated her like a fragile thing. An anxious woman who was always so concerned for Taiye's well-being, she'd treated every scrape or bruise like it were life-threatening.

"You know, I think I'll survive," Taiye would tease her. "I might just pull through this time."

She picked up the hot tray, hands now protected by a tattered dishrag, and put it on the counter. Then she wrapped the pieces of dried fish in sheets of old newspaper from the towering stack on the floor beside the fridge, tied it all together in a black plastic bag, and tossed the whole thing in the deep-freeze. She washed the fish smell off her hands and began whisking butter, eggs, honey, and vanilla extract in a large red ceramic bowl. She let Coca-Cola lick some of the sweet mixture off her fingers when the cat slunk back into the kitchen. Taiye poured in the dry ingredients and divided the batter among three springform pans. The smell of burnt fish wafted into her face when she opened the oven door. She supposed the cake would have a bit of a fishy flavour. Fishcake.

For the caramel, Taiye poured dark golden honey, corn syrup, and water into a saucepan before bringing it to a boil. She moved swiftly between the pan of browning caramel and a double boiler fashioned out of a stainless-steel pot and an orange ceramic bowl filled with chunks of milk chocolate. The bowl just barely fit over the pan, so Taiye had to be careful not to burn her hands on the steam shooting out in livid spurts whenever she moved it. She let the caramel cook down to a deep amber that brought to mind baba dudu—burnt sugar and coconut milk sweets their nanny, Sister Bisi, rewarded them for good behaviour when they were small. Taiye poured some condensed milk into the caramel, whisking until the mixture was near silken, and then added the glossy chocolate. She balanced the bowl in the freezer to cool.

WHILE THE CAKES BAKED, TAIYE BATHED. On her way to the bathroom, she tiptoed to her mother's bedroom door to check on her again. Still asleep.

"Are you my shadow today?" she asked Coca-Cola, who trailed behind her.

She undressed, and the cat promptly lunged atop her clothes and blinked languidly at her. Taiye turned on the hot water, but it trickled out cold, so she let it run until it was tepid—as warm as it was going to get. She let it slowly fill the purple plastic basin, and then entered the tub bottom first, leaving her feet to dangle over the side. She flicked water at the cat, who flinched and widened her eyes before meowing a loud accusation. With a small blue plastic bowl, Taiye poured the lukewarm water from the basin over herself before she remembered the half-full bottle of Dettol sitting on the windowsill next to some liquid black soap that her mother had made. She lifted herself out of the tub, sat on its edge with her back to the cat, and stirred two capfuls of the pungent yellow-brown antiseptic liquid into the basin of water. Then she poured some black soap into her palm and rubbed until the grainy black liquid turned into a slippery white lather. Still seated on the edge of the tub, she rubbed soap into her skin, up her arms and shoulders. She stopped at her chest, her small breasts. Quite suddenly, there was a swell of want in her lower belly.

Perhaps in your life you've come across a force that matched and moved you. Maybe it changed you so profoundly that when you look back at the landscape of your life, you are struck by the indelible the mark it left. For Taiye, that force was a woman named Salomé.

Sometimes, though less and less often with the more time that passed between them, Taiye would become overwhelmed by a thorough thirst for Salomé. To be in her presence, to hear her voice, to be touched by her. Taiye touched her own self, firm and slow. She traced light circles around her dark nipples. Let her hands slide over her belly, across her hips. Traced the lines and dots tattooed on her left hip, zodiac constellations marking the birth months of the people she chose to love, spreading like geometric veins growing around her buttock and up her side. She moved her fingers between her legs, with thoughts of Salomé swirling on the brim of her mind. Salomé's smell, the dark bronze ochre of her skin, her warmth.

Coca-Cola meowed, and Taiye stopped.

"You're right," she said.

It was no use, no good. Her memories turned on her. She winced at flashes of Salomé's crying face and bloodshot eyes, her nose running.

Taiye pulled down her blue net sponge from where it hung on a hook by the frosted glass window, scrubbed her body quickly, and rinsed. She left the bathroom, but the longing never left her.

BY THE TIME TAIYE HAD RUBBED OIL INTO HER SKIN and pulled on a long-sleeved linen kaftan, the cakes were done, and her mother was awake. Taiye found Kambirinachi sitting on the kitchen counter, with a vacant smile on her face as she stirred milk into a white mug filled with hot cocoa. Coca-Cola was on the floor, batting at her swinging legs.

"Mami, good morning." Taiye smiled and kissed her mother's warm forehead.

"Good morning, my love." Kambirinachi beamed up at her daughter as she received her kiss.

"How did you sleep?" Taiye asked, removing the cakes from the oven. She placed them one by one on a tray and put them safely on top of the fridge, away from the cat.

"Dreamlessly," Kambirinachi responded. "And you, my love?"

"Fitfully."

"Oh, darling! What's bothering you?"

Taiye shrugged, and then she smiled. "I'm making a triple-layer cake." She made her eyebrows jump up and down. "Chocolate caramel."

"Yes!" Kambirinachi clapped and squealed. "Let the deliciousness commence!"

Taiye made them a breakfast of fried plantains and eggs scrambled with onions, tomatoes, and peppers. They ate on a blue striped aso oke on the carpeted floor of the parlour.

"What time does your sister's flight come in?" Kambirinachi asked, mid-chew.

"Twelve."

"Uh-oh, cutting it close, are we?"

"It's only after eight," Taiye said. "I'll finish making the cake and go."

"Will you drive?"

"No, I organized with the car hire guy yesterday. He'll pick me up."

"Okay." Kambirinachi smiled wide. "We'll finally get to meet your brother-in-law!"

"Yeah, it's about time."

"What are you thinking?"

"Nothing." Taiye shook her head. "I'm going to make jollof rice." She knew that her mother knew she was being less than honest.

The ceiling fan whirred loud, spinning sluggishly, as if protesting the low power with which it was fed, half-heartedly stirring the heavy air around them. Taiye thought she should ask the gateman to turn on the generator so they could use the A/C when Kehinde and Farouq arrived.

TAIYE FETCHED THE COOLED CAKES from the top of the refrigerator and placed them on the counter by the window looking out into the backyard. Taiye had painstakingly cleared the overgrown mess. She'd spent many many hours on her knees, under a fierce and boastful sun, tension pouring out of her pores in pools of sweat, as she pulled weeds from the hard, clayey soil. She'd wanted a garden, alive with tomatoes, basil, and spinach, but she needed better soil.

She built the frame of a Langstroth hive—a vertical beehive—with salvaged wood from discarded furniture and a manual she'd printed off the first website that showed up in her search. The idea of keeping bees, with gorgeous raw honey as a reward, filled her with a delicate kind of optimism, a tender, pearlescent sort of threshold to joy. She'd thrown herself into home beekeeping; it only took eight months and many fuck-ups, but she'd achieved a considerable healthy hive. The garden, however, remained mostly bare but for tufts of parched grass and purple heart vines that wandered out of their pots by the fence and encroached on her garden beds.

Taiye retrieved the chocolate caramel from the freezer and beat the thick mixture until beads of sweat formed along her hairline and rolled down, tickling the sides of her face. Until the caramel was just stiff enough to be spread without oozing down the sides of the cake. She iced the three layers with a large butter knife and assembled the dessert. Cake, caramel, a sprinkle of salt. Cake, caramel, a sprinkle of salt. Cake, caramel, a sprinkle of salt. She spread the rest of the caramel on the sides of the cake, and then she licked the bowl clean before leaving for the airport.

# Kehinde

EXHAUSTION SHOULD BE STILL, spent, gently beckoning sleep—or better yet, just clocking out. Instead, it is churning inside me with unwelcome vigour. I know, I know, it is more than fatigue that is tugging at me.

The flight from Montreal to Lagos felt incredibly long. Stretched out even longer by the nine-and-a-half-hour layover in Frankfurt. Now I smell foul, like rotten onions or rotten eggs. Just general rot. And there's this sharp throbbing in my temples that won't go away, even though I've eaten a fistful of ibuprofen. I am not prepared for this, not prepared to see my sister, or our mother, for that matter. So much has gone unsaid for so long between us, Taiye and me, and Mami. We've been biting our tongues as if our silences will save us or freeze us in a time that required nothing more than just *being*. Together. More truthfully, I've been biting *my* tongue. Taiye tried, ever long-suffering. But even she gave up after enough time. Throughout our separation, daily calls turned biweekly, turned weekly, and then turned monthly. Eventually, the phone calls turned to monthly emails, turned to a letter now and then, turned to silence. Not that I blame her; I barely responded, and never honestly, and she knew.

We haven't spoken properly in a very long time. Shit.

And there's the box of letters.

Almost a year ago now Taiye sent me an orange shoebox filled with about ninety letters. Some date back as far as eleven years ago. Some are in sealed envelopes, some are on the backs of receipts and flyers, and others are folded pieces of loose-leaf paper. All handwritten. Her hand-writing is the same as always: big looping lines and rounded letters. I started out by reading them slowly, one every few weeks. I haven't gotten very far, and still, I feel apprehensive about delving into them.

The plane landed at noon Lagos time, and Taiye said she would collect us. After the slow wait for bags, and the even slower move through
customs, I spot her among throngs of sweaty, expectant faces at Arrivals.
Hers is my face, only narrower, peeking from between thin waist-length
braids. Her skin is darker than I remember, burnt umber, shiny with oil
and perspiration. I wave frantically to catch her attention, and her lips
stretch into a smile that slightly calms the rapid thrumming in my chest.
We tumble forward and catch each other in a fierce embrace. Her slim
arms wind tightly around me. Her lean body is soft and hot against my
own, and she has the same cocoa butter smell I remember. She pulls
away, just as many smothered emotions begin to well up in my chest, so
I cough to regain composure.

"Look at you," Taiye says, and steps back. "You're here."

I'm here.

"And Farouq." I pull at his arm. "He's here, too."

"I gathered." She smiles. "You exist after all," Taiye says, and hugs him.

The patch of sweat darkening the back of his grey T-shirt grows. The
heat is thick.

"It's good to finally meet you," Taiye adds, looking him square in the
face, no smile. I can sense Farouq's uncertainty, but she means it. Intense
and earnest as always.

"Likewise," he responds, and looks at her with some type of restrained
awe.

Taiye and I, we are identical. Almost. She's always been thinner than
me, even though as a child she ate and ate, everything, often. And she has
this lure that draws people to her orbit; I don't understand it. Our mother
is the same. I am not jealous (anymore), and I am not worried—but only
because I know where Taiye's desires lie in that regard. I don't want to
feel threatened, because I trust Farouq. I *do* trust Farouq, but despite
himself, he's just a man.

We walk outside to find that the sky is too open; the sun pours down
ferociously. Jesus Christ, I need ice water. I watch Farouq struggle to
breathe in the humidity. The heat immediately coats him in a film of

sweat that beads and rolls off his face and neck, catching in the beard he's stubbornly refused to shave for weeks. I watch him decline help from the car hire driver and heave our suitcases into the boot of the silver Camry. It's surreal to have him here; jarring to see him next to Taiye. Who is this man? Brown in Canada, oyimbo in Lagos. What is he doing here? And with me? I don't want to think of my luck and spoil it.

Farouq. He says he loves me, he marries me, he travels to Lagos with me, and I'm terrified. The first time we touched it was innocent enough; his arm brushed my bare shoulder when he reached past me to collect a salted caramel cone from the ice cream man. It was a hot day; it was our first date. His arm brushed my shoulder, and it seared. I felt a swell and a rush inside my belly. I grabbed the hem of his T-shirt to keep him close to me, and I thought fiercely: *Kiss me, kiss me*. The way he looked at me eh, the way he looked at me. He didn't kiss me then.

On our second date, in response to a dry joke I made about godlessness becoming his undoing, he said, "I'm petrified of God. I just don't know that religion will save me from Her inevitable wrath." He identified as a "spiritually open agnostic." At this, all my years of Catholic indoctrination rushed to the surface. I had to stop short of shouting, "Lake of fire!"

Perhaps it's God's wrath that comes down in harsh rays to burn us now. I'm grateful for the air conditioning in the car. I am also thankful not to be alone with Taiye yet.

"I like your hair like that," she says. "It suits you."

Instinctively, I reach my hand to touch my hair, the only feature of mine in which I fail to find fault. It is dyed a light brown that is almost orange, and I have it in loose twists that frame my face and graze my shoulders.

"Thank you." I smile.

"How was the flight?" she asks, looking at Farouq, who has been staring out the window and trying to make sense of the voracious beast that is Lagos.

"It was good, thanks," he says, lifting his round wire-rimmed glasses to rub his eyes, bloodshot with exhaustion. "We had a long layover in

Frankfurt, but it wasn't too bad. Well, except for the shitty company." He jerks his head in my direction, and I flick his arm.

"He thought the cabin crew were especially rude on the flight to Lagos."

Taiye's eyes widen and her eyebrows shoot up. "Right? So you noticed, yeah?"

Her voice is my voice, husky and dulcet at once. But hers has a sweeter lilt, and when she speaks to Farouq, she enunciates her words and clips them like our cousins in London.

They go on about the shitty treatment that Nigerians receive on international flights, and I close my eyes and let myself sink into the cold leather seat.

WE'VE JUST GONE OVER THIRD MAINLAND BRIDGE and are on the Island. The driver takes us into the neighbourhood that is so familiar; the fences are still as high as ever and topped with razor-edged rolls of barbed wire or taut strands of electrical cords. Here, the road is conspicuously void of hawkers, thin children with meticulously piled pyramids of guguru and epa or Agege bread or glass boxes of fist-sized puff-puff balanced on their heads; they'd swarmed the car in the standstill traffic on the mainland. Their sweaty, sun-battered faces and dirty clothes slapped me with shame at how easy my life has been, despite my many woes. In Lagos, there is no bubble thick enough to protect you from the truth of your privilege or your disadvantage; you see it everywhere, every day. Culture is a way of life. I learned that in social studies in primary four, when Taiye and I sat beside each other and would scream and thrash if the teachers tried to separate us. What's our culture? I feel far removed. Untethered. Alone in my head. Alone in a way that is separate from Farouq. I think what I'm trying to say is that I'm embarrassed at how affected I feel by the children selling snacks on the road, mortified that I've been privileged enough to forget.

We drive into the compound, with its towering fences, just as high as everyone else's. I am foolishly surprised that I do not recognize the gateman who drags the heavy metal gates open.

"Where is Mr Suleiman?" I ask Taiye.

"He left a while ago." She shrugs. "I'm not really sure. This guy's name is Hassan."

The house stands three storeys tall. There is a wide balcony jutting out from the master bedroom on the second floor and two narrow ones on the third floor, like bulging square eyes and a straight line for a contemptuous mouth. The house rises above a bungalow used for storage and the security post. Swaying palm trees surround it, so many of them. And mango and pawpaw trees and plantain palms cluster behind it. It's a large compound, a large house; I expected that being back as an adult, everything would seem smaller and less enchanting. The thrumming in my chest proves me wrong.

Our mother is waiting at the doorway, dwarfed by the comically oversized door frame that eats up most of the front wall of the first floor. Her hands are clasped in front of her. She's beaming, rounder than I've ever seen her, round in her cheeks and her belly, and I think it is good because she is glowing. She is wearing an adire bubu with a wide neckline that slips off her shoulder.

We are in each other's arms before I can decide how I feel. We are holding each other tightly, and I don't realize it at first, but I am sobbing into the warmth of her perfumed neck.

"What's going on with your hair?" she asks, as she pulls away from me.

I laugh and say, "Mami, this is Farouq."

"Ehen, so this is the reason you haven't come home since abi?" She clasps his face between her small palms, studying him after he plants kisses on both her cheeks.

"I hope the heat doesn't kill you with this bush on your face," she says to him, and to me, she teases, "He's handsome sha, even though he is oyimbo."

Farouq laughs and says, "It is a pleasure to finally meet you, ma."

"Oya, you people, go and settle. Your sister and I will finish cooking."

I am relieved that she seems lucid, and I choose not to be alarmed by the desperate thing flickering in her eyes. It is so subtle, but I recognize it well.

TAIYE AND ME, our bedrooms are next to each other on the third floor. Mine is a large room with a twin bed covered in brightly coloured tie-dye linens tucked in the corner farthest from the door. The polished wood vanity with an ornately framed four-foot mirror sits across the room from the bed exactly how I left it. On it are my old things: tubes of sticky fruit-flavoured lip gloss, stacks of *Vogue* and *Time*, half-empty bottles of nail polish—their shimmering contents long dried—and a tattered French-English dictionary, my initials written on its spine in thick black marker. On the floor, against the wooden base of the vanity, are stacks and stacks of books: novels and poetry collections; a mixture of secondary school–assigned literature by Buchi Emecheta, Flora Nwapa, Cyprian Ekwensi, Ama Ata Aidoo, Chinua Achebe, Ayi Kwei Armah, and Wole Soyinka; and books that sixteen-year-old me read voluntarily, like *Harry Potter* and *Purple Hibiscus* and *The Sisterhood of the Traveling Pants*. They are covered in a uniformly thin layer of dust. I devoured these books; every single one of them drew me in with its words until I was so deep in each world that any ending seemed too abrupt, and I would just sit with the closed book on my lap, the characters like old friends to whom I had just said good night. I would have to wait a while for the lingering aroma of one story to fade from my mind before diving into another.

I don't think my things have been touched at all since I left. The floors have been swept, the bed made, and the worn red rugs that used to cover the white tile floors replaced with these woven multicoloured square ones, but aside from that nothing has changed. The framed posters of Bob Marley and Fela Kuti still hang above the headboard, and they rattle against the wall when Farouq throws himself onto the bed and moans into the pillow.

"Finally, finally," he says. Then he looks at me with heavy-lidded eyes and asks, "Sleep or food?"

I laugh because I know that he will fall asleep before he chooses, but I suppose that is a choice. I open the windows and the sliding glass door leading out to the narrow balcony, and by the time I turn around he is asleep, with his hands tucked under the pillow and his feet hanging off the side of the bed. When I slip off his shoes and remove his socks, he stirs and mumbles something about being ticklish.

WHEN HE WAS FOURTEEN, Farouq left his mother's tired one-bedroom flat in Aulnay-sous-Bois. She sent him to live in the fifteenth arrondissement with his father, a man she had fallen in love with during her first summer in Paris, a man whose last name Farouq bore but whom he barely knew.

The story goes that his mother, only a few months off a cramped flight from Tangier, met his father at her uncle's café near Parc de Belleville in the twentieth arrondissement. An anti-xenophobia rally had been organized in the dimly lit tea shop. He was slightly older, a thin baby-faced activist with reluctant patches of wiry reddish hair on his face. It was a poor excuse for facial hair, but she found it adorable. She looked at him for a long time and found him beautiful. So beautiful, in fact, that later during the same week, when they were alone in the small flat he shared with two other men, she slipped off her emerald-green hijab, unpinned her thick henna-reddened curls, and let them tumble softly down her round shoulders, so that he could see that she was beautiful, too.

Because her family was devoutly Muslim, they asked her not to see him. Because she was strong-willed and in love—or merely intoxicated by the idea that someone she wanted also wanted her—she saw him anyway. After many secret evenings full of ripe fruit, music, and cheap wine, she became pregnant. I can only imagine the fear that must have gripped her gut when she found out, how difficult it must have been to come clean to her family. She was only nineteen years old. They never married, and apparently, Farouq's father outgrew his activism and settled back into his life as an upper-middle-class white boy.

Farouq traces his interest in racialization and critical race studies to his fifteenth birthday—the year he moved in with his father, who ceaselessly tried to hammer whiteness into him. He couldn't be Farouq and Étienne—the name his father had chosen for him. He had to be one or the other. Maghrebian or French—that is, white. His obsession is the force behind his doctoral research. Three months ago it took him back to

Paris, where he spent weeks holed up in the special collections reading room of the Sorbonne Library, wielding his keen intellect in an attempt to sort out the angst that his family stirs up in him. He Skyped me at four a.m. once, drunkenly ranting about growing up Moroccan in Paris without ever having been to Morocco: the absurdity of the prejudice he endured, the fucked-up way that white supremacy slyly slips a chip on your shoulder, only to turn around and innocently question its position there. A few times, he moved into French and spoke too quickly for me to follow, pausing and smiling sweetly at my interjection of "English, please." This, his obsession, brought him here with me, as part of an agreement we half-jokingly made between glasses of wine on his thirty-sixth birthday: he comes to Lagos with me now, and I'll go to Tangier with him in a few weeks.

I watch Farouq's chest rise and fall in tune with his audible breath, his snores in ragged inhales and silent exhales. Let me tell you a secret: sometimes I scheme, I keep myself scarce from Farouq, but only to stoke his longing. No other reason, I swear. My mother, in dramatically different ways, kept herself scarce from my father, and I have never seen any human being adore another as thoroughly as my father did my mother. I want that so bad, you don't know.

AFTER A QUICK BATH I DRESS AS QUIETLY AS I CAN, walking on the tips of my toes so that I don't disturb Farouq, who has twisted his body into a shape that will undoubtedly leave him hurting when he wakes. I am incredibly tired, but I want to stay awake until nighttime and counter any jet lag. I put on a baggy white T-shirt over shorts and walk past Taiye's room on my way downstairs. I look inside to see two open suitcases with clothes spilling out of them onto the white tiled floor. There is a crumpled orange towel on the red and blue paisley rug at the foot of her bed. She is still so messy. She's been home for months and doesn't seem to have fully unpacked.

A delicious aroma floats up the stairs and pierces the air around me. Downstairs, besides the sizzle and sigh of wet food on heat, the only sound in the kitchen is a melody that our mother is humming. I don't recognize it.

Taiye is at the stove pouring cooked white rice out of a bright green plastic colander into a large stainless-steel pot of bubbling stew.

She looks at me with a smile. "How far?"

"I dey, I bathed, and Farouq is asleep."

Sitting on the counter by the window, our mother looks me up and down, her smile sweet. "My darling, how are you?" she asks. Before I can answer, she adds, "Your sister is preparing a feast—there's even cake!"

"Nice! What kind?"

"Chocolate," our mother says.

"And salted caramel," Taiye adds.

"Fancy," I say.

"Is Farouq allergic to anything, or like, is there stuff that he won't eat?" Taiye asks, a wooden spoon stained dark red in her right hand, her head cocked to the left.

"At all," I scoff. "He eats everything."

Taiye nods.

"I want to help. What can I do?" I ask.

"Uhhh." Taiye absentmindedly rubs her thumb over the finger-length scar that runs from the indent of her right dimple to the faint cleft of her chin. "Yeah, you can fry some plantains." She gestures toward a red plastic basket sitting on top of the fridge.

"Sounds good." I reach up to collect the basket, inside of which are half a dozen large plantains that have ripened to near complete blackness.

"Actually," Taiye says, her eyebrows shooting up in excitement, "we can make mosa!"

"Mosa!"

# Kambirinachi

QUEEN'S COLLEGE IS AN ALL-GIRLS SECONDARY SCHOOL IN YABA, Lagos
Mainland. Kambirinachi hadn't visited Lagos in her present incarnation,
but she remembered it vividly. She had seen it many times. One time
before before, she borrowed the body of a taut and agile dancer at Fela's
Shrine in Ikeja. She longed to feel the thing that made bodies move so
exquisitely, with such blissful urgency. Feet stomping, hips swinging,
waist and ankle beads jiggling and clashing against each other, trans-
forming the dancers into human shekere, percussion in time with the
musicians' cries, chest and body undulating in rhythm to Fela's instru-
ments. It had been quite the time.

Now, she was in Lagos again but confined to the school compound
(confined to a breathing body that required sustenance and upkeep in
fastidious ways that she had not anticipated, particularly now that neither
of her parents were present to scold her).

Kambirinachi had cried until she fell asleep as her mother drove
her along the dilapidated Lagos-Ibadan Expressway. She'd woken up to
the creaky grumble of the pickup's engine and the sound of her mother
chewing roasted groundnuts from a cone of newspaper nestled in the
folds of fabric on her lap.

"Kambi," her mother had said. "You've woken? We've almost reached."
Ikenna handed the half-full cone of nuts to Kambirinachi. "Take."

"Thank you, Ma," Kambirinachi said.

She repeated it when her mother dropped her off at her aunt's two-
bedroom flat in the dusty staff quarters of the school campus. Ikenna
gave her a small wad of faded green twenty-naira notes.

"Keep it well o," she said, voice stern, eyes soft. "Don't let anybody steal
it or push you up and down, okay?"

"Yes, Ma," Kambirinachi said, but Ikenna was worried. Kambirinachi was so small for her age. *Chineke!* she thought. *So small and so strange. These other girls will eat her alive!*

She turned to her sister, Anuli, who leaned against the pickup with a pitying smile curving her plump black-lined lips. Ikenna's expression asked if she was doing the right thing.

Anuli nodded slowly. "Nwanne mu nwanyi enyela onwe gi nsogbu. She's with me. Don't worry, eh?"

Kambirinachi looked unblinking at her mother's face, until tears spilled out of her eyes. She tried her very best not to think about the next time she would see her, lest the voices of her Kin return to drown her.

She asked, "You will come in two weeks?"

"Yes, Kambi, me and Papa will come in two weeks."

THAT WAS A MONTH AGO. Her parents hadn't visited in two weeks like they'd promised, but they had phoned Aunty Anuli to say they would be there that coming weekend, on Visiting Day. It was a difficult thing to refrain from thinking about the future, especially when the present was so ... tedious. Kambirinachi found it tiresome, navigating the social landscape of secondary school, while also trying to understand advanced math and memorize the periodic table. Kambirinachi excelled in part because of her ability to tip herself over like a cup of water and become absorbed in any given moment, but mostly because of her deep terror of the voices. She had already earned a reputation as an efiko, a nerd. She had heard what some of the other girls whispered about each other, the causticity of their words. She did not want to be on the receiving end of that, so she kept her madness, her magic, quiet. So quiet that it was painful.

She was in Dan Fodio House, named for Sultan Usman Dan Fodio of Sokoto. Kambirinachi knew of Dan Fodio from before before. She'd played with his dazzling Fulani Muses—most Muses are dazzling; that is how they inspire. They shared stories of his sheer brilliance, throwing around the term "revolution" quite a bit, but Kambirinachi was preoccupied with his poetry. She started to remember, she laughed about it quietly, and then she stopped, for fear that she would incite a visit from the Muses, her old friends. It had been too long now, and they might condemn her choice to live out this fragile human life. No, they certainly would; it was an unnatural thing.

The thing she loved, the thing she knew would help her manage the waves of tedium interspersed with the angsty melodrama and cruelty of teenage girls, was art class. And Mr Obasa, the junior school art teacher. Kambirinachi patiently sat through forty-five minutes of art history and theory so that she could unleash her mind in the half hour of drawing practice. In still life, she would follow Mr Obasa's instructions: "Draw what is in front of you."

It took several classes for Kambirinachi to remember that the things she saw in front of her were not always apparent to others. Not everyone could see the rot before the rot, growing in small scaly patches around the large green and yellow mangoes arranged on the fabric-draped stool. That kind of decay told Kambirinachi that the person who picked the fruit, whoever they were, had a head full of ill intention. But Mr Obasa appreciated her "imagination." He was impressed by her talent. Only eleven and she had a distinct style, somewhat bizarre and vaguely disturbing but distinct, nonetheless.

AUNTY ANULI LIVED IN A SMALL TWO-BEDROOM FLAT on the ground floor of one of the several bedraggled five-storey blocks of flats in the school staff quarters. She lived with her husband, Ugo, and their six-year-old son, Junior. The three of them slept on the queen bed in the master bedroom, and they used the second room to store all the foodstuffs that overflowed from the kitchen cabinets, some old furniture, and a navy blue and red portmanteau filled with sequined George wrappers and embroidered silks from their wedding a decade ago. The day before Kambirinachi's arrival, Aunty Anuli asked Ugo to cram as much of their things as possible into the cluttered closets and stack the rest against the wall to make room for the new twin mattress she had bought for her strange niece.

Kambirinachi was grateful to be sleeping at Aunty Anuli's place instead of boarding on the other side of campus, where if you weren't claimed by a senior student as a school daughter, you could be awoken before everything alive in the world to fetch bucket after bucket of water for the seniors in your dormitory. Kambirinachi still had to fetch water some mornings, when there was no power for the water pumps. Three full buckets: one for the kitchen, one for Junior, and one for herself. She was slow, but Aunty Anuli never complained.

The thing is that Anuli was afraid of the girl. Even though Ikenna had stopped referring to the child as an Ọgbanje, Anuli could not surrender the thought. She was a pious woman, insisting that her husband and son join her at the crack of dawn in prayer and devotion. On the second or third morning of prayer, she caught Kambirinachi with a vacant look in her wide-open eyes, mumbling something indecipherable under her breath. Maybe she was only praying, but Anuli found it unnerving and decided it was best to leave the girl alone. Best not to anger the thing.

Kambirinachi let the month blur by so that when Visiting Day arrived, she burst with joy at the sight of her father's face and threw herself into his arms. For Ikenna, the distance had made her fonder of her strange child. Kambirinachi tried to commit every single detail of the visit to her knotty, mosaicked memory, so that when the day was over, when her parents had driven back to Abeokuta, and the fear started to slither into her mind, beckoning the voices to join in, she could go back and savour a particular moment. Like sitting in the pickup, on her father's bony lap, her mother smiling, and the taste of Mr Bigg's fried rice and chicken in her mouth.

# Taiye

HOME FROM THE AIRPORT, Taiye retreated to the kitchen to let Mami, Kehinde, and Farouq embrace. Things felt a bit tense, a bit like all the sweetness was a trick, and a rage would rise up soon enough. Though their mother's rage hadn't reared its head since Taiye had been home.

In the kitchen, Taiye checked on the browned pieces of curried chicken roasting on a tray in the oven. Realizing she'd forgotten to stop by the Falomo market to buy tinned tomatoes, she decided to make do with whatever was in the cupboard: maybe palm oil, maybe crayfish, maybe some efirin. Perfect for native jollof, actually.

Rummaging through the cupboards brought to mind a former lover, Kessie, with whom jollof rice had been a topic of heated contention. Kessie was a stubborn woman from Cape Coast, Ghana, whose hedonistic hunger matched Taiye's near perfectly; their perversions complemented each other's gorgeously. They'd dated one stunning London summer and allowed things to peter out in early autumn when Kessie went back to school in Leeds. "Dated" is a bit of an overstatement; they'd slept together, frequently, for four months. For Kessie, it was entirely physical. In her words, she "wasn't a lesbian or anything ..." She had just been "bored with men," and Taiye was "convincing in her advances." Though it was she who came on to Taiye. But Taiye wasn't concerned with the details; their ridiculous chemistry had been enough for her. They'd had many Nigerian jollof versus Ghanaian jollof arguments, but Kessie despised cooking and could never defend her claim. So Taiye always won.

Former lovers aside, this is how you make native jollof rice, or, in Efik, iwuk edesi. Because you forgot to buy tinned tomatoes, but you promised your family jollof rice. Everyone knows that you do not casually break promises of jollof rice and survive unscathed to tell the tale. You will need two cups of rice, preferably long-grain white rice, but really, any type of rice will do. You will also need a quarter cup of palm oil, some smoked fish—eja osan would be your best bet—one large onion, a half cup of dried prawns, ground peppers, two tablespoons of ground dried crayfish, one tablespoon of puréed tomato, a small bunch of chopped efirin, half a tablespoon of salt, and a cup of beef stock or two bouillon cubes.

Taiye washed and set the rice to boil until it was nearly fully cooked. She poured the palm oil into a hot pan and let it smoke and settle before adding the sliced onions. She added the tomato and pepper purée, the crayfish, the smoked fish, the bouillon cubes, and some water. Then she put the lid on the pot and let the stew bubble and reduce. The aroma eh, the depth of flavour that crayfish adds to any dish is incredible. Taiye checked on the chicken again and turned the oven off.

Kambirinachi shuffled into the kitchen. Her socked feet muffled her steps, but Taiye knew her mother's smell.

"So, madame chef," Kambirinachi said, perching herself on the edge of the counter, "did I do well with the chicken?"

"You did well, Ma." Taiye smiled and turned to wash her hands.

"I'm sure your brother-in-law is handsome under that bush he has on his face. Do you think that is his normal look?" Kambirinachi tried to appear sombre, but the smile in her voice gave her away.

Taiye burst out laughing and doubled over at the sink. "You know what? I have no idea, but abeg don't ask him that."

"Well, I'm just wondering what kind of charm he has if that's what he is carrying on his face."

"Oh my God, Mami!"

"Anyway, I hope he eats normal food."

"I'm sure he eats *normal food*."

"I don't know." Kambirinachi raised her shoulders and spread her palms up as if in surrender. "Is he not oyimbo? He might be one of those fussy eaters with all the allergies and special diets, or am I wrong?"

"I don't know for you, o."

"Ehen, what if he's a vegetarian?"

Taiye thought for a moment. "There's efo in the freezer. I'll cook it without meat."

"Okay. I just can't believe you haven't met him before." Kambirinachi was being troublesome. "All that time you were in Canada. I thought you went there so you two could be closer."

"We were in different provinces, Mami. It's a big country."

Taiye hadn't meant to sound derisive, but that was the tone her words took. She began pouring the rice into the simmering stew and was about to apologize when Kehinde walked in. The small talk that followed felt odd to Taiye. There was so much else to say, so much catching up to do. But then it was decided: they would make mosa.

This is how you make mosa with your sister on the day she returns home. You are happy to occupy yourself with this task, as it keeps you from asking if she read the letters you wrote over the years but never intended to send. You will need the following ingredients: several overripe plantains, six heaping tablespoons of flour, four teaspoons of fast-acting yeast, a quarter cup of warm water, Atarodo peppers to your heat preference, a tablespoon of salt, and vegetable oil for frying.

First things first, you'll have to activate the yeast. You can do this while failing to share with your sister the fact that Banke took it upon herself—without your consent or any sense of boundaries whatsoever—to mail the shoebox full of letters that you had poured yourself into with no intention of sharing ever ever. Taiye had never spoken to anyone with as much loathing as she did to Banke after the girl presented her with the mailing slip like it was a gift.

Second, step aside to keep from getting mushy plantain splatter on your kaftan as your sister enthusiastically mashes the plantains in a bowl.

Third, add the salt as your mother sifts the flour into a large stainless-steel bowl.

Fourth, let your sister add the yeast solution and mashed plantain to the bowl of flour, as she seems the most excited of all three of you about this mosa situation.

Fifth, cover the bowl and let the mixture rest for ten to fifteen minutes.

GOLDEN SUNLIGHT POURED THROUGH THE OPEN WINDOWS, making bright swaths on the counter around which the women lingered, waiting for the mosa batter to rise and the rice to cook through. Kambirinachi interrogated Kehinde about Farouq, and Taiye continued to wonder about the letters. The question danced on the tip of her tongue. But how would she ask?

*Are you going to ask, Taiye, or are you just going to carry on torturing yourself?*

She didn't want it to matter so much, but it did.

Time had done what it does; that feral, desperate loneliness that led her to begin writing them had shifted. It had shifted her.

"Such a dreamer." Kambirinachi interrupted Taiye's thoughts with her teasing. She and Kehinde looked at her with identical expressions of amusement. "Where has Taiye gone now?" her mother asked.

"I'm here." Taiye smiled, and ran a finger over the scar on her chin. "Sorry." She stood up. "Let's check on the batter."


TAIYE FILLED A CERAMIC SERVING PLATE WITH RICE AND CHICKEN, and a small bowl with mosa, and handed them to Hassan from the kitchen window.

"Na gode, sister," he said, the words finding their way out through barely parted lips.

"No wahala."

Taiye imagined it was the smell of the food that roused Farouq from sleep. He had changed into a faded blue T-shirt and jeans cuffed just below his knees. The droplets of water trapped in his beard told Taiye that he'd attempted to rinse the sleep off his face. His eyes searched for Kehinde as he descended the stairs. He planted a kiss on her forehead and, looking at the spread on the dining table, exclaimed, "What a feast!"

The four of them sat at the round glass table, set with raffia placemats and cutlery wrapped in batik napkins. Taiye flitted in and out of the kitchen with tray after tray of dishes to be shared. Rice bejewelled with large pieces of smoked fish, crayfish, and aromatic efirin; gorgeously browned chicken; small balls of mosa; and that obscenely decadent chocolate cake. Far more food than the four of them could reasonably consume in one sitting.

Looking unabashedly at Taiye's face, in her eyes, Farouq said, "You're identical, yeah." His eyes darted from Taiye to Kehinde. "But you look *so* different."

His slight lisp endeared him to her, made his beauty less intimidating. She found him beautiful in the same way that she did the pearlescent life-sized marble sculpture of the Virgin Mary at the side entrance of the Falomo Catholic church. The statue was gorgeous to see and easy to fear, but never open to touch. Quite the opposite of her typical instinct upon seeing a beautiful thing. A beautiful person.

"It's the scar," Taiye said, averting her eyes from Farouq's intense gaze. That was it: she found him intense.

"You're acting as if you've never met twins before," Kehinde said, slapping his arm, "Stop embarrassing me, jare."

"No, it's not that," Farouq said.

"Maybe it's because they're different people," Kambirinachi offered with false innocence.

Farouq caught on and smiled. "Ah, I don't know what sort of magic you women have ..."

"Maybe it's because I'm fatter," Kehinde said, and rolled her eyes.

"Oh, darling, why would that matter?" Kambirinachi cooed.

"It seemed to matter a lot when we were small," Kehinde's tone was cold, "and you loved pointing it out."

"Keke, I'm your mother. It's my divine right to tease my children!" As she served herself a generous slice of cake, Kambirinachi added, "Anyway, a bit of fat never killed anyone. Your sister loaded this with butter!" She ate a large forkful and moaned dramatically.

Kehinde looked away.

"Babe, you're perfect," Farouq offered, an attempt at easing the sudden tension.

Then, silence but for the scraping of cutlery on dishes.

Taiye got up and walked to the corner of the living room where old movies on VHS and VCD, and music on cassette, CD, and vinyl were stacked against the wall in precarious towers.

"I found Popsie's records," she said quietly, slipping a shiny black disc from its dusty sheath.

Moments after the needle dropped, the fluid voices of the Lijadu Sisters gliding over a mellow bass on the song "Amebo" filled the room.

"Remember this?" Taiye asked.

Kehinde nodded, a faint smile easing the tightness of her face. "Yes."

# Kehinde

TAIYE AND I THOUGHT WE WOULD ALWAYS BE TOGETHER, when we were small and held hands and whispered secret stories about what must be wrong with our mother. After secondary school, we would go to live with our aunty Yemisi in South London. We would do our A levels together and go to university together and have a flat together. She would cook, and I would run all the errands that required speaking to other people, because back then, she only really talked to me and our parents.

But then a bad thing happened when we were still small, and the plan changed. What I mean is that I changed the plan. I peeled myself away from her rather savagely. One of the multitudes of things I regret.

Our relationship has always struggled against our twinness. "Resentment" is too sharp a word—it's just so unforgiving—but not long after we turned twelve something close to it stained and spread between us, like ink on wet paper. Our mother was plunged deep in one of her episodes—one of the places she sometimes hid when she refused to take her medicine—curled up on the floor or cradled between her bed and the wall, muttering about voices and refusing to be touched.

She was grieving our father's sudden death. All three of us were stunned into a heavy kind of hushedness. As children, Taiye and I didn't understand how our mother blamed herself for it, but we felt that our life, as we knew it before the singular fact of his death, was over. We knew that the season had shifted, that the joy that permeated the air around us because our parents were in love—whatever that meant, we knew it was a gift—had faded. The gorgeousness of our mother's voice when she sang, all of us going swimming at Ikoyi Club, mashing overripe plantains to fry mosa together, the firmness of the ground, the certainty of morning, the assurance that time would wind forward, and mangoes would ripen, all of that was out of our grasp, just as the final wisps of a vivid dream dissipate at the first breath of morning.

Our mother is not well. I can scarcely remember a time when she was. She is a vast garden of water-hungry flowers in a land of perpetual drought. Our father, I imagine, wanted to have something he could save every day, so he married her, narrow-waisted and massive-eyed. She was beautiful in an impossible way, a delicate thing. Too soft for this world, too soft for Lagos and the madness that is its throbbing motor. Too soft for London and its cold, accusatory glares on the narrow sidewalks, in the supermarkets, on the buses. They slayed her, they smothered her, they battered her tongue deep inside of her so that in the eight months we spent there after our father's death, she spoke only to us, at home, in rapid Igbo whispers, until we came back to Lagos. She is flighty, that woman; there are whole worlds inside of her that call for her. It seems the calls have been steadily growing more insistent. Our father kept her tethered to us—he and the quetiapine tablets prescribed by Dr Savage.

All those years ago, after Taiye went away to London for university, it was just me, Mami, and Sister Bisi in the house for almost a year. I'd applied for a Canadian student visa and had to wait many months before it was approved. The house was stifling. Mami seemed to be grieving Taiye's absence; she always seemed to be grieving something, or some-one, that wasn't me. Once, she called me by her name, and I shouted with all the fervour of my teenage angst, "I'm sorry I'm not your precious Taiye!"

The truth is that Taiye had something of our father in her face and gestures. And though I'd been punishing her since the bad thing, I quietly mourned her absence. Alone in my room, I cried for not seeing her face, and my father's, echoing in the subtle mischief of her half smiles, in her leaning gait, in her eyebrows.

That year, our great-aunt visited with massive Ghana must go bags filled with yams, tomatoes, smoked fish—and plantains. She tried to teach me how to make mosa. But without Taiye around to halve the weight of her expectations, they were too heavy for me. I did everything Aunty

Akuchi said, and it yielded glorious puffs. Yet they lacked the lightness of Taiye's touch.

I have not said the word or thought of mosa in years. It's so odd to think that I forgot how much I love the yeasty plantain puff-puffs. We used to have them every Sunday after church. It was a tradition Aunty Akuchi started, when she visited after our father died, and after the bad thing. She promised to reward me with a feast if I got dressed for church. Taiye never needed much convincing; she was always ready on time, quietly waiting in the parlour, while I cried to be left alone.

"No! I don't want anything," I'd sob.

"Not even meat pie?" Aunty Akuchi would ask.

"No."

"Not even jollof rice and chicken?"

"No."

"Chicken suya?"

"No."

"Not even mosa?"

I behaved for mosa.

*Letter no. 101*
*October 28, 2015*
*Agricola St., Halifax*

*Dear Kehinde,*
*I miss you very much. But sometimes I don't know if I miss you or if I miss the person I've needed you to be. The sister I've wanted since you turned cold. I would like to know you as in the you that exists in real life. The one just living her life in Montreal, going about the mundanity of her every day. Anyway, how is Farouq? You live together now, yeah? How's that going?*

*I'm doing all right. Halifax is beautiful, I can't complain. Culinary school is all right, I can't complain. Although I might be going a bit mad. There's this melody that's following me. I no longer know if it is real or imagined. I don't know what song it is, like if it is a popular tune or something that I'm just not* familiar with. The first time I heard it (maybe it wasn't the first time I'd heard it, but it was the first time I noticed it), Elodie, the woman who owned the teaching restaurant I worked at in Montpellier, she hummed it a lot. I heard it again in London, after I moved out of Aunty Yemisi's place. I was waiting for my friend in a café near campus, and the barista started to hum it just as I was leaving. Again, the last time I was in Lagos to see Mami, on my way from the airport, the cab driver was humming it as well! And just this morning, after Mass, I saw one of the altar boys smoking behind the church, and he was humming the same fucking melody. I don't remember it until I hear it again. I've tried humming it myself, but it's always wrong.

Someone told me something about sacred geometry, do you know what that is? I've been thinking that maybe there is a tear in my mind from all my fucking about with drugs, and I'm perceiving this universal melody. I may very well just be mad, but I don't know how else to explain it.

How are you today?

It's our birthday tomorrow, I'll be thinking of you. I'm always thinking of you.

Always,

Taiye

# Kambirinachi

DURING HER THIRD YEAR AT QUEEN'S COLLEGE, Kambirinachi befriended a gaunt, wide-eyed girl named Mercy. The poor thing suffered frequent and harrowing crises because her blood cells—distorted by inherited abnormal hemoglobin—took the shape of razor-sharp sickles and clumped together to block the small vessels in her wisp of a body. On top of that, she was just really quite strange. She mumbled to herself often, with her eyes closed. Kambirinachi worked, to no avail, to decipher the meaning of Mercy's murmuring.

"What are you saying?" she would ask, interrupting Mercy's quiet babbling.

"Eh?" Mercy would respond, her face, meticulously scarred with diagonal lines flaring from the corners of her small lips like wings, a picture of innocence.

"Just now now you were saying something," Kambirinachi would insist.

"I wasn't!" The girl really didn't know she was doing it.

Kambirinachi wondered about Mercy; she didn't recognize her from before before.

Were they the same? Was she lost? Had she forgotten?

The other girls accused Mercy of witchcraft, which was typical of teenage girls. Yet Kambirinachi was astonished at the extreme points of emotion that their collective pendulum hit. Mob mentality, groupthink, call it what you like, but one day their classmates would be moved with sympathy for Mercy the sickler—they'd offer to take biology notes for her and fetch her buckets of water to bathe in the morning—and the next day, after she'd suffered a seizure or screamed from the acute pain of a crisis at the chapel during morning Mass or after lunch break, they would again be sure that she was an Ọgbanje, or a witch, or possessed by an evil spirit. She was just sick.

Once, at break time, not too long after one of Mercy's crises, the girls who'd chosen not to go spend their pocket money at the tuck shop behind campus eyed her. Mercy often spent her breaks asleep with her head on her desk, cradled in the nook of her elbow. The girls whispered silly things like, "Better not wake her up, or she will do juju for you."

"She's not a witch," Kambirinachi said, her small voice calm and even. "You people should just leave her alone."

"Who was talking to you? Anyway, how do you even know? Are you a witch as well?"

"Maybe." Kambirinachi shrugged. "Maybe I'll cut you in your dreams, and you'll never be able to climb out of sleep."

The girls squealed, aghast. They rushed out of the classroom shouting a trail of prayers behind them:

"Tufiakwa!"

"God forbid bad thing!"

"I reject it with the blood of Jesus!"

"No weapon fashioned against me shall prosper!"

"Back to sender!"


SOMEWHERE IN THE FOUR HOURS BETWEEN the French and physics exams in the middle of the junior secondary school certificate exam week, Mercy was in sick bay, writhing in the throes of a violent fever that came upon her suddenly the night before.

The school nurse called the bank where her mother worked as a secretary. The nurse did her best to sound calm, but her voice shook. "Mrs Awoniyi, we are going to rush your daughter to the general hospital this afternoon. Please, ma, will you meet us there so that they can admit her quickly?"

Kambirinachi was sitting on a plastic chair with her legs folded underneath her small body, the skirt of her blue pinafore tucked under her knees, neck-deep in physics revisions. She was in the dappled shade of a mango tree by the science building with several of her classmates, cramming the Assumptions of Kinetic Theory, when she looked up and saw Mercy waving at her from across the quad, a big smile on her face.

Kambirinachi smiled and waved back. "I thought you were in sick bay," she said.

She said it again louder when Mercy didn't answer.

"Mercy!" Kambirinachi shouted. "The nurse let you leave?"

Kambirinachi's classmates looked at her, at first annoyed at the distraction, and then puzzled.

"Who are you talking to?" one of them asked.

"Mercy." Kambirinachi gestured toward their classmate, who stood not even twenty feet away, beaming. She had never smiled so big. Her royal-blue pinafore was, for the first time Kambirinachi had seen, impeccable.

"You're funny. There's no one there."

"She's right there," Kambirinachi said, turning back to see Mercy slowly walking backward, away from them, her face flickering and dimming. Then Kambirinachi understood.

In the humidity of the following Monday morning at general assembly, the principal announced Mercy's death. The wailing and crying that ensued lit a flare of annoyance in Kambirinachi: her classmates were cruel to Mercy when she was alive; what exactly was the purpose of this performance of grief? She felt relief on Mercy's behalf; her body had not been kind to her, had not been able to contain her.

Kambirinachi did not cry. She celebrated that Mercy was free.

FOR THE LONG HOLIDAY BETWEEN HER FINAL YEAR of junior secondary school and first year of senior secondary, Kambirinachi went home to Abeokuta. She packed up her Ghana must go early that day and spent the morning cleaning her aunty's flat. She swept the dark carpet that covered her bedroom floor, washed and mopped the poorly tiled bathroom floor. She scrubbed the toilet with bleach and scoured the discoloured bathtub. In the kitchen, she cleaned the cupboards after politely asking the black, seed-sized cockroaches to leave, and she rearranged the tins of powdered milk and plastic tubs of provisions. Afterward, she bathed in the freshly cleaned tub, oiled her skin, dressed, and waited for Aunty Anuli to drive her home.

The moment she saw her father sitting on the wooden bench on the veranda of their crumbling bungalow, his shoulders drooping sadly, his whole body thinner than she'd ever seen, Kambirinachi knew that something was wrong. She smelled the sickness on him, sharp and sour, when she embraced him. It had only been three months since she'd last seen him; what was working so quickly inside him to undo his body?

"Bigger and taller every time I see you," he said. Even his voice was tainted with the stink of whatever illness was coiled and rotting inside him.

Kambirinachi felt fear like needles down her spine and small bitter bursts in the back of her throat.

"Papa, what is wrong?"

"Ah ahn, tortoise, nothing o!"

He called her tortoise for her precociousness. After the wily character that stole birds' feathers to fly and join a feast in the sky. He angered the birds with his greed, so they pushed the tortoise out of the clouds and he fell to the ground, shattering his shell. Like Kambirinachi on stolen time, waiting waiting to be pushed out of the clouds. But she wouldn't be the only one to shatter.

SHE WAITED UNTIL EARLY THE NEXT MORNING, after her mother left for her provisions shop in the army barracks, before the sun was fully awake with its limbs stretching hot across the sky. She tiptoed across the cold, damp concrete floor of the kitchen toward her parents' room. The brown wooden door was just barely open, and she peeked in to see her father's thin body face up on the old wood-framed bed. His breathing was ragged and loud. She walked toward the bed, careful not to wake him, stood above him, and slowly and steadily, she sank her hands into her father's chest, from her fingertips to her wrist. And then, with all her strength, she drew the sickness out of his lungs. He was fast asleep until she pulled her hands out, then he awoke with a loud gasp, his face broken open in shock.

Kambirinachi ran outside to the backyard. She shook her hands to flick the sickness—black tar that stunk like rotten meat—into the open gutter. The filthy, stagnant muck splashed onto her bare legs, so she rinsed it off with water from a large plastic drum they kept to collect rain. Leaning against the drum, she looked into the water at her reflection, who blinked languidly at her.

"What will the consequence be?" she asked, but her reflection only looked away, with something like contempt on her face.

Kambirinachi went back into the house and knocked gingerly on her parents' bedroom door.

"Kambi, is that you?" her father called out, his voice groggy with sleep.

"Yes, Papa." She stepped into the room that she had fled only moments before.

Her father was sitting upright on the bed, looking around him in a daze. "Your mother has gone?" he asked, on the edge of a big yawn.

Kambirinachi nodded. Already the smell of decay had left him.

"What are we going to eat this morning?" He smiled big.

Ikenna had left a pot of palm oil stew with catfish on the stove, so Kambirinachi peeled and boiled sweet potatoes in salted water. They ate with their hands, listening to the radio in silence that was occasionally interrupted only by her father's laughter; he found the advertisements hilarious.

The voices didn't begin to hound Kambirinachi that day until after her father left the house. He'd decided to surprise his wife at her shop, wanted to tell her that their daughter's return had cured whatever it was that ailed him. Ikenna had taken the pickup, so he travelled to her by bus.

Kambirinachi was lying on a worn red-and-blue raffia mat in the living room, drawing in her school notebook. The moment her father shut the rusty burglar-proof gate behind him, she was overcome by a blank, a savage empty. A yawning hollow, a brief pause, only for an instant, before the howl of voices rushed through her whole self, like harsh, forceful harmattan winds.

*Give it back!*

# Taiye

WHEN TAIYE AWOKE IN THE WARM GLOW OF SUNDAY MORNING, the day felt like it would be yellow and smell bright. She made a cup of green tea with a generous helping of dark honey and sat with her back against the fridge, her bare legs on the cold tiles of the kitchen floor. Coca-Cola cat found her and curled its fat furry body into her lap.

For a long time, even before the bad thing, Taiye felt plagued with, with ... "shame" is too blatant and not quite insidious enough a word for the feeling that she wore, draped over her shoulders like a water-laden blanket. There is a way that she can look up at you through heavy-lidded, dark wells for eyes. It will fill you with this unassailable desire to unburden her. She doesn't know it, but it was this very thing that endeared her to her lovers. The magnetic gravity of the planet that is her.

Among her friends, it wasn't uncommon to hear: "You like her? Of course you do. Everyone likes her."

Even when she was callous about the intimacies she shared like cheap sweets, the women she chose made excuses like, "She's just a bit broken."

Lovers, Taiye'd had many. Too many. She found herself too lustful, too gluttonous. She desired too much. She recognized her weakness for these particular vices early in her life. As an eight-year-old, she quietly consumed helping after helping of beans and dodo, jollof rice, eba and egusi soup. She ate everything, until her stomach stretched well past its limit, and only pain and nausea forced her to stop.

"Oliver Twist!" Sister Bisi would marvel. "Even as you dey chop nothing dey show for your body."

It was true; Taiye was a lanky and wispy child. She grew into a lanky and willowy woman, but she never outgrew her voracious appetite.

*Lucky lucky. Your sister would kill for that figure.*

"It's as if you eat and your sister gets fat," her mother said once, finger on her chin in mock seriousness.

*One moment on your lips, always always on Kehinde's tummy.*

It was a joke—of course it was a joke—and it was a ridiculous notion. Where Kehinde was lush with soft curves, generous hips, and ample thighs, Taiye's skin clung tightly to lean muscle over her athletic frame, narrow hips, statuesque shoulders. This was the extent of their physical difference; they were identical otherwise. They had the same deep dark complexion, the same wide-set brown eyes, the same disarming lopsided smile. Disarming, in part, because it was lopsided and opened to reveal a small gap between their front teeth. Taiye would learn later than Kehinde the effect that particular use of that smile could have on people. Soft manipulation.

But every time Kehinde pinched the soft flesh of her belly, or her round cheeks, the plumpness of her upper arms and frowned, Taiye felt deep remorse for her gluttony.

When Taiye was ten years old, she learned about the seven capital sins. It was at Catechism on Saturday, just after the six p.m. Angelus bell had rung its heavy song, and the sun had begun its slow, reluctant descent. The resting sun cast an orange glow through the high dusty windows of the children's Mass hall. On Saturdays, the white plastic chairs that were usually arranged to face the altar were stacked up high against the stained white walls. And without the lace-covered altar as a focal point, the high-ceilinged hall was exposed for what it was: dusty, old, poorly maintained.

Taiye sat beside her sister on a long wooden bench that they shared with seven other fidgeting children. There were three more benches in front of them and two behind. All filled with squirming but silent pre-teens. Sister Augustina was teaching, and they all knew better than to speak out of turn.

"Okay," Sister Augustina said, adjusting the rose-patterned scarf tied tightly around her head. "We are learning about the seven capital sins that Father Raymond preached about last Sunday. Does anybody remember what they are?"

Eager hands flew up.

"You, Kunle." She pointed at a stout, chubby-faced boy in the second row.

"They are the sins that God doesn't want us to do," Kunle said, his voice scratchy.

"Yes, thank you, Kunle. And which sins are they? Someone else? You, Uche."

Uche hadn't raised her hand; in fact, she had been falling asleep, her head rolling slowly forward. Jumping when she heard her name, she said, "Sorry," high-pitched and trembling.

Sister Augustina looked expectantly at Uche, who stayed silent, her chipped teeth gnawing at her lower lip. Tears pooled in her eyes, defying gravity, until Sister Augustina said in a stern voice, "Uche?"

"I don't remember!" Uche wailed, and the tears poured down, to the laughter of the whole class.

"Olodo!" Sister Augustina scolded. "Okay, I will tell you this time, but make sure you remember tomorrow at Mass."

Vigorous head nods from a chastened Uche.

"The seven capital sins are lust, gluttony, greed, sloth, wrath, envy, and pride. Do any of you remember what they mean?"

Kunle piped up, "Greed is when you want to eat all the biscuits, even if they're not your own."

"No, that is gluttony," another child interjected. More students jumped in, a small uproar as they scrambled to give the right answer.

Sister Augustina whistled to seize their attention and placed a finger across her lips. Silence. She defined each of the seven deadly sins, starting with gluttony, and then, halfway to lust, she hoped she wouldn't have to explain it.

Of course Taiye noticed. "What about lust? What does it mean?"

"You people are just small now, but when you are a little bit older, and you girls start liking boys"—Sister Augustina wagged her crooked fingers and made her eyebrows jump in a suggestive dance, raising groans and nervous laughter from the class—"and you boys start looking at girls' nyash, that is lust. Remember that God doesn't like lust."

Another, louder, eruption of laughter.

Taiye felt a prickly rush run from her chest to her cheeks. Was it lust, the thing she felt when she saw Patra winding her hips in slow motion in the "Worker Man" music video?

*Lusts of the flesh, rotten girl Taiye.*

THAT EVENING, after Catechism, Taiye pulled out the navy blue *Oxford English Dictionary* from the row of *Encyclopaedia Britannica* volumes stacked against the wall by the bathroom door in her parents' bedroom. Her father was sitting cross-legged on the unmade bed, still in his navy blue suit and round tortoiseshell glasses, pawing through a stack of papers on his lap. He worked even on Saturdays.

"What are you doing, Baby Two?" he asked, without looking up from his papers. A Yoruba man, he believed the lore that she was the younger twin. That even though Taiye was born first, her sister, Kehinde, was actually formed first and had merely sent Taiye out before her to make sure the world was fit for their arrival.

"I'm looking for a word," Taiye responded. "What are you doing, Papa?"

"I'm looking for some numbers."

Taiye flipped through the sepia pages of the old dictionary, all the way through to *L*.

**Lust**
Pronunciation: /lʌst/
Definition of lust in English:
noun [Mass Noun]

**1.** Strong sexual desire

**1.1** [In Singular] A passionate desire for something: a lust for power

**1.2** (usually lusts) *chiefly Theology* A sensuous appetite regarded as sinful: lusts of the flesh

This was how Taiye learned that she was sinful.

IT WASN'T JUST PATRA'S DANCING that let Taiye know that her desires lay on the left side of expectations. There was also the quickening in her chest whenever she saw Isabella. Or smelled Isabella. Or heard the dulcet melody of Isabella's voice. They had been neighbours as children and went swimming together at Ikoyi Club. As sixteen-year-olds, during the haze of teenage melodrama, Isabella stopped speaking to Taiye. An abrupt ending to a long-time friendship. Isabella never explained, but Taiye suspected that she'd known something of the warm rush that dizzied Taiye whenever Isabella smiled in her direction.

Thirteen years and many lifetimes later, Isabella was engaged, but she'd been writing and phoning Taiye almost incessantly since they'd run into each other at an Afrobeat concert in Freedom Park.

It was an uncharacteristically cool evening for Lagos when they came across each other again. Taiye had been home for seventeen sluggish days, and aside from a few trips to the market in the Falomo police barracks, she hadn't left the house. So when, on one of her home visits, Dr Savage mentioned that her nieces would be going dancing that evening, Taiye took it as an invitation. She asked if they would pick her up on their way.

Habiba and Kareema drove up in a black Jeep with tinted windows and greeted Taiye with glossy lips and wide white smiles. They sparkled, not with any kind of inner light necessarily; they literally sparkled. Their pin-straight weave-ons shone in the glinting street lights, their bracelets and earrings clinked and shimmered, their lips, their bright eyes. They were perfectly lovely, but Taiye wasn't in a terribly talkative mood. They eyed her as she settled into the back seat.

"Nice to meet you, Taiye," Habiba said, smiling from the driver's seat. "Aunty Folake said you just moved back from Canada?"

"Yes," Taiye said. "Good to meet you, too. Thank you for picking me up."

"Welcome back home." Kareema smiled. "Where in Canada? I have some friends in Toronto."

"Halifax."

"Oh, I don't think I know anybody in Halifax. Where is that?"

"It's farther north than Toronto. There's a lot of Nigerians there, but we're everywhere, so that's not saying much." Taiye laughed; the girls laughed. "It's small, but it's right on the ocean, like the Island," she added.

"How long were you there for?"

"Like two and a half years."

"Really? Aunty Folake said you and your sister had been gone for a while."

"Yeah, I was in London for a bit before I moved to Halifax."

"Oh, okay. How about your sister?"

"She's still in Canada. Montreal." Taiye adjusted the neckline of her kaftan; the stiff opalescent embroidery fell in a deep V down her sternum, revealing the beginnings of a tattoo. She had small breasts that forgave her choice to go without a bra; still, she felt exposed in the cold gusts of air rushing out of the A/C.

"I like your kaftan dress thing," Kareema said, turning her shiny head to flash Taiye a toothy grin. Endearing.

"Thank you." Taiye smiled back. "How about you girls? You're in school?"

"Habiba just graduated from Covenant, pharmacy degree. I'm still there, engineering, one more year. I want to go to Canada for my master's. Toronto, though."

"Congrats, Habiba." Taiye said. "And you, too, Kareema, in advance."

Besides the pulsing rhythms blaring from the speakers, the rest of the car ride passed in smooth silence. There was some traffic in Obalende, but it eased up when they climbed onto the Ring Road bridge. At Freedom Park, Habiba slid the car deftly into the last remaining spot in the crowded lot. They starting walking toward the main stage, where a dense crowd had already formed. Excitement bounced around like an eager contagion. Taiye smiled wide, more to herself than anyone in particular, suddenly grateful for a night out: a desire to become enveloped by the crowd, dance as if she were alone, maybe get a little fucked up. She told the girls she'd meet them by the stage and headed toward what she assumed was the bar. A gin and tonic—maybe three, no ice, mostly gin—would ensure the desired mellow buzz.

Several white plastic chairs were spread out by the open-air bar, all turned to face the stage, mostly occupied. Taiye wove past them. She didn't recognize anyone, but there was a light-skinned woman perched, legs crossed, on a stool by the bar, her heart-shaped face haloed by a short Afro. And she was staring right at Taiye, her eyes widening.

"Taiye Sokky Adejide, is that you?" Isabella asked, a green bottle of Heineken paused midway to her mouth.

Without skipping a beat, as if she'd been expecting to see her childhood friend, Taiye said, "Isa, long time! How far?"

She felt the familiar rush and laughed at herself. She wanted Isabella on sight; that hadn't changed.

"Look at you!" Isabella exclaimed, the smell of cigarettes and alcohol dancing on her breath.

"You look great!" Taiye said, taking in the looping curls, the black V-neck shirt stretched tight, the jeans cinched high on her waist with a leather belt.

"So do you!" Isabella exclaimed. Her mannerisms were oversized, her voice loud. Taiye thought she might be drunk.

"Thank you."

"When did you get back?"

"About two weeks now. How about you?"

"I've been here, o! I was in the UK for, like, two years, at Reading for my master's, but I've been here since."

They looked at each other in silence for a moment. A breeze flapped Taiye's kaftan around her.

Isabella gestured for Taiye to sit on the empty stool beside her. "Are you here on your own?"

"No." Taiye pointed toward the stage, where Habiba and Kareema clutched their purses and swung their hips. From that distance, they looked identical. "You?"

"My people are dancing as well. I'll introduce you later. But we have a lot of catching up to do! How far your sister?"

"She's in Montreal. She'll be here later in the year, actually. Around September, I think."

"Wow, so you guys are moving back for good?"

"I am. I'm not sure about Kehinde. She's coming with her husband, so I guess they'll decide, I don't think so sha."

"Ah! Kehinde is married!" Isabella clapped. "Eyah, to who?"

"This guy named Farouq."

"Muslim?"

"I think so. I'm not sure."

"Nigerian?"

"No."

"Oyimbo?"

"I think, partly maybe. I've seen pictures, he's brown."

"You haven't met him?"

"Nope."

"Na wa for una sha, I don't know sisters that don't talk like you people."

"We're special like that." Taiye shrugged. "How about you?"

"Well," Isabella stretched out her left hand to display a solitaire engagement ring, a delicate silver band with large round-cut diamond, "I'm engaged!"

"Congrats! To who?"

Isabella laughed. "You remember Toki?"

"Of course I remember Toki!"

"We went to UNILAG together, been together since third year."

"Congratulations, Isa, really, God bless. When is the wedding?"

"We're thinking next April, in Dubai."

"Good for you." Taiye wondered whether it was dishonest to express a bit more excitement than she felt.

"What about you?"

"What about me?"

"Ah ahn, how about you, jare? Are you seeing anyone?"

"No." Taiye smiled and looked down at her sandalled feet.

"No one before you came home?" Isabella pressed.

"No, I haven't been lucky like you." It was only a half lie.

"Na lie! I know you." Isa raised an eyebrow to suggest something that Taiye couldn't immediately identify. "I know *of* you."

Taiye sucked her teeth and feigned amusement. "My life is boring. There's nothing to know."

"I know for sure that's not true."

"Whatever. What are you doing for work?" Taiye changed the subject.

"Senior account manager at Adekunle and West!" Isabella laughed. "It's very nine-to-five, but let me tell you, the money is good!"

"Good for you o jare, I'm happy we're not all aimless and jobless."

"How about you?"

"I don't really know. I left a bakery job in Halifax, and now I'm trying to find anything."

"Wait, what did you study at uni again?"

"Chemistry, but I've ended up mostly working with food, so I went to culinary school to try and make it official."

"Culinary school sounds fancy." Isabella lit a cigarette. She ran a free hand through her curls, twisted her mouth to the side to blow smoke away from Taiye. "What are you going to do in Lagos? Any restaurant connections?"

"I don't know yet. If you know anyone that will pay me to cook, hook me up, yeah?"

Taiye wouldn't be able to tell you at exactly what point the quality of the air between their bodies changed. Most of the time, with the women she took or followed home, there was an intentional stirring, mostly her doing. There was a way that she gently, sweetly captured their attention and, with a particular use of that gap-toothed smile, shared her intentions. With very little else, she found that the attraction was mutual. But despite her desires, she hadn't intended anything with Isabella. In fact, all Taiye's memories of Isabella carried a salty scent of shame and some self-loathing that she had spent many years working to unlearn. Taiye wanted none of that. And yet, it had been what? Twenty minutes? Not even. And there it was, that thing.

"Where's Toki?" Taiye heard herself ask.

*Why do you want to know, Taiye?*

"In Abuja."

"For work?"

"Yes, for a few weeks."

Taiye nodded and started to get up. "I'm going to see what those girls are up to, but it's been really good to catch up."

"In a rush suddenly?" Isabella tried to mask her disappointment with humour.

"No, it's just that they brought me here, it would be rude ..." Taiye trailed off.

"Okay, give me your number. We should plan something," Isabella cut in with a wave of her cigarette-holding hand and gave Taiye her phone. "You know, I heard gist about you, Taiye."

"Yeah? What did you hear?"

"I heard that in London you were experimenting with ...?"

"Is that a question?"

Isabella shrugged and arched a meticulously shaped eyebrow.

"Yeah, I'm gay. Is that what you're not asking?" Taiye shrugged. So much shrugging and eyebrow-raising between them; Taiye just wanted to talk plainly.

"Yes," Isabella replied.

LATE INTO THE NIGHT, after Habiba and Kareema dropped her off, and she'd tiptoed up the stairs to keep from waking her mother, Taiye undressed and lay beneath thin covers. She was exhausted from all the dancing, but sleep denied her. Her mind spun and spun. Then a beep from her phone alerted her to a message:

*It was so good to see you today, Taiye. I'm sorry about all the personal questions, I didn't mean to be so somehow. Let me make it up to you. Mumsie is making small chops for an Easter get-together, you should come.*

After Easter Mass and a quiet meal of pepper soup and steamed ofada rice with her mother and great-aunt, Taiye draped her narrow body in an oversized white button-down, tied at the waist, and pulled a tight pair of dark jeans over her hips. She started to apply a deep red stain to her lips but decided against it.

*What are you going for, Taiye?*

She shrugged at her reflection and left.

Isabella's mother, Sabirah, still lived just two houses down from Taiye's childhood home. When Patience, the chubby, wide-eyed maid, led Taiye inside, Isabella was busying herself at the dining table by her mother's side, swaying her hips in a short lace tunic the colour of butter. They were arranging palm-sized samosas and spring rolls on a white plastic tray.

"You came!" Isa exclaimed. "Mummy, remember the twins from down the road?"

Sabirah smiled, faint and shallow. "Of course I remember the twins. Long time no see."

She gave Taiye a very brief embrace, so brief in fact that it was merely a matter of lightly touching her warm cheek against Taiye's and gingerly patting her on the shoulder. Except for a few new fine lines at the corners of her eyes and her plump mouth, Sabirah looked exactly the same as Taiye remembered. Her shoulder-length locs were wrapped in a red silk scarf, and a purple and yellow adire bubu hung elegantly from her slender shoulders.

"Which one are you?" Her voice was a calm, dispassionate purr. To Taiye, she'd always seemed bored and vaguely disinterested in anything other than her only child and their house—both of which she kept impeccable.

"I'm Taiye. Good afternoon, ma. Happy Easter."

"Happy Easter. How is your mother?"

"She's fine. She's at home."

"It's been long since you came home abi? When did you get back?"

"A few weeks ago."

"And your sister, she's back as well?"

"She will be here in a few months."

"Haba so many questions," Isabella interrupted. "Taiye, do you want anything to drink?"

"Water is fine, thank you."

"Okay, come with me through the kitchen. There are people in the backyard."

Taiye trailed her through the old but pristine kitchen to the back-yard, large and covered in lush grass. In the centre stood a white canopy. Under it, a feast and a few people, none of whom Taiye recognized at first glance. She followed Isabella to a blue plastic cooler filled with large jagged chunks of ice and bottles of soft drinks, beer, and water.

"You guys, this is Taiye," Isabella said to the small crowd of guests. "We've been neighbours since we were small."

Taiye tried to be friendly, to seem interested, but she was distracted. In the daylight, on the celebration of Christ's resurrection, Taiye thought she might un-feel whatever it was that had passed between her and Isabella the night before. But she thought wrong. The thing remained; it had marinated in its own fervour (the fervour of an unresolved childhood crush) and become more potent: a childhood crush calcified by rejection into some sort of hallowed wanting. Taiye knew that she should leave. Instead, she took a beer out of the cooler and made small talk.

Despite having spent all the sunlight and a healthy portion of the evening at Isabella's get-together, or perhaps because of that, Taiye's memory of most of that afternoon blurred almost as soon as she left. Isabella followed her out and walked her the five minutes home. She seemed to be vibrating in the night breeze, her face shifting in and out of the air in front of her. They were both considerably intoxicated—Isabella by the numerous drinks she'd thrown back, and Taiye by Isabella's focused attention. So when Isabella invited herself up to Taiye's room, Taiye let her. But when they got up there, she panicked and blurted something about needing some cold water.

By the time Taiye had returned from the kitchen with a plastic jug of water and two small tumblers, Isabella's lace dress was a crumpled pile of soft fabric at her feet. She smiled in a way that swallowed Taiye into a tingle. The air between their bodies—Isa in dark cotton underwear and Taiye fully clothed—bristled electric. Isabella traversed the space that separated them in four languid steps; Taiye counted. Isa kissed a soft line along Taiye's earlobe, across her cheek, to the corner of her mouth, the whole time humming a melody that had haunted Taiye for a long time. A melody that Taiye forgets almost the moment after she hears it.

Isabella looked Taiye square in the face before leaning in for her lips.

Taiye, who'd known this was coming, pulled away. "What are you doing, Isa?"

"I'm trying to kiss you." Isabella was matter-of-fact about it; she was not shy, not accustomed to being rejected.

"What about Toki?"

"What about him?"

"You're engaged."

"Like he's not fucking around," she scoffed.

"Listen, I'm not trying to be part of some kind of revenge plot."

"Chill jare, it's not like that."

"Then what's it like?"

"Are you not attracted to me?"

"You're drunk."

"I am. Are you not attracted to me?" Raised eyebrows.

"It doesn't matter. I don't fuck my friends." Shrug.

"We're not really friends, though, are we?" Again with the raised eyebrows.

"I'd like to be." Shrug.

"I wouldn't." Isabella's pupils were dark discs in honey-brown irises. Her mouth curved in a smile, but her eyes stayed mute as she continued. "But if you say no, I'll put my dress on and leave."

So much silence passed.

Taiye didn't say no.

She was an adaptable lover, quick to intuit her partner's preferences and unabashedly inquisitive whenever desires weren't entirely clear. With Isabella, Taiye took the lead. Isa was pliable, eager, vocal. They were both inebriated well past the point of inhibition.

"Try not to be too loud, my mumsie is asleep," Taiye said against the soft skin of Isabella's throat.

"Oh," Isabella cooed, "you must think really highly of yourself."

"No, that's not what ... I just mean ... actually, well, yeah."

On to kissing, fingers thrusting firmly, tongue lapping, a bite here, sucking, gasping; Isabella came quickly, hard, several times. Then, with her face still resting on the warmth of Isabella's thighs, Taiye drew her own wetness and made herself come.

THE TRUTH WAS, Taiye would have been happy with just a kiss. She realized this, alone again in her bed, moments before drifting into sleep.

Now the affair had lasted longer than either of them could have predicted. Taiye told herself that she didn't want to see Isabella anymore, but follow-through had proven difficult. Her resolve around these matters had always been easy to sway. Just the day before Taiye picked up Kehinde from the airport, Isabella had showed up at the gate of their house in her fiancé's red Honda.

"I'm just here to gist small," she'd said. "Also, I brought suya."

She'd offered up the newspaper-wrapped roasted meat, and then started to undress as soon as Taiye shut her bedroom door. And Taiye, with a plastic bottle of cold zobo hibiscus tea in one hand and two tumblers cradled in the crook of her elbow, had stood there, defenceless.

Afterward, Taiye said, "We need to stop."

"Okay," Isabella replied, and licked a dusting of spice mix off her fingers. "I understand ... I don't even do this. Like I'm not a lesbian, or whatever." She exhaled loudly and lifted her sweaty face to the ceiling. Eyes closed, she said, "There's just ... I don't know. I like being with you, Taiye ..." She shook her head slowly, having heard this from "straight" women many times before.

She hadn't heard from Isabella since. It was a good thing.

*It's a good thing, Taiye.*

Oh, the struggle to be better than oneself.

"Coca-Cola, I won't call her," Taiye said to the cat purring softly in her lap.

"Who aren't you calling?"

Taiye jumped, and the cat flew out of her lap.

"Sorry, I didn't mean to frighten you," Farouq said as he walked into the kitchen.

# Kehinde

TAIYE AND I USED TO BE ONE CELL, one zygote. Isn't that wild? I sometimes wonder if we knew each other before birth, if we were sisters, or the same person who grew tired of herself and shed the parts she didn't want. Perhaps I am the unwanted bits, the chaff, and Taiye the wheat.

She is sitting cross-legged on the floor by the fridge. She doesn't see me yet, though I am just by the kitchen door. Farouq is leaning his back against the counter, his arms supporting him so that his elbows jut out behind him; he doesn't see me either.

Their voices are low. I can't properly hear what they're saying, but Taiye has this look on her face as if she's about to crack open and pour everywhere. She's shaking her head slowly, and Farouq is nodding.

I'm curious, I feel left out, but I don't want to interrupt, so I go back up to my room. I don't understand this jealousy that has crept inside me; I am not usually possessive. Maybe it's the heat.

I married Farouq at city hall with five friends as witnesses. Afterward we went dancing at this tiny Haitian bar I love in the Gay Village to celebrate. I was several tequila shots and a tab of Molly deep, dancing on a mirrored floor with strobing pink lights and a bass so intense I felt my insides vibrate in time to the music. I looked up from the bottom of another shot glass, and Taiye was dancing right in front of me, beckoning me to join her. She was wearing the same black halter dress as I was, had the same waist-length box braids. But I was sure it was her. Even in the dimly lit club, I could make out the scar on her chin. And the way she moved. Taiye moves differently from me. She's not afraid to be seen.

I walked toward her on the dance floor, I tried to take her hand, but in an instant, she was gone, and I was left pawing at my reflection on a mirrored wall.

All this space between us now is dense, heavy. I know that it's not normal for sisters. It hasn't always been like this. Even though I was seething before, I don't think it's supposed to be like this, not anymore.

I suppose this is as good a time as any to tell you about the bad thing, the first thing that split us.

It started after our father's death, with Aunty Funke and the man she brought, Uncle Ernest. Aunty Funke was one of our father's distant cousins—it is only after many steps and ladders that their connection becomes clear. She came for our father's funeral and stayed long after we'd put him in the ground at Ikoyi Cemetery. She claimed that she remained to "help with the children, because a mother should not be on her own at a time like this." After many weeks of her ignoring us, hosting prayer meetings in the living room, and ordering Sister Bisi around, Uncle Ernest came to join her. He arrived with the rainy season, so we were confined to the three storeys of the house.

The day he arrived, Taiye stopped sleeping in my bedroom with me; though we had separate rooms, we shared mine at night. She told me and Sister Bisi that she hated him, but she didn't know why. She would climb into my bed and hold my hand until I fell asleep. Then she would tiptoe down the hallway and curl herself at the foot of our mother's bed.

Aunty Funke and Uncle Ernest slept in one of the guest rooms on the ground floor. Every day after school, I saw Uncle Ernest sitting on a stool outside the black wrought-iron gates of our compound with the gateman. A big smile eating up half his broad face, he often asked, "Ibeji, you've come back already? Didn't you just leave now now?"

I laughed, but Taiye never responded. She always struggled out of his attempts at hugs and ran inside, away from him, dragging me behind her. She said it was the way he looked at us. I didn't see it, even after Taiye whispered into my ear one evening, "I don't like the way he makes his eyes."

It's been almost eighteen years, yet I remember with frightening clarity the first night he came into my room. I still feel the warm breeze from the open glass louvres; I hear the pittering of rain, the whoosh

whoosh of the wind through the palm trees, the way they bowed and made their shadows dance, cast in the light of the street lamps on the bedroom walls. I remember, and it still pains me. Sometimes rage threatens to tear itself out of my body in a sharp scream; sometimes fear freezes me to my bed for days. It still makes me nauseous, makes my skin crawl so that I want to slither out of it. Sometimes I nod at the memories and let them pass as quietly as I can stand it.

It was a Saturday night, and there was no light.

Sister Bisi and the gateman were outside with their torchlights refuelling the generator. I thought Aunty Funke was at night vigil. She usually went on Saturdays, but it turned out she was downstairs the whole time. I think my mother was in her room on the second floor, but I hadn't seen her since Thursday. I was afraid of her then. Taiye and I were in my bedroom, the room we had shared at night since I can remember. She was lying under the bed with a torchlight, reading out loud a story from *Goosebumps* about a living ventriloquist doll. It was supposed to be frightening, and Taiye read it in a low, growling voice to scare me, but I think she was more afraid than I was.

The door was open. I saw Uncle Ernest stumble up the stairs, looking dazed. I felt like there was ice water running down my back, and I sat up quickly. He had never come up that early before.

"Ibeji," he said softly.

Taiye stopped reading the moment she heard his voice.

"Only you on this whole floor?" he asked me from the stairs, looking around at the two rows of closed doors on either side of my open one. "Na wa o," he muttered, and curved his lips down in an exaggerated frown. "Am I talking to myself?" he shouted toward me, quite suddenly very annoyed.

"Sister Bisi sleeps here with us," I lied.

My body was a block of cement when he leaned against the door frame.

"Ehen? Where is she now?"

"Downstairs on-ing the generator."

"Why is your torchlight on the ground?" he asked, apparently unable to see Taiye beneath the bed.

I felt bile rising hot from my stomach when Uncle Ernest came into the room and shut the door behind him. I started to shiver when I smelled that nausea-inducing drunkard smell coming off his damp, wide body.

"You're not allowed to come inside our room." I meant to shout it, but my voice came out small.

It paralyzed me when his face changed, contorted hideously with rage, his eyes widened, his nostrils flared, his mouth twisted into a sneer.

"So this is what happens when your mother is a madwoman, and there is nobody to train you, abi?" His voice was a low growl. "Talking to me as if I'm your mate."

He put his face close to mine, and when I recoiled, he grabbed my shoulders and pushed me down on the bed. I felt his damp palms on my skin. Bile dribbled down my chin, but I couldn't move.

"Please stop," I squeaked.

"Shut up."

He clamped a callused hand over my mouth and shoved his other hand under my nightie. He jammed his fingers inside me, and I bit hard against the sharp pain that shot up through my body. He withdrew his hands and threw a blinding slap against the side of my head.

"Useless girl," he muttered.

I screamed, and he covered my mouth and nose with his big palm so that I couldn't breathe. He pushed my nightie up until it was bunched under my chin.

I remembered my arms, and I flailed them, scratching his face until he removed his hand from over my face. I threw myself onto the floor and screamed. I cried for Taiye, but she didn't come out from under the bed. Her eyes were wide-open circles, both hands covering her mouth, as if to keep her terror from pouring out. She started to move toward me, she reached her hand toward mine, but we weren't close enough to touch. I screamed her name like a question, a plea.

The roar of the generator poured into the room, followed by a flood of light. Uncle Ernest backed away, his bloodshot eyes darting around.

Suddenly, Sister Bisi was there, her breath heavy from running up three flights of stairs. She snatched me from the floor with a strength I didn't know such a soft body could contain. She held me against her, backed away from him. I clung to her while she dragged a sobbing Taiye out from under the bed and took us downstairs to her room. She locked the door and propped a chair under the handle so it wouldn't budge, even when Aunty Funke banged and rattled it, shouting, "What is all this? What are you crying for?"

But Aunty Funke, she must have figured it out, because by morning she was sobbing quietly at the door. She knocked and said, "Abeg make I follow them talk."

"Him don go?" Sister Bisi asked through the door, opening it only when she heard an arrested "Yes" from Aunty Funke.

Sister Bisi said to Aunty Funke, her voice soft but possessing unmistakable undercurrents of rage, "If I see am near this compound again, I go call police. E go better if you sef comot."

Everything moved in molasses that day. I sat on Sister Bisi's bed for several eternities. Aunty Funke left with Uncle Ernest. Taiye stopped shivering and fell asleep. I wailed in the bathtub while Sister Bisi poured warm water from an orange plastic bucket over my head, soaking my braids. I was engulfed in a pitch-black hollowness; it swallowed me whole. Ever since before our father died, since before our mother retreated far from us, I knew without a doubt that I would never be alone. My Taiye was my quiet partner, closer than my shadow, than my own skin. But on that day, I called her, and she hid.

"Taiye didn't come out."

I had nothing else to say.

# 2

# Honey

# Kambirinachi

IT RAINED HARD THE DAY THAT KAMBIRINACHI'S FATHER DIED.

She'd dreamed it just before dawn and woke up during the deep inhale before the sky broke open and poured out. Kambirinachi paused her breathing and rushed to her parents' bedroom to shout that her father mustn't leave the house that day! He mustn't drive on the expressway! But their room was empty. The old green curtains covering the burglar-proof windows flapped and gave way to a warm breeze carrying the scent of rain striking earth: petrichor.

Kambirinachi started to shiver from sheer panic. She heard movement coming from the kitchen and hoped with all her might that it was her father. But it was her mother, spooning thick liquid eko into uma leaves. The spiced aroma of catfish pepper soup woke the air and made it sing. Kambirinachi could identify the distinct scent of each spice: the alligator pepper, the toasted fingers of Grains of Selim, the fragrant aridan. Her mother was making rain food—that's what she called it—food that soothed and comforted when it poured outside. Food to keep you from regretting that you couldn't leave the house. Eko and pepper soup.

Ikenna took one look at Kambirinachi and placed the spoon down by the tray of broad leaves. "What is the matter?" she demanded.

"Where is Papa?" Kambirinachi's voice was small but steady, and sharp with fear.

In reply, the voices of her Kin shrieked, a sound that seemed to pierce Kambirinachi's temples, and was not at all remorseful: *You already know.*

ONLY A SHORT MOMENT BEFORE, Kambirinachi's father was driving, carefully, somewhere between Itori and Wasinmi on the Lagos-Abeokuta Expressway. He always drove carefully. He knew to be cautious of the impending rain by the way the clouds gathered and darkened and swelled. The expressway, usually clogged and choking with traffic, was virtually serene. Not many cars zoomed passed his Peugeot pickup, and he was filled with a hope that he might make it home before the downpour.

Then a shadow came over his eyes, thick, like a heavy cloth draped over his face. He froze, distressed, and when the shadow lifted as suddenly and mysteriously as it had descended upon him, he found his truck facing the rusty mouth of a speeding lorry.

The lorry, transporting Gboko tomatoes, swerved sharply to keep from chewing up the dingy pickup that was sitting there. But there wasn't enough time and space between the two vehicles to prevent a collision. In the end, the sudden swerve shifted the mass of fruit and tipped the metal beast onto the front half of Kambirinachi's father's pickup. He was swallowed up by the lorry. All the burst guts of so many tomatoes hid the slaughter underneath.

SINCE NEWS OF HER HUSBAND'S DEATH, Ikenna could not stand to look at her daughter. She could not bear to hear or smell her, or even know that she was around. The three emotions that dominated her until the day of the funeral, when she decided that her youngest sister must take Kambirinachi away, were grief, rage, and profound fear.

After the burial, Ikenna turned to the youngest of her sisters beside her on the discoloured velvet sofa. "Please, Akuchi, you have to take this child away. Biko, I can't bear it o."

They were in the small living room, which seemed to have shrunk to half its size since her husband died. Everything in it appeared old and dank and worn; she was only just noticing the ugliness of the objects around her. These same objects had seemed so valuable in her husband's presence.

It must have been something in her voice, perhaps in the way that her typically plump cheeks lay flat and deflated. But Akuchi must have seen that Kambirinachi would no longer be safe with her mother. Within a week, Kambirinachi was, again, living with an aunt. She wept, saying goodbye to her mother, who remained stoic, despite her anguish.

Kambirinachi pretended to be asleep for the entire bus ride from Abeokuta to Ife. Akuchi, an agricultural science lecturer at Obafemi Awolowo University, lived in a modest two-storey house covered in a warm terracotta colour that felt welcoming to Kambirinachi.

To get to it, they took a cabu cabu from the bus stop near the university campus. It was only a twenty-minute drive, and the roads were clear. Kambirinachi had never before been to Ife, but to her, it felt the same as Abeokuta had felt since her father died: vast and cold, despite the raging sun.

AKUCHI WAS KIND ON PURPOSE; she believed that it was her duty, as a godly woman, to show the love of Christ through her actions. She understood that kindness was a practice, the same with patience and humility. She had no children of her own, and she loved an unavailable man, so she did not marry. Her housekeeper, Adaora, lived with her, and she frequently had guests visiting from Lagos and Asaba, so she was not a lonely woman. It was unexpected, but she was rather pleased to have Kambirinachi in her care.

Music always played throughout the house, filling the small rooms. Akuchi loved Bob Marley. She loved the thrumming rhythm of Ebenezer Obey, the smoke of his husky voice. Often, she sang along to Fatai Rolling Dollar and I.K. Dairo's Yoruba crooning and swayed her round hips to the Juju beat. She was the youngest of the three sisters, and to Kambirinachi, it seemed that she was the most joyful.

Akuchi set Kambirinachi up in the small bedroom beside hers. She embraced the child, and then, after a moment of hesitation, said, "Don't worry, my dear ... rest, eh, and after, come down and eat, you hear?"

Kambirinachi nodded and waited for Akuchi to leave the room before flinging herself face down on the bed, weeping.

When she was spent, she lifted her head from the hot damp spot on the pillow expecting silence but was met with the soft warmth of Akuchi's singing. The melody found its way from the kitchen where Akuchi was shallow-frying thick rectangles of yam and Adaora was cooking a palm oil stew.

Kambirinachi followed the music.

TWO MONTHS INTO HER STAY WITH AKUCHI, the voices inside Kambirinachi had dimmed somewhat—or perhaps her alive mind had stretched to house them alongside the reality that she had chosen. She heard them on a low volume, always present but not impossible to ignore. She learned to tune in and out as she liked.

Once, she was partially tuned in, listening to her Kin mutter in displeasure, and watching Adaora run after a brown speckled fowl in the backyard. Adaora cornered the chicken and snatched it up by its flapping wings. She flung it onto the concrete slab over the open gutter and fell a knife over its neck so that its head lobbed off and bounced across the grass. Adaora was swift; the fowl likely felt nothing. Still, Kambirinachi shrieked.

The voices paused for a moment, and then just as suddenly poured out again in roaring laughter: *Since when are you afraid of blood?!*

"Wetin?" Adaora scolded Kambirinachi. "Biko commot, dey go inside."

In the living room, Kambirinachi turned on the record player and lay on the carpeted floor. She dozed off to the lulling melodies of Louis Armstrong's "What a Wonderful World."

She dreamed of her parents. They were, all three of them, walking together down a quiet dusty road, hand in hand. Her parents walked on either side of Kambirinachi, her guardians, though in truth, in *her* truth, she was much older than they were, an ancient thing.

She woke up with a start at the sound of a car driving into the gravel-covered driveway of Akuchi's compound. Kambirinachi sat up quickly and rushed to the window to see that it was her mother, stepping out of a navy blue cabu cabu.

She hadn't seen or heard from Ikenna since she'd sent her away with Akuchi. A hard and bitter seed had been rotting in Kambirinachi's stomach ever since. She'd been doing her best to keep from nourishing it. Shaking her head briskly, shaking off the remnants of sleep and spite, Kambirinachi put a smile on and ran out to meet her mother.

IKENNA KNEW THAT THE ONLY WAY TO MOVE FORWARD was simply to *move forward*. She'd learned this lesson many times in her life. Her small bungalow was taunting her, shrinking around her. She'd tried to make space by locking away everything that made her think of her late husband. She'd shoved as much of the furniture, bedsheets, crockery—everything that she could remember him touching—into Kambirinachi's room. Everything except his flattened pillow; Ikenna slept curved like a crayfish, with half the worn pillow between her now-bony knees and the other half cradling her head.

Still, the house taunted her with her late husband's voice, and sometimes it mimicked her daughter's laughter. So the day before Kambirinachi's fourteenth birthday, she packed up a small bag and took a bus to Ife.

The cabu cabu driver had only just pulled into Akuchi's compound when Kambirinachi ran out with a devastating smile on her small face. The girl was already taller. Ikenna embraced her child.

The next day they bought a cake with red icing that tasted as artificial as it looked, but Kambirinachi loved it. Ikenna and Akuchi sang "Happy Birthday" and blessed her with prayers. Adaora fried the chicken she'd slaughtered the day before, and they ate on the floor, joyfully, despite all that lingering grief. Kambirinachi thought of her father, closed her eyes to see his face, and smiled at him with a mouthful of cake. He smiled back.

For years, Kambirinachi would think about that day, and she would scour her memory for signs, examine her mother's features for any indication of the woman's decision to walk out of her life for good.

# Taiye

AT SEVENTEEN, Taiye left home to study chemistry at University College London. During the six-and-a-half-hour flight from Murtala Muhammed to Heathrow, an overwhelming sense of having forgotten something important tugged at her insides. This feeling took the shape of a near gasp in her lungs, or perhaps the brief hollow space before a shiver, but it overstayed and stretched out over her whole self.

Over and over, she searched her backpack for her passports. Her Nigerian and British documents were bound together with a yellow rubber band and tucked away in the inner zippered compartment, next to an envelope filled with cash—crisp pound notes from one of the Mallams outside Ikoyi Hotel. She pushed up her cardigan sleeve to check that her watch was still wrapped around her wrist, still ticking. She touched her chest to feel for the brown scapular that hung from her neck on a thin worn leather rope.

She knew what she was missing, but there was nothing to be done. Kehinde had chosen not to come with her. So she spent the entire flight restlessly checking the same things repeatedly, in a frantic rhythm sustained by her manic grief.

Tears didn't come until the pilot announced that the plane would begin its descent momentarily. Taiye pictured the distance between her seat in row twenty-three and where Kehinde was, at home perhaps—so vast a distance, so much air and space and dust and ground between them. Her tears were silent, yet to keep from waking the grey-haired woman beside her, Taiye covered her mouth with her hand as she cried.

Aunt Yemisi picked Taiye up from the airport and took her to her three-bedroom flat in Brixton. The same flat where Taiye had lived with her mother and sister for the ten months they'd spent in London after their father died. It looked entirely different from how Taiye remembered it. Yemisi had moved in shortly after they'd moved back to Lagos. Technically, it belonged to Kambirinachi and the twins—that was the way Banji, the twins' father, had willed it—but Yemisi needed a place to live after she threw a bubbling pot of egusi soup at her raging ex-husband. It was self-defence, the first and only time she had struck back in twelve years of marriage. She'd run out of the house immediately after and screamed that she would call the police if he didn't let her collect her things and her children and leave in peace.

Yemisi was Banji's younger sister, and in the months to follow, Taiye would learn that Yemisi was the kind of woman who seemed, always, to favour the men in her life. Taiye would also learn that Yemisi did not like Kambirinachi.

Yemisi grew up the youngest child with two older sisters who either ignored or tormented her, and an older brother and father who adored her. So, it was no surprise that she indulged her two sons, Dapo and Jide, and had little patience for her only daughter, Sade. But her impatience for Sade was benevolence in comparison to her treatment of Taiye.

Upon fetching Taiye from the airport, Yemisi was struck by how much the girl resembled her mother. She hadn't seen Taiye in almost seven years. Not since the year her brother died, and Kambirinachi had, for a very brief time, tried to create a life for herself and her twins in London.

Yemisi understood grief, she really did. Still, she detested the way that Kambirinachi seemed to collapse into herself, leaving the girls, only twelve years old at the time, to cling to each other for comfort. Yemisi did what she could, but she had three children of her own to look after, a decaying marriage from which to escape, and a dead brother to mourn.

She noticed that Taiye had her mother's precise features, down to the slight overbite and elsewhere eyes, but her mannerisms were entirely her father's. Her lopsided smile, the sluggish way that she held her lanky frame, her in-toed gait, even the way she moved her features—speaking with her eyebrows, wrinkling her nose—all Banji. This did nothing to endear Taiye to Yemisi—the opposite, in fact. It took very little for Taiye to get on Yemisi's oft-mentioned bad side.

Yemisi started most statements to Taiye with a "Listen, this girl, I don't know how that *mother* of yours trained you, but if you don't want to get on my *bad side*, you better not ..."

Within the first month of living with Yemisi, Taiye knew that she would have to figure out a way to leave. It wasn't just her aunt's volatile moods, or her seeming desire to control everything—she would often barge into the bathroom while Taiye bathed to shout that she was using too much water or to check that she wasn't disgustingly brushing her teeth in the shower. Nor was it the evangelical Nigerian Pentecostal church with which she was heavily involved. Nor the snide and biting comments she made about Taiye's mother. Nor her insistence that Taiye was rotten and spoiled and therefore had to learn "home training" by picking up after her cousins whenever they visited home.

It was the shock of it all. The abrupt contrast of living with a hollow presence of a mother who had rarely surfaced in lucid spells long enough to remind her daughters of precisely what they were missing, to living with a hectoring overbearing aunt who seemed to save her particularly caustic brand of bitterness just for Taiye. Taiye would later grow to understand that the tender mothering she'd hoped to receive from her aunt was unrealistic, perhaps even unfair. As a teenager, though, it was a struggle to see beyond herself.

A FEW YEARS AWAY FROM HER MOTHER'S INCONSISTENT LOOMING, and the shame that drenched her whenever her twin fell into one of her dark moods, Taiye grew into the sort of woman who loved easily. Not foolishly, just hungrily.

It started in Montpellier, Southern France. With Elodie and Guifré, a couple in their late thirties who ran a culinary program marketed primarily to anglophone international students out of their small fine dining restaurant in the Beaux-Arts neighbourhood.

Several years prior, Elodie had come into a substantial inheritance from a great-aunt. She bought and renovated a small restaurant for her Catalan chef husband Guifré's birthday. La Dolça Esposa was doing reasonably well, beloved in the neighbourhood for such a new place, but barely turning a profit. So in what Elodie would come to describe as a *trait de génie*, they started offering cooking classes. They partnered with a language school and had been running the program at a considerable profit for two years before Taiye spotted their flyer on the UCL campus bulletin board, advertising: "Learn French and cook Catalan in Montpellier, France!"

The program cost a little over one thousand pounds more than Taiye could afford with her savings, and she'd decided not to touch the trust account she shared with her sister until they discussed a plan for the money, so she ignored the flyer for a while. But each time she walked past the bulletin board, she noticed that a portion of the leaflet was covered by another poster, advertising for roommates, or sports clubs, or language exchanges. A few weeks more and only the top left corner was visible. Taiye impulsively ripped off the posters that covered it and folded the tattered flyer into her coat pocket.

At home, while emailing the program coordinator, Taiye decided to be honest.

Subject: Inquiry for Funding Opportunities
Taiye Adejide <t.adejide@qmail.com>
March 20, 2009, 6:17 AM
To <margot.sheerin@ucl.uk>

Dear Margot Sheerin,

My name is Taiye Adejide. I'm a final year student here at UCL, and I'm very interested in enrolling in the Culinary + Language Program in Montpellier. However, I am not currently able to afford the £1,250 room and board fee without resorting to selling my blood. I am wondering if it would be possible for me to earn my keep by working either at the language school or the restaurant.

Alternatively, would it be possible for me to pay in instalments? I would be more than happy to take up a part-time job in Montpellier and pay the remainder of the fee during my time there.

I look forward to hearing back from you.

Sincerely,
Taiye Adejide

Though she feared her blood-selling joke might be too much, she sent the email anyway.

Three months after graduation, Taiye was on a train from London to Paris, where she would switch trains to Montpellier.

TWO OTHER STUDENTS HAD ALSO MADE ARRANGEMENTS to work for their housing in Montpellier. One of them was a curly-haired brown boy named Bobby. He was from the US, but in order to avoid having to defend his country's sociopolitical decisions, he travelled with a red maple leaf patch pinned to his backpack. This, however, put him in the unfortunate situation of having to defend another country's sociopolitical decisions, one with which he was much less familiar. It made for many awkward conversations and, often, bashful confessions.

Taiye met Bobby on his first morning in Montpellier, in the large kitchen of Elodie and Guifré's three-bedroom house. She was sitting cross-legged on the kitchen counter, in a white T-shirt and jeans ripped at the knees, writing in a notebook that was cradled in the triangular space between her thighs. She looked up when he walked in.

Her face opened in a beguiling smile. "I'm Taiye." She reached out for a handshake. "You must be Bobby. Elodie told me you'd be coming."

He returned her smile, nodded his head, shook her hand, and knew that he wanted to tell her everything.

"What brought you here?" Taiye asked him.

Bobby answered her, slowly, in the months they lived together. Taiye learned that he was from Coney Island. And that after doing the thing they say you're supposed to do when your single mother loves you sacrificially and suffers to bring you up—excel at school, get a scholarship to university (SUNY Albany), excel there too, and land a junior analyst position at Kohlbrach Ingram Investments; after nearly eight years with the firm, two promotions, a house for his mother, a condo for himself— he married a woman who didn't love him. He was well aware of this fact but, ever the pragmatist, believed that she would stay because he could provide. He was too naive to realize that she could take his provisions without staying with him, until she left with more than half of everything he'd worked for.

That's when the panic attacks started, and then the loss of appetite. Bobby told Taiye that he knew that if he didn't leave, he wouldn't survive. So he transferred a hefty portion of his savings to his mother, rented out his condo, and took nothing but a backpack full of clothes, some cash, credit cards, and a camera. Then he flew to Ho Chi Minh City. From there to Cambodia, Thailand, Laos, and China. He stayed in each place for no less than three weeks, and when he found an opportunity to teach English in Zhuhai, China, he stayed for four months. There, he met a translator who'd just returned from holiday and wouldn't stop gushing about how much she adored her time in Montpellier. So the next month he booked the cheapest ticket he could find and headed out.

"And now I'm here," Bobby said to Taiye. "What brought you here?"

Taiye laughed for a long time. And then she told him.

# Kehinde

I'VE LIVED IN MONTREAL SINCE I WAS EIGHTEEN.

This is the first time I've been home since I left. I was hurt and I needed to stay away. At first, I didn't tell my sister that I'd been looking at universities in Canada when she was working on her applications to schools in the UK. It certainly would have been easier if I'd done the same, owing to our dual citizenship, but I wanted to go elsewhere, away from her. Of course, I wanted to hurt her with this news. And I did. Her face collapsed when I told her.

"But you'll need a student visa. And won't it be more expensive? Are you sure?" she'd asked.

Yes, I needed a student visa. It meant that Taiye was gone for about a year before my visa was approved. Yes, it was significantly more expensive. So I applied for every grant, scholarship, and on-campus job I could find on the university website. Yes, I was sure.

And now.

And now I just want to know what Taiye's life has looked like since we went our separate ways as teenagers. Because—I'm not proud of this—I punished her every day after Sister Bisi snatched me from Uncle Ernest's grasp. I punished her with long silences; I barely looked her in the face.

After we came back from London, Taiye and I went to the same secondary school our mother had attended, Queen's College. We were boarders for less than one term before our mother came to collect us—she couldn't bear us being so far away. I liked Queen's College—the overcrowded dormitories, the classrooms, the fact that Taiye and I were in different houses, me in Emotan, Taiye in Dan Fodio, like our mother had been. All of it gave me space away from our twinness, from the tension of having to keep myself from spewing all my festering feelings at her.

It was a large enough school that, at first, not everyone knew we were twins. We weren't in the same class, so when I met my new classmates, I could just be *Kehinde*, and not *one of the twins*. Without seeing Taiye's face melt into panic whenever a teacher called upon her, I didn't feel that instinctual pull to speak for her like I used to. She had to learn to speak for herself. By the time my classmates found out we were twins they could already distinguish me from her by my personality and my softening body. Even though I was purging often, my body kept widening.

At school I was bubbly. Even after our mother made us become day students, school was my escape from the house and everything it had witnessed. I wanted friends of my own, a life of my own. I was easy to be friends with because I kept it all shallow, light, fun.

"How come you're so, like, nice and friendly and your sister is such a snob?" a girl asked once during biology class.

I didn't defend Taiye. I didn't say, "She's not a snob. She's just painfully shy." I just shrugged.

Another time, I was standing in line to buy snacks from the tuck shop at break time, chatting with the girl ahead of me, when someone from the end of the line shouted, "Ahn ahn this girl, why are you always looking at Isa like you're a leleh?" This was Queen's College slang for lesbian.

I looked to see who she was talking to: Taiye.

My sister stood frozen and stuttering, her eyes searching for me. They found me, and I knew what she was asking, but I looked away. Taiye was gone when I looked back.

There were many such instances of carelessness, too many. They piled up to form a sizable wound. The thing is, Taiye never stopped searching for me. Every time I witnessed other teenager girls inflicting casual cruelty upon her, her eyes always sought me out, always landed on my own. That is how it was until we graduated, and she left.

And now, after all this time, we're home together again.

And all that staying away, I can't say it was worth it. I can't really name precisely what I was staying away from. It feels like a loss.

It's a familiar feeling but much less potent than the one that overtook me that first year in Montreal. There was a lead-heavy and crushing thing that bloomed inside of me then.

It started in the winter, a wretched season. Sharp winds sliced through my insufficient layers, and I was sure all the blood would freeze in my fingers and toes. My skin itched from dryness, and I couldn't seem to get warm enough. To whatever degree my body suffered, my mind was hit tenfold. Something shifted, something cracked. There were many many instances when, walking along the frost-covered sidewalks, I considered throwing myself into the rush of oncoming traffic. I didn't really want to die; I was just tired, and so cold, and so lonely.

At the dining hall, in my quest to feel anything else, I swung between ignoring my appetite entirely and, in a dizzying haze of hunger, eating plates and plates of bland cafeteria food. I made a habit of it, and I continued my habit of purging as much of it as I could manage. That habit was hard to kick; it lasted for some time.

By summer I realized I'd outgrown the T-shirts, jeans, and dresses I'd brought from home. I'd grown bigger than ever before, and I hated it. I'd always hated my body. Well, not always ...

I'd hated my body for a long time, hated all the ways I felt it had betrayed me.

I spent the summer cloaked in shame, seething with jealousy. I envied other women's bodies. I envied fat women who draped their luscious curves without any embarrassment, thighs quaking as they walked. I envied thin women lounging effortlessly in T-shirts and shorts, nothing pinching or pudging, just smooth skin over smooth muscle over delicate bones. I envied anyone who didn't hate their body. People who ate without hesitation or pre-emptive shame at how all those calories would stretch their flesh.

It was about beauty, yes, but it was also about belonging. People treat you with kindness and an invitation to belong if they like the way you look, and every time I looked in the mirror, I saw someone who was almost as beautiful as Taiye, nearly as lucky, but never quite meeting the mark. Body too soft in all the wrong ways—and marked by an invisible unerasable ugliness.

I called our mother often. We talked about nothing, but she was kind.

I hid my number and called Taiye often as well, never saying anything, just listening to her asking, "Hello? Hello? Who is this? Are you okay?"

Sometimes she would stay on the phone saying nothing as well, just breathing quietly on the other end until I hung up.

This is how I knew that she was lonely, too.

FROM MY SMALL SUITCASE ON THE FLOOR BESIDE MY BED, I fetch Taiye's box of letters. Except for my travel documents, some photographs, and jewellery, it's the only other thing I had in my carry-on.

*Letter no. 1*
*September 29, 2005*
*Aunty Yemisi's flat*

*Dear Kehinde,*
*I tried calling you this morning, but you didn't pick up, so I'm just going to write what I was calling to tell you.*

*The flat has changed a lot since we were last here.*

*There are half-empty boxes everywhere, even though they've been living here for long. I don't think Aunty Yemisi likes me, she's very somehow. It's as if she's angry all the time and she's just waiting for me to annoy her so that she can pounce.*

*I've been trying to do everything she asks before she even asks, but she's just too much!*

*They go to church like three times a week! And the Nigerian aunties there only know how to be sending somebody up and down as if I came here to do housegirl.*

*I've just been staying at the campus library longer and longer so that I'm not in her house annoying her with my breathing.*

*Anyway, London feels like Lagos sometimes because there's so many Nigerians here. I like my classes and—*

*Oh God, she's calling me now, I have to go.*

*Love,*

*Taiye*


**Letter no. 3**
*October 29, 2005*


*Our first birthday apart. I hope you're having a better time than I am. Still not answering my calls, not sure what to do. Mumsie called to sing to me. It made me cry. She said you were out with friends.*

*I miss you,*

*Taiye*


**Letter no. 4**
*November 11, 2005*
*Campus Library*


*Kehinde,*

*See me see wahala o!*

*This woman locked me out last night, and she hid the spare key. I rang the doorbell, but she never answered. I ended up sitting on the cold stoop for like four hours before Sade came home from wherever she was.*

*You know what's funny? She didn't even ask why I was locked out; she didn't seem surprised at all. Aunty Yemisi didn't talk to me at all today, surprise surprise.*

*Before Sade left for work, she came into my room and put a key on my bedside table. She asked me not to tell her mumsie and only use it for emergencies like last night.*

*I think she's pregnant. Her mother is going to lose her mind. Anyway, Sade sent me some job postings around campus and one roommate advertisement. She's trying to be subtle, but I get it. I'm grateful sha.*

*Honestly, I feel bad for her. Her mother is a fucking tyrant. She's only sweet to Dapo and Jide, and they don't even live here anymore. They still come every Sunday for supper. It's the only time she's in a good mood.*

*I'm too tired to tell you all the rubbish, but I'll try calling again tomorrow.*

*Love,*

*Taiye*

**Letter no. 15**

*February 18, 2006*

*Asylum Rd., Peckham*

*Kehinde,*

*So are you avoiding my calls or something?*

*I called Mumsie yesterday and asked to talk to you, but she said you weren't at home.*

*I'm worried about Mumsie. Have you spoken to her recently?*

*I've been working so much and saving and doing exams, but I've moved out!*

*I live in a basement room in a house with five other people in Peckham. The house is old and a bit horrible. Cockroaches live in most of the cupboards, and mice live in the walls and floorboards. But you know what's not here?! A wicked aunty who doesn't know how to treat somebody!*

*As for school, I don't know why I'm studying chemistry, I swear. But I did well on the exams, so that's that.*

*That's pretty much my life: school, work, Mass—I've started going regularly, just because it's familiar. I've tried to make some friends, and I've met some all right people. But when we're in a group having a conversation and I have something to add, I feel sooo nervous, and then when I have the courage to say something, the topic has already changed! So, I don't even know. This one girl, Shanti, asked me if I'm shy or just a snob! I wanted to shout that I'm not a snob, people talk so quickly and jump from topic to topic, and they all talk so loud! So even when I say something, they don't seem to hear me. Whatever sha, it's all good; I tried to make pepper soup last night, it wasn't bad.*

*Love,*

*Taiye*

*PS: Sade came to see me yesterday. She IS pregnant. I'm going with her to the clinic. I don't want to think about it too much, for my sake as much as hers. You should have seen her when she asked me to come with her. Her eyes were swollen from crying all day. She didn't want to tell me who the father is. I guess it doesn't really matter.*

**Letter no. 23**
*July 2, 2006*
*Asylum Rd., Peckham*

*K,*

*I just got home. Was at a party. I'm drunk drunk I like it.*

*Oh my God. I danced with someone that was not a boy and I liked it I'm drunk.*

*I want to tell you this thing, which is that I talk to myself sometimes, as in when I need someone to talk to, because you won't answer me and mami can be funny sometimes. So yes*

*I mss you*

*T*

I'M NOT SURE HOW LONG I'VE BEEN HERE in my childhood bedroom, reading these letters. I'm trying to read them chronologically, but they don't seem to be arranged in any meaningful order. I read them silently, and the words bring the sound of Taiye's voice into my mind so that I can hear her hurt.

Sometimes Taiye's letters are funny, or strange. Like this one, from the night Farouq and I got married ...

*Letter no. 64*
*August 10, 2012*
*Somewhere South London*


K,

*I just saw you at this club. I was dancing with this girl I've come home with. I'm rolling, feel incredible. I saw you! It couldn't have been you, but it was. Life is weird as shit, and anything is possible. This girl is fine sha, she has this stainless-steel toy, BUT I'm entirely too fucked up to play with that. And you probably definitely don't want to hear about it! Okay, okay, okay, I have to goooooo. I found this receipt in my coat pocket, it's for chanterelle mushrooms and scallops and organic butter, ha! Why am I such a pretentious twat?!*

*Always,*

*T*

# Kambirinachi

KAMBIRINACHI HAD JUST TURNED FOURTEEN when her aunt Akuchi enrolled her at the university staff secondary school. A much smaller school than Queen's College, this one was coed. She hadn't seen her mother since her birthday just three weeks before. She'd begged Ikenna to stay longer than the three days she'd spent cooking and dancing and braiding Kambirinachi's hair. The night before she was to start classes, she longed to see her mother's face, needed to be reassured. Her mother had been far more tender with her those three days than ever before, and she needed some of that tenderness again.

Her time in Akuchi's home was easy. Her aunt's joy was contagious because she moved in a world saturated with love, despite the rough edges of life in Ife. Akuchi loved her work. She took Kambirinachi to the campus once to show her the school she would soon attend. She greeted everyone with kindness, from the gatemen to the head of her department, a Hausa man in his early fifties named Yusuf.

Yusuf was the man Akuchi loved. He was unavailable for more reasons than his marriage, and Akuchi knew this. There was his faith—he was a Muslim man. There was his age and his seniority in the department. Yet these facts did nothing to dampen her affections. Somehow she'd learned, or perhaps was gifted with, the ability to love without expectation. Kambirinachi could smell the devotion pouring out of Akuchi's pores when she introduced her to Yusuf. And she recognized the sweetness in Yusuf's eyes when he looked at Akuchi.

Kambirinachi's time at the staff school whooshed past her. It was something that she sometimes let happen when the present was just bearable. She was friendly enough but didn't make many friends. She did her work well enough but didn't earn extraordinary marks, except in her fine arts classes. There she poured herself into painting, turning out extraordinary pieces in what was becoming her signature heavily textured and kaleidoscopic style. She continued to listen in on the voices, but she never chimed in to keep from being swallowed up. She cast webs for suitable lovers for Akuchi, but her aunt's desire for Yusuf kept her blind to any potential partners reeled in by Kambirinachi's captivating lures.

She waited for her mother to return for her.

She waited almost a year to ask Akuchi why her mother hadn't come back. Her aunt only looked away, sadness casting a long shadow across her face as she changed the subject.

She let time speed past her like a warm breeze when you drive with your windows down. Three years went by in a languid blink.

On Akuchi's suggestion, Kambirinachi took the matriculation exam for entry to Obafemi Awolowo University. She applied to study in the Department of Fine and Applied Arts.

On the Sunday after her graduation from the staff school, Akuchi threw Kambirinachi a party in the backyard, a large affair. She invited Kambirinachi's entire class, as well as her own colleagues and friends from the university. Kambirinachi, Akuchi, and Adaora spent the whole day cooking: sugary balls of yeasty puff-puff, palm-sized mini meat pies, several batches of chin chin, crispy fried meat in peppery stew, jollof rice with stewed chicken, and sweet golden fried plantains. Akuchi asked Yusuf to bring crates of Coke, Fanta, and Maltina, and he helped her load the drinks into the deep-freeze by the kitchen door.

Kambirinachi was sitting by the phone beside Akuchi's bookshelf in the parlour, willing her mother to call. She walked toward the kitchen to ask her aunt why her mother hadn't called, but before she stepped through the doorway, she heard Akuchi's soft giggles float to meet her. She peeked through the crack of the door, saw Yusuf holding Akuchi from behind, his bearded face buried in the crook of her aunt's plump shoulder. He whispered something that made her aunt beam with so much joy that Kambirinachi didn't dare disturb them.

Kambirinachi felt something waiting for her, paused patiently at a particular point in time. A gift, perhaps, that would justify her choice to stay in this alive way that seemed more about losing to love and eating to stay living than anything else.

BEFORE KAMBIRINACHI MET BANJI, she dreamed of him. It was close to a year after she applied to study fine art at the university, during one of those hazy restless in-between sleeps. She saw only his spirit body, a gentle and curious curve hovering just above the edge of her kaleidoscopic dreamscape. In the morning, she walked to campus with a light giddiness that made her feel almost weightless. It was her first day of undergraduate classes, but she suspected that there was more to her excitement.

So when she stumbled over Banji's black school bag—which he'd slung carelessly at the foot of his chair—and he caught her elbow to keep her from falling on the dusty concrete floor of the lecture hall—she recognized him by the softness of his gaze.

She steadied herself, looked him right in the face, and said, "Oh, it's you."

# Taiye

THE COOKING CLASSES AT LA DOLÇA ESPOSA WERE DEMANDING, on account of having to learn new cooking techniques in a new language. Besides Taiye and Bobby, there were eight students. Four white undergraduate students—two from upstate New York, one from North Dakota, and the other from Connecticut—a Japanese woman, Kaoru—she was pregnant and would only start to show as the course progressed—a middle-aged Austrian woman and her brown teenaged daughter, and a very pale Scottish girl with fuzzy orange dreadlocks.

Naturally, the students broke off into smaller groups. The Americans stuck with each other; the Austrian woman seemed to gravitate to the Scottish girl, while keeping a sharp eye on her young daughter, who always drifted to Taiye's side, likely because she was the only other Black person present. Taiye harboured an obvious empathy for Kaoru since her pregnancy gave her a weak stomach.

All of them, except for Bobby, had at least an intermediate command of the language and seemed to excel not only at deciphering Guifré's rapid French but also maintaining their composure when he scolded them sharply for improperly descaling fish or facing the partridge in the wrong direction when preparing a perdreaux á la catalane.

During one of their early classes, Taiye broke her intense focus, caught Bobby's eye, and smiled at the expression of pure bafflement on his face. He smiled back. At their fifteen-minute break, he joined her where she was smoking at the back door of the kitchen.

"You smoke," he said. He'd meant it as a question, but it came out flat.

"Only in France." She smiled and offered him a cigarette.

"No, I'm good. Thanks, though."

"How are you finding this?" She jerked her head toward the restaurant.

"Fuck, I don't know ..." Bobby stretched his lean body. "My French is shit, so I don't know what he's saying half the time."

Taiye dropped the rest of her cigarette on the ground and put it out with her sandal-clad toes. "I can help you out if you want. Take the station next to mine on Wednesday."

EVEN AS A YOUNG CHILD, Taiye recognized when her father started earning more money because they switched from using margarine, the kind that comes in a yellow plastic tub with a blue lid, to butter imported from Ireland, the salted kind that comes wrapped in gold foil. Kehinde didn't seem to notice, but Taiye's palate sang in response to the butter's superiority. In London, she didn't buy butter unless she could afford the organic cultured kind from health food shops. It was a treat when she could spare the money, and she could make an eight-ounce block last well over a month.

In Catalan cuisine, though, it was all olive oil.

"Ici, nous ne mangeons pas toujours du beurre comme les stéréotypes français. Dans la cuisine Catalane nous utilisons l'huile d'olive," Guifré announced at the beginning of a lesson on sauces and condiments.

At La Dolça Esposa, the dishes on the menu—designed to resemble humble parchment paper—were all written in Catalan, with their descriptions written below in French. The curriculum of Elodie and Guifré's culinary course covered how to make every item on the restaurant's seasonal menu. During the summer that Taiye studied under them, it was a small selection of five starters, five main courses, and three desserts. The wine list was three times as long as the food menu.

The first starter they learned to prepare was a fair-style octopus dish: *pop estil a feira*. The dish involved curling the tips of the octopus's tentacles by dipping it in boiling water for fifteen seconds a few times. Kaoru ran out of the kitchen to vomit at that particular point; Taiye grabbed the octopus that Kaoru had flung aside in her haste and continued dipping its tentacles in the bubbling pot so that she wouldn't fall behind.

They had to cook the octopus, sans head, with onions, garlic, and salt, until tender—but not too tender, or Guifré would eye them as if they'd just insulted his mother. While the octopus simmered, they set some potatoes to boil. Then they thinly sliced and layered the octopus over the potatoes before drizzling a generous helping of extra-virgin olive oil and sprinkling with coarse salt—or, as Guifré preferred, smoked black salt—and both sweet and hot paprika.

"Done!" Taiye exclaimed, after she'd assembled her dish on a black slate plate.

Guifré looked over her dish and did his best to conceal a smile. "Pas mal," he said, and went to inspect Bobby's to the left.

"AW, MAN, YOU KILLED IT!" Bobby said, handing Taiye a small glass of gin and tonic with a bright green lime wedge fizzing at the bottom.

"Merci; merci," Taiye said. "How did you guys find it?" she asked the table.

It was Friday evening, the end of their first practical exam. Taiye had loved it.

"I hate to be this person," the Scottish girl said. Her name was Fiona, though Taiye had taken to referring to her, rather unkindly, as white-dreadlock-girl.

"Then don't be!" one of the Americans, a boy named Evan, retorted. The table erupted in laughter.

"No, no, I must," Fiona continued. "Octopus—wait, what's the plural for octopus?"

"Octopi!"

"Yes, thank you. Octopi are actually quite brilliant."

"You mean delicious?" Kaoru asked. Her belly had swelled well past her small breasts by then.

"No, like really intelligent." Fiona said. "They recognize people, they open jars. Some organization in Ireland is trying to make it illegal to eat them."

"But they're so yummy," the brown Austrian girl said. Her name was Johanna, she was seventeen, and her mother had reluctantly left her in Taiye and Kaoru's care that evening.

"You know what's also yummy?" Evan asked. He'd thrown back four beers within the first hour at the Cuban bar somewhere off Place de la Comédie in downtown Montpellier.

"What's also yummy?" Johanna asked.

"Human flesh!"

"Ew, no!" another American, Tabitha, exclaimed.

"What?! It's true. Cannibals call human flesh the 'long pork.'"

"Why? Why would you tell us this?" Fiona asked in mock annoyance.

Evan shrugged. "I'd give it a try."

"That's because you're disgusting," Fiona said. "I need the loo."

"Wait, I'll come too," Kaoru said. The two women waded through the crowded bar in search of the toilets.

Taiye felt responsible for ensuring that Johanna got home before midnight and Kaoru made it to her flat before exhaustion wiped her out, so she kept it to two drinks that evening. The group left the bar at a quarter after eleven and split up. Taiye, Kaoru, Bobby, and Johanna headed toward Kaoru's neighbourhood, which was a short walk from the tram station, and the rest of the group went off to find more music. Taiye and Bobby walked Kaoru to her flat and took a tram with Johanna to the house her mother had rented for the summer. Then they walked the forty-five minutes to their neighbourhood.

The walk was mostly silent. To Taiye, Bobby seemed much drunker than she'd seen him before. She allowed it when he reached for her cold hand.

"Your hands are freezing, girl," he said. "You cold?"

"A little," Taiye said. "This seems like a dumb choice now." She gestured at her white button-down. It was sheer silk, bought second-hand as a gift to herself a year prior. Underneath it, she wore denim shorts and a sports bra.

"You look beautiful." Bobby took off his dark denim jacket and gave it to her. "Here, let me," he said, and draped it over her shoulders.

"Thank you, but now you'll be cold."

"Nah, I'm good."

They walked the rest of the way home in more silence.

When they arrived at Elodie and Guifré's place, Taiye waved Bobby toward the kitchen. She switched on the pot lights above the shiny stainless-steel gas stove, filled a glass with water from the tap, and handed it to him.

"You know," she whispered to keep from waking up their hosts, "you're probably the most soulful boy I've ever met."

Bobby gulped the water down and placed the glass on the counter. "Soulful?" he asked.

"Yeah."

"What does that even mean?" He stood closer to Taiye and took her hand again.

She let him kiss her hands, her voice shaking with uncertainty. "Like, I don't know ... soulful."

Bobby leaned in and lightly touched his lips to hers. She didn't move away, so he kissed her with more firmness and moved his hands to her waist. Still, she didn't move away, but she didn't kiss him back, either.

He stopped and looked at her. "No?" he asked, wincing as if in preparation for a blow to the face.

"I'm sorry Bobby, I ..." Taiye inhaled sharply and looked away for a moment before settling her eyes back on his.

"No, no, it's all good." He pushed back the dark curls that framed his face. "I guess I just, ah ... misread the situation?" He stepped back and took a seat at the counter. "I definitely thought you were into ..."

"No, Bobby, I'm sorry." Taiye struggled with the words. "You're lovely, and I would probably want to kiss you if ... but I'm gay ... that's all."

"Oh."

"Yeah, I'm totally into you, but just as a friend. It's nice to feel close to someone."

Taiye realized the truth of her statement as the words came out of her mouth. It had been a long time since she'd felt close to anyone. She'd figured out fairly quickly that Bobby harboured feelings for her. She relished his attention and the intimacy that developed with their late-night conversations on the balcony.

"Okay," Bobby said, looking at her. "Okay ..."

"Yeah ..."

Taiye took a seat next to him, and they rested in silence for a long while.

"So, you're like full-on homo, huh?" Bobby said and gave her a playful nudge with his elbow. He put his hurt away quickly; he wanted to make it okay.

"Yeah." Taiye chuckled softly. "Yeah, it's like the first time I've said that out loud."

"For real?"

"Yes."

"Wow, okay. Well, I feel pretty special." He flashed her an impish grin that was entirely at odds with the sadness of his eyes.

Upstairs he gave her a hug and said, "Well, good night."

Taiye asked, "Bobby, would you like to have a platonic sleepover?"

"Right now?" he asked, eyebrows raised.

Taiye nodded. She didn't want to sleep alone.

"All right, get in here." He let her into his bedroom ahead of him.

Taiye undressed down to her sports bra and underwear. They held each other tight in the centre of his soft mattress. Taiye started to snore shortly after they climbed into bed. But Bobby never slept.

CLOSE TO THE END OF HER STAY IN MONTPELLIER, Taiye was eager to figure out the "gay thing," as Bobby phrased it. So, on his suggestion, she began to make eyes at women she found attractive.

Taiye and Bobby had managed to recover from the awkward phase of their friendship after he came on to her, and she came out to him. They stayed close. Although Bobby tried and failed to have firmer emotional boundaries, he was still very much in *something* with Taiye.

On his last night in Montpellier, they stayed up all night together. They drank many tiny cups of espresso and talked about what they would do next. Taiye planned to return to London, and then maybe go home to Lagos to be with her mother for a few months before looking for proper work. Bobby had been travelling for over a year by then, so he thought that he might go home to Brooklyn to see his mother. He definitely didn't want to go back to working as an actuarial analyst, so maybe he would go back to school, or if he could manage to get a gig, work as a line cook somewhere in the city.

When it was time, Bobby said a quiet goodbye to Elodie and Guifré, and then walked with Taiye to Saint Roch train station. They sat together in silence at a café in the already bustling station, and shared a stale chocolate pastry and even more coffee, before heading toward his train. They hugged tight and for a long time. Taiye couldn't keep her tears back.

"Well, love," Bobby said, pulling away, "if you're ever in Brooklyn, you definitely have a place to stay."

"Likewise." Taiye wiped away her tears with the back of her hand, which shook from all that caffeine. "I mean, if you're in London, or Lagos, for that matter." They smiled at each other, stalling.

"Bobby," Taiye kissed him soft on his dry lips, "thank you for being my friend."

"Thank you for letting me," he responded. Then he turned and ambled toward his train.

"THANK YOU, ELODIE, I'VE, UH, THIS HAS BEEN A GREAT OPPORTUNITY." Taiye wound her red knit scarf snug around her neck. The evening air was cool—nothing compared to the dampness of London, but still, she shivered. "I appreciate it very much. I've learned a lot."

"De rien, Taiye. You are a very hard worker, thank *you*," Elodie replied.

She'd seemed, to Taiye, curt throughout the semester, but with just the two of them here, Elodie's eyes lingered on Taiye's face, her body.

Now and again, Taiye caught her looking, and she'd only smile, startled, and carry on with her errands.

Just over three weeks since the program ended and Bobby left, Taiye had stayed on to help at the restaurant. She felt that nothing awaited her in London and was in no rush to leave. But the restaurant was closing for a few weeks, and Elodie and Guifré were going to Barcelona to see Guifré's family. They'd had a hectic summer and needed the rest, Elodie said.

Guifré took a train a few days before his wife, leaving left her to pack the car and take the nearly four-hour drive along the A9 autoroute. Taiye helped Elodie load her car with their suitcases. They were both leaving the following day and Taiye didn't have a lot to pack—a satchel for her computer and papers, a duffle for clothes, and some presents for her mother and great-aunt—so she joined Elodie for supper that evening. They shared a duck confit cassoulet that Taiye found outrageously delicious, largely because it reminded her of Sister Bisi's ewa agoyin.

Several glasses of red wine after they ate, Elodie grew blatant. On the sofa in the spacious living room with the south-facing glass doors that opened onto a flourishing garden, Taiye's body clenched tight when she felt Elodie's hand glide up her jean-clad thigh. Pausing her breathing for a moment, Taiye leaned in to discover how she felt about it, and then relaxed into Elodie's touch.

"So, the American boy, Bobby, is your boyfriend?" Elodie asked, one hand still on Taiye's leg, the other cupping a half-empty wineglass, its deep garnet contents swishing dangerously close to the rim as she moved.

Taiye shook her head. "Just friends."

"I think he like you," Elodie said. She let her eyes linger on Taiye's lips. "I mean, no surprise. T'es tellement belle."

"I'm gay," Taiye said bluntly, awkwardly. She'd been practising saying those words out loud. "Elodie, may I kiss you?"

Elodie laughed, her whole mouth stained purple from the wine she'd been sucking down like water. In response, she leaned forward and parted Taiye's lips with the tip of her tongue. They kissed voraciously on the sofa until Elodie said, "Upstairs?"

AS ONE WOULD EXPECT FROM A LOVER'S FIRST LOVING, Taiye was eager and clumsy. She asked before slipping her fingers inside Elodie, "Let me know what feels good, yeah?"

Afterward, Elodie, with a smile spread across her face, and her eyes closed, said, "Taiye, you are a very ... sincere lover."

She rested her head on Taiye's bare lap and played with the ends of her braids, coiling them around her red-tipped fingers, unravelling and rebraiding them.

"Oh God, sincere?" Taiye said, self-conscious about her enthusiasm just moments before, her heart still racing.

"It's very good. How is it you say 'inattendu'? I didn't ... ah ...?"

"Expect? Unexpected!" Taiye said.

"Yes, c'est ça. Because you are like, eh, timide, but not so shy. You don't say too much, but in bed just now—"

"Oh God, I was talking too much?"

"No, no ... you ask questions, pay attention. It was very nice."

"You liked it?"

"Yes." Elodie rolled off her back and stretched. "Your other lovers, they have not told you this?"

"I haven't ... really had other lovers."

"Ah! I am the first?"

"A little bit." Nervous laughter escaped her.

"Well, I think that you will have many." Elodie got out of bed and stretched again before beginning to dress.

"Elodie?" Taiye said sweetly; from her mouth, Elodie's name was a question.

Elodie smiled and raised her eyebrows.

"Will you stay in bed for a little while longer?"

Elodie pulled her T-shirt over her head and fell back into Taiye's lap. She lightly traced a finger from the shallow cleft of Taiye's lower lip, all the way down her throat and between her breasts, where she paused to tap a rhythm on Taiye's sternum. She hummed a drowsy tune in time with the slow tapping. That melody again.

"What's that song?" Taiye asked.

Elodie paused to think. "I don't know. I just think of it now."

"Elodie's melody." Taiye smiled the words.

She hadn't known until that evening with Elodie just how intoxicating it could be to have another person engulf you with their scent, their self. She wouldn't be able to tell you if it was merely the naked act of sex, the warmth, the pleasure of it, or if it was something else, equally as simple: to be wanted in return by someone you want. No obligation, just desire. To be chosen. It was her first dose of the thing she would spend a long time pursuing. A sense of belonging like with Bobby but viscerally enrapturing.

After Elodie, quite like falling off a narrow ledge, accidentally but perhaps a little intentionally, sauntering backward, with that soft impish smile spread across her dark face and her eyes half-shut sleepy moons, Taiye plunged deep into hedonism.

# Kehinde

I AM LYING ON A TATTERED RED RAFFIA MAT under the palm trees in the backyard, only a few feet from Taiye's hive. I can hear the steady buzzing of her bees, a lulling, low hum. Besides the foot and car traffic outside the gate on the opposite side of the house, the compound is silent. I don't know where anybody is. It's good this way because the painful throb in my temples has returned, and I don't want to talk to anyone just now.

And Taiye's letters ...

I open an envelope dated two years ago. It isn't sealed or stamped, but it's addressed to my place in Montreal. It's one of those small white envelopes that are blue on the inside, with red-and-blue striped borders along the outside edges. Taiye's voice is distinct. I can hear it in my mind. Her voice is transparent; she hides nothing. In this letter, she tells me how she is learning to make sourdough bread. I can read her excitement in her handwriting, which is slanted and sloppy, and some of the words aren't entirely spelled out.

*I'm a little bit in awe of how little this recipe needs. It's simple and complete. Flour, water, and time. That it! Well, I think the real magic is the bacteria floating in the air and wild yeast in the flour. Breadmaking is my favourit part of Culinary schoo so far. I butchred a pig the other day, and it was intense. Intense is a good word.*

*Fresh sourdough and butter is everything*

I also have a pig story. Isn't that funny? Or strange? I'll get to that.

I close my eyes, wanting to sync my breathing with the hum of the hive. By the mercy of shady trees, the air is almost cool. There is a patch of earth near the hive, about seven feet by eight feet; it wants to be alive with green. Someone took pains to prepare it, to weed and till the red-tinged soil for seeding. Yet it is barren, waiting.

Barren, but waiting.

There is this cold envy slithering in and out of my ears; although I know it is misplaced, I cannot will it away. Taiye does not want Farouq, Farouq wants me, but the thing is that Taiye has always been lucky. I don't want to be the sort of person who resents that; I don't want to be the sort of person who punishes her twin for over a decade for something that neither of us could control. But I am; I have been. And this envy, perpetually pained, remembers everything, hisses the question: *Why did it have to be you?*

I shiver, though I am not cold.

It answers its own question: *Because she left you.*

Always the same answer.

I haven't had a bad life. The privilege of our class, our money, shielded us from just how severe the pain could have been. To deny it would be dishonest.

And I've been so lucky in love.

Before Farouq, I loved a boy named Wolfie. Even now, in the rare thoughts that I keep from Farouq, I cradle my memories of Wolfie with tenderness.

We met during my fifth year in Montreal. I was still working on my undergrad degree in international development. The dark fog that had rapidly enveloped me that first winter started to lift slowly at the beginning of the second year, after I switched dorms and started living with new roommates who would become good friends. It lifted some more when my new friends suggested that I see a counsellor at the student centre. I saw the counsellor, a middle-aged white woman named Corinne, bi-monthly, and we rarely talked about where I came from, just where I was at the moment. It helped.

By the time I felt that I could see clearer, my grades were unsalvageable, and I had to start over. So I did. I was focused. It didn't matter that the program was revealing itself to be rooted in neocolonialism. Or that there seemed to be no solutions for issues like child labour, human trafficking, or environmental degradation, or exploitative economic policies that didn't breed more trouble. Or that those issues are rooted in the systems that are perpetually *attempting* to undo them, even if only half-heartedly.

These were melodramatic spirals I found myself descending into, but I did the work.

My scholarship money had run out after four years, and my job at the school library wasn't nearly enough to cover tuition and rent. So I lied about having serving experience and dropped my cv at Milas, a tiny casual fine dining restaurant in Mile End.

Wolfie was a line cook at Milas, and for well over four months he barely said four words to me, and I pretended not to be sore about it. He had a scar on the right side of his upper lip, where the split from a cleft palate had been sewn together. He was fair-skinned, even for a white boy, so pale, and he blushed easily. He kept his blond hair buzzed short and let his beard grow in a dense reddish bristle just long enough that you could imagine grabbing it in a tight fistful. At family meals before the dimly lit restaurant opened for dinner service, the employees ate at one of the worn communal mahogany slab tables under mismatched vintage crystal chandeliers. The chef and owner, Luca, led a small staff of eight: sous chef Baptiste; line cook and pastry chef Saoirse; line cook Wolfie; bartender and Luca's wife, Genevieve; three servers: me, Uma, and Billa; and the dishwasher, Ezra.

On hectic nights, when the Mile End crowd craved twenty-two-dollar smoked mushroom and chicken liver tarts, or eighteen-dollar head-cheese pâté with habanero basil jam on a fresh baguette, or any of Chef's overpriced, undeniably delicious experiments, the kitchen line was tense. Chef barked orders like a drill sergeant, and Baptiste, Saoirse, and Wolfie turned out impeccable dishes with fury at the servers. On nights like that, Wolfie oscillated between harsh and indifferent, and I always took offence.

"I don't know what his fucking problem is," I'd mutter to Uma whenever we got a moment to breathe.

Sometimes she'd respond, "Back of house folk are always taking the piss. Don't take it to heart, love." Other times she'd roll her eyes and say, "Fucking cunt."

She was my favourite.

On one of those nights Uma suddenly became violently ill. She draped herself over the staff toilet, heaving the contents of her stomach into the bowl and crying. Genevieve called her girlfriend to take her to the emergency room. Genevieve and Billa stepped in to help me whenever they could, but the narrow bar was crowded with the hungry, impatient, and aloof. I was a spinning top, and the night went by in a blur. I broke three wineglasses and emptied a whole bowl of beer-steamed mussels onto a patron's lap. I was lucky she was kind, but I still had to pay for her meal.

When we finally closed for the night and I cashed out, I cried at the bar and sucked down a gin and soda with the rest of the staff before cleaning up the dining room. Everyone chipped in with the tidying and left one by one as they finished their tasks. I was mopping the floors, so I had to be the last to go, but Wolfie stayed with me.

"Good work today," he said from the bar as he upended the thin-legged wooden stools.

"Thank you."

"Pretty wild shift, eh?"

"Yeah."

"You know if Uma's all right?"

"No idea. I'll give her a call in the morning."

"Can I help you with the mopping?"

"No, I'm all right, thanks."

He walked across the small dining room and took the mop from me. "Please, let me."

"You know this is the longest conversation we've had?" I asked, stepping out of his way.

"Yeah?"

"Mm-hmm."

"Well, I've never really had a chance. We've never been alone before."

"We don't have to be alone to have a conversation, Wolfie."

"You never talk to me either," he said playfully, defensively.

"I do! You're just too cool to pay attention."

"Cool?"

"Indifferent."

He looked right at me, his eyes such a pale grey they seemed almost clear, and flashed a devastating grin. "I'm not indifferent now, am I?"

"No." I smiled back.

THE DAY HAD BEEN WARM AND HEAVY WITH HUMIDITY, but the late-August night was too cold for my lace sundress. Even with a thick pashmina wrapped around my bare shoulders, I shivered as we walked west of the restaurant, toward my bus stop. It was a little past two a.m., and I was hoping to catch the last bus to Shaughnessy Village. Quiet and still for a Friday, as if the night, with its blinking street lights, had blanketed the entire neighbourhood in calm.

"You all right?" Wolfie asked, breaking the silence between us.

"I'm good, a bit cold."

He pulled off the black knit sweater he was wearing over a long-sleeved T-shirt and, despite my protests, handed it to me.

"How long you lived in Montreal?" he asked, shoving his hands into the front pockets of his jeans.

"Five-ish years."

"And you still haven't learned?" He chuckled and nudged me gently with his elbow. "Where do you live?" he asked.

"Concordia ghetto. You?"

"Just there." He pointed to a two-storey red-brick house a few buildings ahead of us.

"Oh, okay. You live pretty close," I said, trying to hide the disappointment in my voice. I'd hoped for a longer walk together.

"Would you ..." He gestured toward his building. "You want to come up for a bit?"

I nodded. "Yes."

WOLFIE LIVED IN A SPACIOUS TWO-BEDROOM.

"Bienvenue chez moi."

"Nice."

The air was dense with a mixture of musky incense and the sharp, distinct smell of some sort of fermentation. The apartment was minimally decorated, with white walls and no drapes on the bay windows that looked out onto the sleepy street. The bareness of the room seemed curated, and I was surprised by it. I had spent many idle moments wondering about what Wolfie got up to outside of work, where he slept. I hadn't pictured this.

"Make yourself comfortable," he said.

"You live by yourself?" I asked, curling myself into a soft corner of the sofa.

"No, I have a roommate. She's away, though."

"Where?"

"Thailand. Yoga teacher school, or something like that." He pulled a stool right up next to me. "Would you like something to drink?"

"Maybe. What are you offering?"

"Wine, some pop probably." He walked across the room to the kitchen, and I followed behind him. I jumped and yelped in surprise at the fat black and white cat that sped across my feet. Wolfie turned quickly, saw the cat, and laughed at me.

"That's Lulu," he said. "I found her scratching at my window last winter. She's annoying as fuck."

"You took in a stray cat?"

"Yeah." He shrugged. "She wanted to live here."

In the kitchen, a filthy jellyfish-looking thing floated in a large glass jar on top of the white refrigerator. The sour smell seemed to originate from there.

"What is that?" I asked in mild revulsion.

Wolfie laughed again. "It's a SCOBY," he said. "For kombucha."

"I don't know the meaning of any of the words you just said." I couldn't tear my eyes away from the funky jar.

"It's a fermented tea. The SCOBY is the mother."

"I don't think you understand how horrible that sounds. The *mother?*"

"Yeah, yeah, it's a yeast and bacteria culture that ferments the tea." He laughed at my horror. "It's good for your gut, like yogurt."

"You drink this?" I asked, aghast, looking at the cloudy liquid in the jar.

"Yeah, it's my roommate's, but I do a batch here and there."

He opened the fridge door and took out a cobalt-blue flip-top bottle. "This is mine. It's blueberry basil." He flicked open the top of the bottle with his thumb and handed it to me.

I sniffed: fruity and sour. "I don't know about this." I sipped tentatively. It was fizzy and sweet and tangy.

"Oh."

"'Oh' good?" he asked.

"Well ..." I took another sip. "I taste the basil. I don't hate it."

He took out another bottle. "Try this one. It's peach, mint, and cardamom."

He opened the bottle, and the contents rushed out in a frothy explosion, right in his face. "Tabarnak!" he swore, slamming the bottle down on the white tiled counter.

Wolfie pulled his T-shirt off to reveal a well-worn V-neck undershirt that was also wet. He had a swimmer's body, lean and broad, with a belly that protruded noticeably past the bunched waistband of his red tracksuit bottoms. We had never shared such a small space before, and I struggled to seem unaffected.

"You did that on purpose, just so you could take off your shirt, didn't you?" I teased.

He blushed deeply and tried to suppress a smile, but the rounded apples of his cheeks betrayed him. "And to what end, Kchinde?" he asked, eyebrows raised.

I shrugged. "Maybe you're trying to charm me," I said, in hopes that my nervousness would pass for cockiness.

"Is it working?"

"Maybe if I weren't so hungry I'd be able to tell."

"I can feed you."

"Yeah? What do you have?"

Wolfie rummaged through the fridge again. "Kimchi, some sausages, and ... smoked beets!"

He placed the items side by side on the counter: a large glass jar of kimchi, sausages wrapped in pink butcher's paper, and a blue-lidded plastic tub filled with wedges of smoked golden beet.

"Let me guess, you made all of this yourself, yeah?"

He just laughed.

He took down a cast-iron skillet that hung from a hook by the window. With deft hands, he placed the pan on the gas stove, chopped up some onions, and threw them in with a hefty helping of coconut oil. I watched, dazed with sleep climbing into my eyes but the delicious aroma of sizzling onions keeping me awake. Wolfie sautéed thick slices of sausage, tossed in some beets, and seasoned the whole thing with salt and freshly ground pepper. He served it to me on a chipped china plate with a spoonful of kimchi on the side.

He ripped a half-eaten baguette into large chunks and handed one to me. "Eat up," he said.

We ate in the kitchen. Me sitting on the counter, cradling the plate of food in my lap, him leaning against the refrigerator across the small room. He shovelled the sausage, fried onions, and kimchi medley into his mouth with a piece of bread. I made a sloppy sandwich, tearing my hunk of bread in half and filling it with the chunky mixture.

He'd made the kimchi himself and was very proud of it. He was close with Chef Luca, and they'd spent the summer experimenting with different preserves and fermentation. As for the sausages, his stepfather owned a small pig and poultry farm in Chateauguay Valley, just outside of Montreal, and he paid Wolfie in meat whenever he helped slaughter or butcher an animal. Wolfie had spent the weekends and holidays of his teen years working on that farm. After he turned nineteen, he moved away and worked at an abattoir for a little over a year. In his early twenties he moved to Montreal to apprentice in a butcher shop until the first woman he loved took their dog and left him. He decided that healing would only come through time and distance. Since he had zero control over time, he chose to move across the country to Vancouver. He stayed there for a while, found work, and took some part-time courses to get his Red Seal cook certification. Afterward, he spent a few years working in various resort kitchens in different parts of the Caribbean, but he moved back to his stepfather's farm when his mother got sick.

The farm delivered meat to Milas, which was how Wolfie met Luca. And it was close enough that he got to see his mother a couple times a week.

We moved back to the living room to share the couch. I sat with my back against the arm of the sofa, my legs almost fully extended on the plush seat. Wolfie sat on the other end, and my toes grazed the fabric of his trousers. We passed a bottle of his home-brewed kombucha between us. With each exchange of the bottle, our bodies softened and escaped the rigidity that nerves bring when bodies want, badly, to touch. We drew closer to the centre of the sofa until my legs were well nestled in his lap, and his arm was draped around my shoulder. It all felt inexplicably familiar.

"How old are you, Wolfie?" I asked.

"I'm twenty-nine. Can I kiss you?"

I was surprised by his directness, but I liked it. Still, I continued to feign impassiveness. "*Can* asks if you are capable, *may* asks permission."

"May I kiss you, Kehinde?" He offered a smile that faltered after only a moment.

I nodded. Practically on top of him, I didn't understand why we weren't kissing already.

He leaned in until I could feel the warmth of his breath on my face. "May I?" he asked again, and I pulled his scruffy face into mine. We kissed softly at first, gentle pecks that melded into something else at once intense and urgent and playful. He pulled me closer so that I was straddling him, and his hands ran up and down my back. He moved back, and we looked at each other for what felt like a long time.

"This is okay?" he finally said.

"Yes. Why did you wait so long?" I asked.

"Honestly, I wasn't sure if you were into white guys. I didn't want to make it awkward at work."

"Well," I said, "only the good ones. In fact," I continued, "I don't really date them. I just make out with them on the very first night that we have a full conversation."

"Nooo." He shook his legs so that I had to hold on to his shoulders to keep from tumbling off.

I laughed and laughed. "Okay, okay," I said.

"For real, though." He cupped the side of my face with his right hand, kissed my cheek, kissed my shoulder. "I want to see you more, like this, outside work." He held his face close to me so that our noses touched. "Will you see me?"

I liked myself when I was with Wolfie.

Again, I nodded. "Yes."


WOLFIE DIDN'T LOOK THAT BEAUTIFUL, BUT HE WAS. He was generous and kind. Moody when drunk, but other than that, his flaws were forgivable; I never had to do more than my fair share.

He wasn't my first lover. That goes to a boy named Wale, the TA from my third-year conflict and development class. Wale was a Nigerian who had never been to Nigeria. He'd grown up in Toronto and was thrilled to know that I'd never been with anyone before him. We went out once, when I felt reckless and deserving of a wound. It hurt when he put himself inside me; otherwise, the sex was unremarkable.

Perhaps I fled my body out of habit. Later, in the shower, I scrubbed and scrubbed my skin raw. I suppose I wasn't ready.

I think Wale intended to ghost me afterward, but I honestly felt indifferent toward him, and that seemed to pique his interest. I spent the remainder of the semester gently eschewing his advances. We became friends later.

Wolfie shaved his beard the first time we slept together, but the two incidents weren't necessarily related. It was early November. I'd worked a ten-hour shift at Milas the night before and woken up barely five hours afterward to catch the bus to campus for an early class. Later in the afternoon, after three back-to-back courses, I tumbled into his bed, leaving my jeans and cardigan in a rumpled pile on the floor.

Wolfie kissed my forehead and let me sleep. A few hours later, I awoke to the smell of fried plantains and, for a very brief moment, forgot where I was. I found myself at home in Lagos. Then I found my way to the kitchen and was startled by the clean-shaven man sautéing onions for sauce.

"Hey," he said.

"No, who are you?" I joked, eyeing him suspiciously. "What did you do with my man?"

"Damn, I love that." He smiled to reveal the dimples his beard had hidden.

"Love what?" I asked, still feigning suspicion.

"When you call me your man."

"Well, you were, before you"—I waved my hand around my face—"transformed."

"Aw, come on." He put the wooden spoon down and reached for me. "Tell me you like it."

I pulled a face and let myself be dragged into him. He smelled freshly showered, like the citrus body wash I'd left at his place just the week before. I held his newly shorn face between my palms, held his gaze for a long time, kissed the scar that ran from his lip to his right nostril, kissed both cheeks, the spots where his dimples formed. "You're beautiful, my beautiful man."

He yielded to me, to something in my voice. He said my name in this way. We kissed like a fervent prayer until we smelled the onions burning. Wolfie turned the stove off, and we went to the bedroom. He sat on the edge of his rumpled bed, and I stood before him. I stroked his hair as he unbuttoned my shirt to kiss my belly.

We had been naked together before; in fact, since our first kiss, we were naked countless times, but there was only so far I was willing to go. I'd told him about the bad thing, about Wale and the scrubbing. I wanted him just as much as he did me, but I was afraid that the memories of Uncle Ernest—which I'd shoved to the furthest corner of my mind—would spill out and touch my space with Wolfie, corrupt it.

They didn't corrupt it. I mean, the memory reared its scaly head for a brief moment, but the hum in Wolfie's throat as he kissed me, it brought me back before I could panic. I felt a sudden sharp pain and heavy pressure when he put himself inside me, and it was delicious, like relief from a deep longing I hadn't realized was there until he filled me up. It took some time for our rhythms to sync, but the space between was playful.

"I don't want you to think I'm just saying this because we fucked, Kehinde."

"But ...?"

"But I'm really into you."

"That's all right. It only happened because you shaved your face, so we're both horrible shallow people."

He laughed and his whole body shook; I had to move my head from its place on his quivering chest. "I suppose."

He rolled onto his side so that his body was facing mine. I looked him up and down, and he blushed. He put his hands under the covers in which I'd wrapped myself, found my legs, and nudged them apart. He asked, "You okay?"

"Yes," I answered, and then I guided his fingers inside me again.


"STAFF EXCURSION!" Luca shouted from the driver's side of his black truck. "Next week's menu is all pork, all the way, so we're getting a big ol' piggy!"

"It's only about a half hour away," Genevieve said, as she hauled a bright red duffle bag into the back of the truck, "but we like to make a night of it, camp out on the farm, butcher and freeze the meat, get a little high."

"High?" I asked.

"Yeah. No pressure, though." She smiled.

"So we pick the pig and have it killed?" I asked.

"*Have* it killed?" Luca asked incredulously. "*We* kill it."

Luca shot the massive pale-skinned creature right in the head. I wasn't expecting that. I'd seen livestock slaughtered before—goats, rams, chickens, killed for Salah and Christmas. I thought he would slit its throat and let the blood drain out with a prayer, halal, like we do at home.

After Luca shot the pig, he and Wolfie strung it up and used a blowtorch to singe the translucent hairs covering the animal. The pig's body shuddered when the flames touched it, and I felt my breakfast rise in my stomach. I looked away and clutched Genevieve's arm. I almost cried when I asked her, "It's still alive?"

"No, love." She was sympathetic. "It's just its nerves still reacting, but it's dead, promise."

AFTER THE BONFIRE HAD EATEN ITSELF DOWN TO GLOWING EMBERS, Wolfie and I kissed until the cold drove us into his tent. Inside the tiny space, his skin felt hot against mine. We undressed quickly and pressed against each other. He flexed his fingers inside me like he always did when we were naked together. We kissed sloppily and my toes curled, but quite suddenly, I remembered the pig.

The memory of the sound the rifle made when it slugged the bullet into the animal's head reverberated in mine as though I'd just heard it. The way it hung from the hook, blood pouring out into the dirty plastic bucket, flashed again and again in my mind. The way that Wolfie handled its bloody, hideously lifeless body; the animal's blood coated and dripped off his callused hands, thick like molasses, chunky, already coagulating.

The wetness that slicked my thighs was blood, pig's blood! A small squeal escaped me, and I shoved Wolfie off me.

"Wha ...?" he asked, his face flushed, confused.

I sat up and grabbed his hands to check for blood. There was nothing. I touched myself and brought my fingers up to see. Nothing.

"I'm sorry," I said. "I had a scary thought."

He leaned away from me, cautious and concerned. "What did you think?" he asked.

"I don't know; I'm sorry." I reached for him. "I just imagined there was pig's blood on your hands."

"My hands?" He held both of his hands up to show me: clean. "I washed them."

"I know, I know."

"It really bothered you, eh?"

"More than I thought, I guess."

"Okay." He looked at me for a long time before asking, "Can I touch you?"

I nodded, and he showed me his hands again, smiling. He was gentle. He touched my shoulders, my neck. He ran his hands through my thick braids. He kissed my temples, the tip of my nose, and said, "We could shower together."

"Right now?"

"Yeah, there's a guest washroom in the house."

"Okay, yeah."

"You can watch me wash my hands again," he joked.

IT DIDN'T OCCUR TO ME THAT I MIGHT BE PREGNANT until the vomiting started. Most things I ate returned in vicious spurts. Everything at the restaurant smelled vile. Everything at Wolfie's place smelled vile.

I didn't want to be pregnant, and, true to form, Wolfie said he would do whatever I wanted.

I didn't want to be pregnant, yet when I miscarried just a little after eleven weeks, I felt something more than clotted blood drain out of me. The cramps were horrendous, and the clinic visit to clear out what was left inside me was a cold, fluorescent blur. I felt this caustic shame that coloured everything; it was clear to me that the almost-baby knew that I didn't want it, so it dissolved away.

Internally, I tripped on something—I tripped and landed a long way down a damp and lonely hole. So far down that Wolfie's voice became a faint echo. His care seemed pointless. I seemed pointless. I'd never felt such a downward-pulling hollow inside myself before. I stopped taking shifts at Milas and genuinely wasn't sure if I should take the semester off school. My sadness seemed melodramatic, but the consistency of classes gave me a reason to leave my room four times a week. I was shocked to learn later that it was my most successful semester.

I wanted Wolfie to go away because I wasn't doing anything for him. I felt smothered by his affections. I felt like an empty vacuum, and I started to despise myself too much to let him look after me. I tried to break up with him, but he fought me on it. "Kehinde, please don't do this, we can make it work ..." he pleaded.

That just made me furious, and I shouted at him often. After scouring self-help blogs online, Wolfie found testaments on journaling as a healing practice. He brought me an unlined brown leather-bound journal and suggested I write about my sadness. I started many sentences, but the writing was peeling me open and unearthing questions I didn't want to think about, so I let my pen glide over the smooth pages in meaningless lines and loops. I doodled for what seemed like ages, page after page, in a soothing flow, emerging hours later feeling rested.

I started attempting to render objects in ink, simple still lifes of dirty plates, stacked books, fruit. Eventually, I grew more interested in drawing faces, so I looked through my things for family photographs. I was looking for a particular portrait of my father as a boy, the one with his hair picked out into a glorious Afro, a toothy smile stretched wide across his round face, the embroidered neckline of his dashiki peeking through, just barely in the frame. I found the photo, browned to sepia by time, and it struck me how much of Taiye's face I saw in his.

There was another photo stuck behind the portrait, and I peeled them apart to find a photograph of our house, in the vivid colours of the late nineties. It was taken within two months of our father's death and funeral, when our great-aunt Akuchi had us paint across our black gates and fences: THIS HOUSE IS NOT FOR SALE. BUYERS BEWARE. I overheard her say to Sister Bisi in rapid Yoruba, "We have to make sure Banji's useless family don't try and sell this house from under this poor woman's nose."

The "poor woman" was our mother. Distraught, she just sat in her room, alternating between wailing and silently rocking back and forth.

Sister Bisi took the picture of us: Taiye and me on either side of Aunty Akuchi. Miniature replicas of her in our matching orange and black ankara bubus. Smiling smugly at having graffitied our own house, faces shining with sweat. We stood by the lopsided words, brushes in hand, paint weeping down the corners of our freshly written warning.

Looking at that picture, I couldn't pick out which one of the little girls I was. Both of them looked like Taiye. I chose to draw that picture, over and over again, until I could tell which one was me. I filled the journal with ink and pencil drawings. Then I attempted several renditions in cheap watercolours, then pastel crayons, then beeswax encaustics, then collage, then glass beads ...

I don't think Wolfie realized the gift he gave me with that journal. Or with his kindness. He made me cups and cups of woody St. John's wort tea, because he'd read somewhere that it was a natural antidepressant. Once, I was rummaging through his kitchen cabinet in search of some honey. I found it by his computer on the small dining table in the corner of the cramped kitchen. I sat down to check my email, and it was still logged in to his account. Everyone knows you mustn't snoop, everyone knows, yet I did. And there sat an email from the head chef of Grégoire, a restaurant in Paris that Wolfie and Luca had prattled on about since I'd worked at Milas. Wolfie had visited the year before, and then sent a long and eager message asking about opportunities for an apprenticeship. Many months later, the chef was offering him one, to start in eight weeks. Wolfie had received the email over a month ago.

Simultaneously, joy—incredible amounts of it for him—and a deep dread for myself filled my body. The corners of my chest, the overgrown cuticles of my toes, every inch of me vibrated with that fight.

The next morning, before sunrise, I initiated sex. We'd barely touched since the miscarriage. Wolfie was gentler than usual, leaning his forehead against mine to kiss me over and over. He told me that he loved me and asked, with a catch in his voice, if I loved him too.

It had all happened so quickly between us, from nothing to everything in the span of a few months. I'd opened the door of myself to him so wide and so quickly, and now I was on the verge of closing it.

Afterward, as we lay tangled under the covers, I confessed that I'd read his email from Grégoire. "You have to take it."

"Only if you come with me."

"I can't come with you, Wolfie."

"Kehinde, please come with me," he pleaded. "I can make you happy again."

He took my hands in his and said the things you say when you're afraid to let go. I said nothing. We held each other until I had to leave for school.

It wouldn't have been right, if I'd gone with him. It just wouldn't have been right.

*Letter no. 59*
*January 3, 2011*
*On a train from Paris to London*

*Dear Kehinde,*
*Happy New Year!*
  *I didn't have any place to be, so I went to Paris for Christmas.*
  *On Boxing Day, I left the place I was staying to explore. I was loitering around the Fontaine des Innocents. Just staring at the relief sculptures on each corner of the fountain, trying to hear only the water and just generally appear like I wasn't lost. I failed because I definitely looked lost when I let a Romani woman read my palm for eight euros.*
  *She told me some things about you and Mami, and she told me that I would see the "wolf that loved you." To be fair, my French is only just fine, so I only understood "wolf" and "love" and "you." But the things she said about you and Mami were too real, and I got scared. I gave her money and rushed*

*away on the first bus that came by. It was just about to leave the stop when I saw this very pale white bloke with wild eyes. He saw me too and somehow got even paler. He started to run after the bus, so I pulled the thing for the next stop and got off to look for him.*

*We found each other, and he looked me up and down for a bit before calling me by your name, like a question. I told him that I was Taiye, and his head nearly exploded. He told me that you never told him we were twins. We shook hands, and he said that his name was Wolfie. I remembered the palm reader's words and my head exploded.*

*We walked together and talked for a long time. He was very eager to share his time with me. I think he was having difficulty separating the two of us. At one point, we stopped at a tiny Syrian place for falafels, and while we were waiting for our food, he touched the scar on my chin and said, "Kehinde doesn't have this."*

*He told me about the miscarriage, and the depression.*

*I'm sorry. I'm just so sorry.*

*We went to the restaurant where he works. It's a bit avant-garde (a bit pretentious, if you ask me), but the food is weird and fantastic, I can't lie. He says he loves it, that he's doing well and they like him, but he misses you all the time.*

*Wolfie has this warm energy. He seemed kind. I'm sorry that things didn't work out between the two of you.*

*He invited me to a party at his restaurant on New Year's Eve. The party was in a greenhouse on the rooftop of the restaurant. The whole place was draped in string lights, and there were trays of canapés everywhere. It felt posh and magical.*

*But yeah, it was special. Wolfie kissed me when we said goodbye, and I had to remind him that we—me and you—are different people. He was a bit drunk, confused. He started to cry when we hugged, and we held each other for a long time. He needed it, and I think I needed it too.*

*I hope that you are doing better than he is.*

*All my love,*

*Taiye*

# Kambirinachi

IT WASN'T THAT BANJI'S FAMILY DIDN'T LIKE KAMBIRINACHI. Rather, they were concerned by how thoroughly she seemed to consume him. His older sisters, Folasade and Olayinka, joked that she'd charmed him with wild sex. His younger sister, Yemisi, resented that his attention was further divided to include another woman and thus diverted away from her even more. They watched with caution as this strange person magicked their brother into becoming the kind of man they'd all wished for him to be, the man he always almost was.

Before Kambirinachi, Banji was kind but never on time; he was generous but never on time; he listened attentively but, again, never on time. With his new lover, his internal clock shifted, or expanded. It grew to accommodate other people's rhythms. You could say that he became more considerate. Quite simply, he considered Kambirinachi before himself. Dangerous, yes. But this also allowed him to consider his mother, sisters, friends, and colleagues with more generosity, too.

Their courtship was long. It took many months after they met in the lecture hall before Kambirinachi chose to sink herself into a life intertwined with a person outside of her blood and Kin. That sort of thing required sacrifice, and she wasn't yet sure of the price. But she liked him. She liked him. In five months, he'd asked her to join him for lunch seven times; each time, she declined with a smile and a subtle shake of her head.

By the eighth time he asked, the harmattan semester was over, but having charmed Mrs Ijisakin, the intro to fine and applied arts lecturer, Kambirinachi had a set of keys to the second-floor studio. She was alone in the dim workroom, with its large burglar-proof windows, the sun streaming in vivid slits to spark floating dust particles alight. She'd set up a still life of bright green guavas, avocados, and mangoes whose colours danced between warm orange, red-yellow, and spotty green, mounted her canvas sketch pad on the wooden easel, and then perched herself on a tall stool. Damp paintbrush had just kissed eager canvas with its watercolour-tipped bristle when Banji knocked on the open door.

"Kambirinachi," he said, sonorous voice rising to fill the room. "I don't mean to disturb you."

Kambirinachi put her paintbrush down and looked up at him, his lanky body framed in the doorway, round tortoiseshell glasses reflecting the light.

"Banji," she said. "How far?"

He walked into the studio, and she nodded at his outfit—indigo adire button-up, long sleeves rolled up to his ashy elbows, hem tucked into ripped acid-wash jeans. "I like what you're wearing," she said.

The compliment startled Banji and spread a coy smile across his face, setting his pearly teeth in stark and gorgeous contrast to the deep dark of his face.

"Thank you," he said with a nod. "I saw that you've been coming here to paint—"

"You've been watching me?"

"No, yes, a little bit," he stammered. "I'm working at the agric department brooder house over the holiday, so I see you when you walk across campus sometimes." He flung his hand behind him, gesturing toward the Agricultural and Environmental Engineering Department on the other side of the sprawling campus.

Kambirinachi picked up her brush and turned back to her canvas, but her skin sang, hyperaware of Banji's gaze.

"I'm wondering," he said, "if you'd like to join me for lunch after you finish painting."

"Yes," she said, without turning to face him. "Tell me where to find you."

THEIR LUNCHES BECAME WEEKLY.

And after four months of these weekly dates, Aunty Akuchi asked to meet the person who stirred in Kambirinachi a desire to oil her skin and braid her hair with more attention than her aunt had ever witnessed. Kambirinachi suddenly started spending more than mere moments looking into the mirror. Instead of leaving her hair in its usual poof, she split parts in and anointed her scalp with fragrant Indian hemp hair pomade before weaving her dense coils into thin intricate braids.

Banji joined Kambirinachi, Akuchi, and Yusuf for supper. Yusuf hadn't officially left his wife but had nonetheless become, more or less, a permanent fixture in Akuchi's home.

Banji arrived two minutes and twenty seconds into King Sunny Adé's "Ma Jaiye Oni." Adaora had just led him into the living room when the slide guitar licked a slinky melody on the track.

He said, "Good evening, ma" to Akuchi, "Evening, sir" to Yusuf, and prostrated in greeting, lying down with his chest to the carpeted floor: dòbálẹ̀.

"Welcome o!" Akuchi smiled warmly and embraced him, and Yusuf shook his hand.

Supper was simple: ofada rice with palm oil stew and moi moi. Akuchi asked the usual questions: "Where are you from?" "Who are your people?" "What are you studying?" "What church do you attend?"

Banji answered graciously: Oṣogbo. Third of four children, only son. Father passed away four years ago, mother was an assistant lecturer in the biochemistry department at OAU, where he was in his second year of an accounting degree. Our Lady of Perpetual Light, right by the campus.

He was respectful and warm and honest. Akuchi liked him, but she was hesitant about the idea of Kambirinachi dating. The girl had until now shown no interest in romance, or sex, for that matter. Even when her classmates exchanged Valentine's Day gifts or were caught kissing in empty classrooms, Kambirinachi had seemed entirely indifferent to the teenage iterations of love and attempts to tame their lust. Yet, that evening, it was clear to everyone present that the thing between Banji and Kambirinachi was heartier than any easily quenchable passion.

Late at night, after Banji had left and they'd cleaned up, after Adaora had gone to her room and Yusuf to sleep, Akuchi knocked quietly on Kambirinachi's bedroom door and let herself in before she was invited.

It didn't take much to rouse Kambirinachi from sleep; Akuchi simply had to say her name no louder than a whisper. When Kambirinachi sat up in the narrow bed, Akuchi flicked on the lamp on the night table and sat beside her.

"Aunty, is everything okay?" Kambirinachi asked, rubbing the remnants of sleep from her eyes.

"Yes, Kambi. I just wanted to talk to you about something ..." Akuchi sank her full frame into the soft mattress and leaned her back against the wall. "You like that Yoruba boy, yes?"

Kambirinachi offered a small smile and nodded.

"He seems well trained," Akuchi continued. "You must be careful, you know. You are a young woman now."

"Yes, Aunty."

Akuchi was silent for a while. The lamp dimmed and brightened, dimmed and brightened, making all the shadows in the room shrink and grow as if alive. Power had been on and off all day, and when it was on, the current ran low. Kambirinachi knew that there was a story coming, but her body was drooping into sleep again when her aunt's voice pulled her out.

"You know I was married once," Akuchi said finally. "A long time ago, before you were even born. My husband was a good man, but he wanted children and my body wouldn't ... cooperate. It was my fault anyway, because when I was a girl, one or two years younger than you are now—you're eighteen?"

"Yes."

"Yes, so I was about sixteen. I became pregnant, you know. I was sleeping with my first boyfriend, and yes, you know, the natural order of things, it just happens like that sometimes. But, em ... my father, your grandfather—he had passed by the time you were born, may his soul rest in peace—he wouldn't have stood for it, you know, he was very active in our church. It just ... anyway, there was a nurse in the area who used to perform abortions ... it was terrible, Kambi. So when I was married and ready to have children, my body was damaged from that ... anyway ... I just want you to know that you can tell me anything."

Akuchi picked at a mole on her upper arm.

"Tomorrow I'm going to the pharmacist. I will buy some condoms and leave them here. You don't have to, but you can tell me anything ..."

She was no longer looking at Kambirinachi, instead fixing her eyes on a point on the wall across the room. Akuchi sat like that, not moving, barely breathing, tears rolling down her plump cheeks, until Kambirinachi placed a hand on her elbow. "Aunty, are you okay?"

"Yes, my dear." Akuchi shook her head, as if to loosen the grip of her memories. She'd forgotten where she was.

"Yes," she repeated. "Okay, sleep well." Then she got up and left.

Kambirinachi did not sleep well.

She thought backward, thought of a young and terrified Akuchi. She felt the memory of her aunt's pain slither under her own skin, and she finally understood why Yusuf seemed like a good fit for her—he didn't require her to be a promise or potential for anything because he already had a family. Also, quite simply, Akuchi loved him.

Kambirinachi considered loving Banji in a way that didn't make space for consequences. Foolish, maybe. Especially considering what the implications for a being like her might be. She sank her senses into the air beyond the air around her, sought out her Kin, her selves, to ask them, "What will be the cost?"

But, annoyed by her refusal to return home, her Kin turned away and continued to speak of and not to her. Loud enough for her to hear, they said, *She is always choosing them. She will soon learn.*

Four years after Kambirinachi dreamed him, the day after she graduated from OAU with a fine arts degree, Banji placed a plain gold band in her palm and covered it with his own. He held her hand this way, tight, with the ring between their palms, and said, "I want to learn to love you better every day. I want to marry you and have a family that is our own. Do you want this? Will you marry me?"

Kambirinachi ignored her Kin roaring inside herself and chose Banji's voice to be her anchor. She smiled at him, so bright, so yielding.

She nodded her head: *Yes.*

Then she spoke it: "Yes."

# Taiye

LONG BEFORE SHE WOULD GO BACK HOME TO LAGOS, before her beehive, before the meals she would make to appease—more truthfully, avoid— her sister, there was a Sunday morning in South London, drowned in the wet sanguinity of spring, when Taiye woke up next to a girl she'd met late the previous night. The girl shared her MDMA with Taiye before they danced together at a tiny queer club with walls covered in mirrors and multicoloured neon lights, in the basement of a fried chicken place. They'd danced wildly, sweating and grinding their bodies against each other. In the mirror across the room, peeking from between other flailing bodies, Kehinde appeared, in a slow-motion ethereal surfacing. Even later that night, only moments before the girl started to undress her, Taiye scribbled a note to Kehinde on a receipt she found crumpled in her coat pocket.

The following morning, from the throbbing haze of a comedown, Taiye tumbled out of the unfamiliar bed and dressed quickly. If she rushed, she could make the ten a.m. Mass at Our Lady of La Salette and St. Joseph Church, which was two, maybe three, blocks away. She'd never been there before but had seen it on her inebriated saunter to the girl's flat. Taiye thought she remembered the schedule posted in the glass-enclosed bulletin board, beside the arched marble doorway, announcing ten a.m. Sunday Mass. Or had it said 10:30? Either way, Taiye had to leave this stranger's home.

The girl's name was Eden—or Aida, or Aisha. And she was snoring lightly under a bright yellow duvet ripe with the musky scent of nag champa incense and sweat. Her hair was a short curly Afro, dyed a yellow-tinged blonde, with a tight undercut fade. Twin gold studs glittered in each nostril. She was from Cardiff and had moved to London the previous year to study painting at Slade.

It wasn't a huge flat, not as small as Taiye's attic studio but not much bigger. Unlike Taiye, however, Eden—or Aida, or Aisha—seemed to keep it immaculate so that the white walls and tiled floors appeared vast. Furniture was sparse, except for the pile of clothing on the floor beside the low platform bed, a worn red leather sofa, and a stack of sketchbooks by an empty easel near the bathroom door. Everything else must have been tucked away behind the white closet doors or was non-existent.

"Morning." Eden—or Aida, or Aisha—sat up. She stretched, exposing pierced nipples and a triangle tattoo on her sternum between her small breasts. "You're leaving?"

"Yeah, I just have to rush ... somewhere." Taiye smiled and said, "I had a good time last night."

"Yeah, same. I'd hoped we could get breakfast or something."

"That would be lovely, but ... I left my number." Taiye gestured toward the wall on the left side of the bed, where she'd posted a yellow sticky note with her name, phone number, and a colon and wobbly bracket for a smiley face.

The girl took the sticky note off the wall and smiled. "Cute."

"Call me whenever. We can do this again, or something else ..." Taiye kissed the girl on her hot, dry cheek and stood up to leave.

"There's a great little café down the road called Poppy. They have a smoothie concoction, vitamin something. Helps with the comedown." The girl yawned.

"Thank you." Taiye smiled again.

"Just your friendly tip of the day." The girl winked, the studs in her nose glinting in the cold morning light pouring in from the skylight above her bed.

TAIYE FOUND THE CRUMPLED RECEIPT with her barely legible letter to her sister in the right-hand pocket of her black fleece jacket. She would smooth it out later and put it in the box of letters that she'd already more than halfway filled. Tripping down the stairs, she fell outside into the quiet day, which was colder than the previous night. A dull pain pulsed through her temples in an incessant rhythm; drained of serotonin, she felt her whole self tipped toward the void. She pulled the hood of her jacket up over her braids and shoved her hands into the snug pockets of her tight jeans as she walked quickly, almost passing the café. It was a small, unassuming place with an indistinct white placard on the side of the entrance that read in red block letters, POPPY. TEA AND TREATS. The narrow space held three mismatched tables and clusters of wooden chairs. A middle-aged white couple sat silently with a steaming pot of tea between them at the table closest to the counter. They shared a red plate of honeyed pastries, eating with faint smiles, their bashful eyelashes fluttering at each other.

At the counter, a light-skinned woman with a gorgeous large orange halo of Afro stocked the display case with baked treats. She swayed slightly to the electronic rhythms pulsing on low volume from a radio on a shelf behind her. She flashed Taiye a wide smile to reveal a gap between her two front teeth, greeting her, "Hiya, you all right?"

"Good morning," Taiye croaked, her voice still laden with sleep. "I was told that you served a vitamin smoothie type thing, good for hangovers?" A coy smile.

"Ah, yes! The Vitamin Aid." The woman pointed to the chalkboard menu on the wall behind her. "Bit cold for smoothie, though, innit?"

"Yeah, I was wondering if maybe you had a hot version or some kind of tea that works the same magic."

"You know what?" The woman tied her hair into a coily bun atop her head. "The real magic in the smoothie is ginger and ashwagandha infusion." She took down a jar of what looked to Taiye like small grey wood chips. "We make a really strong tea with this, with some fresh ginger, and loads of lemon. It'll be nice and hot." She offered the same wide smile, and the only word that could come out of Taiye's mouth was "yes."

Taiye stood at the counter and watched the woman make her tea.

"I'm Zora," she said, as she poured ginger and lemon juice into a steaming cup of green tea.

Zora's brown skin was covered in a generous scattering of dark freckles that grew denser and denser, until they formed a nearly solid birthmark, a misshapen oval, just above her right eye, before disappearing into her hairline. Her tight white shirt had long sleeves that showed the colourful, intricate end points of what Taiye imagined to be a sleeve tattoo. Zora was a full-figured woman whose big hips spread out over the sides of the lace apron tied around her thick waist. She spoke with a mild lisp that had Taiye wondering about slipping underneath her tongue. She imagined a warm kiss between them and smiled to herself. The café smelled like most cafés must: earthy burnt coffee, hot butter, warm bread. But here, there was also the distinct sweet spice smell of cardamom.

A denunciative thought danced across Taiye's mind: *The art student's sweat still lingers on your skin.*

The night with Eden/Aida/Aisha/pierced-nipple girl had been fun.

*She's probably never going to call,* Taiye replied, to excuse whatever her desire demanded.

"I'm Taiye," she said. "So what's this ashwagandha thing?" She knew what it was; she just wanted to hear Zora speak with her lisp.

"Oh, it's a miracle herb that's used in Ayurvedic medicine, and this is actually just the dried root." She shook the jar, rattling the ashwagandha chips. "It's great for your immune system, helps with anxiety and what-not." Zora shrugged with a sudden and subtle coquettishness that startled a dopey smile onto Taiye's face. She handed Taiye a medium-sized paper cup, white with an olive-green plastic lid. "Sip slowly, it's scorching."

"Thank you." Taiye reached for her wallet in the back pocket of her jeans. "How much do I owe?"

"This one's on me."

"Thank you." Taiye chewed her bottom lip. Zora just shrugged and smiled. The silence that followed held a glimmer of recognition.

"I have to go," Taiye said, jerking her head toward the door. "But if you're here tomorrow, I'd like to stop by and let you know how this tea works out for me."

"I'm here tomorrow."

TAIYE'S TEA WAS STILL TOO HOT TO DRINK by the time she walked to the high-ceilinged chapel of Our Lady of La Salette. The massive oak doors were propped open by a white sandwich board that read ALL WELCOME. Taiye slipped inside as quietly as she could, tiptoeing to keep the chunky heels of her boots from striking the floor, and sat at the end of an empty pew. It was a modest brownstone church with stained-glass rose windows on either side of the vaulted archway. She sipped the tea, burning her tongue.

Mass had already begun. She'd arrived just at the start of the Penitential Rite, and the small congregation was standing. Taiye placed her cup beside her on the bench and stood as the prayer began. The sound of the congregation praying together, many voices rising and falling in unison, sounded like a rushing brook. It felt like warm water pouring down her skin.

Taiye hoped they would sing instead of reciting the Kyrie eleison, and they did. She sang with an abandon she typically reserved for her vices, her voice rising high in tune with the small choir and sleepy congregation. They sang "Gloria in Excelsis Deo" in English instead of Latin, and Taiye remembered home. She remembered the church in Falomo, recalled how this particular hymn was often accompanied by rhythmic drumming and fervent clapping—a celebration. In London, the prayer felt subdued, sombre, like the grey sky that hung low to darken the morning.

ON HER WAY OUT OF THE CHURCH, Taiye took a pamphlet containing the brief history of Our Lady of La Salette. She sat on a stone bench in a small sorry park across the cobbled street. The seat was cold and slowly numbed her bottom, so she sipped the tea, which had grown tepid. On the cover of the pale blue pamphlet was a detailed drawing of a woman, Our Lady, in flowing garments, sitting with her elbow resting on her knees and her face buried in her open palms. She was praying, or weeping, or both.

In the district of Grenoble, southeastern France, there sits a small village called La Salette-Fallavaux. In 1846, it was a farming community, and on the evening of September 19, two children—Maximin Giraud and Mélanie Calvat—climbed the slopes of Mount Sous-Les-Baisses, driving a small herd of cows. They lay down to rest for a moment, but having spent the morning working in the fields, their little bodies faltered, and they fell fast asleep. The children awoke to find that all the cows had wandered off, and in their frantic search they found a woman within a circle of light, sitting and weeping into her hands. Through her anguished tears, the lady warned the children that a great famine would come if her people refused to turn to Christ. Then she told each child a secret, walked away from them, and vanished into the light.

In the months following the apparition, there was a famine throughout Europe, in which the people of Ireland suffered most severely. Taiye wondered why Our Lady didn't warn a couple of Irish children. A blasphemous thought, probably.

She folded the pamphlet and put it with her wallet in her back pocket. Her stomach grumbled, so she walked quickly toward home.

TAIYE'S FLAT WAS A CONVERTED ATTIC in the home of a Trinidadian widow in her late sixties named Cherelle Baptiste. Cherelle was kind to Taiye, if slightly overbearing. Although a narrow flight of wrought-iron stairs led to her own entrance separate from the main house, Taiye tiptoed to keep from alerting Cherelle, who routinely rapped on the window, waved Taiye toward the front door, and talked about the joys of her relationship with Jehovah, and the brilliance and generosity of her son: Kevon, a very handsome engineer.

By the time Taiye undressed and bathed the night and sex, and holy smoke, off her skin, Our Lady of La Salette had made herself at home in Taiye's mind, stretched out on the plush sofa by the garden window of her thoughts.

Taiye kept a palm-sized satin pouch of weed in the back of her freezer. She reached in behind bags of frozen sweet corn, peas, and chargrilled vegetables from Tesco, found her pouch, and returned to her bed to loosen up and crush the tight buds on a narrow leaf of thin hemp paper. Then she added wrinkled and petrified petals of pink lotus flower and wound the paper into a slender roll. Curled up at the edge of her mattress with her face toward the open window, Taiye lit the joint and sucked the smoke deep into her lungs. She held in the smoke for a long pause and turned her attention to Our Lady, who watched Taiye with pale, lazy eyes from the corner of her mind.

"So, where did you come from?" Taiye asked, as she exhaled a dense plume out the window.

*Come from ...? I suppose the answer is you. You just offered me a shape today.*

Taiye nodded, already high. "Was that you last night at the club?"

Our Lady gave a half smile and lifted her chin slightly, as if to say, *I think you know who that was.*

"I really don't," Taiye responded. "It looked like my sister, but she hasn't spoken to me in a long time, so I don't think she would bother with an apparition."

Our Lady blinked, silent, that faint smile lingering on her glowing face.

"It was just drugs doing drug things to my brain," Taiye concluded. "I'm hungry."

Our Lady leaned forward, stretched her hand out, and placed a holy finger on Taiye's scar, a shiny slice starting from the soft dip in her right cheek and running all the way down in a diagonal swipe across her chin.

*Eat something ... and call your mother.*

TAIYE HEEDED OUR LADY'S WORDS. She sautéed roughly chopped shiitake mushrooms, slivers of sweet shallots, Scotch bonnet peppers, juicy corn kernels, and garlic in bacon fat. She let the mixture simmer in rich coconut milk, added a chicken stock cube, ground crayfish, and a generous handful of fresh basil. Then she poured the sauce over a steaming plate of couscous, sat down with her meal by the window, and called her mother.

"Hello." Kambirinachi's low voice climbed with smoothness through Taiye's earphones and, despite all their difficulties, placed a calm in her core.

"Mami, happy Sunday," Taiye said, her voice a song.

"Keke, my dear, happy Sunday o," Kambirinachi said, her voice wavering.

With a mouthful of couscous, wondering if her mother has just woken from sleep, Taiye said, "No, Mami, it's Taiye."

"Eh?" her mother asked.

Taiye raised her voice slightly. "It's Taiye, not Keke." Worry tightened twin knots in her temples. Her mother was not always *well*. Sometimes small things like mixing up her twin daughters' voices swelled to become signposts of an impending descent. Into the sort of thing that, two years prior, had Taiye on the first flight home to Lagos, where she found her mother with broken ankles, a fractured right tibia, and a thoroughly implausible story about how she had not, in fact, jumped off the third-storey balcony.

"I know." Kambirinachi exhaled loudly so that it sounded as though she was blowing directly into the receiver. "How is your sister?"

"I don't know."

"Ahn ahn?! Keke, you should be calling her o. You should be calling her. You know that she misses you."

"Mami, it's not Kehinde. It's me, Taiye."

"Eh now, call Taiye. You are sisters. My sisters and I don't go one day without greeting each other."

"Mami." Taiye closed her eyes and slowed her speech. "Mami, which sisters? Sister Agnes from church?"

Her mother laughed something sharp, like good china shattering on a tile floor, and Taiye understood that it would be right to carry on the conversation as though she were Kehinde.

"Which sisters?" she asked her mother again.

"You know, my sisters, they tell me about the wound between you two, make una fix am o! Anyway, Dr Savage has just arrived. We have to go and greet her."

"Okay, please greet her for me," Taiye said, and then added quickly, "Who is 'we'?"

"I can't hear you well." Kambirinachi raised her voice to a shout but still sounded far away. "I think my credit is low, but I'll phone you after, okay?"

"Okay, okay, call me after." Taiye's voice was dampened by emotion.

"Phone your sister. Greet her for me!" Kambirinachi shouted into the phone before hanging up.

Taiye turned an accusatory glare toward Our Lady, but the apparition's holy head was rolled back, eyes closed, and a gentle snore—like a purr—escaped her parted lips. Taiye laughed at herself and finished her meal.

AFTER HER TIME IN MONTPELLIER, Taiye had a string of restaurant and bar jobs, from dishwasher to server to line cook. But the late nights, and the easy access to utter and blissful intoxication, proved too seductive and risky for her. So she polished her resumé, highlighting her chemistry degree, and found work as an analytical chemist in the quality control department at Green Key Pharmaceuticals, where she tested luxury cosmetics for allergens. The pay was decent enough for rent, food, transportation, and very meagre savings, but it did not suffice for weekly benders with seductive strangers because she insisted on living alone, drinking too much, was precious about the grade of weed she smoked, and liked organic butter.

As Taiye wandered toward the taxi stand outside the hotel, she attempted to calculate how much she'd spent on drinks and taxis the night prior. She shared a trust account with her estranged twin—their late father had set it up when they were children—but she didn't dare look into it. She was very much at odds with her own self, a pendulum striking extreme and opposite points; it made for an abundance of emotional self-flagellation.

She caught a glimpse of Our Lady on the glass entrance doors and muttered, "I know" to the impassive expression fixed on Our Lady's pale face.

It was Saturday, six days after Our Lady had first appeared to Taiye, who supposed at this point that she was going to be a long-term guest in the room of her mind.

She turned away from the taxi stand, having decided to walk the forty-five minutes to her neighbourhood.

The morning fog settled and sank into her thin jean jacket. She dug her numb hands into her pockets and sped up. Her phone beeped a message; it was Eden/Aida/Aisha, whose name was actually Aiden. Taiye had learned this halfway through the week, when Aiden sent her a message to ask how the vitamin aid smoothie worked for her. They'd chatted briefly, and it culminated in an invitation to a gallery opening in Peckham. Taiye had been keen to go, honestly. But when she got close to the gallery and peered through the massive glass windows, she'd seen that the brightly lit room was crowded with mostly white people; people who looked like they could afford the cosmetics she mindlessly tested at work. She hadn't been able to spot Aiden, so she'd chewed her nails and listened to the stream of chatter that poured out of the open doors. Then she turned around and left.

Instead of looking at art, Taiye had gotten drunk on her own at a rooftop bar around the corner from the gallery, before sharing three thin lines of blow in the bathroom with a hot Korean girl wearing head-to-toe neon orange, before they took a near half-hour taxi ride to a club in Chelsea with a genderqueer Argentinian DJ. She couldn't recall which one of them had paid.

All that to say that she hadn't intended to blow off Aiden, so after she read the girl's message of *You alive?* she responded, *Hey, I'm sorry about last night.*

*Oh, you're alive then. Great.*

*I'm sorry!*

*You could've just declined my invitation to gawk at mediocre art*

*No, I really wanted to come*
*But ...?*
*But I'm a shithead ...*
*I see ...*
*I'd still like to see you again*
*You had your chance*
*For real?!*
*Jokes! Sober soirée ce soir chez moi if you're keen. A few friends, someone's*
*bringing a juicer.*
*I can do sober*
*Rough night?*
*A night*
*Tell me about it when you get here*
*Can I bring anything to atone for my bad behaviour?*
*Ha, bring yourself. We'll talk.*

Taiye smiled at her phone. Our Lady rolled her eyes.

"What?!" Taiye asked her, but Our Lady only raised both eyebrows and rolled her eyes again. *Just dress warmly.*

Taiye didn't take offence at Our Lady finding her irksome. She, too, was incredibly sick of her own shit. But one cannot abandon oneself, try try try as one might.

AT 7:37 IN THE EVENING, Taiye was bundled up warm in an oversized sweater, a red scarf wound loosely around her neck, and a large denim jacket. She turned up at Aiden's door with a mesh bag of grapefruits and a small honeydew melon. Wearing a tender smile as a shield.

Somebody who wasn't Aiden opened the door, looked her up and down, and said, "You look lumpy," as he rolled his soft neck. He was beautiful, fat, and femme in the way he flicked his wrist and gestured to her outfit, in the soft smirk that lifted the edges of his glossed lips. His large eyes peeked out from beneath luscious mascaraed lashes; his brows were arched elegantly to frame them. His dark skin glistened in the evening light. Gold dust highlighted his cheekbones to make them appear higher, but when he smiled, his cheeks plumped and gave away his youth.

"I'm Timi," he said. "And you're the one that didn't show up last night, yeah? Rude."

"Very rude," Taiye replied. "I'm Taiye."

"I know." Timi stepped back to let her into the small apartment, where more than a dozen people sprawled on blankets on the floor, on Aiden's low bed, and on the sofa tucked by the window. In the middle of the room, a South Asian girl with a mass of dense curls sat on a stool with a gorgeous dark mahogany cello resting wide between her open knees. She gestured wildly with her slender bow above her head as she spoke.

"That's Avani," Timi said, gesturing toward the cellist, "and Tuzz, Hannah, Catie, Biyi, Neil, Adanna, Seyi, and Alanna ..." He continued to name the party guests until Taiye spotted Aiden sitting on the floor by the window, listening intently to Avani's story. Taiye caught her eye and smiled wide; Aiden raised her right hand and waved before getting up to meet her.

"Hiya, you all right? You made it!" she said, after they attempted a hug that was awkward but settled all right in the end.

"Yeah, sorry about last night."

Aiden waved away the apology. "No worries, you're here now. And you met Timi." She stood on the tips of her toes to drape her arm over Timi's shoulder and plant a kiss on his smooth cheek.

"We met," Timi said, smiling derisively.

"Oh, Timz, be nice!" Aiden smacked his arm and laughed.

"I am nice!" Timi retorted, rolling his neck again. "Fine. Madame King Emperor Taiye, would you like anything to drink? We have juice, water, and tea."

"I'll have some juice," Taiye replied. "I heard there'd be a juicer, so I bought some fruit."

"Oh, lovely." Aiden took the bag from Taiye and led her into the tiny excuse for a kitchen. She emptied the fruit into a deep sink and rinsed them in cold water that trickled out of the limescale-stained tap.

While they cut the fruit, pushed it through the feeding cylinder of the juicer, and watched through the clear plastic body as the grinder pummelled chunks of melon and grapefruit, Avani's cello began to sing something mournful and assuaging.

In the living room, Taiye joined the rest of Aiden's guests sitting in a semicircle around Avani and Timi. Avani plucked a rhythmic melody to accompany Timi's drumming on a small brown dundun slung over his ample shoulders. Toward the end of their song, Avani's cello simmered to a gentle chant, Timi silenced his talking drum, and his voice rose in a high and glorious soprano: "Gbe mi mì ninu omi tutu, sweet water, sweet water, swallow me."

Aiden passed around a tray of chocolate truffles after the applause, half the plate labelled 5 MG THC, the other half, .75 G PSILOCYBIN.

When the dish came her way Taiye declined. She turned to Timi and said, "I thought this was a sober party."

"Yeah, but only alcohol sober." He chuckled and shook his head. "Aiden just doesn't like drunk people in her place."

"Oh, okay, fair enough." Taiye nodded. "I think I'm good to keep it sober tonight, though."

"How about a joint?" Timi asked.

Taiye laughed. "I could fuck with a joint."

Timi led the way across the loose maze of bodies, through the tiny kitchen, and onto a narrow ledge of a balcony. The wrought-iron railing seemed far too flimsy to be leaned upon; they were only three floors up, but Taiye didn't feel up to testing its integrity. She sat cross-legged on the floor, and Timi mirrored her.

"You're Yoruba?" Timi asked, as he ground the potent buds in a gold-plated grinder.

"Yes, on my father's side. My mother's side is Igbo."

"You always lived here?"

"No, came for uni, like eight, nine years ago. You?"

"Born and raised. Are you out to, like, your family?"

"I mean, I'm not really in. I don't have a lot of family here so ... like, I don't really have anyone to explain anything to."

He gutted a cigarette and mixed its contents with the weed before rolling it up tight and narrow in hemp paper. Handing the joint to Taiye, he said, "Do the honours?"

Taiye obliged. On her exhale, she asked, "How about you?" and passed it back.

"My mother is a pastor at Unchained Ministries—what do you think?"

"That's intense."

Timi threw his gorgeous head back and roared in laughter. It was infectious.

"Intense is fucking right, innit?" Timi sucked the smoke deep and held it for a long time. He coughed with the same force as his laughter when he finally released the cloud.

They sat in silence until the music from Avani's cello floated through the kitchen, out onto the balcony, and met with the night. Timi closed his eyes and swayed slightly. "I play the keyboard at church, but I would love to learn the cello or the violin."

"You have a gorgeous voice. Do you sing at church?"

He shook his head.

"Are you a believer?" Taiye asked.

"In Unchained? No, not at all. There is zero percent room for someone like me to be out in Nigerian Pentecostalism. I am a believer in God, though, like in a divine goodness that loves us and wants us to love each other, blah blah." He laughed, this time with a calm sincerity.

"I think that God is definitely femme, though. I mean, look at flowers! Anyway, are you?" he asked Taiye.

"What?"

He rolled his eyes, and Taiye saw Our Lady in a quick flash. An uncanny feeling settled in her stomach. She shook her head and pursed her lips before saying, "I mean, I think I'm similar to you, maybe. I believe in a much bigger light than I can see. I have to believe there's something looking after me." She looked down at her wide palms; her hands felt cold. Our Lady's suggestion to dress warmly was proving to be worthwhile. "And I like going to church. I like the smell of incense at Mass. Does that make sense?"

"I hear you. You're Catholic?"

"I go to Catholic Mass," she corrected him.


AGAIN, TAIYE SPENT THE NIGHT WITH AIDEN. It was a much less frenzied affair, with considerably more space for Taiye to unfurl herself, and that frightened her.

The following morning, they ate crepes with salted brown butter and blackcurrant compote. They drank hot Ribena from misshapen mugs that Aiden had made in a beginners' ceramics course. Afterward, they lay with swollen bellies on her bed and shared a joint of sticky sativa buds and lavender.

"Would it be totally weird for you if I wanted to be friends with one of your friends?" Taiye asked, her head resting on Aiden's soft belly.

"Timi? He said to give you his number. You two are too cute." She swiped open her phone screen and sent Timi's phone number to Taiye.

"Thank you."

"Hey, so we just met, and I'm moving to Barcelona in a few weeks."

"Oh damn, what for?"

"To study. There's this incredible refugee and migrant-worker art scene. I got an Erasmus grant to check it out."

"What will you do there?"

"I wrote some shit about documenting the most prominent artists of the movement, and art as its own sanctuary, and learning frameworks, blah blah. All rubbish. I just want to witness it, you know."

"Nice. Good for you. Are you excited or ... nervous?"

"All of the above. Super premature, but I'd love it if you would visit. Maybe you and Timz could take a romantic trip down one weekend?"

Aiden looked at her hands when she said that, picked at her nails, and didn't look up until Taiye asked, "Why are you interested in that—I mean, it obviously sounds incredible, but I'm just curious why that's your thing in particular."

"Oh man, yeah, like my mum's a refugee. I mean, she came here from Eritrea as an asylum seeker when she was quite young, much much younger than I am now, and she married this, like, working-class Welshman from Swansea, and they moved to Cardiff and had me. And like," she gnawed at a hangnail on her left thumb, "I can't go to Eritrea, yeah, and I can't afford to go anywhere in Africa, at least not yet, so this way—like with this project—I'm a bit closer to the, like, handiwork of people with a similar experience to my mum. I think." She laughed after a brief moment of silence. "You know, I could've just written that for the Erasmus grant."

"Yeah," Taiye said, nodding, "that's a lot more fucking real than anything with the term 'frameworks.'"

Aiden laughed. "You done much travelling?"

"A little bit, not really," Taiye said. "Most recently I spent some time in Montpellier. That was few years ago. And I went home to Lagos to see my mum like two years ago, I think."

"Oh, Montpellier is right close to Barcelona! Why were you there?"

"There was this Catalan culinary program ... I also really wanted to improve my French." Taiye shrugged, feeling sheepish.

"You learned to cook Catalan food?!" Aiden sat up, her face broken open with enthusiasm. "That is random and fucking cool!"

"Yeah, random, I suppose." Taiye laughed.

"Tell me what you learned!" Aiden exclaimed.

"I'll cook for you sometime."


"SOMETIME" WAS THREE DAYS BEFORE Aiden was scheduled to board a train to Paris, and then another to Barcelona. It was a dinner party she'd dubbed Glitter Goodbyes, where she hosted a handful of close friends and required that they dust themselves with gold glitter from a compact case glued below the peephole on her front door before entering the flat. Taiye promised Catalan food, but at the last moment, she enlisted

Timi's help, and they made food from home. "From home" meant different things to each of them, but the food was mollifying, the aromas and flavours familiar.

In the cramped space of the kitchen, they danced around each other casually, with unexpected ease. They worked smoothly in soothed silence; Taiye offered gentle orders to purée, grind, pour, chop— "Careful careful, don't touch the pepper seeds with naked fingers!" Timi responded by doing. He knew his way, had done so many times, with his mother and sisters, and the occasional lover.

They soaked, rinsed off the chaff, and ground beans for moi moi: They mixed the mealy ground beans with pale red onion and tomato purée, sharp slivers of Scotch bonnet, chicken bouillon cubes, palm oil, and crayfish powder. They poured the thick batter in oiled ramekins— turquoise, white, black and gold, yellow. Because Aiden didn't have a large enough pot, they baked the moi moi in a *bain-marie*, with a broad sheet of foil cinched around the tray to keep the steam inside to cook the savoury bean cakes.

Taiye and Timi peeled, sliced, and fried overripe plantains in fragrant coconut oil, squealing and jumping away when scalding oil spat from the pan. They oven-roasted skewers of marinated beef covered in homemade yaji—a valiant attempt at suya. They laughed at this, at their diasporic angst, as they dipped yeasty balls of puff-puff in glossy melted dark chocolate.

When they served their offerings, Taiye glowed, proud to be feeding Aiden and her guests a meal that conjured memories of her twin and their mother. Of a time in which the hollowing echo of loneliness didn't ring so loud in her steps, her voice, and her body. None of her indulgences had yet silenced the shrill call of such a vast empty; still, she latched, she let go, she consumed, unhinged the jaw of her soul to drink whatever was given. And, still, nothing satiated.

Aiden changed the music from the relentlessly cool poetics of Digable Planets to Sérgio Mendes's sultry bossa nova. Beside the billowing lace curtains, Our Lady swayed her ethereal body in rhythm with the percussion.

Taiye smiled at her. Timi caught her smile and saw only lace curtains fluttering in protest of the cold breeze that poured through the open window. He raised his flawlessly arched eyebrows at Taiye and smirked. Taiye's smile grew bigger at Timi. They ate in the comfortable din of conversation.

WEEKS LATER, Taiye went to Unchained Ministries in South Norwood to watch Timi sing in the church choir for the first time. This Timi was a watered-down version of the one she'd met at Aiden's party, the one with whom she had spent many of her evenings since Aiden's Glitter Goodbyes. They'd made a tradition of meeting on Wednesdays after work to cook together or watch Yoruba films online or traipse around galleries, giggling at contemporary art. In Aiden's absence, they developed a fast friendship. The kind of kinship established due to a common sadness, shared loneliness that becomes bearable through laughter and food and the good company of one who understands.

At church that Sunday, Timi's voice rose past the din of Taiye's anxieties. When he sang a solo rendition of the chorus and a couple verses of the hymn "It Is Well with My Soul," she closed her eyes and prayed the lyrics in earnest.

Only moments after the service ended, they snuck out of the church and spilled onto the damp road ahead of the crowd of worshippers that were sure to corner Timi and, unwarranted, share their thoughts on his singing. On their walk to Eko Mama Takeaway, Taye hugged Timi, saying over and over, "You were amazing."

Timi looked like an entirely different person in his blue button-down and dark-wash jeans, but once they'd crossed the road and were farther away from the church he allowed some of his femmeness to resurface. He rolled his neck and exclaimed, "I was, innit!"

By the time they ordered rice and goat stew to be eaten with plastic forks on the first park bench they found, bodies huddled together, sharing warmth and good meat, Timi's body had relaxed, and his smirk returned.

"I love singing," he said between mouthfuls. "I want to do that all the time, even if it's at that place."

"You looked so happy."

"I was ... I am." He laughed his laugh, with his head thrown back, and Taiye felt happy along with him. Then she saw a familiar orange Afro floating across the street, attached to the lovely head of a fat, freckled woman.

Zora.

And Taiye, prone to sinking in the face of beauty, lost her thoughts at the sight of her. Timi's voice faded as Zora came closer into view. Her arms were full of grocery bags, close to tumbling out of her grasp. She teetered in black high-heeled pumps and smiled when she caught Taiye's eye.

And Taiye, she sank.

THE TROUBLE WAS THAT ZORA WANTED MORE than Taiye could give. She was hungry for a full meal, but Taiye offered only appetizers, delectable hors d'oeuvres, mouth-watering desserts, fine sweets, and rich wine. Zora wanted nourishment, so although their few months together were torrid, they were also tumultuous and exhausting for both women. Once Zora clocked that there would be no real lasting relationship with Taiye, she left, and that was that.

By the time Taiye emerged from that most recent collapse into lust, or a self-delusion of potential love, she couldn't find Timi.

She called often. She left apologetic voice messages that stayed unreturned:

"Hey, love, I'm sorry I've been M.I.A. How are you doing? Let's catch up."

"Timmy Timz, miss you, lovey. Let me know what you've been up to."

"Heya, Timmy, I'm so sorry I've been a rubbish friend. I'm sorry."

Then text messages:

*Baby boy, we NEEEEEED to hang out.*

*Bruhhh! I miss you, bruh. Let's sneak wine into the cinema and watch white people release ancient curses from Egyptian tombs.*

*Timi, I'm sorry that I disappeared for a bit there. I'd like to see you, please let me know.*

Then she took to leaving heart eyes and sweet comments on his social media posts.

The weeks crawled by in Timi's absence. Taiye was outrageously stoned, splayed on the floor of her shoebox flat, nibbling on cold spring rolls, ignoring the apparition that had become her only companion, basking in the stink of her self-loathing, wondering how she managed to take so many lovers yet failed to keep *one* friend.

She was mulling over all the specific ways she was, in fact, a mistake, when she heard her phone beep.

A message from Aiden:

*Heya, sorry for the out of the blue text, wasn't sure who else to ask. Have you heard from Timi? I'm a bit worried. He hasn't responded to my messages or any of our mates'. And hasn't posted anything in a bit. I think something happened. I'm scared he's gone and done something daft. Please let me know if you know anything.*

Taiye bolted upright so quickly her head became a helium balloon, and she had to pause to keep from falling back.

*Call him again,* Our Lady directed.

Taiye called, over and over. She fell asleep cotton-mouthed and light-headed, to a ringtone. She woke up the next morning and called in sick to work. She spent the day calling. She took the tube to Norwood junction and walked to Unchained Ministries, calling Timi's number the whole while. The church was closed, so she sat on the front steps for the duration of fifty-nine unanswered calls.

Our Lady placed a holy hand on Taiye's shoulder, and she shivered. She asked, "Is he okay?"

But Our Lady only pursed her lips and sighed.

Taiye carried on walking.

Forty-five minutes to Croydon, Aiden's neighbourhood, her fingers insistent on the redial button, and still no answer from Timi. Taiye felt frustration build tension in her right shoulder. She fought the impulse to throw her phone into the glass windows of a Chinese herb store. With her phone still against her ear, she entered Wandle Park. She perched on a cold low stone fence across from a placid pond. There she peeled the hot phone from her face, and instead of redialling Timi, she called her mother.

After four rings, the phone went to voice mail, and the coincidence of her mother being unavailable at the same time as Timi arrested Taiye's breath in her throat. She called her mother again, and when it went to voice mail again, she cried into the phone, "Mami, I'm alone."

Across from her, Our Lady shook her head.

Taiye said, "I make things *bad* with people, I don't know ... I'm just alone ..."

The phone beeped. She dropped her face into her hands and let her body heave with sobbing.

"Zora was right," Taiye said to Our Lady. "I have nothing that nourishes."

Our Lady lifted Taiye's chin and said, *You haven't eaten today.*

TAIYE WALKED SLOWLY, still calling Timi, time warping around her—a gift from her mother—until Our Lady shimmered at the entrance of a café with a mustard-yellow awning and a sign that read ABEILLE in bronze lettering. It was late afternoon with the sky hanging low, laden, and grey, refusing to give in and just break open in the drizzle that everybody was expecting.

Taiye had talked, more than once, with Timi about the "something daft" Aiden had mentioned. Always in semi-jest, always as something they would never do, *never.*

But: "You know, sometimes a queen gets tired." That's how Timi put it.

Taiye knew that she would never go there, not while Kehinde was alive in the world. She would never leave her sister alone, even if they never spoke again. But Timi was an only child; he was his mother's miracle. He took form after she'd spent many years casting and binding every evil spirit and every curse that kept her womb tied shut. He took form and filled her life with purpose, that's how she put it when, seven months pregnant at age forty-three, she gave testimony at Unchained Ministries. Timi's mother meant well; really, she loved him like a vice. But her words started to take cruel shapes when she saw the softness in his gestures. He had never been exceptionally masculine, but that was fine in boyhood. She expected a certain level of toughening up as he grew, but no. No, he leaned deeper into femmeness, until she highlighted the parameters of her love. She made it clear that neither she nor the church would protect him from the inevitable wrath of God if he didn't stop all that rubbish and behave like a normal man. So he became two people. One person for God and his mother, and another for himself. And he shared himself with his queer friends like Aiden, like Taiye.

Her food had grown cold. Taiye started to think that perhaps the sharing had all meant more to her than it did to him. Maybe she was making a fool of herself, harassing this poor boy who really just didn't want to be her friend anymore. Who did she think she was, anyway? She sat there, sniffling into her scarf, thinking what an utter—

Her phone rang. Timi's name and number blinked on the screen.

"Hello?" Taiye answered, out of breath from surprise.

Silence.

"Hello?" she said again.

"Taiye?" Timi's voice was hoarse.

"Timz, hey, yeah, it's me ..."

"Girl ...?" he slurred. Taiye envisioned his right brow cocking up, in preparation for some juicy gossip, but he mumbled as if he'd just woken, or was on the brink of sleep.

"Timmy Timz, how far?"

"I dey like dele." He laughed in slow motion.

"It's been a minute. I'm sorry."

"No worries, babes ..."

"You all right, love? You're slurring your words a bit."

"I had a bit to drink."

"So early, how come?"

"... Well ..."

"What happened? Maybe you can tell me in person. Where are you?"

"Been s-staying at Aiden's old flat."

"You there now?"

"Mm-hmm."

"You all right?"

Silence.

"Timz?"

"Taiye ..."

"You all right, love?"

"... Not really, my mother hates me." The laughter that followed was jarring. Its joylessness was painful to hear.

"I doubt that, darling."

"No, really ... and you know what's fucked up?"

"Everything?"

"Correct ... but also the bloke that told everyone ..."

"Yeah?"

Silence. Followed by sniffling. Followed by sobbing. A guttural cry that sounded as though it were ripped forcefully from the back of his throat.

Something dropped fast from a high place in Taiye's chest. It dropped down to her gut and sat there heavy and hard and hot.

"Timi?"

"He forced me ..." Timi hiccupped.

"Who?" Taiye asked, her voice forceful, already licking at the rage that smouldered in her gut. "Who, Timi?"

"The choirmaster, Wasiu .,. he forced himself on ... then he told the elders ... he showed them my Grindr profile ... they told the whole church."

"Timi, I'm so sorry."

He responded with that cutting laughter. "My mother told me I was a disgusting abomination." His voice started to sound far away, leaving Taiye with a sense of sand pouring out quickly from between her fingers.

"Never, Timi. You are not."

"But what if ...?" The far-awayness persisted.

"No."

Silence.

"Timi?"

He slurred something unintelligible, and fear spiked up Taiye's neck.

"Timi, you're drunk. Are you alone?"

"I ... hope so ... Taiye. I took some pills ... I'm tired."

Taiye's pulse quickened. "Timi?"

Silence.

Taiye waved the server over and mouthed that she needed a pen. She stilled her hands and wrote Aiden's address, Timi's name, and the words, *Please call an ambulance to this address. Overdose attempt* on the unused paper napkin. The server nodded and pulled out a cellphone from her apron pocket. Taiye watched her read out the address to the dispatcher before leaving a crumpled twenty-pound note and running out.

She ran, following Our Lady's directions. She still had the phone pressed against her face as she jogged through the door, out onto the cobblestone sidewalk. The sky finally broke open and drizzled cold rain on everything. The wind whipped against her skin as she ran.

Timi was silent on the other end, and the panic made Taiye speed up until she tripped and fell face down onto the damp, filthy sidewalk, scraping her knees and palm. But she barely registered the pain. She pushed herself up, picked up her phone, and continued to run.

"Timz," Taiye said into her phone, but there was no answer.

She kept running, her legs pumping despite the sharp pain steadily building in her thighs. She sped past the church where she first met Our Lady, past the small park, past the café where Zora worked. She got to Aiden's apartment just as the ambulance was driving away.

"Is he okay?" she asked one of the many neighbours loitering on the front lawn. "Is he alive?" she shouted.

"Think so, love," said an elderly woman in a red headwrap and a green terry cloth housecoat, her face a mask of concern. "They had that little oxygen mask thing on the boy's face. I think he's all right."

The woman kept talking, but Taiye stopped listening. She leaned against the brick wall and slid down until her bottom rested on wet grass. Her heart raced to a rhythm that seemed infinite. Bile rose up, bitter, from her queasy bowels to her tight throat. She coughed, and her face crumpled and her head fell into her trembling hands.

She closed her eyes, and Our Lady was there. The apparition folded Taiye's damp and shivering body into her own holy one, held her tight, and whispered a secret in her ear.

# Kehinde

*Letter no. 79*

*Kehinde,*

*It's a clear night in London. A gift. My eyes aren't big enough to see the whole night. The sky seems impossibly close, if I reached up right now I could probably touch it. I'm on this tiny balcony that I'm sure will collapse at any moment, but alas, it seems that I cannot move.*

*I've been sitting here for what feels like a long time. I've eaten sooo many edibles. I found them in the fridge, chocolate truffles.*

*I wish you would pick up my calls. I called at least a dozen times, at least.*

*I made a new friend this year, a real friend that I wasn't sleeping with, or taking anything from. Yesterday he tried to end his life because something bad happened to him. He was tired.*

*An apparition set me up, I think. She set me up to find him. I haven't seen her since yesterday. I hope she comes back soon. She told me something good, something glorious. I will tell you when I see you.*

*Things line up funny sometimes; madness has its purpose I suppose.*

*The last time I spoke with Mami, she thought I was you.*

*Always always I love you,*

*Taiye.*

*Letter no. 86*
*August 11, 2014*
*Heathrow Airport*
*Terminal 5*

*Kehinde,*
*I'm about to catch a flight to Canada.*
    *Halifax, Nova Scotia, to be exact.*
    *Don't worry, I'm not following you. Your silence has spoken, I'm not running after you anymore.*
    *I no longer want to be in London. My job was meaningless, and I felt like I was burning through people only to find myself fucked up and alone.*
    *I've enrolled in a culinary program at Nova Scotia Community College because cooking is something I know for a fact that I can do well. Meaning: I have not yet found a way to spoil it with my rubbish.*
    *How have you been?*
    *I did a bit of reading on Nova Scotian history: Did you know the first big group of immigrants to Nova Scotia (except for the dodgy white settlers—do they count as immigrants?) were Black Loyalists who came to the area as refugees after the American Revolution? Afterward, a group of exiled Jamaicans settled. They helped build the city's citadel and served in the military.*
    *African Nova Scotians have a history of more than four hundred years. I read that on a government website. I'll let you know what else I learn.*
    *I tried to visit Timi in the hospital; the nurses told me that he's alive, but his family insisted he not be allowed to see any friends. His phone was disconnected; his Insta was deactivated. I've written a few emails just updating him on my life and letting him know I miss him.*
    *I miss him very much. I feel powerless and foolish.*
    *I don't know what else to do, so I'm going away.*
    *I'm boarding now, I have to go.*
    *Love,*
    *Taiye*

**Letter no. 97**
March 25, 2015
Central Library, Halifax


Dear Kehinde,

What's the weather like in Montreal?

Today Halifax is covered in a thick grey fog, but it's humid, and it's one of the warmest days I've experienced in the last three weeks. The sky here can be pretty indecisive, I think that's why people talk about it so much. Everyone I've met so far is atypically friendly. So far the Canadian stereotype is proving to be accurate, but they aren't necessarily warm, more like polite. That's more than I can say for South London folk. I do miss it, though. I miss the grit and honesty.

I've been staying out of trouble. My apparition buddy is still with me, though she's not quite an apparition anymore. Anyway, I have to go. Today's free event at the library is a mini conference put on by one of the universities here called, "Who Belongs Here: Conversations on Race and Space in K'jipuktuk." K'jipuktuk is the Mi'kmaq name for Halifax. Mi'kmaq is the name of the Indigenous peoples of the Atlantic provinces like Nova Scotia, New Brunswick, and some other areas I don't know too much about yet. I've been learning a little bit about the way Canada was formed as a nation. Like about the European colonizers, and the way they straight-up killed and stole and raped (as they do) and attempted to destroy the original people on this land.

The conference should be interesting, and if not, then I hope they have snacks.

Love always,
Taiye


I THINK TAIYE IS AVOIDING ME.

Which is ironic. And extremely irritating, considering how often she used to write to me when we were a whole ocean apart. But I know I have no right to be annoyed, or demand more than she's giving, considering how absent I've been. Ocean or bedroom door or unspoken hurt, something always remains lodged between us.

In the week I've been back, she has spent most of her days tending to her beehive or knee-deep in the patch of soil in the backyard, hoping to turn it into something more alive. Also, she cooks. Large feasts that are too much food for the four of us. She makes plates for Hassan and the security men at the estate gates. Sometimes I help her, and she delegates tasks with swift authority: "Julienne these. Thinner than that." "Crush this." "Please put a lid on that." "Is it burning? Don't let it burn." "A heaping spoonful. Heaping." "No, leave it. It's supposed to char."

But we barely speak otherwise. Don't get me wrong, Taiye is warm. She touches me: a hand on my shoulder, fingers picking fluff out of my hair, hands rubbing my arms when the a/c turns on suddenly and the chill raises goosebumps on my skin. But words are scarce.

Most evenings, she massages a mixture of ori and Tiger Balm into our mother's feet, ankles, and back.

Always, she ignores her phone, which beeps so incessantly that I want to snap that she must switch off the volume.

It's the heat and the house, and this rootless, untethered feeling that they spark inside me, that's making me so irritable.

I've occupied myself, mostly, by reading Taiye's letters and attempting to have lucid conversations with our mother. She is a whole other character. This morning, for example, while we were tucking into a breakfast of masa and catfish stew that Taiye woke up before the sun to prepare, our mother asked if I still worked at the gallery.

"Yes," I said, "but only part time."

She didn't ask, "How come part time?" or "What do you do the rest of the time?" She just nodded and said, "Lovely," then took a big bite of her breakfast.

"How about your art?" Taiye had asked to fill the awkward silence our mother had plunged us into with her half-assed interest and typical distractedness.

"Good—how did you know ...?" I'd asked.

I'd sent our mother pictures of my work from my first group show. Four pieces of the same picture in different media: white charcoal on black paper, black ink on white paper, watercolour on canvas, and a glass bead collage in beeswax encaustic. Trying, failing, to make myself emerge from the picture. Always, it was Taiye's face. I only recognized her.

I'd sent pictures from my first group show—a few years ago now—to our mother, but not to Taiye.

"Google." She shrugged, her face a mask of nonchalance. But I recognize this mask; I have the same one.

"She just scored gallery representation!" Farouq exclaimed. The poor guy was trying to navigate the sudden and perplexing web of unspokens between the lot of us.

"Congratulations," Taiye said with a smile, always a warm unfurling flower on that face. "Well done. What gallery?"

"Galerie d'Or, in Old Montreal." I wanted to tell her about my art, suddenly, I want her to find it, and me, interesting.

"Very cool." Taiye nodded and she said again, "Well done."

"And these are for the drawings of the house you sent me pictures of?" asked our mother.

"Yes, but I've evolved the concept since then. I've been doing larger pieces." I wanted to tell her more, describe how I'd been combining the intricate beadwork and beeswax encaustic with life-sized photos to make murals. But she was no longer looking at me, and my words stuck in my throat.

"So lovely. Your hair is interesting these days, isn't it?" she said.

Taiye stifled a giggle.

Farouq raised his eyebrows in confusion.

I shook my head, rolled my eyes, and ate my catfish stew in silence.

Farouq stayed in the kitchen after breakfast to help Taiye clean up. I probably should have done the same, instead of running up to my room like I've done after every awkward conversation, but here I am again, in my childhood bedroom, trying to recall why I've chosen to come home after all this time. After the bad thing, I stopped sleeping here. I would get dressed and do my homework in my room, but as soon as it was time for sleep, I went into the empty guest room across the hall and locked the door.

Farouq comes in just in time to keep my thoughts from quietly devouring me. He finds me sitting cross-legged on the vanity, with my back resting against the mirror. Only a week in Lagos and already, he is burnt and browning. He is also clean-shaven.

"You decided against the beard, huh?" I ask, reaching out to hold his face.

He sucks his teeth like I showed him. "It's too hot for all that jor," he says in a poor interpretation of a Nigerian accent and Yoruba vernacular.

I laugh, and he laughs. He uncrosses my legs and wraps them around his waist so that I'm straddling him. He kisses me, carries me to the bed, and starts to untie the straps of the adire halter dress that I stole from my mother's closet.

"No," I whisper against his mouth. "Not now."

What I mean is, *Not here. Not in this room, in this house.*

He rolls off me. "It's been almost a month," he says, and leans his forehead against my sternum; gently, he taps it there.

I sit up, and he rolls his head onto my lap. From here, I can see out the mosquito-netted window to Taiye crouched over in her garden. I kiss Farouq on the forehead and leave him to go outside and join my sister.

She is barefoot, in a faded black T-shirt and old aso oke shokoto folded up at her ashy knees. She doesn't look up when I walk out onto the damp grass. Beside her, seedlings are sprouting out of old paint cans: basil, spinach, onions, waterleaf, and a few other plants that I don't recognize.

"You're going to plant all these?" I ask her.

"Yeah," she answers, and picks up one of the cans. "I started it when I first came back. I thought Mami would get into it and come out a bit. But I never got to it until now."

"Come out?"

"Yeah, she wasn't doing so well."

"What do you mean? Was she sick?"

"Her body was probably fine." Taiye finally looks up at me. She taps her temple with dirt-covered fingers. "She was struggling here. I thought a garden would help, but ..."

"You've planted a garden before?" I ask, because for the life of me I cannot think of any other direction to take this conversation and keep it light.

"Not really." She is gentle with the seedling, her deft hands tender as she transfers it into the ground. "I figured I'd throw some seedlings in and say a prayer," she jokes, and to me, it is a sign of hope.

"And maybe add some water?" I ask, and it lights a smile in me when she looks up and chuckles softly.

Brown dirt is smeared on her cheeks and chin. She tries to shake a fly that has landed on her nose, and her braids tumble down from the loose bun that was tied on top of her head.

I touch them gently, thin and long. "I don't miss sitting for hours to get these in," I say.

She starts to say something when the back screen door creaks open. A light-skinned stranger peeks her head through the doorway.

"Can we help you?" I ask, just as Taiye stands up abruptly. "Isabella, what are you doing here?" tumbles quickly out of her mouth.

"Isabella?!"

"Kehinde!" Isabella exclaims, and reaches out to embrace me. "Your sister said you were coming. How long have you been back?"

"A week!"

"O girl, welcome back to Lagos!" Isabella is stunning in a slim-cut navy blue skirt suit, her hair slicked back into a small poof at the base of her neck, makeup miraculously immaculate in this humidity. She says with what stinks of forced cheer, "I'm just heading to work, but your sister hasn't been returning my calls, so I'm here, in person, to invite you all to my engagement party!"

"Congratulations!" I look at Taiye, who is attempting to mask a pained expression with a forced smile of her own. "Taiye didn't tell me you had seen each other."

"Well," Isabella says, "it's on Saturday at my mumsie's place, starts at three. Actually, it starts at four thirty, but I'm telling people three because ... well, you know."

"Thank you so much for the invite. We'll definitely be there," I say.

"Perfect! I can't wait to meet your husband!" Isabella yells, as she rushes back through the kitchen.

The silence is thick when I turn to face Taiye, who is pouring her attention back into her seedlings. I crouch to join her closer to the soil. "How can I help?" I ask, but she stays silent.

Just as I get up to leave, she says, "There's a watering can by the fence. Can you please fill it with water?"

While I fill the green plastic container at the kitchen sink, I come up with things I must say to Taiye.

*I've been reading your letters and I would like us to talk seriously.*

*I'm sorry I've been so unavailable. I'd like us to talk like sisters now.*

*So we both saw apparitions of each other. That's fucking wild, no?*

*About Wolfie ...*

But when I go back out, Taiye is chewing the corner of her bottom lip. "So Isa and I have been sleeping together."

I can only blink at her. "Ah ... I didn't know she was ..." I start to say.

"Yeah, well ... yeah, so I have a problem ..." Abruptly she sits in the soil. "I sometimes don't know how to ... say no ... to myself or other people ... other women." She looks down at her palms as she continues, "I want to be different ... better. Anyway, we've been fucking for a few months, and I told her it had to end because ... yeah, she's engaged."

This may be the most truthful she's been since I've come home.

"Anyway, I just wanted you to know ..."

"Do you not want to go to her engagement party?"

"No, I mean, yeah, we should go. It's only right." She wrings her hands like a rag, rubs her cheek, and smears more dirt on her face.

I smile to ease her, and she mirrors me.

"Tell me about your bees," I say.

And with a sigh of something I can only name as relief, she tells me. "Well, I wanted to plant a garden, something lush, with edible flowers. But, then, um, I got nervous that, like, nothing would grow."

"What do you mean?"

"Just like, you know, that I'm cursed and nothing I plant would grow."

"Well, that seems reasonable," I joke.

She laughs and continues, "So I started reading books on gardening, learning about plants native to Lagos Island, plants that might thrive. Books and articles and podcasts of Nigerian gardening and urban farming. This one book, *Organic Farming in Urban Jungles: Lagos Edition*, had a chapter on beekeeping."

"Yeah?"

"Yeah, it reminded me of someone I used to see ... and also that bees are dope." She shrugs.

"You've always been a bit obsessed with bees," I chime in. "At least you were when we were small."

"I was, wasn't I?"

I nod, and we smile at each other.

I remember when her honeybee obsession started. One Saturday afternoon, after swimming lessons at Ikoyi Club, when Taiye and I were back home with our skin and braids still soaked with that astringent smell of chlorine, the peppery bite of suya on our tongues, our hands sticky with melted cotton candy. And our father came home with two plastic bottles filled with thick brown honey.

"Good honey from Abeokuta!" He smeared a spoonful on a soft slice of Senegalese bread.

The honey sank into our tongues, a deep earthy malt flavour that didn't exist in the glass jars of imported honey we bought at Goodies Supermarket. Taiye took to ripping off hunks of bread and dipping them into a shallow bowl of honey that our father set on the dining table for us. Between mouthfuls, she asked about honey, about bees and their hives, about beekeepers. *Do wasps make honey too? Do ants and cockroaches?*

Our father answered all her questions with the sincere solemnity of a
priest and plenty of laughter in his eyes. Then he placed a heavy volume
of the *Encyclopaedia Britannica* on the table in front of her, the entries for
honey and bees marked with two yellow wooden rulers.

"Read, Baby Two," he said. "It's all here for you."

So she read about bees and honey, and talked about bees and honey,
and looked for pictures of bees and honey. Our father even took us to
Abeokuta to meet a beekeeper acquaintance of his, Kenneth Bello, an
entomologist trained specially in breeding queen bees. Our mother
stayed behind; she said that Abeokuta was a sore place for her and went,
instead, to visit her aunt in Ife.

My memories of the beekeeper and his hives are murky with the scent
of jealousy—yes, even then, I was jealous of our father's attentiveness
to Taiye. But with shining eyes, Taiye tells me now that she remembers
everything. The beekeeper is still there—that is where she went to learn
to finish building a hive of her own. When our father took us to Kenneth's
apiary all those years ago, the entomologist owned no more than six hives.
Taiye remembers they were perched on a slight hill in spacious clusters
under the mango, almond, and guava trees that bordered his small farm.
When she went back, almost two decades after first gorging herself on
honey from his hives, she found that the size of both his farm and apiary
had more than tripled.

"It's an outstanding operation," she says, "with a training and apprenticeship centre, and a shop selling beekeeping supplies, raw honey,
pollen, propolis, royal jelly, and beeswax. When I called the number on
Kenneth's website he didn't remember who I was, but he said it would be
better if I visited to talk in person."

"You went?"

"I did." She nods. "He recognized me, or rather, recognized Popsie's
features on my face. He was much nicer in person than on the phone.
Gave me a quick tour of the apiary, asked where I was planning to keep
my hive, mentioned that he'd suggested Popsie turn our house into hotel.

He talked about him a lot, told me that it was Popsie who loaned him money to buy his farm back in the day."

Kenneth sent her back with wooden frames and wired wax foundations, a smoker with a replacement bellow, a hook end hive tool, bee brush, and frame grips. He promised to pay the house a visit in the following week with the remaining supplies and a nucleus colony.

"I asked how much I owed, but he refused to take my money. It took him over five weeks to make it to Lagos with a nucleus colony and fully set up my hive. It was all good, though, because it gave me plenty of time to build the rest of the hive and fit the frames. Mami was here when he showed up—there was some ... tension." She raises her eyebrows and smirks.

"What do you mean?"

"Mami had finally emerged from her room after many days of ... well, not leaving her room. And we were out here listening to music when he came. They both seemed stunned to see each other, and then she rushed back inside after an awkward greeting."

"What do you think that was about?"

"Fuck knows." She shrugs. "Anyway sha, even with the delay, it was probably the only straightforward transaction I've had since I've been in Lagos."

"For real?" I ask.

"For real," she replies, swatting a fly away from her face. "Although, it was less of a transaction and more of a favour."

"I can't believe he hooked you up for free."

"Babe, neither can I."

"You didn't tell me about your bees, though." I sit in the dirt beside her. "You just told me how you got the hive."

"Oh yeah." She laughs. "My bees are ... tempestuous."

"Like you," I tease her.

She laughs. "Anyway, I'm pretty sure there's a story with that Kenneth bloke, though."

"Yeah? Has he been around since?"

"No, but there's always a story when Mami is involved."

# 3

# Pig

# Kambirinachi

THE SUN SWELLED MASSIVELY AND HUNG LOW on the day of the wedding. To the immense chagrin of Banji's family, the ceremony was neither traditional nor Christian but a simple matter of signing a marriage contract at the local government office with his parents and Aunty Akuchi as witnesses. The whole time, Kambirinachi did her best to put aside thoughts of her mother, whose absence had grown into a bleak yawn of longing in her life.

Afterward, they drove the bumpy road to Banji's family's compound to celebrate. His family tried not to sully the party with their disappointment, at not only his choice to eschew a traditional ceremony but also his choice of bride. Again, it wasn't that they didn't like Kambirinachi; they were just concerned by her strangeness and the fact that her family constituted only a childless aunt in a relationship with a married man. The whole thing was quite shameful, really, but should the girl be punished for her lack of respectable family? She was beautiful—bewitching, actually. Massive eyes that beguiled merely by looking. She was trained well enough: greeted her elders, never waited to be asked before rushing to assist, generous with what little she seemed to have. Perhaps it was just that—the fact that she seemed to possess so little—that stoked their doubt.

Regardless, Kambirinachi was striking in her crimson, cream, and navy blue striped iro and buba, head crowned with an elaborately wrapped and fanned-out gold gele, as she clasped the lean kaftan-clad arm of her new husband. Her aunt Akuchi and Yusuf—"the woman's shameless lover"—shared a table with Banji's mother. A dozen rented plastic tables dotted the compound, decorated with indigo adire tablecloths gathered at the legs with pale pink satin ribbons tied into large bows that wilted in the heat. Each table held an offering of aromatic schnapps and kola nuts, and was occupied mainly by Banji's family friends, many of whom eyed his unknown bride with awe and confusion.

Kambirinachi remained unfazed. With her gaze fixed on Banji, she hardly registered anyone else. They danced and danced and ate, and when they knelt at the feet of their elders to receive prayers of long life, prosperity, and fertility, she didn't close her eyes as one ought. Instead, she kept them fixed on Banji's knuckly hands clasped over her own.

THE YOUNG COUPLE spent their first night as husband and wife in the somewhat arbitrarily dubbed honeymoon hut at Apatala Village, a spacious compound lush with palm, coconut, mango, hibiscus, and almond trees. Among all the greenery, ten large thatched-roofed huts surrounded an artificial fish pond the size of a small swimming pool. Apatala Village was built to replicate a picturesque rural village experience for European travellers who desired just a taste and not a full meal of rural living in Ife. However, the taste was only a facade; the huts were air conditioned, their tiled floors covered in gorgeously patterned raffia mats. The only difference between the honeymoon hut and the other nine on the property was the bed—a lopsided heart covered in red satin bedding that made Kambirinachi burst into laughter upon first sight. Banji's sisters had booked the place and Kambirinachi really couldn't decipher if their choice was sincere—which would mean they had questionable taste—or cruel. Either way, once they were finally alone there was too much joy simmering beneath her skin to spare even a moment indulging thoughts of anything other than her husband and his beautiful body.

As soon as they set foot in the honeymoon hut, Banji became uncharacteristically shy. He averted his gaze and scratched his head, distractedly looking around from the cane furniture to the shiny sound system stacked against the wall across from the bed.

"Banji," Kambirinachi said from where she was already perched on the bed.

"Mm-hmm?" he responded, avoiding her gaze.

"What music do they have?" she asked.

"Erm ..." He fingered the collection of cassette tapes and vinyl records. "Bob Marley, Manu Dibango, Angélique Kidjo, Ebenezer Obey, King Sunny Adé, Stevie Wonder ... there's plenty."

"How about Manu Dibango?"

Banji pulled out the record *Soul Makossa*, placed it gingerly on the dusty turntable, and dropped the needle. By the time he turned around to face his bride, she was already dancing where she sat. With her eyes closed and shimmying her shoulders, she slowly unwound the gele from her head and let her thick braids tumble down her shoulders. Kambirinachi stood up and danced toward her husband, smiling the whole while, inviting him to dance with her. His shy smile widened, and he stepped in rhythm to Manu Dibango's beat. The two of them, they danced toward and away from each other in turn. Until one of them—hard to say who— grabbed the other and planted a kiss on the lips.

Yes, they had kissed many times before, sloppy, impatient, but nothing like this, nothing that hinted at a much larger hunger. Kambirinachi took the reins. She undressed Banji slowly and requested that he do the same for her. They looked at each other for a long time, and by the time they kissed again, Banji had forgotten to be shy.

THE CLOUDS WERE INCONSOLABLE the Sunday that Kambirinachi and Banji moved to Lagos. But the weeping sky did not sway them. Neither did Akuchi's pleas.

"Won't you consider waiting until tomorrow?" she asked, her eyebrows knotted in concern as she watched Banji pile their bags into his friend's rusty tan van. "I'm worried about you people driving in all this rain."

The downpour sounded like applause as it beat against the windows.

"Don't worry, Ma." Banji's touched her shoulder with a damp hand. "We'll be very careful."

He meant to reassure her, but the rainwater soaked through his red T-shirt and did nothing to assuage her anxieties that they would veer off the dilapidated roads and into a ditch. Or face opportunistic robbers on the Lagos-Ojoo Expressway or collide with any number of drunken idiots driving in the wrong direction. Her imagination ran amok with countless possibilities that all ended with her niece hurt, or worse. In truth, in her deepest self, she was distraught to see the girl go.

But Banji had an interview on Monday at the accounting department of a microfinance company, a new business started by a middle-aged Austrian expat. It was a development project to appease his philanthropic wife's guilt at their luxurious standard of living in such a politically turbulent country. During the fifteen years the Austrian couple had lived in Nigeria, one head of state was deposed after ruling for over eight years. The one who followed was assassinated just shy of two hundred days in office. The next one resigned after nearly four years. Then there was a break from military regimes, the dawn of a Second Republic. However, that lasted all of four years and ninety-one days before that president was deposed. And it was back to military rule.

The expat's wife insisted that her husband hire young graduates and support the local economy, as apparently, their government would not be doing very much in their favour. Banji's uncle did business with a man who did business with the expat, put in a good word for the boy, and scored him an interview. Banji would not be missing it, even if it started to rain shards of glass. He needed a stable job; he had a new wife to look after.

So, sheltered by the blue plastic awning that arched over the burglar-proof entrance to the house, Banji hugged Akuchi goodbye and stepped into the van to give the women some space.

Akuchi enveloped Kambirinachi in a snug embrace. She whispered a prayer over the girl and planted a kiss on her wet forehead.

"Go well, eh, my dear," she said. "Please call me as soon as you reach Lagos."

"Yes, Ma." Kambirinachi sniffled before joining Banji in the van.

They had already driven through the gates of Akuchi's compound before she asked him to stop. She hopped out into the rain and ran across the gravel driveway, back into her aunt's arms, and said over and over, "Thank you, I love you, thank you."

THE RAINFALL WANED TO A DRIZZLE and then climbed to a torrential deluge several times during the five-and-a-half-hour drive to Lagos Island. With a soft hand on Banji's bony knee, Kambirinachi watched the view change from the greenness and open-skyness of Ife—which she hadn't left since her mother abandoned her there seven years ago—to the grey muddiness of the expressway. Then she slowly fell asleep with her head against the window. She didn't wake up until they were in Yaba. She blinked the sleep out of her dry eyes just as they drove past the worn blue gates of her old secondary school. Memories of her former schoolmates flooded her mind. Memories of Mercy were most vibrant.

She'd never told Banji much about her life before they met. Nothing about all of her misfortunes being a punishment for her choosing to live in this realm and abandon her Kin. Nothing about the way their voices sometimes plagued her—rare occurrences these days, but still. Moreover, when Banji asked about her mother, in those early days of their courtship, Kambirinachi said simply, "The grief from my father's death was too much for her. It, maybe, broke her."

Nothing about the fear that her mother blamed her, that she knew, somehow *somehow*, that his death was Kambirinachi's doing.

The traffic from Yaba to Surulere, their final destination for the day, was incessant, as was the rain again. They would stay with Banji's childhood friend Toyosi Awosika. Toyosi was halfway through her year with the national youth service corps and living in a sizable two-bedroom flat in a newly renovated complex rented by trusting parents who believed she was subletting the spare bedroom to a fellow corper to supplement her meagre service corps allowance. In truth, she was seeing a secretive married man who preferred that the place remain a private sanctuary for their trysts, so he paid for her to keep the room unoccupied.

Banji was one of three people privy to the affair. He'd asked her over the phone a week prior, "Are you sure he'll be okay with us staying?"

"Yes, jare! In fact, he'll be out of town, so no wahala at all."

By the time they drove through the compound, the sun had begun its slow descent, painting the low-hanging clouds in orange and magenta streaks. Kambirinachi had never met Toyosi in person, but she liked her voice on the phone, and she liked all the stories of Banji's childhood in which she featured as a brash fearless lizard catcher, or agbalumo thief, or general cheeky trickster. As an apology for missing their wedding, Toyosi sent Kambirinachi presents of delicate lace lingerie and pearlescent waist beads. The accompanying card joked that it was actually more of a present for Banji, and Toyosi signed off with many Xs and Os, and a PS expressing how eager she was to meet Kambirinachi in Lagos, finally.

And when they did meet at the front door of her flat, Toyosi squealed and wrapped her plump arms around Kambirinachi. "So good to finally meet you!" She pulled back, squeezed her shoulders, tilted her head to the side, and added, "And you are fine, sha!"

To Banji, she said, "Well done!" with a playful slap to his shoulder.

"Thank God you arrived well o," she said, and led them into the sparsely furnished living room where a ceiling fan spun lazily. The lights dimmed and brightened, dimmed and brightened.

"Toyo, this whole place for you?!" Banji exclaimed and dropped their bags by a sofa painted in giant red hibiscuses. He gave her a proper hug before he collapsed, exhausted, into a chair and pulled Kambirinachi into his lap.

"Yes, ke!" Toyosi replied. Then she said to Kambirinachi, "You're always so quiet?"

Banji laughed. "She's not o, don't be fooled."

Kambirinachi rolled her eyes at him and smiled demurely at Toyosi. "Sorry, I was just distracted, thinking. I really like this sofa."

"Thank you, my bo—the person I'm dating had it made for me." She placed a manicured hand on the arm of the chair; her glossy red nails matched the flowers.

"It's very beautiful," Kambirinachi said, and stifled a yawn.

"No sleeping before supper." Toyosi wagged her finger at Kambirinachi. "I hope you two are hungry."

"Three." Banji winced. "Kenny is coming to get his van. He'll join us for supper, jor no vex."

"That mugu owes me petrol money!"

KENNETH RANG THE SHRILL DOORBELL and let himself into the flat. Kambirinachi was very smugly beating Banji at a game of Ayo, and Toyosi had disappeared into the kitchen to heat a pot of egusi soup.

"Baba Banji!" Kenneth shouted from the door as he slid off wet squelchy sandals. "Longest time, brother!"

Banji flew off the couch and embraced his old friend. They did an elaborate handshake that involved a few finger snaps and finished with a lean back and a whistle.

"Longest time!" Banji exclaimed. He stretched his hand out toward Kambirinachi and said, "Kenny, this is my wife, Kambi. Kambi, Kenny and I went to primary school together."

At the sight of Kambirinachi, Kenneth's features arranged themselves in an expression of utter bewilderment. He was confident he knew this woman—and knew her well, down to her smell and the white flecks on her fingernails—but for the life of him, he couldn't say from where.

Kambirinachi ignored his slack-jawed ogle and shook his outstretched hand. "Nice to meet you, Kenny."

"Sister, no vex, but don't I know you from somewhere?"

"I don't know. Did you go to OAU?"

"No, UNILAG."

"I grew up in Abeokuta ... maybe there ...?"

"My father's people are from there, but I grew up in Ife with them Banji and Toyosi."

"Well, I was in Ife as well, so maybe that's where." Annoyance was climbing up and down her neck and shoulders. Kambirinachi did not like the way he looked at her face, an intense stare that was certain of something she could neither confirm nor deny.

"Bros, abeg leave my wife before I woze you." Banji stepped in, as confused as Kambirinachi was annoyed.

"Jor, no vex ..." Kenneth reluctantly tore his eyes away from Kambirinachi's face. He scratched the back of his neck, as if to disperse the awkwardness that was clouding the spaces between their bodies, and asked, "Where Toyosi dey?"

"Kitchen." Banji motioned in that direction with a sideways tilt of his head.

After Kenneth vanished into the kitchen, Banji turned to Kambirinachi with raised eyebrows. "Have you met him before?"

Kambirinachi shook her head and shrugged. "No."

"He's funny," Banji said, but it was clear by his tone that he meant something considerably more serious.

BETWEEN SWALLOWS OF EBA made with yellow garri and the peppery egusi chock-full of stockfish and chicken, the three friends and Kambirinachi played a tight game of Ludo. All except Banji had successfully moved all four of their tokens out of their yards and were in a close race for the finishing square. Sade Adu's silky voice poured out of a cassette player and filled the living room with the sultry rhythms of "Smooth Operator."

"Where is your interview tomorrow?" Toyosi asked Banji, as she rolled the dice to determine how many squares forward her token could move.

"On the Island, Ikoyi."

"What time?"

"Nine thirty."

"Ah, you better leave here around seven, just to be safe."

"I can drop you off," Kenneth offered. The young man was making a valiant effort to not look at Kambirinachi. "What is the name of the company?"

"Dasha Microfinance, it's a ne—"

"Are you joking?" Toyosi asked, cutting him off, her eyebrows knotted in a sudden tight frown. She handed the dice to Kambirinachi and sat back with her arms crossed over her chest.

"Yes now, why? You know it?"

"That's my"—she waved a hand vaguely—"you know, my person's new company."

"Are you serious?" Banji asked.

The game paused.

Kenneth and Kambirinachi looked from Toyosi to Banji and back again.

"How did you even find out about it?" Toyosi asked.

"One of Popsie's connections ... wait, why didn't *you* tell me about it?"

"Ah ahn, sebi, you know I don't like to mix my life with his life like that now." She pouted ever so slightly, a mixture of embarrassment and annoyance playing out across her heart-shaped face.

"So, is this *somehow* for you?"

"Well, I can't be the one to tell you not to interview for the job."

"No," Kenneth piped in, "but you *can* put in a good word for him with your Oga and make sure he gets it."

"Kenny, no," Banji interrupted. "Toyosi, you don't have to do that—"

"She doesn't have to, but it would be nice if she did," Kambirinachi said softly.

All three of them turned to look at Kambirinachi, surprised that she had spoken up after her near silence for the majority of the evening. The rain was coming down hard again, and the pittering sound merged with the noise from the traffic below and the din from many nearby beer parlours. So it wasn't quite an awkward *silence* that enveloped the room but a disquiet that refused to be quelled when Toyosi finally said, "Well, he's out of town anyway, so he won't even be the one interviewing you."

"He owns the company," Kambirinachi scoffed. "You could always call and let him know that your dear childhood friend—"

"Kambi, stop." Banji was firm.

Kambirinachi only shrugged, put the dice down, got up, and sauntered to Toyosi's spare bedroom.

BANJI, EVER CHARMING, IMPRESSED THE VICE-PRESIDENT of Dasha Microfinance, convincing her that what he lacked in experience he compensated for with sheer enthusiasm and keenness to learn. Granted, the vice-president happened to be the disgruntled wife of the founder; acutely aware of her husband's indiscretions, she decided that at the very least she could have a beautiful boy to look at.

Moreover, despite her hesitation and new-found dislike for Kambirinachi, Toyosi did put in a good word for her childhood friend. Although, if you asked Kambirinachi, she would say that while her husband slept, she whispered prayers of luck and favour into the starched cuffs and collar of the striped button-down he would wear to the interview. She would add that she sweetened his path with a heavy dusting of crushed sugar on the soles of his brown leather loafers, and that, she would explain, is why he got the job.

The point remains, however, that he did get the job. The considerably well-compensated job that, because he had to relocate to Lagos, included housing. The housing was a rather modest one-bedroom bungalow in the dusty boys' quarters of Banji's new employers' recently acquired property in Ikoyi.

Banji and Kambirinachi were thrilled to be securing a life for themselves in the nation's capital. Before moving into the bungalow, Kambirinachi clapped and prayed into every corner in all four rooms to clear away whatever spirits belonged to its previous residents. And to invite only goodness into her new home. Then, with their sparse belongings still mostly packed, they celebrated on a raffia mat spread on the pale yellow linoleum tiles of their tiny living room, drinking palm wine—a gift from Kenneth—and digging into catfish pepper soup—a gift from Toyosi.

# Taiye

OUR LADY'S VOICE BECAME A FIXTURE IN TAIYE'S MIND, a kindly inquirer, never mocking or cruel but always honest. Her voice grew so similar to Taiye's that the two became quite indistinguishable. Her ethereal embodiment merged with Taiye's reflection so that all Taiye had to do was look upon any reflective surface and there Our Lady would be: skin a deep dark brown, eyes widened and darkened, face narrowed, exactly like Taiye's. So that Taiye would never be alone.

During those first few lonely months in Halifax, with its salty fogs and gorgeous ocean and monuments to cruel colonizers, Our Lady was Taiye's only companion. She followed Taiye on the charming ferry, across the dazzling harbour, to the Akerley campus of the community college, where Taiye took culinary courses. She whispered encouragements when Taiye's body felt too heavy and entirely uninterested in crawling out of bed to engage with the world, sometimes for whole weekends. She suggested that Taiye attend free lectures at the public Central Library on Spring Garden Road, if only to be around other people, if only to share the same air and hear other voices. Our Lady joined Taiye on long evening walks from where she rented the finished basement in a four-bedroom house on Creighton Street in the North End of the small city. Like her attic flat in London, her place had its own separate door and a tiny afterthought of a kitchen. She only had to share a bathroom with the rotating roster of roommates upstairs.

Their walks invariably included a perch on one of the picnic benches by the harbour, the cold breeze from the ocean whipping through Taiye's insufficient layers of clothing, raising goosebumps on her skin. It was a simple matter of loneliness. The same grief that drove her to seek respite in the beds of willing women, that drove her into nearly anything that paused her whirling mind, and most recently, that drove her abruptly out of London. It was always the same creature, creeping up and dressed for different occasions, and it felt somewhat matched by the vastness and dramatics of the ocean.

On a particularly frigid Wednesday evening, after a tiresome knife skills class revisiting technique that she'd already learned, Taiye cried cold tears on her bench by the ocean, and then continued her walk up traffic-clogged Barrington Street and onto Argyle Street. She walked down the cobblestoned sidewalks and considered the bars. Many Irish pubs, a Mexican bar, at least two oyster bars, a karaoke bar, a French bistro, a wine bar. She was considering the soothing silence of intoxication when Our Lady said to Taiye, *Look at this sweet little place. Check it out.*

Taiye turned toward the small tea shop at the back of an old Marriott Hotel, with the words GOOD TEAS displayed in large grey lettering across its bright red ·awning. She walked inside, smiled at the blue-haired woman at the counter, and scanned the wall behind her for a list of teas.

"We have smelling samples on the wall over there," Blue Hair said.

Taiye stood, holding small glass jars of tea to her face, mmming at the feast of aromas, losing herself in the green tea section for nearly an hour. On the adjacent wall: black tea blends. She selected a sample jar of lapsang souchong and the deep earth, glowing fire smokiness blossomed ideas of smoked rice, chicken marinated in the potent brew, a glaze made of tea reduction with honey and fish sauce. Taiye, eyes closed, nose buried in the jar, a half smile on her face, was oblivious to the woman watching her with amusement.

"Good?" someone asked, startling Taiye out of her tea-fuelled reverie.

Taiye looked up, saw the owner of the voice, and her smile widened, bashful.

"Really good," she replied to the woman whose dark skin and sloe eyes roused in Taiye a familiar longing. She turned away, entirely unaware that this person would scrape through her poorly hidden wounds to reveal something worthwhile.

HALIFAX IS A SMALL CITY, beautiful and old. If you visit during the sweltering height of summer, you can prance along the crowded boardwalk
and sway your hips to the music of many buskers performing in the salty
breeze of the harbour. You can stop along the waterfront for a variety of
full-fat ice creams; salty, saucy, cheesy poutine; sugar-coated beaver tails;
fish and chips; and an assortment of taffies, cakes, and sweets. Downtown, you can visit the public gardens, where you may enjoy the pretty
flowers, the fountains, and the comical sight of fat bumbling geese in the
bird enclosure. If you wander north, to any of the many microbreweries
and bistros, it might be difficult to ignore the glaring scars of gentrification, but you must, if you have any intention of savouring your Jonah crab
bao, or your mezcal and tepache cocktail. And if while nursing the afore-
mentioned cocktail, you start to wonder where all the Black and Indigenous people are ... well ... we'll have to get back to that.

If, like Taiye, you turn up in September and are lulled into sentiments
of warmth and wellness by all the torrid gorgeousness of red oak trees
aflame in autumn, don't lose hope when the brittle cold descends swiftly
and without notice. If you feel discouraged by the severity of that wet
winter cold seeping right down to your core, hold tight until spring; it
all comes alive again. In the meantime, there will be hot tea, wool socks,
warm bread, and soups to tide you over.

By mid-March, after a lonely Christmas that included Catholic Mass,
a two-hour video call with her mother, and the drunken preparation of a
Christmas feast that she lived off for over a week, Taiye found her rhythm,
just as the air started to warm and the trees slowly clothed themselves in
green again.

Her culinary skills program was chugging along; in a Protein and
Sauce Foundations course, she learned the basic techniques of butcher-
ing a pig and how best to cook its various cuts.

The first step is to break the hog down to its five main cuts: shoulder,
belly, loin, ham, and head. Then you can whittle the beast down further
to steaks, chops, and bacon. Cuts like the loin, sirloin, spareribs, and
shoulders are ideal for roasting, whereas the blade steak, chop, tenderloin,

and arm steak are better braised. Pan broiling ham slices and bacon does those cuts the most justice. Very little is wasted, especially not the fat. Lard, Taiye discovered, was much less challenging to make than she'd anticipated. It was, in fact, a simple matter of using the leaf fat from around the pig's kidneys, as this particular kind of fat produces a versatile white and mildly flavoured lard. First, you must dice the fat in small pieces or, perhaps, grind it up. Then place it in a heavy pot, something that distributes heat evenly, like a cast-iron Dutch oven. Simmer over low heat. The fat will begin to melt, and it will smell blissful. Then the cracklings will sink, rise up again, and start to crackle and sigh—only then can you turn off the heat and thoroughly strain the oil.

Good lard is divine, unless you take issue with the killing and consumption of sentient creatures. Taiye had no problem with it. So when the instructor suggested that each student keep some of the lard they'd rendered, Taiye eagerly obliged. She was holding the warm sixteen-ounce Mason jar of pig fat in her lap as she sat on the top deck of the ferry from Woodside to Halifax when she saw the woman from the tea shop again.

The woman had a boyish demeanour and was leaning against the railing, beside a sign that read DO NOT LEAN OVER GUARDRAIL. Beside her was a lanky child with chunky chin-length locs, also leaning against the railing. They wore matching black patent leather boots, the kind that Taiye associated with American punks. Both pairs were covered in chalky white salt stains. Taiye was sure it was the same person from the tea shop, if only by the deep belly gnaw of attraction she felt toward her.

The child said something in a comically animated fashion that Taiye couldn't hear from where she sat. And when the woman threw her head back in laughter, her hood fell to reveal a short tapered Afro with a sharp undercut. As if she was suddenly aware of Taiye's gaze, the woman turned in her direction. When her eyes settled on Taiye, she raised a thick brow and offered a small smile that illuminated her fine-boned features.

Taiye's smile in return was much more tentative—feeble, in fact. She was uncharacteristically cautious: keeping to herself at school, keeping off dating apps, keeping away from most of her favourite vices. Yes, she routinely got profoundly stoned alone at home, masturbated to the kind of hentai that made her confident she was a disgusting pervert, and ate copious amounts of meat and pastries. But the point was that she did all this alone. No cocaine with strangers, no shrooms with new lovers, no booze with beloved friends, no sex with anyone but herself. No one to abandon, and no one by whom to be abandoned.

By the time the woman looked in her direction again, Taiye was gone. Down to the interior of the cabin, perched on a seat close to the exit. Ready to jet off the ferry once it docked, before she could convince herself to ride out her desire for touch.

ON ANOTHER DAY, during another monotonous week, Taiye took Our Lady's advice and went to a free conference at the public library.

*Of course*, Taiye thought, when she saw the woman from the tea shop and the ferry. The woman stood addressing the overflowing community room on the third floor of the public library. With all the seats occupied, many people stood against the white wall at the back of the room, and others sat on the carpeted floor at the front.

As Taiye walked in, the woman said, "I just want to start by acknowledging that we are on unceded Mi'kmaq territory." She pushed up the sleeves of her white button-down. "I would like to request a moment of silent reflection on the violence and injustice that Indigenous peoples have suffered historically and currently face in this country."

The woman's voice was silver smoke; it carried through the crowded glass-walled community room, which fell silent at her request. After a long pause, punctuated by the rustling of shifting bodies, she continued. "I'd like to encourage us to put our time, money, and energy where our ethics lie. What I mean is that solidarity requires action. If we say that we are in solidarity with Indigenous people, then we must act in line with that. Over at the table is a donation box for the Mi'kmaw Native Friendship Centre. Give them your money. Donate to the pipeline and railway protests. Join the movements." This was met with head nods and murmurs of agreement from the room.

"The students presenting today have shown incredible dedication, resilience, curiosity, and care in their research." The woman couldn't seem to keep still: she nodded as she spoke and her hands moved from the folded cuffs of her sleeves to the pockets of her tapered burgundy corduroy trousers and back again.

"These papers have themes ranging from analyses of race and space in Nova Scotia to queering Indigeneity. From racism within queer spaces to gentrification of Black communities in Halifax, and many of the in-betweens."

Taiye stood at the back of the packed room, close to the door. She shrugged off her oversized jacket and leaned against the wall, but her shoulder hit a switch and turned off the flickering fluorescent lights above.

"Shit, sorry," she muttered to no one in particular and turned to flick the switch on again.

Perhaps everyone turned to look at her. If Taiye had noticed, it might have incited a desire to shrivel up and disappear, but she only saw the woman's eyes move to where she stood. And really, if she had to be honest, Taiye wanted to be seen by this woman. There was that gnaw again, deep in her belly. Taiye put her jacket back on.

With her eyes still on Taiye, and an expression of amusement on her face, the woman continued. "We're grateful to be hosted by the public library today. It's an opportunity for many of our students to engage with the community outside of campus." She took a sip of water from a glass on the stand before her.

"We often talk about how the theories we engage with in the classroom and during research do not exist in a vacuum. No, they function and play out in communities, in our communities. So thank you very much for being here."

She ran a hand over her hair and chuckled. "I've talked for a million years now, so I'll wrap up this introduction with a brief description of what to expect in terms of the conference format. The students will present their work according to the themes highlighted in the program, which you can find on your seat and in a stack at the table there." She gestured to the back of the room.

"Then there will be time for questions and discussion before we move to the next theme. Again, thank you very much for being here, and have an enlightening evening."

The room erupted in applause as a student took the woman's place at the front of the room and said, "Thank you very much, Professor Colette."

Taiye's eyebrows shot up. Of course, the woman who'd incited that visceral pull in her gut was a fucking professor.

"And thank you to the Department of Sociology and Social Anthropology for organizing this conference. My name is Amara Patrick, and I'll start this presentation with a clip from a short doc titled *Come from Away, Who Gets to Stay*." The student gestured to the white projection screen behind her. "This project is part of my research on Blackness and belonging in Nova Scotia."

Professor Colette walked toward Taiye, a faint smile on her face, and gestured toward Taiye's right shoulder. Taiye looked at her shoulder, then back at the woman, muttered something incomprehensible, and regretted it immediately.

"Just the light switch," Professor Colette said to Taiye when she was close enough to be heard without having to raise her voice. Close enough for Taiye to smell the blend of incense-scented oils, she would later learn, the professor ritually applied to her temples, the back of her neck, and the scoops of her collarbones.

"Yeah ..." Taiye said, and turned to switch the lights off again, this time on purpose.

"Thanks," the professor whispered. "I didn't get your name."

"Taiye."

"Nice to meet you." She nodded. "Enjoy the conference."

Taiye could only nod in return. Feeling foolish, she waited for the documentary to start before slipping out of the room.

The walk home took an eternity. Halfway to Taiye's place, Our Lady took her hand and asked, *What are you afraid of?*

# Kehinde

TAIYE DOESN'T REMEMBER HOW SHE GOT THE SCAR ON HER CHIN, BUT I DO.
It happened after our father's death, when Uncle Ernest and Aunty
Funke were with us, and she had stopped sleeping in my room. Taiye
used to walk in her sleep, traipse down the stairs in an eerie daze. I discovered her one night, swaying slightly in the kitchen, eyes closed, a thin
line of blood dripping down her chin. Our mother was before her, silhou-
etted by the cold light of the open fridge. She was gaunt, her thin body a
curve made sinister by the glint of a small paring knife in her right hand.
The blade was clean; it must have been a swift slice. Her eyes shifted,
unfocused, as she muttered under her breath.

Terror seized me, and I grabbed Taiye's cold hand and led her out of
the kitchen. Our mother gasped low and horrified as we rushed away.

Our mother is insane.

No, I should say this instead: I believe that our mother is insane and
occasionally has moments of vibrant lucidity. In those small windows of
clarity, she is tender. Outside of that, she dances between catatonic and
grieving.

There's also the rage. The first time I witnessed it was after our father
died, after the bad thing, but before we went to London. During that
incident, Taiye woke me up by shaking my shoulders. I was still angry
with her and started to turn away when I saw the glint of tears in her eyes.

"What?" I asked.

"It's Mami."

Just then, I heard our mother screaming, and loud thumps, and crash-
ing. We rushed downstairs and saw her smashing a dining chair against
the door of the guest bedroom where Uncle Ernest and Aunty Funke had
stayed. Her thin arms lifted the hefty chair above her head and crashed

it against the door over and over, until there was nothing left but two splintered legs.

Her face was a blur. It looked like her features had been rubbed by an eraser. Does that make sense? My mind still cannot comprehend it, but that is what I remember. I turned to Taiye to ask if she could see our mother's face, but her eyes were shut tight and she was holding her breath.

Sister Bisi rushed over to lead us back upstairs.

God, there were so many nights like that, it just became *normal*.

Now our mother is cooing at us as we prepare to head out for Isabella's engagement party, smiling with a genuine light. It is infuriating.

"Mami, you won't come?" Taiye asks and ties her braids in a bun. I don't know why she bothers; her braids will tumble down in a few moments, and she'll be right back where she started. She is wearing an oversized kaftan in cream-coloured floral damask with gold embroidery on the hem and a low neckline that reveals lines and tendrils from what I can only guess is a chest tattoo. Her tight jeans are cuffed all the way up her shins. Her eyes are lined in black kajal; otherwise, her face is bare.

How she manages to make such a slapdash mismatched outfit seem chic, I'll never know. She looks effortlessly cool, and I feel like an over-stuffed dumpling in my satin polka-dot dress, with balloon sleeves that are supposed to flatter my figure but only make me feel like a misshapen pillow. I must be getting my period soon; I'm just so irritable.

Our mother is going on about how pretty we both look and how we mustn't forget to take the zobo and isn't it so lovely how Taiye put it in these beautiful carafes with the cork stoppers.

"Okay, Mami." Taiye kisses her on the cheek. "Rest well, call if you need anything, my ringer is on."

I lean in and hug her quickly before heading out with Taiye and Farouq. I try not to look at her face, but I catch a glimpse and am stung with shame at my inability to embrace her properly just now.

We walk out into the breezy evening. Taiye holds two glass carafes of ruby-red zobo glinting in the light of the slowly setting sun, one bottle spiked with a floral gin and the other with white rum. I hold Farouq's hand and a small purse with my phone and wallet.

"How are you feeling?" I ask Taiye. I want to acknowledge the fact that she confided in me about her affair with Isabella.

"I don't really know," she says. "But I'll let you know if I need to duck out, yeah?"

"For sure."

Farouq squeezes my hand gently. I have my sister on one side and my husband on the other.

"ANEMOIA" IS A WORD I FOUND A FEW YEARS AGO on a website called the *Dictionary of Obscure Sorrows*. It means nostalgia for a time you've never known. I scribbled it in my journal, and in the years since, when I started taking my art practice seriously, I would write it all over my canvases before priming. Because even though I couldn't taste the feeling at the time, I knew that I knew it, that I'd felt it before. I feel it again now, at Isabella's engagement party. I taste its full-bodied flavour: pungent and salty. It is unmistakable. I've never been surrounded by old friends and family the way that Isabella is right now, but I feel nostalgic for this moment. I am watching, in slow motion, as Isabella—wrapped in a sheer coral maxi dress that shimmers as she moves, her Afro a glittering halo—laughs and playfully slaps Toki on the shoulder. Some familiar faces surround her, secondary school friends with whom I failed to keep in touch. Isabella kept in touch; she tended to the garden of her life and grew a community. A community that shows up to her engagement party and packs her backyard dense with swaying bodies. Perhaps this is what happens when you stay home instead of eagerly launching yourself into the diaspora and disappearing from everything that shaped you. You get a celebration, familiarity, home.

Isabella spots us and exclaims, "Ibeji! The twins are here!" She hurries toward us, hugs us, and ushers us deeper into the celebration.

Taiye's body stiffens at Isabella's touch; I sense it more than see it. She is cordial when she offers the spiked zobo and smiles politely at Isabella's squeal of delight.

"Isa, this is my husband, Farouq," I say. Up close, I see that I didn't imagine it—her hair is dusted with gold shimmer.

"So lovely to meet you," Isabella says. She waves Toki over.

Tokunbo Pedro swam with us at Ikoyi Club when we were children. Unlike most other boys in our cohort, he wore Speedos instead of swimming trunks. When he wasn't following Isabella around like a lost pet, he swam many laps to the deep end and back while the rest of us splashed around the shallow end playing Marco Polo. He was such a small-framed crusty-nosed boy; I remember towering tall over him until I left for Canada at eighteen.

So I am stunned at the broad-shouldered polished mahogany heft of a man that walks toward us. Toki is all grown up.

"Toks," Isabella says, "remember the twins?"

"Of course." His voice is still slightly nasal, a remnant of the sniffly child that vied for Isabella's attention, but more assured. He kisses Taiye and me on our cheeks with a distracted, "Long time, how far?" Then he offers Farouq a firm handshake.

"Long time indeed." I smile and attempt to locate something genuine in the smooth skin of his face, the shallow curve of his distant smile, his commanding demeanour. It's not very difficult to spot a hardened person. Thickening one's proverbial skin can only be a natural response to the causticity that life sometimes visits upon us. But there is a unique type of hardness, a single-minded drive to thrive through whatever the fuck, to tear through whoever, to get what you want, that levels everything so that nothing is sacred. Someone else might call it sharp, masculine, capable of getting anything done. But I knew Toki when we were children, and if you ask me, something happened between then and now that took some light away from him. Perhaps it's just what happens when we grow up. Could he look at me and come to the same conclusion?

"Please make yourselves at home," he says coolly. "There is plenty to eat."

"Thank you," Taiye says to a spot on his shoulder. "And congratulations," she adds, and then walks away from us, toward the buffet table covered in platters of small chops and glistening pastries.

Our eyes follow her until the silence teeters on awkward, so I say to Farouq with as much cheer as I can muster, "We grew up together," gesturing to Toki and Isabella. "Toki has loved Isa from day one. It's special to see them make it official."

Isabella rolls her eyes and forces a smile.

"Congratulations," Farouq chimes in. "My childhood crush spat on me and told me I was ugly, so I had to find a different chump to marry me!" He puts his arm around me and squeezes.

Toki smiles. Isabella laughs and asks, "How long have you been married?"

"Just over four years," Farouq answers.

"Any advice for us?" Isabella tilts her head to the right, and her eyes wander for the briefest moment. I imagine she's looking for Taiye, who has moved farther into the heart of the party.

"Stay lucky," Farouq says, and his eyes are smiling into mine.

"That's nonsense." Isabella's eyebrows shoot high up on her forehead. "Give us some concrete, useful adv—"

"Please excuse me," Toki interrupts. "I have to go welcome some other guests, but it was a pleasure to meet you." He shakes Farouq's hand. "And to see you again, welcome home," he says to me. Then he leaves, and Isabella's face becomes a wound.

"Please don't let us keep you." I place a hand on her bare shoulder. "Go and do your hostess things, show off this stunning dress!"

She forces another smile and says, "Okay ... make yourselves at home." Then she goes in the opposite direction from Toki.

THE PARTY ROARS ON AS THE SKY DARKENS, lit by strings of soft orange fairy lights and torches that emit a light scent of citronella. Afro-electronic rhythms pulse through the warm night air. Farouq and I wander through the garden, squeezing between the impeccably dressed and heavily perfumed bodies of Isabella and Toki's guests. We walk past the buffet table, grazing on peppered gizzards, crispy spring rolls, and charred skewers of chicken suya. We swat away mosquitoes and gleefully receive cold glasses of beer and malt when we reach the bar. I smile at all the people I recognize but feel shyness like a thick spider's web, keeping me from initiating conversation. Most people are stylishly aloof and exude an air of profound disinterest in anyone who isn't already comfortably situated in their circle—social and literal. I'm sweating through the satin of my dress, and my feet throb from standing in heels, so I take my sandals off. The grass feels warm and dry; memories of barefoot cartwheels in this very backyard flash through my mind. Swiftly followed by memories of Taiye bawling into her pillow the holiday when Isabella stopped talking to us.

Farouq dances behind me, his arms encircling my waist. He is taking it all in stride, committed, as ever, to having a good time.

"Ça va?" he says into my left ear, and his warm, alcohol-laced breath tickles me.

"Ça va," I say, just as I spot Taiye sitting cross-legged on the grass by a moss-covered fence. She is on the periphery of a small circle of party guests, laughing along at something a slim light-skinned man is saying.

I pull Farouq toward the group, and we sit by Taiye. She smiles at me, and her eyes are bloodshot sleepy slits. She takes my hand in her own. "This guy is funny," she says, swats away a mosquito that is buzzing by my nose, and turns her attention back to him.

"Na so I been tell this my friend, 'O girl, if you get sense you go stop to dey wear pant go man house.' But she no like to dey hear word," the light-skinned man says, tugging on his right ear for emphasis.

"This kind world where we dey," he continues, with hand gestures I identify as femme only after I notice the black matte varnish on his nails, "these men dey use their girlfriend pant dey do juju, dem dey try teef person destiny."

The group carries on in riotous laughter, and I attempt to translate for Farouq between bouts of my own laughing.

"He's saying he has this friend, and he keeps trying to warn her to stop wearing underwear when she goes home with the men she's fucking with because some men do juju with women's undies."

"Juju?" asks Farouq.

"Black magic," I explain, "to bring them good fortune—no, more like to steal the women's good fortune for their own."

"That's a thing?" Farouq asks too loud so that the light-skinned man hears him and replies, "Yes ke, it is something o! Who oyimbo be dis?"

"That's my brother-in-law, Farouq," Taiye says. "And my sister, Kehinde."

The whole group turns to look at us.

"Ah, where dem come from?" He laughs. "I didn't even see them sit down. Me, I'm Star."

"Good to meet you, Star," Farouq says. "I want to hear more about this juju." Juju in Farouq's accent sounds like *joojoo*, and that's enough to stoke more laughter.

"Ah, Kehinde, your oyimbo bobo wan sabi do *joojoo* for you! Na to run now!" Star claps at his own joke and we all laugh.

Isabella is here suddenly. "Dem no sabi now." She laughs. Eyes bloodshot, perspiration darkening the soft coral of her dress along the neckline and armpits. She continues with a hiccup. "Na ajebutter dem be, posh girls, innit." She sways before plopping herself on the grass beside Star.

"Wetin *you* sabi?" Star says and puts his arm around her. "As if you sef no be ajebutter." Carefully, he takes the half-full green bottle of Heineken away from her clumsy grip.

Isabella rolls her head onto Star's shoulder, then looks at me with languid eyes. "Kehinde, are you happy?" she asks.

"Me?" I ask obtusely, feeling the warm wash of everyone's eyes on me.

"Yes, you," Isabella confirms. "Are you *happily married*? Were you happy before you married? Are you happy now?" she slurs, eyes fixed on my steadily warming face.

"Erm ..." Taiye's grip on my hand tightens slightly. "I am happy in my marriage, yes." I look at Farouq, and he smiles at me. Pearls of perspiration dot his forehead and roll down the sides of his face.

I continue, "And, like, separate from my marriage, I'm happy sometimes and sad sometimes and neutral sometimes ... same as before I was married. Sometimes, I think, when painful things happen, my emotions reflect that ... and painful things have happened ..." Taiye brings my hand to her mouth, and her lips are warm and dry when she kisses my knuckles. "But that's just life," I finish, just as Taiye gets up to leave.

Isabella watches Taiye walk away, and then she slaps Star on the arm. "You see that?" she asks, her voice climbing in pitch with each word. "See as she dey look am, as she dey look her husband? You no fit buy am, that *look*, you no fit buy am for market."

Her voice is shaking, and the group is silent as she continues, "You know when I was in uni, in Reading, I wanted to kill myself." She clenches her fists for emphasis, and then she tries to stand, but Star holds on to her shoulders. "I carried myself to a psychologist because I didn't understand." Tears are streaming down her face, making dark, muddy streaks of her mascara and foundation.

"When I told my mother what was happening, she said that it's because I haven't suffered in life, because I'm half-caste, and everything has been easy for me. So any small trouble and I just want to kpeme." She draws a finger across her throat before bursting into a bout of breathless laughter that veers on hysterical.

"Half-caste?" Farouq asks me in a whisper.

"Mixed race, part white," I reply. "It's a bit fucked, but we don't use it as a slur here."

"You know something," Isabella says, "I'm *not* happy. I'm not looking forward to *anything*." She throws her hands up in surrender. "I wasn't happy before I was engaged; I'm not happy now; I won't be happy after I get married. I know we're never supposed to admit it, but na so we see am."

Two women in the circle mutter something unintelligible and get up to leave. We watch as Isabella unravels at her own party. I feel sad for her, like a gaping wound in my belly. I want to reach for her and take her away from this audience, but she continues, "This thing, happiness, is it actually a luxury? Am I a fool to want to be happy in this life? I feel as if, say, if you open my body, nothing go dey inside. As is say I be empty box!" She slaps mosquitoes off her bare arms and turns to face Star. "Abi I dey craze? I no fit pretend now," she pleads. "I no wan live my whole life just dey pretend pretend. I no say we go never gree say sometimes no matter how much money, how many connections person get, if something just no dey correct inside here"—she taps her temple with two fingers so forcefully her head tilts, she taps her sternum. "But nobody ... nobod ..." She drops her face into her hands and bawls.

It's hard to make out what she says next, her voice muffled by her hands, but I think she says, "I just want to be happy ..."

Star holds her tight.

I want to reach out and touch her arm. The circle disperses slowly, stiffly, as she cries. Some people offer confused words of sympathy, rub her shoulders gingerly, before departing to less dismal regions of the party. I think the music is louder than Isabella's cries. I'm reasonably sure that most guests are unaware that their host is presently in the volatile throes of an emotional meltdown. Still, I scan the party from where we sit. Yes, a few furtive glances shoot our way, but otherwise, most guests seem cheerfully unaware.

Then there is Toki, sitting among a handful of friends on white wicker garden chairs, drinking cognac from small tumblers. He is looking straight at Isabella as she trembles in Star's arms. His face gives nothing away, his features neatly arranged, opaque.

I tug at Farouq's arm. "Babe, let's go find Taiye."

Before we leave, I hold Isabella's hand and invite her to our place for breakfast, or lunch, or dinner, or a swim at Ikoyi Club sometime during the week. She looks at my face for a long time and nods her head before saying, "Tell Taiye I'm sorry."

# Kambirinachi

IN THE YEAR AFTER KAMBIRINACHI AND BANJI LEFT IFE they found their rhythm as a couple. Banji was exhausted but happy and well paid at work. During the week, he took a cabu cabu from their place on Osborne Road, Ikoyi, to the Dasha office on Saka Jojo Street on Victoria Island. There he assessed some of the most desperate loan applications, wishing he could approve them all.

While he worked, Kambirinachi alternated between taking slow walks around the neighbourhood and painting vibrant acrylics of the views from the small burglar-proof windows of their place. From the kitchen window: plantain palms with their fanned-out leaves peeled apart like fingers waving in the breeze and bunches of unripe fruit, still starchy and green, hung low and heavy at their base. From the bedroom window: in much deeper shades of green, unkempt Ixora bushes burst with clusters of tiny red flowers. As a child, Kambirinachi gingerly pulled the delicate needle-thin stigma out of the heart of the flower and sucked on precious droplets of tangy-sweet nectar. As a young woman, she only painted them. From the living room window: mature frangipani trees with flowers that started yellow at the core and whitened as their fragrant petals curled out.

Her paintings were stunning, highly stylized renderings that bore minimal resemblance to plants. Because she saw all the life of them, from seed or cutting to seedling, to flowering, to fruit, to dead and drying. She captured each phase of the plants' lives in layers of bold brush strokes until the resulting pieces were vivid, abstract, and very textured.

Once a week, she went to the Falomo Mammy Market for food. Not an experimental cook, never having been properly taught, she bought produce that was straightforward to prepare: yams to be boiled and pounded or fried. Eggs to be hardboiled or fried. Groundnut oil for all that frying.

Okra for soup. Tomatoes, peppers, and onions puréed right there in the market to be made into stew. Beans, plantains, and as much of whatever fruit was in season as she could afford.

The day she felt the first murmurings of a small life begin its delicate unfurling in her body it was agbalumo season. She was haggling with the fruit seller—a woman about her age with a fat infant asleep on her lap. Kambirinachi paused her playful haggling, distracted by the strings of tiny amber beads that clung to each of the baby's pudgy ankles. In the silence, she was struck by how fragile and gorgeous the sleeping baby's feet were, struck by the glint of sunlight on those amber beads. In the silence, she heard a soft murmur coming from inside herself. No, it wasn't the sound of her wounded Kin; it was a different language, a different pitch altogether, one that resonated with her core. She dropped the two unusually large agbalumo she'd been holding, and they rolled across the dirt into an open gutter.

"E jor," she said to the fruit seller, "no vex." Then she paid eighty naira more than the cost of the fruit in her bag and ran home.

Kambirinachi was negotiating with her Kin for less palpable madness. "Negotiating" is perhaps too gentle a word for what was happening between them; a combat of wills more aptly describes it.

Here it is: Kambirinachi's Kin—her many aspects, the core being from whom she'd attempted to sever herself by choosing to stay alive all those years ago—they wanted her back. Quite simply, they desired to heal the wound of her leaving, and this healing required her return. She knew this, she felt it in her marrow, heard their rageful whisperings, cried knowing that rage was only hurt untended, hurt ignored and cast aside. This is how you make fury. She made this fury, this dark spirit, howling, feral, and bloodthirsty. She made it by turning her ears from their cries because she yearned to weave herself into the fabric of aliveness.

So her Kin willed her to their presence, willed her ears to turn to them, willed her hands to sharp objects, willed blood. They willed her fragile body to stop its pointless rotations, pointless because alive bodies must die. They die slowly or swiftly, in pain or in sleep, but they die, nonetheless.

*How could you want this?*

*How could you leave us?*

*How could you turn away?*

So you can imagine the fear it cast over her, this murmur of life in her body. She didn't know how long it had been growing inside her, only that one day she heard nothing but her Kin howling and Banji's sweet words, and the next day there was another voice, a mewling, a request to be born.

Kambirinachi was pregnant.

"PETRICHOR." The word had been swimming around in Kambirinachi's mind. She had to speak it out.

"What's that, my love?" Banji asked, rubbing circles on the small of his wife's back.

They were in their living room, wrapped around each other on the sofa, a gift from Banji's employers that they had reupholstered in deep burgundy crushed velvet. Listening to the soothing pittering of rainfall on the corrugated roof of their bungalow.

"The smell of rain on dry earth," Kambirinachi replied. "Petrichor, from the Greek word 'pétrā,' which means 'stone,' and 'īchōr,' which, in Greek mythology, is the fluid that flows through the veins of their gods."

Laughing, Banji asked, "And you know this how?"

"I'm smart, Baba, that's why you married me."

"Is that why?" Banji teased. "I thought it was because of your big nyash."

"My nyash isn't even that big!"

"But it will, it will grow with Baby."

Baby.

Baby was growing.

Baby was three and a half months formed.

Baby's murmuring was rising into a gentle song, a soothing loop of a melody, a travel song, rejoicing.

Kambirinachi's spirit body, her mind, was becoming a vessel of immiscible elements. Her Kin wanted her, Baby wanted her, but they would not have each other.

Her Kin: *This will tether you to them, this will tether you to them, this will tether you to them, this will tether you to them, this is not how it's supposed to be, we will not allow this.*

Baby: a comforting melody, a promise, life and life and life ...

Kambirinachi: *I choose life.*

Her Kin: *And the cost—can you pay?*

She answered: she ate fruits and vegetables and seeds and good meat and prenatal vitamins. She and Banji went to a private clinic in Victoria Island on referral from his employers, whose family friend ran the place almost exclusively for expats. They glowed as Baby grew.

And then Baby stopped growing. Abruptly, the song ended, in its place a starving, clawing void.

Banji grieved quietly, lit many candles at the chapel in Falomo Catholic church, wept silently, kneeling in the pews.

"Let's try again," he said to Kambirinachi. "Let's try again."

But Kambirinachi raged. A week after the clinic scraped out what was left of Baby from inside of her, she stumbled out of bed before dawn. She blundered in the darkness to the cluster of plantain palms and scratched open the welts on the back of her neck, opened the wound her mother had given her in an attempt to keep her tied to this realm. A guttural wail rose from her throat, echoed loud and ringing as she dug her bloody fingers into the soil by the root of the plants to call her Kin.

They came to her, a multitude of her own self, plenty of them—of her. They were the same as her. Down to her bloody fingers, to the weeping wound at the base of her neck. They surrounded her.

"Why did you do this?" she asked.

*That was the price.* They spoke in unison, in perfect alignment, with their eyes fixed on her.

"But I've already paid. You took my papa."

*It was his time. You altered that. We only corrected it. Death did her work. She always collects, you know this.*

"I cast you!"

*You cannot cast us.*

"I reject you!"

*You cannot reject us.*

"I bind you!"

*You cannot bind us. We are not a demon, or evil. We are you.*

"I reject you!"

*Kin ...*

"I reject *me*!"

*Don't do this.*

"I reject myself! I reject myself! I free me now!"

*You will forget yourself. You will be so lonely.*

"I. Reject. Myself." Her voice rose, distraught and resolute.

Her Kin exhaled in unison, their faces drooped in immense sadness, and they said, *You may leave us, but we will never leave you.*

Kambirinachi woke up beside Banji after the sun had risen to find that her mind was silent.


SO HOW DID THE TWINS COME TO BE?

Kambirinachi would tell you that she chose them. Like with Banji, she dreamed them. She dreamed them many times, and in these dreams, she saw a spot of light, something akin to a small orb the size of her palm, that floated above gentle, rippling waters. The light flirted with the water, occasionally dipping down to touch its undulating surface, sometimes immersing half of itself, but always, it rose back up to resume its buoyant dance.

When she claimed them, Kambirinachi mistook the orb for one spirit. She glided across the water, scooped the orb in her hands, and swallowed it in one swift gulp. It wasn't until she felt the weight of the light travel through her that she realized that it was two beings intertwined. That through birthing, she would destine them to a painful separation.

EIGHT MONTHS AFTER BABY STOPPED GROWING, after Kambirinachi attempted to sever ties with her Kin, and three months after she swallowed the orb of light in her dream, Kambirinachi placed Banji's palms on the slight swell of her belly.

"This one." She smiled at him. "This one will stay."

They were in a cabu cabu, on the way to Murtala Muhammed airport. Banji's employers, who were generous and wanted to be known as such, were sponsoring his six-month managerial finance professional development course at the London School of Economics. Banji was thrilled at the opportunity, and seeing his joy at the prospect, Kambirinachi was also thrilled. She'd meant to double his happiness by telling him of her pregnancy, but he grew ambivalent about leaving.

"Kambi, this is wonderful, but I can't leave now!"

"Yes, you can, and you must," she reassured him. "There's nothing to do here but be pregnant, and I'm already taking care of that."

"Maybe you can come, too," he responded. "Before you're too big?"

"I don't think we can afford that."

"Not yet, but I could ask my boss for a loan. They like me, so if I tell them you're pregnant and explain why we're worried they might be open to—"

"Baba, don't worry," she insisted. "You'll be back just in time."

But Banji *did* worry. He gutted their savings, asked his mother for support, and asked his generous employers if they would contribute to flying his pregnant wife to join him in London.

Within two months, he was meeting a five-months-pregnant Kambirinachi at London Heathrow. He dropped his coat across her shoulders and squeezed her tightly, thinking his joy was complete. And it was still multiplying, growing with his child inside Kambirinachi.

Upon learning a few weeks later, at King's College Hospital, that his wife was in fact carrying twins, Banji marvelled at his blessings. Ibeji are a blessing, divine twins, one soul contained in two vessels. The offspring of Sango and Osun, they are the orishas of abundance and joy. And mischief.

THE LIGHT THAT KAMBIRINACHI HAD SWALLOWED was two beings of one spirit intertwined in the sort of bliss into which, within the short window of living, many seek to awaken. Inside Kambirinachi, they began their painful separation: monozygotic twins form when one zygote splits into two embryos. Monoamniotic twins develop when an embryo does not divide until after the formation of the amniotic sac. The splitting is excruciating, but neither will remember it acutely. All that will remain is a disorienting echo of the wound that the twins would spend a lifetime attempting to locate. Monozygotic twins are physically identical because they share identical genes; they may even have similar personality traits.

Patience is not one of the personality traits that the twins shared; for example, the twin that would be named Kehinde was eager to be born. She coaxed her counterpart, the one that would be called Taiye, to share her enthusiasm for the world into which they would soon be spit. Reluctant, Taiye longed for the blissful quiet they'd shared before before, not wanting to be snatched, swallowed, and forced apart, not wishing to be thrust into the world and its harsh artificial lights.

But, you see, because of this thing we call love, Taiye would always concede to Kehinde. So, five weeks too soon, upon Kehinde's request, Taiye burst forth from Kambirinachi to see what awaited them, and Kehinde eagerly followed.

KAMBIRINACHI FELT A WARM LIQUID flow out of her body and splash onto the pale yellow tiles of the kitchen floor. It was 10:47 a.m. on October 29, 1987, in their cramped flat in Brixton—a community still recovering from the devastating riot between police and protesters that had occurred earlier in the decade. Banji was at school, a half-hour tube ride away. In the nearly three months that she'd been in London, Kambirinachi hadn't made any friends outside of a handful of Banji's classmates. They'd made plans for Banji to spend what they'd assumed would be the last three weeks of the pregnancy at home, but the twins were early. Kambirinachi had no one to call.

She breathed deeply and found a rag to mop up the amniotic fluid. She hummed a soothing melody, Baby's song, knowing all too well that these were different beings altogether who were tunnelling their way through her body. She was a portal. She hummed Baby's song and paced around the kitchen. She considered going to the neighbours, a Bajan family of many children and a stern matriarch, but when she moved toward the door, the first contraction caused her to double over in tremendous pain. She sank to the floor, still humming Baby's song, until the tightness in her abdomen passed, and then she rocked herself back and forth in preparation for the next one.

The second contraction was slow coming, so she got up and swayed to Baby's melody. She moved to the bedroom to search for her photo album among the sparse belongings she'd brought from Lagos. She slipped her favourite photos out of the album's plastic sleeves and rested them against the windows to keep watch over her. A picture of Aunty Akuchi smiling in her kitchen, and a black and white one of her father leaning against his bicycle, dwarfed by a row of tall palm trees behind him, stood side by side against the small kitchen window over the sink. Against one of the living room windows, Kambirinachi placed a faded picture of her mother in a bright blue gele. By the other window, she put a picture of river Orisha Osun's shrine, which she took at Oṣogbo sacred grove when she visited with Banji three years before. Leaning against the bedroom window above their bed was a picture of Banji on their wedding day; his smile was electric and yanked her back to that day in his family's compound. She smiled at the memory just as the second contraction doubled her over again.

When it passed, she resumed her swaying. Her alive body was an intelligent creature that knew what it needed. She decided to trust it, to move however it desired. Time was a loyal friend. Time had always loved her, so it wound forward quickly, past the pain of the many many contractions that would eventually squeeze her babies out.

Banji returned home in the late afternoon to find Kambirinachi on her hands and knees on the kitchen floor. She was cushioned by a mound of towels and blankets, a plastic jug of cold water stood by her face, and by her side a few feet away, sat a large bowl of steaming water. Banji looked at his wife, stunned. It took a moment for the scene to arrange itself with meaning so that he could make sense of what he was seeing. The splotches of bloody fluid on the kitchen floor brought it all into clear focus.

"Kambi!" he cried out, dropping his satchel and rushing to her side. "Oya, oya, let's go to the hospital."

But she shook her head. Kambirinachi rose up from her arms so that she was squatting with the pile of towels between her open knees.

"Too late for that, Baba," she croaked. "Jor wash your hands quick quick."

Banji protested while obeying, too shocked to register that the hot water was burning his hands. He returned to Kambirinachi just as she was pulling Taiye out from between her bloodied thighs. The screeching newborn entered the world with her tiny hand clasping her sister's. Too hesitant to separate them, Banji held Taiye, in awe, while Kambirinachi pulled out the rest of Kehinde.

"WHAT A FIERCE MAMA YOU ARE!" the nurse exclaimed.

They were back at King's College Hospital, this time on the fourth floor, in the neonatal intensive care unit. Banji, panicked by the smallness of his newborn daughters and the bloodied state of his wife, called an ambulance moments after Kambirinachi pulled Kehinde out of her body.

The nurse was a heavyset brown man with an incredible smile that revealed his gold-capped upper incisors. "You did a great job bringing these little impatient ones here. They're late preterm, but they're looking good at nearly four pounds nine ounces each, which is quite normal. We'll have to monitor them here for a couple weeks ..."

Midway through the nurse's words, Kambirinachi's eyes closed without her consent, her body convulsed, and the machines to which she was tethered by tubes and wires emitted shrill beeps.

SHE AWOKE TO THE SOUND OF HER MEWLING INFANTS. They were alone in the whole ward, she knew this. Still, there was a considerable distance of white tiles and flickering fluorescent lights between them. She rushed toward her babies, who were swaddled together in a cot across the ward. She rushed to them and found them entangled. Rail thin, emaciated, like miniature skeletons carved from splotchy mahogany, raspy whimpers escaping their small crusty mouths.

She wailed something grotesque, picked her infants up gingerly, wept salty tears onto their gaunt faces.

Then she woke up again, in the hospital, with Banji sitting by her side. His face lit up in relief at the sight of her.

"Oh God," he said, standing up quickly. "Oh, thank God, she's awake!"

The gold-toothed nurse came back through the privacy curtains.

"Where are my babies?" Kambirinachi croaked.

"Don't worry, Mama, they are in the incubators, just down the hallway." The nurse looked at her closely. "You can go visit them soon. How are you feeling?"

"I want to be with them."

"Yes, love," Banji piped in, "but how do you feel now?"

"Fine."

"You had a seizure," the nurse said, "and then you passed out."

"I'm fine. I want to be with my babies."

"Of course, we're just running a few tests."

She turned to Banji and asked, "Baba, can we go home?"

"Of course," he replied. "As soon as you're discharged."

"But can we go back home to Lagos?"

"As soon as I finish my course, then, yes, just a few more weeks. And by then the babies will be stronger, and you'll be stronger ..." Banji was looking at the nurse as he said this.

"We'll need to run a few tests," the nurse resumed. "And once we're in the clear, then you can be with your babies, okay?"

"Okay."

"Why did she have a seizure?" Banji asked.

"That's what the tests will tell us." The nurse placed a firm hand on ˉ Banji's shoulder.

The doctors found nothing. Although the image of the emaciated twins was seared in Kambirinachi's memory, she held and fed her infants, the ones who existed outside of her mind, in the same world as Banji. Within two weeks, they were discharged, and six weeks later, they were on a flight back to Lagos.

# Taiye

WHAT WAS TAIYE AFRAID OF? Though dull and lonesome, the rhythm of the life she'd found in Halifax was safe.

*Safe from what exactly?* Our Lady asked.

Taiye only replied, "You know."

When she got home from the conference at the library, she drew herself a bath. Zora had made a ritual of baths, using Himalayan salts and dried rose petals and geranium and ylang-ylang oils, whispering blessings into the hot water with each drop. Taiye, however, used the least expensive lavender-scented Epsom salts she could find at the drugstore. She didn't want to think of Zora—thoughts of her led to thoughts of Timi, pushing sadness to the surface.

Instead, after settling into the tub, she let her mind wander to thoughts of Professor Colette and her holy smoke scent.

"Of course she's a prof," Taiye said, a bubble of laughter escaping her.

*And why does that matter?* Our Lady asked.

"She's likely too good for my bullshit," Taiye replied. "Too smart." She closed her eyes, slid under the surface of the perfumed water, and touched herself with no intention of climaxing but to feel fully in her body.

*We all have our bullshit, baby.*

INDEED, WE ALL HAVE OUR BULLSHIT. Although Taiye was still convinced she owned a disproportionate share of said bullshit, she found that immersing herself in any of her favourite vices provided some respite. Unfortunately, her favourite vices involved other people: their drugs, their bodies, their attention. So after her bath, she settled instead for immersing herself in a recipe using her new lard.

Something savoury, filling, crusty: empanadas!

For the dough, she scooped approximately four ounces of lard from the jar and melted it in the oven, and then left it out to cool slightly. She mixed the warm fat, a tablespoon of salt, a splash of vinegar, and two cups of lukewarm water in a large bowl. Gradually, she added six cups of flour, mixing it with firm hands to form a shaggy dough. She transferred the dough to the narrow flour-dusted Formica kitchen counter and sank her fingers into it, kneading until it became mostly smooth with no remaining dry spots. Then she let it rest and moved on to the filling. Taiye rifled through her small refrigerator and all the way to the back of the tiny freezer, where she found a Ziploc bag of peeled and deveined shrimp and a small Tupperware of shito.

"Fuck, yes, shito!" she exclaimed to Our Lady.

Then she thinly sliced and sautéed an onion and four garlic cloves in fragrant olive oil and a bit of lard. While the alliums browned, she finely chopped the shrimp, along with some sad soft carrots she'd found in the vegetable crisper, and tossed it all into the sizzling pan. She used shito as a seasoning and waited until most of the shrimp had cooked to pink before setting the filling aside to cool.

The rest of the process was a simple matter of rolling out, cutting, and filling the dough, and then crimping the edges. Taiye fried the pockets in a deep pot she'd found at the Salvation Army, and when she set them aside to cool, she counted fourteen shito shrimp empanadas.

By the time she'd packed them up to share at school the next day, there were only eight left. They were delicious; she regretted nothing.

"DAMN, GIRL, YOU'RE THE REAL MVP FOR BRINGING THESE EMPANADAS." Taiye's classmate Ryan chewed loudly with bits of crust spewing out as he spoke.

"My pleasure," Taiye replied, tying the belt of her white apron. They were standing at the doorway of their classroom kitchen, Ryan holding Taiye's glass Tupperware of empanadas.

"What's that seasoning ...?" he asked, rubbing his thumb and forefinger as he tried to place the flavour he was relishing.

"Just whatever was in the shito." Taiye shrugged. "I made it a while ago."

"Fuck is that?" He said, laughter shaking his large body.

"What's what?"

"Shido?"

Taiye laughed. "*Shi-to*. It's a Ghanaian condiment: peppers, ginger, onions, and crayfish, all fried up."

"Yo, that's delicious!"

"Thank you." Taiye smiled.

"Hey, what are you doing tonight?"

"No real plans. Might try out a pork belly recipe."

"Sounds dope," he said, handing the empanadas back to Taiye so he could tie his locs back and slip on a hairnet. "Also dope, my girlfriend is deejaying at the Odette tonight, and I'm trying to get a crowd going, posted it on the Facebook group."

"I'm not on Facebook."

"Oh yeah, no wonder! I've been wondering why you haven't been coming to social stuff."

"What's the Odette?"

"It's this gallery space by the waterfront, great for dancing, too."

"Text me the info?"

"For sure!"

THE ODETTE, a small artist-run gallery and music venue on the waterfront, was a glass building, not unlike a large greenhouse. It sat slightly off the edge of the pier so that if you stood before the east-facing wall of glass, it seemed like you were moments from tipping into the ocean.

Taiye walked into the warm space, aglow with dim fairy lights hanging from the glass ceiling and lo-fi beats pulsing through massive speakers tucked in the front corners of the rooms, to find Ryan working the door.

"You came!" he exclaimed, embracing her in a sweaty bear hug.

"Thanks for inviting me." Taiye squeezed him back. "What's the cover?"

"Nothing for you, girl." He waved her away. "Go get your dance on!"

She wriggled between warm flailing bodies until she was smack in the middle of the packed floor, and dance she did, with a measure of abandon. She swayed her body with her eyes closed, and time moved the way it always did whenever she got stoned—though she wasn't stoned that night. She was bright-eyed, sober, thrilled, as if something good was waiting for her around the corner.

She opened her eyes and found herself looking past the people in front of her and down to the bar. And, of course, the professor was there. Taiye squeezed past bodies again until she was at the bar, where she smiled and nodded at Professor Colette.

"I've seen you around a lot lately," the professor said, smiling back. Roguish in an oversized black jumpsuit and sipping water from a white plastic cup.

"Yeah," Taiye agreed.

"Taiye, right?"

"Yeah."

"I'm Salomé."

"Herod's daughter."

"Yeah, stepdaughter." She chuckled.

"You're a prof, yeah?"

"Yeah, you?"

"Student." She tilted her head toward the twinkling lights beyond the water. "Culinary program across the harbour."

The volume of the music swelled after the drop of deep bass and a bored-looking woman beside Salomé tapped her shoulder and gestured toward the exit. Salomé nodded at the woman and shouted to Taiye, "I want to call you sometime, or text, whatever. What's your number?"

"Give me your phone," Taiye replied. She laughed at the brick of a phone—a relic from the early 2000s—that the woman handed over. Taiye fumbled with the tiny keypad and typed in her number. "Call me," she said, handing the phone over.

"I will," Salomé replied, and smiling, she headed out.

"HEY, THIS IS SALOMÉ, uh, from the Odette. I'm calling to ... um ... invite you to an event, uh, this Thursday at the North Memorial Library. It's a monthly Black film series thing at seven p.m. Not school related at all, just a ... uh ... thing. Um, yeah, we're watching Daouda Coulibaly's *Wùlu*, it's a Malian film, should be good, I'm rambling. Yeah, I hope you can make it, and ... I'll get off the phone now."

Taiye listened to the message four more times. She enjoyed that Salomé seemed nervous. She listened to the message again as she stood outside the building with the words HALIFAX NORTH MEMORIAL PUBLIC LIBRARY inscribed high on its red-brick walls. Taiye lost herself, despite her eagerness to see Salomé. She became stuck fast in the rigid jaw of her anxieties. It took Our Lady's gentle nudging to encourage her to go inside. A few steps into the library lobby, she saw Salomé standing at the entrance of the Terry Symonds Auditorium. She wore a black ball cap with gold sunflowers embroidered along the rim, and the words DESTROY WHITE SUPREMACY across the front. A black T-shirt hung loosely around her boyish frame, and a smile curved her lips as she welcomed people into the auditorium.

"Hey, Salomé." Taiye waved meekly. She couldn't help the smile brightening her face.

"You came!" Salomé exclaimed. "Welcome, it, um, it should be good tonight."

"Yeah."

"I saved you a seat," Salomé said, "in case you showed up ... which you did ... as you're here."

They both laughed, looking at each other and nodding, until Salomé said, "Let me show you."

Taiye followed her to the front row of the small auditorium, which was filling up quickly.

"Taiye, this is my kid, Hachim." Salomé placed her hands on the shoulders of a tall child with thick locs and the same brown eyes as his mother, the same kid from the ferry. He looked to be about eight or nine years old.

"Nice to meet you, Hachim."

"You too." Hachim's smile was a mirror of Salomé's. "Wha-what are your pro-pronouns?" he stuttered.

"My pronouns?"

"Yeah, m-mine are he/him and th-th-they/th-them."

"Oh, I'm ... uh, my pronouns are she/her."

"Coo-cool, I'll remem-remember that." The kid had an undeniable sharpness, like sparks bouncing off his body in the quickness of his gestures.

"One of my favourite things about life right now," Salomé said, as they settled into their seats—Taiye to her right in the last place on the row, and Hachim to her left— "is that my kid is obviously far better and more interesting than me."

Taiye smelled the smoky fragrance on Salomé's skin and noticed the slight bend in the prominent bridge of her nose—aquiline. Taiye wanted to trace her finger along that sloping line, wanted to do away with all the preamble of getting to know each other and be kissing already.

Our Lady scoffed, *Calm down.*

The film was brilliant and devastating, entrancing Taiye with its astute storytelling. It was a skilfully executed roller coaster of a narrative that had Taiye quite literally perched on the edge of her plastic seat. Yet, even in the partial darkness of the auditorium, she was still acutely aware of Salomé's warm body next to hers. She wanted to pause, magnify, and live in the split seconds when their arms brushed against each other.

And that was her principal vice, wasn't it? Desiring to be entirely consumed by any and every moment that quenched the hungry howling loneliness that sat curled down down inside herself. If she could climb down the throat of an orgasm and rest, eternal, in its belly, and if she could sink into and be sealed beneath every delicious bite of every delightful thing—oh, how she would, she would, she would. But life pushes forth, persistently, the afterglow of even the most transcendent climax will fade; every tasty thing is digested and turns to shit. Mundanity is persistent. Periods must be dealt with, blood rots, dishes must be done, everything tarnishes and ends. It's just that beginnings are so seductive, the promise of possibilities.

Taiye comforted herself with the hope that she was at the start of what she prayed would be a particularly delicious thing with Salomé. The credits rolled on the screen before her, but her eyes were fixed on the lines of Salomé's angular profile. She didn't avert her eyes when Salomé turned. Instead, she leaned in closer and whispered, "Probably weird timing on my part, but I'd like to take you out for a drink sometime, if you're not terribly busy ... or dinner, or whatever you're into?"

Salomé's big smile accentuated the dimple at the top of her right cheek. She chuckled and said, "I don't drink, but I'm very into dinner ... and *whatever.*"

CROWS ROOST IN THE LATE SUMMER, FALL, AND WINTER; they gather from many many kilometres to form collective night perches. In Halifax, they flock, in small groups, in pairs, or alone, just before dusk, to perch in the trees near Mount Saint Vincent University.

Taiye was on one of her routine walks around the city, looking through the wide windows of The Page bookstore on Spring Garden Road. As she read the colourful titles of new releases, she felt her phone vibrate in her coat pocket.

*Hey, hey, super last minute, but Hachim and I are going to see the crows now-ish. Interested in joining?*

Taiye smiled wide. *Sure!*

Then added: *Are these actual crows? A band? An art performance?*

*Haha! Actual crows!*

She looked up from her phone, her lips chapped from the cold wind and curved into a bashful smile. She caught her reflection in the window, saw Our Lady wink at her, and then stepped into the bookstore to wait for Salomé to pick her up.

So there they were, Salomé, Hachim, and Taiye, the three of them bundled up, leaning against the warm hood of Salomé's car. Their heads

craned toward the darkening sky, which was awash with a stream of cawing crows flying into the trees just ahead of where they stood.

"Incredible, eh?" Salomé asked.

"Yeah, incredi-di-dible," Hachim replied.

"Yeah ..." Taiye said.

For decades, thousands of crows had congregated in those trees, scuf-
fling and filtering down through the branches as the late arrivals forced
the early birds down to lower limbs, cawing an incredible cacophony all
the while.

"It's how they share information and find mates," Salomé explained.

"That's c-cah-cute," Hachim replied.

Salomé chuckled, and Taiye echoed Hachim, "It *is* cute."

Now, Salomé reached into the canvas tote on the hood of the car, pulled
out a small jar of brown liquid, unscrewed the metal lid, and handed it to
Hachim. She retrieved another similar jar and asked Taiye, "Would you
like to share?"

"Please." She took the warm jar from Salomé. "Hot cocoa?"

"Yup." Salomé was, again, reaching into the canvas tote. She offered
Hachim then Taiye bright orange strips of dehydrated mangoes from a
wax paper bag.

"Thank you," Taiye said, exchanging the jar of hot cocoa for a small
handful.

"What do you think they're saying?" Salomé asked, taking a sip. She
was wearing the floral embroidered DESTROY WHITE SUPREMACY cap. She
handed the jar back to Taiye.

"Th-they are s-s-saying, 'Save m-me a spot!'" Hachim replied.

The navy sky was rapidly deepening to black. The crows' music was
dimming. They populated the bare trees like black leaves dancing in the
cold late-winter breeze.

"How was your d-day, Taiye?" Hachim asked, turning to look up at her.

"Good." Taiye smiled at them. "The class I was supposed to have got
cancelled, so I job-searched a bit and walked around."

"It was a n-nice d-day for walking, sunny." Hachim seemed to Taiye like a child who spent a lot of time with adults.

"It was. How was your day?" she asked.

"I went to th-the D-d-discovery Centre with An-Annie."

"Annie's their sitter," Salomé added.

"What's the Discovery Centre?"

"It's so cool!" Hachim exclaimed. "There's, there's a me-m-meteorite from Mm-mars, and a, um, a Meg-Megalodon sh-sh-shark jaw, and th-the tallest m-man in the—in the wor-world!" Their face filled with an excitement so endearing that Taiye giggled with them.

"It's a children's science museum," Salomé said, just as her phone began to ring. She smiled at the screen and announced to Hachim, "It's your other momma," before she flipped it open to answer the call, "Hey Jaz."

Salomé's smile quickly melted into a frown. She said, "We're looking at the crows ... no, love, today is Wednesday, you said Friday." She walked a few steps to the left, away from Taiye and Hachim, and conceded, "Okay, okay, fine, I'll um ... I can bring him down. Halfway? Yeah, okay ... okay, okay. My love to your parents. Drive safe."

She returned to them with her lips pressed together. "Hey, I'm really sorry, I have to take Hachim down to the Valley."

"B-but I'm with-with you until F-friday," they protested.

"I'm sorry, baby. Jaz mixed up the dates, but, hey, Oma and Opa are down to see you."

"B-b-but, it's s-so late, Sal!"

"I know, I know." She squatted down to match their height. "But that's why we have to head out now." To Taiye she said, "Hey, I'm sorry about the abruptness."

"No worries."

"Can I drive you home?"

"Yes, please. I'm not sure how to get back from here."

"Of course, um, can I hit you up when I'm back? Maybe we could grab that dinner if it's not too late."

"Yeah, yeah, let me know when you're back."

"It shouldn't be *too* too long. We're meeting up halfway between here and—" She chuckled. "Sorry, you don't care."

"I do, actually," Taiye said, and climbed into the car after Hachim.

WHILE SLEEP EVADED HER THE NIGHT BEFORE, Taiye had filled a bowl with cleaned wrinkly dehydrated shiitake mushrooms and a potent brew of smoky lapsang souchong tea, fish sauce, tamari, rice wine vinegar, and honey. Upon returning from seeing the crows with Salomé and Hachim, she found her mushrooms reconstituted into plump, firm caps, which she sliced into thick ears and set aside.

Our Lady tapped her on the shoulder.

"What's up?" Taiye pushed a knife through the thick middle of a large sweet potato.

*What are you making?*

"I'm not sure. I've been meaning to use this tea." She cut the sweet potato into cubes. "I'm going to stir-fry the mushrooms, roast these pota-toes, maybe make some brown rice ... What do you think?"

*Are you even hungry?*

"Not really ..."

Our Lady laughed. *You had a nice time with the prof?*

"Yeah, cut short, though."

Taiye ran cold water over a half cup of brown rice, and then toasted it in a pan of hot coconut oil until a nutty fragrance wafted up to indicate it was time to add water.

*I think she's calling.*

"What?"

Our Lady pointed to the bedroom, where Taiye's phone was rattling on the red bedside table. She rushed out of the kitchen to answer the call.

"MAKE YOURSELF COMFORTABLE," Taiye said to Salomé as she let her in. "I'll only be a moment." Then she disappeared into the bathroom to change out of her sauce-splattered T-shirt.

Salomé took in the view of the small sparsely furnished space. A low platform bed, with a wide colourful swath of aso oke draped over a white duvet. Beside the bedside table, sat stacks of cookbooks: *Larousse Gastronomique; Joy of Cooking; Classic Indian Cooking; The Soul of a New Cuisine: A Discovery of the Foods and Flavors of Africa; Mastering the Art of French Cooking; The Boston Cooking-School Cookbook; Ottolenghi: The Cookbook; The Complete Caribbean Cookbook;* and *Afro-Vegan: Farm-Fresh African, Caribbean, and Southern Flavors Remixed.* And many many potted plants: tiny clay pots of succulents, hanging spider plants, devil's ivy with vines cascading down the sides of the planters, purple variegated wandering inch plants.

"You have a lot of plants," Salomé shouted so Taiye would hear.

"Yeah," Taiye replied. "I try to get one every time I go to the supermarket." She walked back into the living room in a fresh T-shirt and an oversized cardigan. "It's a bit obsessive."

"Cute."

"Me or my plants?"

"Um, both." Salomé laughed bashfully.

They stood by the closed front door and considered each other.

"Are you okay?" Taiye asked.

"Yeah, sorry." Salomé ran a hand over her head. "I just hate saying goodbye to my kid."

Taiye nodded.

"I mean," Salomé continued, "don't get me wrong, it's really convenient being a part-time parent. Goodbyes just always feel really hard."

"I'm sure." Taiye stepped closer. "I'm sorry."

"It's all good." Salomé leaned in when Taiye touched her hand.

"Is this okay?" Taiye asked, rubbing her thumb in light circles on her forearm.

"Yeah ..."

"When next do you have him?"

"Next week ..."

They stood that way for a slow moment, Salomé considering the scar on Taiye's chin, Taiye refraining from taking Salomé's fingers to her mouth.

Then Taiye asked, "This ...?" her fingers running up and down Salomé's arms, their faces a breath away from touching.

"Yes," Salomé said, barely audible. She leaned her face closer to Taiye's for the kiss they'd both been keenly awaiting.

It was an upsurge, their kiss. Tongue licking tongue, prying lips apart to the steady rhythm of longing. Their bodies pressed together; Salomé's back pushed up against Taiye's front door. A crescendo..

Then Salomé pulled her face away. "We should talk ... a bit ... like at a restaurant or ... somewhere ..." she said, catching her breath.

"Sure." Feigning nonchalance, Taiye shrugged and stepped back. "I'll just grab my coat." But she didn't move any farther away.

"Yeah," Salomé said, firmly holding Taiye's gaze, not moving away either. "Or," she continued, "we could just ride that first impulse ...?"

Taiye nodded and launched forward. They were kissing again, fiercely. Who can say how much time passed like that, Taiye's knee wedged between Salomé's thighs, both their hands groping, seeking the warmth of bare skin? Salomé's hands moved under Taiye's shirt, touching her breasts, digging into the soft skin of her back. Taiye pulled away and asked, "What do you like?"

"Uh ..." Salomé sighed. "Like, um." She bit the corner of her bottom lip.

Taiye smiled encouragingly.

"Well, I like being bossed around ... a bit," she said finally.

"Yeah?"

"Yeah ... you?"

Taiye ignored Salomé's question and stepped away from her. "Cross your arms over your head," she said firmly. When Salomé hesitated, she smiled and added, "Now."

Salomé obeyed, a startled smile spreading across her face. Taiye grazed her teeth on the hot skin of Salomé's neck. She pushed her shirt and sports bra up over her chest to reveal small breasts, dark nipples pierced with tiny gold hoops, a quarter-inch thick vertical line tattoo bisecting her torso from midway down her sternum to just above her navel. She kissed Salomé's breasts and fumbled with the metal buttons of her jeans until Salomé broke her bondage to help Taiye undo them.

"Hands back up," Taiye commanded.

Salomé eagerly obliged.

Then Taiye sank her hand inside Salomé's jeans, seeking her clit, where she rubbed her fingers in firm circles until she felt warm wetness.

"I want to ... may I go down on you?"

"Please, yes." More of a moan than two distinct words.

Taiye fell to her knees, licked, and sucked, and flexed her fingers inside Salomé, until the woman came, trembling and calling on her god.

AFTERWARD, TAIYE FED SALOMÉ THE STIR-FRIED RICE and marinated mushrooms. For dessert, frozen cherries, warmed in the heat of their mouths before biting into sweetness. Then they were kissing, that same urgency.

Then Salomé asked, "What do *you* like?"

"I ... I don't really know."

"Come on," she kissed her earlobe, "tell me."

"I—" Taiye hesitated, shook her head, and chuckled. "I like you."

"Oh." Salomé's face softened. She held Taiye's gaze for a long time.

At the core of it, for Taiye, it was a simple matter of closeness. Two people, sometimes more, feeding a hunger to touch and be touched, kissing, naked—it was the intimacy of it that she found most arousing. Though varied, her appetites weren't terribly sophisticated. Beyond the fact of pleasure, it was merely the thrill of being with someone. Being with an entirely separate universe of a person who wanted to be with her in return. And the ways that it could, even if only until the delicious edge of an orgasm, quell the loneliness in her skull.

So when she said, "I like *you*," to Salomé, it held many meanings.

"GOD, I USED TO BE A MESS," Salomé said. "I mean, I still am, in many ways, but ... I was probably about your age when I had Hachim; he's almost nine now. Hachim's other parent and I had been together for a while, and we were pretty open, but, fuck, I definitely managed to violate the few boundaries we had. I was, um, consistently fucking people on her 'no' list. I was using a lot, too, and lying about it. I mean ... I loved her, it had everything to do with my shit and not her, but still, no one deserves to deal with that." Salomé shifted her gaze from Taiye's face, nervously chewing her bottom lip.

"We'd been trying for a kid, like sinking our savings into IUI, and then IVF, treatments because Jaz—Jasmin—really wanted to carry ... anyway, it didn't work out, so in a last-ditch effort, we did the IUI on me. It took right away. So, of course, karma is a bitch, as they say, and six-ish months into the pregnancy, Jasmin met someone. Like someone she wanted to be monogamous with, definitely a healthier, kinder person than I was. And, like, I couldn't be mad! You know, after all the garbage I'd put her through, I couldn't hold anything against her. The woman she met, Corinne, lives in the Valley, so they moved in together, opened up a feminist used book-store ... they're definitely living some kind of queer fantasy."

Taiye took Salomé's hand as she spoke and pressed her fingers against her cheek, kissing her open palm.

"Anyway, they were really supportive during the pregnancy and birth. And we've been co-parenting ever since. It sounds wildly cliché probably, but it changed me ... like it didn't make me better or anything, it just made me *want* to be better. But I also knew that I had to get properly clean. Like, if my body was going to be a halfway decent home for a growing fetus, and then if I was going to be a halfway decent parent, I couldn't be doing coke and fucking around with pills or whatever ... anyway, I guess that's why I got sober." Salomé smiled at Taiye. "That was the question, right?"

"It was." Taiye planted a kiss on her temple.

"I rambled a bit there."

"No, it was perfect."

"Tell me something."

"What do you want to know?"

"Everything."

"There's not much to tell."

"I know that's a lie."

"Okay, ask me a question."

"Mmm ... what's most on your mind?"

"My sister." Taiye's answer jumped out of her mouth before she could consider it.

"Yeah? Are you close?"

Taiye shook her head, and a shadow crept across her face.

"Tell me about her."

"I didn't talk very much when we were small." Taiye remembered it vividly. "I had words, I just didn't ... I don't know." She shook her head. "So Kehinde would speak for me. She always knew what I needed to say ..."

"Taiye and Kehinde—you're twins?"

"Yeah."

"And you're not close?"

"No." Taiye shook her head again, this time to shake the grief away. "Now you tell me something."

"Hachim and I have a secret beehive."

"Do you really?!"

Salomé nodded. "It's a secret, though."

"May I see it?"

"Absolutely."

Salomé untangled herself from Taiye, stood up, and stretched her wiry body, throwing her arms up with a satisfied grunt. She sighed and dropped her head into Taiye's chest. "I don't want to," she moaned, "but I have to go. I have an early class tomorrow."

"Good luck."

"Thank you." She planted a kiss on Taiye's forehead before saying, "I've had a really good and really unexpected time with you this evening, Taiye." She scanned the floor for her discarded jeans and underwear. "I'd like to see you again, like as soon as possible." She pulled her T-shirt over her head and stuffed her sports bra into the back pocket of her jeans.

"Likewise."

Taiye stayed under the aso oke and waved shyly at Salomé as she left. She touched the warm spot where Salomé had kissed her forehead, left her fingers there as she fell asleep with thoughts of belonging with a woman like that, with a family like that.

*HOLD IT GENTLY, THIS HUNGRY BEAST THAT IS YOUR HEART. Feed it well.*

Taiye awoke to Our Lady's words. The apparition sat at the edge of her bed, bathed in ethereal light, smiling sweetly at her.

Taiye climbed out of her bed, felt her body, after having been touched so thoroughly for the first time in a long time. She felt her body close to the surface of the skin of the day. Early-morning sunshine poured through the slits of the thin turquoise curtains that hung over the small basement windows. Taiye stood in the stream of sunlight and stretched backward, smiled at the warmth on her belly, the tenderness of her nipples.

She moved slowly to the kitchen, feeling the weight of her body on her feet, the stretch of her legs with each languid step. In the kitchen, she made a pot of zobo, a tea of dried hibiscus flowers, cloves, dehydrated ginger, lemon, cinnamon, and honey. Then she drew herself a bath and climbed in with her tea and thoughts of her mother. Memories swam in the pit of her mind, deep below murky waters. She feared they bore no good news, so she skipped over them like she'd learned to do after her father died. Taiye skipped passed blurry flashes of Mami with a paring knife, of blood dripping down her own chin, into her small palms. Of being in a dream, and then being awake, in the kitchen, the tile cold underneath her feet ...

The bathwater grew tepid. Ever constant, time wound forward. Taiye turned her thoughts to the night with Salomé. She bit her bottom lip, hard on the right side, just as Salomé had done, and she smiled.

She smiled all the way to the ferry, all the way across the harbour to Woodside, all the way to her Cold Kitchen class. She smiled through the salads, dressings, and cold sauces course, whipping bright egg yolks with oil with the poise and enthusiasm of a gifted violinist. Smiling all the while, laughing at her crush-induced giddiness.

On her evening walk home, a text from Salomé: *Hey hey, free for a quick tea or something?*

They met at a small café named Grind on a side street off Gottingen. Taiye found Salomé sitting at the counter in a black velvet T-shirt and slim-cut khakis, sipping from a bright yellow espresso cup.

"Isn't it a bit late for caffeine?" Taiye asked, pulling up a bench beside her.

"Hey." Salomé put her cup down and leaned in to kiss Taiye on her cold cheek.

"I have some papers to grade," she chuckled, "so I, um, so I need this." She touched the copper buttons on Taiye's shoulder straps and added, "This is nice."

"Thank you." Taiye shrugged off her jacket. "I like your shirt."

"Hachim picked it out for me." She chuckled nervously again. "What will you have? Let me get you something."

"A London fog," Taiye told the barista. "Coconut milk and honey, please." To Salomé, she said, "Thank you."

"Hey, so, um ..." Salomé started to say, her expression sliding between apprehensive and concerned. "Last night was ... excellent, but it was a bit unexpected, and I usually prefer to talk a bit about my ... situation," she curved her fingers in air quotes around "situation," "before being intimate in that way."

"Spit it out, mate." Pre-emptive hurt was bringing shame along with it, and Taiye was responding with curtness.

"Um, well, I'm non-monogamous, which means that I do—"

"I know what non-monogamous means."

"Here's your London fog." The barista placed a steaming mug of tea in front of Taiye.

"Thank you," Taiye said.

"Right, well, yeah ... so I'm not seeing anyone here seriously. I have a lover in Montreal that I see about three times a year, usually less actually. So other than her ... um ..."

"Okay, I get it." Taiye started to get up.

"Hey, wait." Salomé touched Taiye's hand, and her voice was gentle. "Please, wait a sec. I don't think you do get it."

Taiye relaxed into her seat, averted her gaze, and took a sip of her tea.

"I like you, and I want to get to know you, um, properly, like go on dates or whatever you like, and keep talking, if you're into it."

"Oh."

"Yeah," Salomé continued, "I just wanted to, um, I was just really excited about what happened ... and what could happen. I just wanted to be up front right away, because I'd really like to see you again. If you'd like to see me again, too ..."

"I would."

Salomé couldn't hide the relief that swelled from inside her. "Cool," she said.

"Cool," Taiye replied.

# Kehinde

I DON'T NOTICE THE EXTENT OF FAROUQ'S DRUNKENNESS until we're walking home from Isabella's engagement party. Each step seems hilariously laborious, and he's laughing at everything. It takes us more than twice as long to get back as it did to get to Isabella's place.

We walk arm in arm, and thanks to the electronic mix of Fela's *Expensive Shit* album, which played in the last moments before we left the party, he's singing, "Water water water no get enemy e ee" over and over, until we arrive at the gates of our compound.

"Good evening," I greet Hassan, as he pulls the gates open and nods at us. "Good evening, ma. Good evening, sah."

"Mr Hassan, has my sister come home?" I ask him.

"Yes, e never too tey wey she come back, maybe one hour."

"Thank you, good night."

There is no power, and the generator is turned off, but the orange glow of candlelight illuminates the kitchen window. And half a dozen inflatable solar lanterns, brought by Taiye, light the way to the front door, the stairs, our bedrooms, and the bathrooms.

Farouq undresses and collapses into bed. "That party took an odd turn at the end," he says, as he pulls me onto his body. "But I had fun. You had a good time, babe?"

"I did." I kiss his sweaty brow. "You're drunk, love."

"I am." The lopsided tilt of his smile and his drunken half-moon eyes send a warm rush through my belly. "You're drunk?"

I shake my head. "Not even a little bit."

"I miss dancing with you." He wipes the sweat off his face with the batik pillowcase.

Many of our first dates ended in dancing, an honest way of touching each other, familiarizing ourselves with each other's unique rhythm, a kind of sensual inquiry. A declaration of desire before a more complete consumption. And when we did finally sleep together, it *was* a thorough consumption. Yes, I only had Wale and Wolfie to compare it to, but with Farouq, there was a distinct focus on the mouth: he sucked my fingers, my nipples, licked my lips, my neck, bit delicious bruises into the soft flesh of my inner thighs, ate me out thoroughly. Before he flexes his fingers inside me, he licks them, and then puts them in my mouth. He always licks his fingers afterward as well. All that licking ...

And the snacks: small bowls of cut-up melon and frozen berries often sat on the nightstand. "In case we get hungry," he would say, and we always did.

Living together hasn't dampened my desire, but his dissertation steals his time and energy, forcing me to behave the way a patient person might. I am not a patient person. Now, during this emotionally fraught excuse for a holiday, we should be taking advantage of the break in his writing, but this house haunts me with memories that do not incite sexiness.

"Let's dance more often," I say into his chest.

"Yes," he says, closing his eyes.

"I'll go get some water." I untangle myself from his arms and get up.

"Yes, water," he mumbles, already at the threshold of sleep.

Downstairs, I find Coca-Cola cat trailing Taiye in the kitchen. I meow at her, but she ignores me and stays wound around Taiye's bare feet. The old asshole cat has shown no interest in me since I got back. Our mother says it's just because she doesn't recognize me, but I don't believe that; I think she's punishing me for being away so long. She used to belong to me. I felt jealous about our father and Taiye's honeybee excursion, so he got me Coca-Cola cat to cheer me up.

Taiye meows at me, and it's so believable that the cat looks up at her as if she's just been insulted.

Taiye is holding a large pawpaw in one hand and a glass of water in the other.

"You disappeared," I say, and it comes out far more accusatory than I intended.

"Sorry, I got a bit too high and couldn't be around ... all that."

"Oh, who had weed?"

"That queer bloke, Star." She takes a large gulp of water before handing me the glass. "You all right?"

I nod and drink. "How do you know he's queer?"

"We talked a bit before." She rolls her head from to side to side, stretches her neck.

"Isa is ..." I start to say but trail off because I really don't know.

"Aggressively depressed?" Taiye offers with a smirk.

"Yes."

"That's what I look for in a lover," she jokes, placing the pawpaw on the counter.

"She said to apologize to you."

Taiye only shrugs and pulls her kaftan over her head so that she is wearing just a bra and jeans. She has the body I've always wanted, even though she eats like a pig. Well, I don't know what she's like now, but growing up, she had a huge appetite. The front clasp of her black bra dissects a detailed botanical illustration of an onion rendered in fine lines of black ink on her sternum. The roots of the onion creep down the centre of her ribcage, the leaves like gnarled fingers climbing up between her small breasts. I'm surprised by the tattoo, surprised by how little I know of my sister, despite all those letters.

"This is interesting." I point at her chest.

"Oh yeah." She looks down at it. "It's my most recent one."

"Why an onion?"

"You might think it's dumb." She laughs. "I read an essay about an onion."

"An essay about an onion?" I'm not sure I heard her correctly.

"Yeah, it's more about faith, the reflection on the onion is just the vehicle ... I think, anyway."

"What's it called?"

"'The Heavenly Onion,'" she says, "by a priest chef dude named Robert Farrar Capon."

"So, you read it and decided to get an onion tattoo?"

"Yes," she says, deadpan, "that's the kind of life I'm living." She bursts into laughter at the look on my face, and I laugh with her.

"Do you have any tattoos?" she asks.

"No. Not yet anyway. I don't know if it's my thing."

"Fair enough."

"Which other ones do you have?"

"Mmm." She purses her lips, then says, "I'll show you later."

We look at each other for some time. Taiye has a faint smile on her face, and I feel my face mirror hers. She still seems stoned, lighter, and her words are flowing easy.

"Do you think Isabella suffers because she's closeted?" I ask.

"Maybe." With a broad, red-handled knife, Taiye cuts into the soft yellow-green skin of the pawpaw. A firm push down and the fruit falls open in two even halves, tiny juicy black seeds glistening in the candlelight.

"Maybe her brain just doesn't make enough serotonin, and she needs help," Taiye continues. "But you know our people. Nigerians don't get depressed. She really should just pray it away." She chuckles as she guts the fruit.

"How about you?" I ask her.

"What about me?"

"Are you okay? Was it okay to see her?"

A shadow crosses her face and takes the shape of a joyless smile, a sneer. She doesn't say it, but I hear the faint words, *Now you're concerned?*

"I'm okay," she says, and hands me one half of the fruit with a spoon. "Eat up, you have to stay healthy for this one." She gestures to my belly.

"For which one?" I take the pawpaw, an inexplicable wave of annoyance climbing up from my stomach to my throat.

Eyebrows raised, Taiye asks, "Or am I wrong?"

"Wrong about what?" My tone is biting.

"Maybe I'm wrong." She shrugs again. "I just thought you were pregnant."

My feet are stuck to the kitchen floor, and my voice is stuck in my throat. But Taiye doesn't notice. She plants a soft kiss on my cheek and leaves the kitchen, Coca-Cola cat close behind her.

"Don't forget to blow out the candles before you leave," she calls from the stairs.

I CANNOT SAY PRECISELY HOW LONG I'VE STOOD, alone, in the kitchen, running through the last few times that Farouq and I had sex.

How would Taiye even know? What is she even talking about? Just a stoned woman's ramblings. Or, I'm pregnant. My last period was ... my last period was last month? I remember I had it when we bought our flights to Lagos, and that was, maybe seven weeks ago, maybe eight. Then I got it again, I think, I can't remember, I don't keep track. No, Taiye is fucking with me.

I run out of the kitchen and up the stairs to her door. I push it open without knocking. "Why would you say that?" I demand.

"Huh?" She sits up in bed, a dazed look on her face, a chunk of pawpaw paused midway to her mouth. "What? Say what?"

"You said I was pregnant," I say in a forceful whisper. "Why?"

"Oh." She relaxes back against her pillow. "Kehinde, I don't know, I just ... *are* you pregnant?" She takes a bite of the fruit.

"I don't know!" I throw my hands up.

"Well, maybe you should take a test, then." She puts the hollow shell of pawpaw skin down on the nightstand. "You just had the same ... like, vibe as Sade when she was pregnant."

I am very truly at a loss for words.

IT APPEARS THAT I AM, INDEED, PREGNANT. I don't understand how Taiye knew, but she fucking did, like the unwittingly witchy weirdo that she is. And now I must tell Farouq. I think he will be happy. I think.

I'm annoyed that Farouq is still snoring in bed with the covers pulled up over his head. The loud hum of the A/C doesn't seem to disturb him at all, so I slam the door shut when I leave the bedroom. Walking past our mother's room returns me to years before, when our father was gone, and I was small, and her door was perpetually shut.

Downstairs, Taiye is puttering about in the kitchen—she's *always* in the kitchen.

I wonder what it's like to exist in her skin. I'm the nearest to that, the closest to understanding the particular contours of her psyche, perhaps, yet still, I wonder.

"Look!" I say to her in a low voice, clumsily spreading a rag over the counter and laying seven positive pregnancy tests down vertically, side by side.

"Morning, love, how did you sleep?" she asks from across the kitchen where she is stirring something aromatic on the stove.

"Come look!" I say, louder this time. "Please." She's not moving quickly enough.

"Oh," she says, when she finally walks the four steps from the stove to the counter and sees the tests. Her eyes grow wide, and her expression is only moments away from breaking open into a smile. I can see her stop herself instead and ask, "How are you feeling? What are you thinking?"

"I think," I take a deep breath to clear my mind, willing something true to float to the surface, "I think that this is good ... right?"

"And how do you feel?" she presses.

"I feel a bit shocked." As I say it, I understand that it's true. And something else, something I want to grasp on to, but not too tightly, just in case.

"I'm afraid," I tell Taiye.

She nods, eyes squinted with such raw empathy I feel a ball of heat unfurling in my chest, the preamble before tears. She takes my hands in her own damp ones and asks, "Have you told Farouq?"

I shake my head. A familiar scent overwhelms my senses, and Wolfie's face bobs across the surface of my mind. Last time, I was with Wolfie, and I wasn't ready. Things are very different now ... I must remember that things are different now.

"What are you afraid of, Kehinde?"

"I was pregnant once before."

"Yeah."

"Miscarriage."

"I'm sorry." Taiye chews her bottom lip, her expression dancing from sadness to hope and back again, and back again. The mid-morning sun streams through the slatted louvres of the kitchen window, and a faint but steady hum pours in with it.

"What are you cooking?"

"Catfish vindaloo. How far along do you think you are?"

"I don't know."

"Do you want a baby?"

"I think so ..." I think that I have to be a lot more certain than that or I might lose it again.

"Yes," I say. "I want this baby."

She nods again, and then gestures toward the stove. "Help me with the rice."

I follow Taiye to the wide pan where halved cinnamon sticks, cloves, cardamom, and small black specks of mustard seeds are sizzling in shallow oil. She adds a generous handful of chopped onion and asks me to set a kettle of water to boil. I obey and lean against the counter by the oven.

"What's this?" I ask, lifting the lid off a bowl with fleshy chunks covered in a fragrant red paste.

"Catfish." Taiye pours a cupful of brown liquid through a small sieve over a red mug. "Marinating in turmeric, ginger, garlic, and stuff ..."

"And that?"

"Tamarind juice." She puts the juice aside and adds the catfish to the simmering pan. "What will you name her?"

"What?"

"What will you name her?"

"Her?"

"Your baby?" She hands me a tiny jar filled with a cloud of red threads. "Put two pinches of that in a quarter cup of boiling water to steep for a bit."

"I haven't thought of names," I lie, and add the saffron to a mug, still waiting for the kettle to boil.

I have thought of many names. I have wondered about the ingredients that make a family—a *good* family. I have desired so deeply to create a good family, with Farouq. I have thought of names for girls: Habiba, Ayomide, Azuka.

"Will you please put a pot on with some oil?"

"A big one?"

"Yeah. It's for the rice, so big enough for about five or six servings."

"Why so many?" I ask. "You always make so much food."

Taiye just shrugs and smiles.

"So," I say after some silence, "will you go to the wedding?"

"Isa's wedding?"

"Yeah."

"Maybe. If I'm invited."

"Do you still have feelings for her?"

"Really, really not." Taiye laughs. "Not in that way." She pours the tamarind juice in with the simmering catfish, lowers the heat, and covers the pan. "Tell me about your wedding?" she asks, and hands me a large onion, adding, "please mince."

When the fumes sting my eyes, I let the tears run down my face and drip from my chin onto the wooden cutting board.

"It wasn't much of a wedding," I tell her. "Some friends joined us at city hall, and a court clerk officiated."

"No dancing?"

"There was some dancing later that evening."

I want to tell Taiye that I saw her dancing the same day she saw me, tell her how impossible and frightening it is. But I don't.

I want to tell her the truth about my miscarriage as well. The truth is that, almost exactly a week before my pregnancy failed, I named it. I will not say the name. The truth is that, after I named it, I wanted it more than I remember wanting anything before. The truth is that, as much as I loved Wolfie, I already loved the possibility of that pregnancy more, and I felt committed to making a go at a family, with whoever that baby would be. I can't bear to recall the pain of that time, but I must remember that the flip side of that pain was a gift. Through that grief, I birthed a version of myself who creates. I hesitate to name myself as an artist, but yes, I birthed a version of myself who makes art. It was a coping mechanism that has become my livelihood.

"I wish I'd been there," Taiye says, disrupting the silence that has fallen between us. "At your wedding, as a witness, or just to dance with you afterward."

She adds my shoddily minced onions to the pan of hot oil.

"I would have loved to be there." The longing in her voice is palpable enough to rise over the loud sizzling.

Silence emerges again, as onions caramelize to a translucent golden brown, and then she asks me to add the rice and sauté it for a moment before adding the saffron liquid, three cups of water, and salt.

In the time it takes the saffron rice to cook through, the catfish vindaloo is ready, and Taiye has made us black tea with evaporated milk and honey from her hive. We are sitting at the table with the pregnancy tests between us, but she is elsewhere, receded into herself. I recognize this trait of hers, the way her pupils widen, regardless of the light, as she slips behind them and dips herself away to away. She's done this since we were small, but it grew more frequent after our father died.

"I've been reading your letters," I say, to bring her back.

"You need to go to a clinic for checkups and stuff," she says quietly, "to see how far along you are and get vitamins ..."

"I've been reading your letters," I say again, though I'm sure she heard me the first time.

"Mami will be so happy about the baby." Still ignoring my revelation, she takes a sip of her tea.

"Taiye," I say, my tone forceful now, "I said I've been read—"

"I heard you." Her voice stays soft, but she looks away from me.

Before I can respond, I hear heavy footsteps descending the stairs. At the same moment, a stir begins in my stomach and grows more vigorous with each breath. I am bent over in my chair, combatting an intense wave of nausea, when Farouq crouches beside me and starts rubbing my back. When the nausea passes and I sit up, I see his eyes dart from the tests on the table to Taiye to me before he says, "Uh ... babe?"

# Kambirinachi

KAMBIRINACHI BLOSSOMED in the gaze of her growing babies. She was suited to motherhood. Those first few years back in Lagos were truly blissful.

Banji's employers, the Austrian couple, however, were unsatisfied with their own marriage, and thus poured all their affection into renovating their property. They transformed the deteriorating block of flats into a three-storey home with massive windows to swallow all that Lagos sunshine. They ensured there were many bedrooms for visiting relatives, a high-ceilinged kitchen, a spacious backyard. But the new home failed to coax new love out of them, and the government—another military dictator had taken office—the heat—the Island humidity!—the failing business— who would have thought that small-time traders wouldn't be able to pay back microloans?—were making their time in Nigeria unbearable.

The wife left first. She returned to her home city of Klagenfurt. The husband followed two years later, after Toyosi called things off. She'd met someone else, a soft-spoken pastor and sharp businessman who would go on to start one of the city's largest megachurches. Weeks before leaving, the boss called Banji to his office to tell him they would be closing shop. And he was giving Banji the house.

"So I'll be jobless, but we'll have a home," Banji reported to Kambirinachi that evening while she peeled old yams for fufu.

The six-year-old twins were playing hide-and-seek by the plantain palms, Kehinde squealing whenever Taiye found her, poorly hidden under the same canopy of leaves where she'd hidden the last three times.

"And he wants nothing in return?"

Banji shook his head, slicing fingers of okra for soup. "Nothing."

"This is a gift!" she shouted. "Why do you seem stressed about it?"

"Isn't it too big a gift?"

"Don't be ridiculous." She waved his anxieties away and set the large chunks of yam to boil on the stove. "Somebody wants to dash us a house, and you're panicking."

"People don't do things like this for free, Kambi."

"Rich oyimbo people who feel guilty about leaving you jobless and are leaving the country do." She laughed. "Have you talked to Toyosi?"

"No, I don't want to say anything until I've signed the papers and he's moved out, and we've moved in."

"Probably wise."

"Not that I think she'll have an issue with it."

"So what else are you worried about, worry worry?"

"It's just," he chuckled softly, "it's a whole house, Kambi."

She smiled and took his hands, slippery with okra. "It's a gift. Let's just say thank you."

"Mami!" Kehinde ran into the kitchen, out of breath. "I can't find Taiye!"

But Kambirinachi lifted her eyes to see Taiye perched on the knobbly limb of the frangipani tree outside the kitchen window, giggling at having successfully disappeared.

OH, HOW THE TWINS LOVED THAT HOUSE! So many rooms in which to play hide-and-seek. So much space to twirl and dance. Such high ceilings to carry their voices when they sang. So many corners to in which to whisper secrets. Inseparable, they shared the same room, slept in a tight ball, clutching each other in the soft centre of their small bed. They were a small family of four, but they filled the house right up.

Aunty Akuchi came to visit, and she brought her music; it mingled with so much laughter, rose up to coat the ceilings of the home with joy. They hosted a small housewarming party with Kenneth, Toyosi, Banji's mother and sisters, and a handful of new Lagos friends. A lovely celebration of blessings or luck or whatever benevolent force had seen fit to hook them up so well. During the party, Kambirinachi escaped the buoyant chatter for a moment of quiet in the well-appointed kitchen she was still getting used to. There she found Toyosi looking up at the ceiling. "It's so big," she said, when Kambirinachi came into her view.

"It is," she replied, and sat cross-legged on the cold tile floor.

Toyosi sat across from her, and Kambirinachi could read the taut lines of envy on her face.

"Maybe I would have got it if I wasn't trying to be a pastor's wife," she said, intending her statement to come off light, a joke.

But Kambirinachi understood scarcity and the fear it invokes. "Maybe."

"You just have it all," Toyosi said, "don't you?"

"I do?"

It had been almost eight years, and they had not grown close.

"Gentle husband, twins—your tiny waistline after birthing twins." She laughed. "In England, for that matter. And now, a beautiful, newly reno-vated house on the Island."

"I suppose I'm fortunate." Kambirinachi smiled.

"Or blessed." Toyosi returned the smile, albeit tight and insincere. "Or something else ..."

"Is there anything else?"

"Kenneth seems to think so."

"Kenneth finds me attractive and doesn't know what to do about it." Kambirinachi was frank, but her smile didn't falter. "What do you think?" she asked Toyosi.

"How are you going to furnish this whole house?" Toyosi deflected.

"With time," Kambirinachi answered, and she asked again, "What do you think?"

"I'm a woman of God." Toyosi shrugged. "So I think you're highly favoured."

"You lost nothing, Toyosi." Kambirinachi unfolded her legs and got up. "If it's wealth that you want, the man you chose, he'll attract plenty. If it's children that you want, you'll have many."

"How do you know?"

"What is yours is yours, no one can else can claim it."

Toyosi looked down at her palms and muttered through sudden tears, "Thank you for the blessing."

"We're all creatures of the cosmos," Kambirinachi said. "It's only the law." Then she returned to the party.

BANJI KEPT HIS PROMISE to love Kambirinachi every day. In many ways, his love looked as one might have been taught to expect from a man, a husband, a provider. For over a year after Dasha Microfinance folded, he exploited every connection he could to find another job. Until, with a fine dusting of sugar coating the soles of his shoes, he walked into an interview with a corporate law firm in desperate need of an accountant, their last one having attempted to flee with a considerable portion of the firm's previous year's earnings. That man was sitting in a filthy jail cell as Banji was being interviewed.

"Despite the fuckery of this country, we value honesty and integrity here." The interviewer was abrupt. He looked no more than a decade older than Banji and was the newest partner at the firm. "That is the culture of this firm: honesty, integrity, diligence. We won't waste your time if you don't waste ours. I've interviewed eight other candidates today, and everyone has been rubbish, barely able to string a sentence together. I see you have a certificate from LSE, and you worked in microfinance, not bad. You're a bit young. You have a family?"

"I do." Banji leaned forward in his chair. "A wife and twins, they're eight years—"

The interviewer cut him off. "The hours here are long. We have international clients who expect fu—"

"Apologies for interrupting," Banji said. "I'm exceptional at what I do. I may not have done it for very long, but I work smart, I work quickly, and my numbers are flawless. I want this job."

Pleased with Banji's forwardness, the interviewer took a long pause before asking, "When can you start?"

"That depends on the salary."

The interviewer flipped open the paper file on his desk and pushed it toward Banji. There was a work contract with the salary highlighted in yellow. Banji looked down at it, cleared his throat, and then looked up at the interviewer and said, "I can start tomorrow."

Banji's love also looked more tender than one might have been taught to expect from a man and a husband. He hung Kambirinachi's paintings all over their new house and suggested she consider selling them.

"It's incredible!" he would gasp whenever she churned out another kaleidoscopic piece.

Work consumed his hours, but despite exhaustion, he stayed awake to cuddle the twins while Kambirinachi told them stories of magic people in Abeokuta. Whenever they fought, he conceded, if only because he didn't want to waste time divided by anger.

"I don't care who's right," he would say. "I'm sorry, I'm sorry, tell me how to make it good again."

Banji was there, he was loving, and he was content.

And then he died.

A LITTLE OVER FOUR YEARS AFTER HE STARTED AT THE LAW FIRM, Banji was on his way home from the work. He was driving a new car, a company car, on the Falomo Bridge. The sun had only just sunk beneath the horizon— he had watched it from the standstill traffic—when a group of robbers surrounded the car and demanded that he roll the windows down. Banji shook his head and honked, but every other car was honking, too. The driver behind him noticed what was happening and honked as well.

"Oga open, or we go shoot o!" one of the robbers shouted. Their faces weren't even covered; their eyes were red, lips blackened and chapped. Five of them, all armed with black assault rifles. The youngest one was shaking; he was thin, and the gun looked heavy in his spindly arms.

"Open the door!" the shortest one shouted. He must have been the ringleader; he was muscular and the least shaky of the lot.

Banji closed his eyes and whispered the Lord's Prayer. He opened the door and stepped out of the car with the keys in his hand.

"Take it," he said. His whole body shook. "I have twins," he said. "They are only twelve years old. And a wife. She's waiting for me at home."

"Shut up!" The ringleader snatched the keys from Banji's outstretched hand.

They entered the car. Two of them leaned out the windows with their rifles out. They revved and honked and waved their guns so that the other drivers would move out of their way, driving their vehicles up onto the sidewalk, fear of violence clearing the traffic. Banji leaned against the concrete barricade and exhaled.

The driver who had been behind him rolled down his window, his eyes wide, and said, "Jesu Christi, bros abeg enter my car. Where I fit take you?"

"E-e se o," Banji stuttered. Dazed, he started toward the car, until he saw the youngest robber running toward him, crying. Banji froze, his mind screamed, but he couldn't move. In slow motion, the young robber raised his rifle and shot Banji square in the chest.

A scared nineteen-year-old, still a child, newly recruited into armed robbery, fingers twitchy with nervousness, was asked to prove his loyalty, or be killed.

Does it matter what made him a killer?

On the bridge, Banji wheezed as his lifeblood poured out of him. He closed his eyes so that the last thing he would see was his wife's face, smiling at him, welcoming him home.

On the other side of the bridge, Kambirinachi squeezed Kehinde's shoulders between her knees and braided the squirming girl's dense coils in the living room. In the kitchen, Taiye helped Sister Bisi, the housegirl they'd hired when Banji got the job at the law firm.

Kambirinachi was lifting a glass of water to her lips when the young robber pulled the trigger. And when the bullets tore open her husband's chest, she gasped. She felt a swift force slam her own breast and dropped the glass of water to shatter on the floor beside Kehinde. In the kitchen, Taiye crumpled onto the tiled floor in a sudden convulsion.

Something you must know is that Kambirinachi and Death were no strangers—no, but certainly not friends, either. Kambirinachi knew Death from before before. And regardless of what Kambirinachi thought about her, or what the world knows about her, Death is not, in fact, a dreary, hooded, scythe-bearing bore. She is a doorway personified, vibrant and hilarious, quite whimsical, actually. But she takes her job very seriously, more diligently than the tides that pull back the ocean's skirts. She is prompt and focused, and this is what Kambirinachi loathed about her. Having done it herself, Kambirinachi knew that one can deny one's nature, and she believed that one ought to, sometimes, decline the pull of one's blood to run its course.

After Banji was killed, Kambirinachi called upon Death and presented her petition. She pleaded, "Just this once, I beg you, don't take him."

"Ha!" Death exclaimed. "Just once? As if you haven't attempted to cheat me before." She sucked her teeth and cut her eyes at Kambirinachi.

Kambirinachi whimpered, "But you still collected what was due."

"After," Death raised a glowing finger in accusation, "after you *stole* time from me!"

"Please ..." Kambirinachi begged, "please, please."

"I won't hear, I won't hear it," said Death. "You know that I am the marrow. This is my work. If I sway for you, then everything will falter. It's all meaningless if I'm a bad worker, easily moved by passionate petition."

"I beg you, take me instead, please."

"What you're asking me to do is an abomination. But it seems you are more comfortable with that, now that you've become an abomination yourself."

Kambirinachi swallowed the insult. "Please take me instead."

"I don't want you," said Death. "I collect only what I'm owed. Otherwise, everything unravels."

Kambirinachi's wailing was hard to hear, even for a dedicated worker like Death.

Death had nothing soothing to say, yet she tried. "You have little ones. He lives in their faces, in their blood, too. Look there and be content."

KAMBIRINACHI'S GRIEF WAS PERMANENT.

The whole house grew cold. The windows seemed to shrink and the ceilings rise higher.

Her Kin rushed forth to comfort her, and she let them, basking in the soothing numbness of dissociation. But, as is their nature, they tried to lure her home again. Remembering her daughters, Kambirinachi turned away from her Kin once more. At Banji's funeral, she held the twins' small damp hands and stood still in the unrelenting sun, held their hands tight as the casket lowered into the dry earth. The twins wept quietly on either side of their mother. Taiye hadn't spoken since Kambirinachi told the girls their father was dead. She cried when Kehinde cried; otherwise, she seemed to recede into herself. She never came all the way back after her convulsion in the kitchen.

For over a week after the funeral, the house was flooded with Banji's relatives. They trickled out slowly only after Banji's mother and Aunty Akuchi gently suggested over and over that they allow the widow and her children to mourn in peace. Everyone left except Funke, Banji's fourth cousin from his late father's side of the family. She insisted on staying to help Kambirinachi with the twins, and within a few days, her boyfriend, Ernest, joined her.

# Taiye

SALOMÉ LIVED IN A TWO-BEDROOM, two-storey semi-detached home on Dresden Row in the South End, which was a fifteen-minute walk from Saint Agnes University, where she worked as an associate professor in the sociology department. On the days she had Hachim, dinner was simple: stir-fried veggies and rice, tofu scramble on molasses seed bread, baked sweet potatoes with tahini and black beans. Hachim was two years into veganism, a choice he made after a class visit to a small pig farm where they learned the origin of bacon. He had come home distraught and determined not to eat animals.

On this particular night, however, Salomé wanted to impress Taiye, who was, much like her, a voracious meat-eater. She ordered pork belly kimchi stew and had it heating on the stove when Taiye arrived.

The sultry melodies of D'Angelo's *Brown Sugar* met Taiye when she arrived. "I like this song," she said, as she stepped in through the heavy wooden doors. "It's ... smooth."

"Yeah, I'm trying to seduce you." Salomé chuckled. "I can't compete with your cooking, so I've enlisted the help of D'Angelo and the other Soulquarians."

"Who, or what, are the Soulquarians?"

"Girl, what?" Salomé cut her eyes playfully at Taiye, who smiled sheepishly and shrugged her jacket off.

"The Soulquarians are Questlove—you know Questlove, yeah?"

Taiye nodded.

"So, um, Questlove, Bilal, Common," she counted the names on her fingers and frowned, trying to remember, "J Dilla—rest in power—um, Mos Def, Erykah Badu, Roy Hargrove, D'Angelo ... um, James Poyser, Q-Tip, Talib Kweli, and Pino Palladino." She laughed on an exhale and clapped her palms together. "These brilliant, brilliant artists formed a neo-soul collective in the late nineties. They produced some of the sexiest, most provocative music to date, in my not-so-humble opinion."

"Oh, my bad!"

"Your bad indeed." Salomé placed a shy kiss on Taiye's cheek, her mouth cold from the soda water she'd been drinking. "Bienvenue chez moi." She smiled and attempted subtlety, as she looked Taiye up and down while sipping from her glass. "What would you like to drink?"

Salomé led Taiye from the narrow foyer into the spacious living room, which, except for the mess of Hachim's schoolbooks strewn across the coffee table, was neat. The two black leather couches tucked in the corner of the room had small stacks of books piled at their feet. Taiye recognized Audre Lorde's *Zami*, Patricia H. Collins's *Black Feminist Thought*, Christina Sharpe's *In the Wake: On Blackness and Being*.

"What do you have?" she asked.

Salomé looked into the fridge. "Water, tea, guava juice, soda water, and chocolate oat milk in a juice box."

"Guava juice, please."

"Ice?"

"No, thank you." Taiye took in the warmly lit space: stainless-steel appliances, glass stovetop, solid butcher block kitchen island, heavy-laden pan rack above it. Pale coral walls covered in many framed photographs of Hachim in every stage of growth. Infant Hachim and Salomé; toddler Hachim and a round-faced light-skinned woman Taiye assumed was Jasmin; laughing images of people Taiye assumed were friends and family.

"Your place is lovely."

"Thank you." Salomé handed her a tall glass of cloudy pink juice. "We've lived here a while."

"What am I smelling?"

"Do you like it?"

"Smells incredible."

"Oh, good. It's kimchi stew with pork belly."

"Ooh, fancy," Taiye teased. "You made it?"

"Um, yes, I definitely painstakingly made an order from Song's Korean." She laughed and scratched her head sheepishly. "I am cooking rice from scratch, though. In a rice cooker, but still."

Taiye laughed with Salomé. "But still, well done."

"And, and, I got some crostini and was just about to caramelize some onions and mushrooms for appies, because we're fancy bitches."

"Can I help?"

"Absolutely not." Salomé pointed at a padded bar stool at the kitchen island. "You get cozy over there and tell me about your day—um, in one second." She disappeared into the pantry beside the fridge and returned with two red onions and a small paper bag of cremini mushrooms. She scooped softened coconut oil into a red plastic measuring cup, and then scraped some of that into a cast-iron skillet.

"My day was uneventful," Taiye said, as Salomé started to peel the papery skins off the onions. "I was in class this morning, I spoke to my mother, I heard back from a bakery job, and I have an interview next week."

"Well done! Where is this?"

"A bakery on Quinpool. Bird's Nest, or Birdie, something bird related."

"How do you feel about it?"

"I think I have a good shot. It's a part-time baker position. They have their own recipes, so pretty straightforward."

"I hope you get it, if you want it."

"I do." Taiye curved her back in a stretch.

Salomé scraped the roughly chopped onion, garlic, and mushrooms from the cutting board into the skillet on the stove. The oil wasn't hot enough, but Taiye kept this observation to herself. Instead, she watched Salomé wash her hands and wipe them on the front of her black jeans.

"What are you smiling at?" Salomé asked when she turned around.

"You." Taiye couldn't help her smile if she tried; her lips were doing whatever they wanted. "Come here."

Salomé walked right into an open-mouthed kiss. She sighed and sank into it, just as the deep bass began its thrumming on D'Angelo's "Shit, Damn, Motherfucker." She pulled away halfway through the second chorus.

"You okay?" Taiye asked.

"I feel, um, I feel a bit nervous," Salomé confessed, her lips brushing Taiye's.

"Me too."

"Yeah?"

"Yeah."

"You know, I've been thinking of all the things I'd like to do to you," Salomé said, with charged frankness. "With you."

"Like what? Tell me."

"I'd rather show. May I?"

"Please."

"Get up and turn around." From behind, Salomé unzipped Taiye's plaid trousers and slid a hand past the band of her underwear. She pressed her body against Taiye's back, kissing her neck and working her fingers until soft moans escaped her.

Onions and mushrooms sizzled in the cast-iron skillet on the other side of the kitchen island. Taiye thought it was time for some salt and maybe some of those chipotle pepper flakes, but the thought lost traction. She reached a hand under her shirt to squeeze her breasts. The stew smelled incredible; the rice was fragrant, like basmati or jasmine. She sank into her body, into the delicious whorls Salomé's slow fingers traced inside her underwear.

Salomé's breath warmed Taiye's ear. "I want to fuck you so bad, Taiye."

"Yes?"

"Your arms—rest your arms against the counter," Salomé commanded, and as Taiye obeyed, Salomé pulled her trousers down urgently, slipped her fingers inside Taiye and thrust, encouraged by her eager yeses.

Taiye could have lived there forever—the air thick with her moans and Salomé's heavy breathing and the aroma of delicious things. The island shook with the force of their rocking. Salomé moved her free hand from its position on Taiye's shoulder; clumsily, she dipped it into the measuring cup of coconut oil that would eventually fall off the island and clank loud against the floor tiles. She smeared the oil on Taiye and carried on, thoroughly aroused by the deep hunger of Taiye's moaning. And Taiye was where she liked to be, on the exquisite brink of climax; she could gorge on this, on and on—but the onions were starting to burn, so she rubbed herself, let herself come, and collapsed on the counter.

"Oh shit." Salomé rushed to turn off the stove. "Well, that's gone." She covered the skillet and slid it off the burner. "Sorry about that." She returned to Taiye.

"Don't apologize," Taiye said, still dazed. She pulled her trousers up and dragged Salomé by the arm toward her, saying, "Few things smell as good as frying onions."

"You should read this sweet essay on onions and faith," Salomé said, and fell into another kiss.

"Onions and faith?"

"Yeah, it's called 'The Holy Onion,' or something like that ... and I have no business talking about essays right now."

"You really don't." Shaking her head, Taiye reached her hands to feel the dampness between Salomé's denim-clad thighs. "I'm into how wet you are right now." She smiled.

"Yeah, that was hot for me."

"I didn't want it to end." Taiye exhaled loudly.

"I know the feeling." Salomé pulled her T-shirt shirt off, tossed it aside, and took Taiye's hand. "Let me show you the bedroom."

AFTERWARD, THEY FINALLY ATE. In Salomé's bed, an entangled pile of limbs and lips, sharing the same plate of rice and stew. Salomé had the smaller of the two bedrooms. There was a plush mattress dressed in white sheets sitting in a low frame across from the door, a desk and stool against the opposite wall, more photographs, more books, a full-length mirror hanging on the door, and the musky fragrance of incense.

Taiye slurped. "This is so good."

Salomé, her mouth full, nodded in agreement.

"Was it worth the wait?" Taiye asked.

"The stew or the sex? Because this stew is worth anything," Salomé teased.

"Haha."

"Yeah, totally. For you?"

"Mm-hmm." Swallowing a mouthful of rice, Taiye asked, "Why was it important to slow down? On sex, I mean."

"Um." Salomé wiped sauce from her chin with the back of her hand. "I, um, I'm in recovery, yeah, like I'm an addict. So even though I've been sober for a while, I have to be careful. And—this is just for me, I can't speak for anyone else's experience—but I just have to be cautious about things that have been, um, like triggers or associations in the past. Or things that I enjoyed a lot while using, so, like sex and general reckless-ness ... early in my sobriety even going out dancing was kind of scary."

Taiye chewed on her bottom lip and nodded.

"Was that too real?"

"No such thing." Taiye shook her head. "How do you stay sober?"

"I'm in one of those anonymous twelve-step programs." Salomé winked. "I go twice a week, more on the weeks I don't have Hachim."

"That works?"

"For me, yeah, but it's one part of, like, a larger wellness practice. Like I try to stay busy, especially when I don't have Hachim. Idleness is my kryptonite. And I try to end the day exhausted to keep my mind from wandering at night, so I run. Um ... I meditate, as well, that helps a lot."

"What kind of meditation?"

"Mindful breathing, sometimes loving-kindness meditation. Do you meditate?"

"No, I don't know too much about any of that."

"I might have a book you can borrow, if you'd like?"

"I'd like, thank you."

"For sure."

"Salomé, you're really interesting."

"I'm really not." She smiled, both embarrassed and elated by Taiye's gaze. "I've just lived a decade longer."

"That's not it; don't be patronizing."

"My bad." Salomé took Taiye's hand. "I like that you find me interesting. I find you really interesting, too. And mysterious."

Taiye laughed. "No mystery here."

"No, really, I know very little about you."

"What do you want to know?"

"Mmm, tell me about your family."

"Oof." Taiye collapsed backward into the bed. "My family is my sister and our mother."

"Your father?"

"He died when we were small."

"I'm sorry."

"Ça arrive."

"French for ...?"

"It happens."

"How did your father pass?"

Taiye considered how honestly she should respond to the question. "He was killed. Robbed and killed."

"I'm sorry."

"Yeah, me too. He was ... I remember him to be quite sweet. You?"

"Me?"

"Your family?"

"You didn't finish telling me about yours!"

"What else would you like to know?"

"What's your mother like?"

"She's ... tender. And unwell."

"Yeah?"

"Salomé."

"I like the way you say my name."

"Your turn."

"Okay, what do you want to know?"

"Everything."

"Ha!"

"Tell me." Taiye held her gaze and smiled that lopsided smile that made it difficult for Salomé to deny her.

"Um, well, I was adopted," Salomé said as she put their plate—licked clean—away at the foot of the bed and fell under the covers beside Taiye. "It was a closed adoption, so I don't know my birth family." She placed her head on Taiye's chest and closed her eyes.

"Did you ever try to find them?"

"Yes, in my early twenties. I had this fantasy that everything about me would make sense when I met them, but I couldn't find them."

"I'm sorry."

"No, it's all good. Everything is on purpose."

"What's your adoptive family like?"

"They're very lovely people. Deeply prejudiced, but lovely."

"White?"

"Yeah."

"Racist?"

"Inherently, but, you know, the well-meaning kind." She laughed.

"Damn."

"No, I had a charming childhood. My parents adopted a whole brood of Black and brown kids and raised us on a gorgeous farm in Upstate New York. It was mostly a good time."

"Sounds very sweet and vaguely culty," Taiye joked.

"It was a little bit, yeah. We were heavily involved in the Mormon Church. We were kind of the poster family ..."

"Are you close to them?"

"I'm in contact with two of my siblings, close to one, but that's it."

"How come?"

"Um ... I kind of, I got cut out of the church, and ... yeah."

"Fuck, I'm sorry."

"Oh no, it was, um, it was a good thing, actually. I was always a bit militant." She laughed. "I'm sure my parents saw it coming."

"What happened?"

"It was a long process of questioning. I started getting really interested in learning about my Blackness early on, so as soon as I turned nineteen, I applied for and got my call to serve, um, which is like a call to become a missionary. I went to Haiti, met a woman, you know how it goes."

"So, you fell in love and walked away from your faith?"

"A little bit." She chuckled. "It was a bit more drawn out than that, but at the end of the day, my companions reported what happened, which was actually very little. Oh man, my attraction to her was just undeniable. Um ... but, yeah, we held hands and kissed once, and my companion saw and rightfully clocked that it wasn't terribly righteous."

"Righteous," Taiye echoed.

"Yeah, so it was back to Palmyra."

"Palmyra?"

"Yeah, that's the name of the town where I grew up. I denied it, of course, but my parents begged me to tell the truth, promised that it wouldn't matter, so I told them."

"What did you tell them?"

"Just that I'd always known that I was queer, and had been prepared to put it away, but meeting this woman who was Black and queer, and liked me back, um, I couldn't ignore that."

"What did they say?"

"They were devastated. They're devout, and they'd done everything right by the church, and here I was, throwing a wrench into their whole situation."

"They disowned you?"

"Not quite. Sort of. They didn't have much of choice, I don't think. I agreed to conversion therapy, but after the first few sessions, I refused. I couldn't ... it was sick. I told my family I wouldn't continue, and I knew I had to leave them. They were never cruel, but we didn't stay in touch after I left."

"I'm sorry, Salomé." Taiye stroked her face, traced her fingers along the edge of her jaw.

"It's all good. It's been so long, and when I got sober and pregnant, I reconnected with my older sister, and have slowly been reconnecting with one of my older brothers who I suspect is closeted, so it's not entirely sad."

"What happened with the Haitian girl?"

"Oh, we reconnected after I left home and figured out social media, but we just stayed friends. She's married now, lives in Oakland."

They lay together in silence for a long moment. The quiet was soothing. Taiye held Salomé tight, rubbed firm circles on her back, kissed her forehead. "Thank you for sharing that with me," she said.

"Thank you for listening." Salomé kissed Taiye's knuckles. "It was a lot, I'm sorry."

"Don't apologize."

"I've been officially Canadian for six years, it's my patriotic duty to apologize for everything all the time."

"You're a patriot."

"I am," she said in a yawn. "Are you out to your family?"

"I don't really talk to my mother about that."

"And your sister?"

"She doesn't really talk to me." Taiye's voice quavered. "So there hasn't been much of an opportunity."

"What's she like? I mean, as kids, what were you two like?"

"We're identical, you know, well, we were. I haven't seen her face-to-face in a while."

"I don't think you stop being identical." Salomé laughed.

"I guess not. She's a bit bigger than me, like fleshier. Our mother used to tease her about it, just as a joke, but it really got to her. She's beautiful."

"Very modest of you," she teased.

"No," Taiye chuckled, "I didn't mean it like that. She's just brave, like more ... just more. She used to look after me, speak for me when I couldn't find words ..."

"What does she do?"

"She's an artist these days." Taiye smiled. "I don't have Facebook or anything, but sometimes I look her up. I found her portfolio online. It's funny because she never did art when we were younger, but our mother used to paint all the time." She shook her head. "Anyway, the stuff in Kehinde's portfolio is really incredible, a bit similar to our mother's, which makes sense."

"Did something happen between you two? Sounds like you used to be close."

"We were close when we were small." Taiye closed her eyes and searched her mind, travelled back to their house in Lagos, to those nights.

"According to our mother, I started sleepwalking after our father died. She thought I was searching for him in my sleep, but, you know, she's funny sometimes. We had an aunt, really just a distant relative who came to live with us. She came with her partner, this alcoholic guy we called Uncle Ernest. He was a real disgusting person. I couldn't stand the sight of him. It's like I could never really see his face, it just kept, like, shifting or flickering ... I ... we were small, like eleven or twelve, I'm not sure ... I was under Kehinde's bed, reading a book to her or something; the power was out. And he came into her room. I don't think he knew I was there. He attacked her. He tried to rape her."

Taiye tried to control her breathing. She wanted to slow down her inhalations, feel the cold air enter her lungs, let it out slowly, but she couldn't seem to grasp the air. She choked, and Salomé moved to hold her, wound her arms tight around her.

Taiye continued, despite the tightening in her throat. "I have these memories. They are muddy, but sometimes I get these glimpses. I think I heard him—" her breathing bypassed her attempts at control and picked up a panicked pace.

"I think I heard him raping her." She tried to talk through hyperventilation, stuttered, "I-I, I think I used to sleepwalk and hear it, but I swear ..." She sobbed with her eyes closed, her chest heaving, her face contorted in desperation. Deep sinking devastation wound tight in her gut. "I swear

I didn't remember. I barely remember now, but I think I knew ... somewhere inside inside, I think I knew. Am I not truly sickening?"

Salomé looked at Taiye, stunned.

"This is too much," Taiye said suddenly, barely able to catch her breath. "I'm so sorry. I know it's too much." She started to untangle herself from Salomé, to climb out of bed, to leave.

"No, don't go," Salomé pleaded. "It's not too much. Will you please sit down?"

Taiye obeyed, still struggling to breathe.

"May I hold you again?"

Taiye nodded. "I'm sorry."

"You don't have to apologize for anything." She held Taiye's clammy, shaking hands in her own. "He—"

"I can't catch my breath," Taiye wheezed.

"I think you're having an anxiety attack." Salomé's voice was gentle. "Breathe with me, okay?" She took a slow, exaggerated breath, and Taiye mimicked her. Then slowly let it out. They inhaled and exhaled in sync until Taiye calmed down.

"I'm so sorry, Salomé," she said, as shame flooded her chest.

"You have no reason to apologize." Salomé stroked her face. "I'm so sorry that happened. My heart hurts for you. It's not your fault. You know that, right?"

But Taiye was silent.

THE MORNING THAT FOLLOWED OFFERED A PROMISE OF LIGHTNESS. The early sun sent soft rays filtering through the curtains of Salomé's bedroom and made luminescent pools of light on the white covers. Taiye woke from dreamless sleep while Salomé still snored loudly. She pulled on her shirt and tiptoed to the kitchen, taking the empty plate with her. She cleared the sink and loaded the dishwasher, wiped the stew stains off the stove, scraped the burnt mushrooms and onions into a compost bucket under the sink, and wiped down the counter. The electric kettle refused to switch on, so she set a small pot of water on the stove to boil, and then searched the cupboards for tea. Salomé's tea collection was impressive. She had bags and boxes of loose-leaf English breakfast, South African rooibos, lemongrass, lemon verbena, herbal blends that Taiye didn't recognize, licorice root, valerian root. Most of them with labels from the tea shop where they'd first seen each other. Taiye selected a matcha, and with a quick peek in the fridge, found some coconut milk. A rummage through the cutlery drawer proved fruitful: she found a small whisk and was frothing bright green matcha in hot water and coconut milk, just as a groggy and topless Salomé joined her in the kitchen.

"Hey," she said. "Good morning."

"Morning." Taiye smiled and continued to whisk.

Salomé looked at the clock above the stove: 6:33. "Why are we up so early?"

Taiye smiled. "Matcha?"

"Yes."

"Do you have some honey?"

"Yes." She fetched a small jar of dark honey from the cupboard, placed it beside Taiye, and kissed her cheek. "I don't teach until later this afternoon, so if you're not busy, I'd like to show you this breakfast spot I really like."

"Yeah, let's do that."

"Great." She stretched and yawned loudly, arching her back in a deep bend.

"Here you go." Taiye handed her a frothy cup of hot matcha.

"Thank you."

"So, I feel embarrassed about last night. I apologize for getting intense." Taiye took a sip, licked green foam off her upper lip, and averted her gaze to the close-grained wooden countertop.

"I hear your apology, but I don't accept it." Salomé kept her gaze steady on Taiye's face—she still had sleep crust in the corners of her eyes. Salomé dusted it off and continued. "Only because you have nothing to apologize for. I understand why you feel vulnerable, and I empathize. Thank you for sharing that with me."

"It was a lot."

"Sure, but you're welcome to share a lot with me."

Taiye nodded. "I don't think I want to talk to you about that for a bit."

"Fair enough."

"It's all good. But hey, remember what we did before I cried on you and had a panic attack?"

"Yeah, that was dope."

"It was. Let's do that again."

"You're trying to change the subject."

"I am."

"It's working."

THEY PAID A VISIT TO THE BEES ON THEIR WAY TO BREAKFAST. Salomé and Hachim kept a short Langstroth hive, painted in green and yellow stripes, sitting on a frame of wood and cement blocks. It stood in the corner of their garden, in a stream of sunshine dappled by the leaves of mature poplar and maple trees that populated the backyard.

"Let's see what they're up to." Salomé led the way through the screen door. "They get real busy minding their business, trying to find that nectar."

"That's how I'm trying to be," Taiye joked.

"They zip into the sky and travel about five kilometres in either direction to get all that good good nectar and pollen." She placed a hand on the flat roof of the hive.

"You're so lucky!"

"Yeah, I know." Salomé smiled wide. "We got a complaint a couple weeks ago, but they can suck my dick."

They laughed all the way out of the backyard and into Salomé's car.

The breakfast spot that Salomé liked was a hole in the wall near Alderney Landing in Dartmouth, a Greek diner that served large portions for cheap without skimping on flavour. It was one of her favourite places, and Salomé shared it only with friends and lovers she intended to keep. And she very much intended to keep Taiye; she told her as much over a platter of buttered toast, Loukaniko sausage, falafel, eggs, tomatoes, and beans.

"I, um, I'd like to keep doing this," she said, "um, with you ... if you're into it?"

Taiye chewed slowly, relishing Salomé's shyness. "Even after my freak-out last night?"

"Yeah, even after you expressed emotions like any other human being would."

Taiye laughed at this, took another bite.

"No pressure at all," Salomé continued. "I'm just having a great time, and I wanted to say it out loud."

"That you're having a great time?"

"Hey, stop being a dick." Salomé took Taiye's free hand. "I'm trying to say that it's been some time now, and I keep liking you more."

"Your lover in Montreal," Taiye said. "What's her name?"

Salomé didn't flinch. "Her name is Angharad."

"What's it like between you two?"

"It's good, we've known each other a long time."

"Why non-monogamy?"

"Monogamy hasn't worked for me."

"What would it look like, you and me?"

"Like this," Salomé said, taking a sip of her coffee. "With the freedom to see whoever else you'd like, well, um, except my students or colleagues."

"That's your only boundary?"

"My only non-negotiables, yeah."

"Non-negotiables ..."

"What would yours be?"

"Honesty."

"Well, that's a given."

"I like you."

"I know."

"I'd like to keep seeing you."

Salomé smiled and relaxed into her chair.

Later that night, back in the quiet of her place, Taiye turned to Our Lady and confided, "I don't think I'll be the same."

*After her?*

"Yes," she replied, wishing there would be no after.

BUT THERE IS ALWAYS AN AFTER, ISN'T THERE?

For the better part of a year, Taiye and Salomé, they had this real good love, though they rarely named it that. Instead, they said things like:

*I've been thinking about you, missing you.*

*Did you eat yet? I brought you food.*

*How is your heart? How is your body?*

*How can I make your day better?*

*Let me help. Let me take that for you.*

It was a salve for both their wounds, a tender balance between their respective demons.

So what happened to change it?

Taiye's least-favourite vice, the brittle glass beast that is Envy, she reared her fragile head when Salomé spent a couple of weeks in Montreal, presenting at a decolonial Black feminist conference, and visiting Angharad. And Taiye, instead of tending to this particularly unyielding creature of her own concoction, scorned and suppressed it, until it imploded.

The morning before Salomé flew to Montreal, while she and Taiye unfolded fresh sheets to make the bed, she asked, "You want to check in about my trip?"

"Why are you asking?"

"I just want to know how I can take care of you while I'm—"

"While you're taking care of Angharad?"

"Well," she shrugged, "I guess that's not an inaccurate interpretation. So ... um, is there ... how are you feeling?"

"What does her name mean?"

"Angharad?"

"Yeah."

"I'm not sure. It's Welsh, I think."

"She's white?"

"Her dad is, yeah. Her mother is Black, Scotian from Preston."

"What does she do?"

"She works as a veterinary assistant. What do you *really* want to know, Taiye?"

"What's she like?"

"A bit like you, actually. Intense, funny."

"I don't think of myself as funny."

"Well, you are, babe." Pulling Taiye with her, Salomé collapsed onto the freshly made bed.

Taiye nestled into Salomé, ignoring Our Lady's suggestion that she simply tell her: *I feel jealous. This is new for me.* She closed her eyes and basked in the affection of Salomé's warm hand, stroking her cheek.

The first week of Salomé's absence stretched near-infinite to Taiye. Restlessness found her fretting at the thought of being forgotten. Surely, she was only a momentary distraction from whatever else Salomé had going on with that Angharad woman, not unlike Taiye's own convenient trysts with hapless lovers who had inevitably wanted more than she was willing to offer. Surely the proverbial tables had taken a swift one-eighty, and Taiye had become the hapless, pining lover. It didn't help that word from Salomé was scarce and slow to come. Intellectually, Taiye understood—she knew the rules of the game and, in fact, had enough in her own life to fill the space of Salomé's absence. But emotionally, she wrestled with the unwieldy jaw of her envy.

Taiye lost the fight and snooped through Salomé's social media profiles in search of photos of Angharad. Seeing the woman's round face, framed by a mass of dark curls falling on ample copper-coloured shoulders, the many pictures of her in magenta scrubs with bandaged animals, a handful with Salomé smiling brightly at the camera, arm in arm, kiss pressed into cheek, she understood what drew them to each other. Believing that she couldn't compete with their history—thinking, erroneously, that there was any need for competition—she slammed her laptop screen down in a flash of jealous anger.

As a distraction, she turned to an old itch. She pulled up her Tinder profile, swiped right and left, right and left. Then there was a familiar face on her screen, a right swipe, an immediate match, quick conversation, plans to meet up the following night.

With flickering tea candles that cast sultry dancing shadows against the dark walls, and twinkling fairy lights draped high and reflecting off the stained glass of the atrium, Cloud Oyster bar set an alluring ambience for a first date. Taiye walked in with the intimate scent of guilt dusting her shoulders. Telling Our Lady that she was doing nothing wrong, she settled into a seat at the bar, ordered a fragrant gin martini with sweet vermouth, and waited for her date.

Taiye dating—as in the verb—was all good. In fact, Salomé would likely have been thrilled that she was venturing outside of their relationship for sex or companionship or whatever. Taiye's date—the noun—was a whole other issue. She walked in all high femme with thigh-high stockings and platform Mary Janes. They had a few too many drinks, made small talk— Taiye's date did much of the talking—and shared a charcuterie board before going back to her date's place.

"Your family know about you?" her date asked, as they stumbled through her front door.

"What about me?"

"That you're, like, queer."

"I don't think that they're super concerned with who I'm sleeping with."

"You know what I mean, though. You're Nigerian as well, right?"

"Yeah."

"So, like, are they cool with it?"

"I'd rather not talk about my family right now ..."

"Okay, okay." She kissed a sloppy trail from Taiye's lips down her neck to her shoulders as she unbuttoned her shirt. "I normally go for more masculine types. You're, like, softer. Soft butch? Futch?"

"Funke, I—"

"Banke," she corrected.

"Sorry, Banke. I don't know what you're talking about. Take your top off."

Banke obliged. "You know, like, how do you identify?"

"I don't know, girl. I'm a human animal who's just trying to fuck you right now. Is that okay?"

"Absolutely." Banke smiled wide, utterly delighted. "You definitely have a toppy vibe."

Taiye slurred, "You're just talking a lot. I have to ... direct the situation."

"Ugh, yes, direct me."

"Skirt off."

Banke came with a high-pitched moan. She started to return the favour, but Taiye apologized and hurried out of her place, awash in the hollow feeling of having just broken something priceless.

"BANKE?" Salomé asked. "My new TA?"

"Y-yes," Taiye stuttered.

Salomé nodded and got up to leave. She'd driven straight from the airport to Taiye's place, eager to hold her. And Taiye had met her at the door with an expression that made her heart sink.

"Please, Salomé, wait, I'm sorry." Taiye's words sounded empty even to her own ears.

"Were you unhappy with me, Taiye, with us?" Salomé paused but didn't sit. She shook her head, her eyebrows knotted tight on her forehead. "Because I'm *so* happy—I mean ... I was."

"I am. I just ..."

"And you knew, right?"

Taiye wanted to lie, but she nodded. She had known. Not at first, but pretty soon into the date, she knew.

"Why?"

"I didn't mean to ... I don't know."

"But I think you do, Taiye." Salomé clasped her hands tight, her voice strained. "I made my boundaries clear."

"I know." Taiye felt something bubble in her chest, and she choked. "I didn't mean it. I was just ..."

"What?" Salomé's voice took on a sharp edge. "You were just *what*?"

"I'm sorry, I was just ... you were with Angharad."

"Fuck." Salomé collapsed back into the couch. "That's what this is about? You lashed out because you were jealous?"

Taiye couldn't bring herself to answer. The bubbling in her chest grew vigorous.

"You said you were cool with non-monogamy ... I thought we had something *really good*. I ... I'm so in love with you, Taiye."

"I am, and we do," Taiye said weakly. "I'm so sorry, Salomé, plea—"

Salomé inhaled and exhaled slowly, deliberately. Then, as calmly as she could manage, she said, "You know, I, um, I know where you are ... I know this place, I've been there. I can't go back there ... put my sobriety on the line like that. A decade ago, I would be diving right into ... you, even after this." Her voice was ragged, and she wiped away her tears quickly. "But I have Hachim now, I can't risk it." She shook her head. "I have to go."

# Kehinde

IT'S BEEN THREE DAYS since the tests confirmed that I am pregnant. I smile at my reflection, and she smiles back at me. My body is a home. It is a tool. A collection of intelligent components, each with a unique function, the overall goal to grow this life inside of me and bring it forth safely. Unlike Taiye, who just grew taller and filled out with small breasts and slightly fuller hips at puberty, I was driven to intense negotiations with my body when my breasts ballooned, my hips followed suit, and Taiye and I couldn't share clothes anymore. The abundance of my body was foreign to me, unfamiliar and frustrating. I feel like I've been trying to wrangle it into surrender ever since. No need to suck in my belly now, because someone lives in there. I can be a good home. I can treat my body as any good host would treat their home. I can be a good host.

Listen, I know my body is more than that, more than a *temple*, more than a home for this fetus growing inside me, but it helps to think of it this way. To consider it as more than the flesh casing that attracted that disgusting man. It has taken me so long to understand that my breasts are not to blame for what happened. So, yes, I know that I am more than my body, and my body is more than a host, but just let me be good the way I can be for this baby.

Farouq is thrilled about the pregnancy. He cried and insisted on a celebration.

I haven't mentioned how we met. It was at Satsuma, an artist-run centre that I joined after Wolfie moved to Paris. I volunteered twice a week, to bartend, set up and clean up after events, or run the door. It was early autumn, and the centre was showcasing the work of five photographers as part of the city's photography festival. The director made an error in her welcome email to the artists that had them arrive to set up at the gallery at six a.m. instead of nine. After a frantic call from her, I rushed over to let them in, and I don't think I could have possibly had a worse attitude. It wasn't their fault they were early, but I was stuck on a painting— Taiye's face continued to reveal itself when I tried to create my own image. I retreated to the tiny bar to make myself a London fog, sat on the narrow marble counter, and watched the photographers with barely concealed scorn as they carved out sections of the freshly whited walls and began mounting their work.

They asked each other's opinions on their setups and rearranged their pieces based on the feedback. I intended to seem utterly unapproachable. But Farouq walked up to me and, running a hand through his unruly curls, asked in fast French if I would share my thoughts on his wall. I barely understood, but his smile stunned me, so I followed him.

Farouq's photographs were black and white, about seventy of them, and palm-sized like Polaroids. Mounted in thin tarnished copper frames, the pictures were high contrast and pristine, mostly images of body parts captured separate from a whole. Close-ups of henna-covered hands clasping beloved objects, scarred chests and forearms, tattooed shoulders, faces contorted in consuming emotions, eyes that pierced you suddenly with fierce passion, feet, some bare and digging into sand, others seemingly in motion, in heels, running shoes, heavy boots.

The collection was intense and stirring, surprising. He watched me look at his work for a moment before saying, "This is my first, and probably my only, exhibition. I'm not sure what to expect."

I didn't know how to respond to the earnest way he spoke to me, or the way his thickly lashed eyes settled so comfortably on mine, so I asked if he would like some tea.

"Why is it likely your only exhibition?" I asked, as I poured hot water over loose mint leaves and licorice root.

"I'm not really an artist."

"No? What are you, then?" I added a lavish amount of honey to the tea and handed it to him.

"I'm a student." He blew steam off his cup, and I couldn't un-notice the shape his lips made. I became acutely aware of my breasts and arms, of my body as a hunched-over mass. I straightened my back and worried that my many layers of clothing made me look lumpy and unattractive. After Wolfie, I'd entirely forgotten how particularly potent the power of yearning can be. Yearning to be seen, to be desired, to lust and be lusted after. After all that trouble, the puckered pout of a certain plump-lipped, brown non-artist was all it took to reignite a familiar want.

"And this?" I gestured toward his wall of photographs with feigned coolness.

"I asked those people to show me what best represents them." He kept his eyes on me and sipped his tea. "That's what they showed me. It's how they want to be seen."

"And how do you want to be seen?" I asked.

As an answer, he smiled wide and revealed crinkles at the corners of his dark eyes. And I was satisfied.

Even though he "wasn't an artist," he kept coming by Satsuma long after the exhibition closed. He signed up for many workshops, volunteered a few times. Once, he walked in just as I was leaving; he looked at me with raised eyebrows, and waited until I smiled and nodded, before falling into step with me. We headed out onto cobbled roads and walked to the shawarma stand a few minutes from Satsuma.

When we sat on one of the stone benches facing the port, he said with laughter in his voice, "This is a bit like a date, isn't it? You're eating, I'm paying, you're wearing a pretty dress under that old-man sweater."

"We know nothing about each other," I responded.

He shook his head, saying, "Isn't that what first dates are for?"

He fetched a pack of cigarettes from an inner pocket in his dark blazer and lifted one to his mouth.

"You'll have to ask me out properly," I said.

He fumbled with a black lighter until it sparked and flamed and gave light to the end of his cigarette. "Can I take you out on a proper date sometime?"

"What does your name mean?" I evaded his question and took the cigarette from him to test my lungs. They failed terribly, and I almost coughed up my falafel. I should have been embarrassed, but I laughed when he laughed. He patted my back and left his hand there well after I'd stopped retching.

"It's a derivative of Al-Farūq, Arabic for redeemer," he said, taking the cigarette back.

"Arabic is such a beautiful language. I'd love to learn it one day." My voice was hoarse from coughing and laughing.

"I'll teach you, come out with me," he responded without looking at me; instead, he fixed his gaze on the sun as it dipped into the heaving river ahead of us.

"How come you speak Arabic?"

He shrugged. "I grew up speaking it. I'm Moroccan. My mother is from Tangier ..." he trailed off and crushed the cigarette on the arm of the bench. "Anyway, we could go see a film." He moved closer to me on the bench and waited until I nodded before seeking out the curve of my waist with his warm hand.

BUT THERE IS MUSIC NOW. Someone is playing Lagbaja downstairs. The house is buzzing with a new life. I am a house buzzing with new life. And Farouq is shouting my name. He rushes up the stairs and into the room.

"Kehinde, Taiye and I were talking—we should have a wedding party here!" he exclaims. "A celebration here with your mum and your sister. Would you like that?" He is out of breath. He takes me in his arms and asks again, "Would you like that?"

"Yes," I say. "I really would." And I mean it.

# 4

# Bread

# Kambirinachi

AFTER BANJI'S DEATH, grief wound its tense muscles around Kambirinachi's mind. It squeezed, squeezed until it split a hairline fracture that ran the length of her—

*Stop, I want to speak—*

. It ran the length of her—

*We—I—will tell—*

It is not an uncommon thing to be cut open like tha—

*I will tell my own story now.*

*I am not insane. I may be mad with this life, but it's an intoxicating thing, wouldn't you agree?*

*Life is an ambivalent lover. One moment, you are everything and life wants to consume you entirely. The next moment, you are an insignificant speck of nothing. Meaningless.*

*But I am not insane. Imagine this:*

*You are made unbound, birthed from everything glorious and fermented and fertile and free. Unbound. You visit this binding, this flesh cage. It's sacred and robust but a cage nonetheless. You visit because it's your nature. The visitations blind you, yes, but they also pierce new eyes into you, and you see you see you see.*

*Imagine you made a choice to stay bound in this cage indefinitely, despite your nature. Imagine your purpose began to fade from you because this cage cannot hold it. Lost in translation from pure light to flesh ... so many fluid channels ...*

*There are moments when I remember, so lucid and sweet. This purpose keeps me grounded. There are moments when I forget. Still, I am not insane— whatever meaning you give to that word. Don't insult me. I am more massive than you can fathom.*

*There are so few ways to transmute grief through this cage, and all of them merely ease the seed rotting inside you. Imagine living with a rot inside you. Perhaps you don't need to imagine. Is this the condition of living? Tell me, how do you make the seed grow? How do you make it bloom into something beautiful?*

*You may understand this: the people I love are taken from me. They are taken by death or wounded until they leave me. My father, my Banji, my mother, my Kehinde—taken, taken, wounded, wounded. And when Kehinde is wounded, Taiye drowns in the pain.*

KAMBIRINACHI'S KIN DISPATCHED THE SISTERS, mercenaries to lure her back to them. Strategically, they chose her season of grief to attack. The Sisters came as a pair each time, alternating between cruel and kind.

The kind pair came first, encouraging her to rest. She was wounded with sorrow; she needed the rest. The twins were okay; they had Sister Bisi, and Aunty Funke. They knew where to find her—all they had to do was push her bedroom door open. *Sshhhh*, she must rest.

Kambirinachi heeded their counsel and curled under the covers in her darkened room. Everything smelled of Banji; she hadn't changed the sheets in the nearly three months since he'd died. His toothbrush still leaned beside hers in the cup on the bathroom sink. His razors and oils, his clothes, dirty socks, dirty underwear, all still sat where he'd left them. Kambirinachi let herself sink into the mattress, the pillow damp from tears. There was nothing to do but dissolve.

One night, Kambirinachi rose from her bed to find Ernest, sitting at the kitchen table, snoring, his head rolled back, empty Star Lager bottles on the counter, a half-finished one on the floor beside the chair in which he was slumped. A sleepwalking Taiye, blank-faced, her eyes only white slits, stood stock-still, pressing a paring knife against his throat.

Kambirinachi moved slowly and deliberately toward the two of them and removed the blade from Taiye's firm grasp. She hummed Baby's song as she cut a small slit across Taiye's chin and smeared the blood over her eyes, so the girl could sleep in peace.

Then the cruel Sisters came, with the same faces as the pair before them, but they smelled of rotten oranges—sweet sweet, then, just at the head of the scent, corrupt.

The day Taiye witnessed the bad thing happen to Kehinde, the Sisters sat, one on either side of Kambirinachi, and whispered in her ears.

*And you are still lying here, pathetic, while your children are being devoured.*

They laughed like sharp needles clustered at the base of her skull. They slipped images into her mind, pictures of the most horrifying things, being done to her twins by a person whose face was shrouded in a red mist. The images were so revolting, so frightening, that Kambirinachi bolted upright in bed, retching until bitter bile dribbled down her chin. She rushed out of her bed, forcefully opened the door to the hallway, only to find another door, and behind that another, and another. No matter how many doors she flung open, there was always another one keeping her from getting to the hallway, from getting to Kehinde's bedroom. She heard screams: Kehinde's; she heard a soft, frightened whimper: Taiye's. She turned around to face the Sisters, demanded to be set free, but they only said, in that uncanny unison that Kambirinachi so detested, *We're not holding you.*

Defeated, she climbed back into her bed. And there they were again, saying: *And you are still lying here, pathetic, while your children are being devoured.* Again, with the grotesque images, the retching, the cycle so many times in that single night.

By the forty-third time the Sisters forced the poison images of her twins upon her, Kambirinachi was weeping silently, rocking back and forth. "Why are you making me suffer?" she asked finally.

The Sisters laughed, long and mocking. *We're not making you suffer. You chose this.*

"But not for my babies ..."

*Don't be so naive,* one of them said, caustic and sharp, her beautiful lips turned down in disgust.

*You know the basic arithmetic,* the other one joined in, her lips turned up in a sneer.

Then together they said, *Ti o ba yan lati jiya, awọn ọmọ rẹ yoo jiya bi daradara.*

*If you choose to suffer, your children suffer, too.*

Kambirinachi woke up to crusty bits of dried vomit smeared on her chin and along the right side of her face. There was a loud series of knocks on her door before Sister Bisi let herself in. Her eyes were swollen and bloodshot.

"Madam," she said, kneeling at Kambirinachi's bedside, "the aunty wey been dey stay with us, Sister Funke, she don comot." Sister Bisi sniffed and wiped her swollen eyes. "Her and that her husband, dem don comot, dem no good." She shook her head and looked fiercely into Kambirinachi's eyes.

"Madam, you understand wetin I dey try tell you?" Tears welled up in Sister Bisi's eyes, but she blinked them away. "You understand?"

Kambirinachi understood. A gasp escaped her, and then a loud piercing wail: "My children!"

She tried to scramble out of bed, but her weak body couldn't support her; she hadn't eaten in many days. She fell back into the bed.

RAGE BECAME HER FEAST. Kambirinachi gorged herself, but it had nowhere to go. In wraths so blinding, she moved fluidly around the house, destroying anything that smelled of the man who had hurt her daughters. Regretting that she'd stopped Taiye from slaughtering the man in her sleep like the pig that he was. It would have been wrong, yes; it wasn't the child's pain to eat. Still, she regretted.

The first time her twins witnessed her explode, she was at the door to the bedroom where Ernest had slept with Funke, empty now. She lifted the closest chair and smashed it against the door. A sturdy chair, a solid door. She lifted the chair above her head and down over the door. Over and over. Chunks and splinters of wood flew about her. A sound came out of her, a wail from somewhere in the pit of her stomach, poured out like a swirling blackness, as she hammered the door.

She didn't see her twins cowering behind her before Sister Bisi led them away.

And after that, a seal of silence befell all of them. Kehinde no longer spoke for Taiye. She saved her words for the bouts of terror that seized her at night. Taiye rarely spoke at all.

They spent eight months in London, leaving Sister Bisi and Aunty Akuchi in the house in Lagos. Kehinde begged for Sister Bisi. Taiye begged for Kehinde. Kambirinachi begged for the strength to stay caged, if only for her twins.

THIS CAGE IS AGING.

*London was unbearable. When we returned to Lagos I took a job at the Church of Assumption bookstore. Money was not an issue, thanks to Banji, but I needed a place to pass the time away from my daughters' wary eyes. Besides, I liked the smell of the church. I find the holy smoke soothing. I couldn't bring myself to paint, without hearing Banji's voice and feeling this relentless wave of sorrow wash over me, so I put my brushes, my papers and canvases, and my easel away.*

*The years wound on. My girls grew up and ever more apart. It pained me to witness, but I was afraid to interfere. The way Kehinde switched off from Taiye, and Taiye, ever faithful, watched Kehinde for a sign of forgiveness. It was all wrong, you see. I didn't birth them to be pain-eaters, but that is all I seemed able to teach. I couldn't blame my Kin for that—they surrounded me when I wept, they sang Baby's song to help me remember why I chose to stay and stay. It all pained me too much ... so I started to take the medicine that Folake Savage prescribed.*

*Kehinde was distraught after Taiye left, though she wouldn't share the burden with me. She refused to share anything with me.*

*When Kehinde left, she cried in my lap when she said goodbye. I could have clutched her close forever, but she got up as abruptly as she had collapsed into my embrace and ran to the taxi waiting to drive her to the airport.*

*My sweet Taiye started to send me money as soon as she started working in London; the poor thing worries about earning her place. It's a wound, you know, this thing that has her believing she is shameful. It won't heal without her sister's words: "I forgive you." She never tried to keep her love of women from me, though I suspect she uses it to hurt herself. These alive bodies ... so adept at turning even the most precious things into vices.*

*And Kehinde, my Kehinde, is home after all this time. I want to show her something ...*

# Taiye

SOME NIGHTS AFTER FAROUQ AND KEHINDE AGREED to a wedding party Taiye lies awake in her bed, her mind crowded with thoughts of Salomé.

"How long has it been?" she asks Our Lady.

*Some time.*

"A year? More?"

*More or less.*

"You're not being very helpful."

*You don't need any help.*

Sleep evades her, her thoughts taunt her, so Taiye turns to her phone for distraction. A new email alert flashes across the screen, the name attached to it sending her heart lurching forward.

Subject: Old Friend, Long Time
Timi C. Lawal <t.c.lawal@qmail.com>
June 13, 2017, 3:38 AM
To <t.adejide@qmail.com>

Taiye, it's been very long.

First, I have to apologize for only now writing to you. I didn't have access to my emails while I was in treatment, and I was honestly terrified to look until only a few months ago. And even after I read your emails, I just didn't know how to start to reply. I kept putting it off and off until I could pay proper attention and well ... it's been a long time now, three years? Oh, girl, true true, where I suppose start?

My life looks very different now. I imagine yours does too—you moved to Canada!

I left London, just like you. I had to. I was in Barcelona for a while after my treatment, stayed with Aiden, you remember her? I started teaching English, it was nice, gentle times, good for me.

Can we talk on the phone? I have so much to tell you, but everything is seeming quite daft as I write it.

I think about you a lot. I am grateful for every voice mail and email you sent me. Please call me.

Love,
Timi

"Hello?" Taiye's voice is shaking, her palms so damp with perspiration that her phone slips in her nervous grasp, threatening to fall to the ground.

"Hello, who's this?" Timi asks.

Taiye's breath catches in her chest. "Timi? It's Taiye."

"Girl!" he shouts. "Oh my God! You got my email!"

"Yes." She hiccups, a sob quietly rising out of her. Clearing her throat to keep her voice steady, she continues. "Yes, I did. How are you, love?"

"Bitch, I'm in Amsterdam. Where are you?"

"Of course you're in Amsterdam!" She laughs, full-bellied and joyous. "I'm in Lagos."

"The motherland."

"You should come visit so we can catch up properly."

"Are you kidding? Because I'll come. I have some time off, and I'm trying to do my gay African *Eat Pray Love*."

"I'm not kidding. Are you kidding? Because I'll cover half your flight, and you'll have a place to stay and food to eat." ·

"I'm not kidding if you're not kidding."

"Bitch, are you about to come to Lagos?"

"If you're not kidding, I'm coming."

"I'm not kidding." Her tone stills to serious. "It's been so long, and I've been so worried. I won't actually believe you until I see you."

"Well, you're about to be a believer, chile!"

"Hallelujah! Hallelujah!"

HEAVY RAIN FALLS SIDEWAYS the day that Timi arrives in Lagos. The potholes on the road to the airport hide beneath filthy muddy puddles, and the only option is to move slowly through near-standstill traffic punctuated by drenched and exhausted hawkers, most of them with gaunt child faces, hawking their wares of roasted groundnuts, Gala sausage rolls, plantain chips. In her eagerness, Taiye left the house a solid six hours before Timi's flight was to land, gifting herself ample time to sit in the traffic listening to the steady thrum of rain above her and smiling with gratitude because she will see her friend again.

At Murtala Muhammed airport, Taiye pushes through expectant crowds to meet Timi at the arrivals gate with a small black bag hot with beef suya, which gets squished between their bodies as they embrace. In the cluttered din of arrivals, they hug for a long time, and Taiye doesn't realize that she's crying until they pull away from each other and Timi wipes tears from her hot face before wiping his own tears away. He is leaner, his shoulders seeming broader now that the rest of his body is trimmer. A short thick beard covers the bottom half of his face, yet his gestures are the same, and so is the roguish light that sparkles in his black kajal-lined eyes when he smiles.

"Tell. Me. Everything," they say simultaneously, and throw their heads back laughing.

"Okay," Taiye says, handing him the bag of suya, "you go first."

On the drive back to the Island, Timi tells Taiye that almost a week after he failed to end his life, he woke up in the ICU hooked to an IV, to the sound of his mother's soft voice crying prayers at his side. Fear and grief had aged her rapidly so that her face was slack with deep laugh lines carved like brackets on either side of her mouth, and fine wrinkles creased her forehead. She praised the Lord when she saw his eyes flutter open, and then she told Timi that her kind and merciful God had given him another chance at life, and she would not stand by; in fact, it would render her an utter failure as a mother if she couldn't guide him away from his life of homosexual sin. All this within five minutes of him waking up.

"I knew then that I'd rather stay in the psych ward than go home with her," he says with his eyes fixed on Taiye.

"I'm sorry, love."

"No, don't be." Shaking his head, he continues, "I left London after I got back on my feet."

"She ... I think she just wanted to protect you. She loves you." Stating the obvious leaves Taiye feeling daft. She touches Timi's arm and offers an apologetic smile.

"I know. Her love is just too heavy, that's all." He shrugs, looking out the window at the drenched cacophony of contradictions that is Lagos.

They move on to lighter topics, more laughter—despite the bass thrum of heartache, deep belly rumbling laughter. And then Timi sees the house and says, "Damn."

Taiye sees her childhood home through Timi's eyes: the three storeys, the massive windows slatted with frosted louvres, the wrought-iron balconies, the oversized mahogany front door, the magnificent trees—almond, palm nut, mango, guava, coconut, hibiscus and frangipani, plantain palms, rows of Ixora hedges.

"Welcome," Taiye says, and brings the car to a halt under the blue-canopied garage.

IN THE LATE EVENING HUSH OF THE LIVING ROOM, Kambirinachi is sprawled on the sofa reading the day's *Punch* newspaper. Kehinde is on the floor near her mother's feet, her knees drawn up to her chest with a sketch pad resting against them. And Farouq is hunched over his laptop at the dining table, typing rapidly. A woman's voice rises from the old radio on the floor beside Kehinde, breaking the nine o'clock news, just as Taiye leads Timi inside the house.

"Family," she says, though the word ambles its way awkwardly out of her mouth, "this is Timi," with an arm wound around his waist.

"A boy?" Kambirinachi raises an eyebrow, mischief all over her face.

"A friend," Taiye replies, tilting her head and rolling her eyes at her mother.

"Good afternoon, ma," Timi greets her with a hand to his chest and a slight bow.

"Welcome." Kambirinachi smiles. She gets up to embrace him, saying, "I rarely meet my daughters' friends."

"That's because we have so few of them for you to meet." Kehinde rises and shakes Timi's hand. "Nice to meet you," she says. "This is my husband, Farouq."

Farouq removes his glasses distractedly and joins them, shaking Timi's hand as well. "Good to meet you. How was your flight?"

"It was a flight." Timi is flirtatious, his words music. "I hear we're planning a party?"

"Yes." Farouq takes Kehinde's hand. "I guess we're renewing our vows?"

"Is that a question?" Kehinde snaps playfully. "It's just a small wedding party because Mami and Taiye missed the last one."

"I don't think we had a choice in the mat—" Kambirinachi starts to say, but Taiye interrupts with a gentle, "Stop, Mami."

"Anyway," Kehinde continues, "it's also a baby shower."

"Congratulations!"

"Thank you."

Kehinde is showing, though her bump is hidden underneath the bright flowing fabric of one of their mother's tie-dye bubus. Her joy is undeniable now.

AS IF ON REQUEST, dazzling sunshine is coupled with a cool breeze on the day of Kehinde and Farouq's wedding party. The guests are few: Isabella and Toki (seemingly reconciled), Star and a blindingly handsome friend he introduces as Mukhtar, Dr Savage and her nieces, and a handful of Kambirinachi's friends from the church bookstore. The guests join the twins, their mother, Farouq, and Timi under the tree-dappled late-afternoon sunlight in the backyard to eat and shower the couple with good wishes.

Kehinde is a vision in a pale coral tiered eyelet lace dress that lifts at her belly. Her thick hair muscled into a coronet braid and adorned with tiny Ixora flowers that match her lipstick. Farouq is in a white kaftan embroidered at the edges in gold thread, he is clean-shaven, and beaming with his eyes fixed on his wife.

The smile of sheer delight on Kehinde's face at the sight of the feast that Taiye and Timi prepared sends a thrill of satisfaction through Taiye.

"Taiye, thank you for making all this food," Kehinde says to her sister. "For putting this whole thing together."

Taiye waves Kehinde's sincerity away.

"Thank you, everyone, for coming," Kehinde continues. "I haven't been home in a long time, I didn't dream that we"—she gestures to Farouq—"would get to celebrate with my sister and our mother."

No one but Taiye and Kambirinachi hears the subtle strain in "mother," something like a sarcastic emphasis.

"We're very grateful," Farouq adds, resting a gentle hand on the swell of Kehinde's belly.

"Congratulations!" Kambirinachi cheers, and the guests follow her lead and bless the couple.


"CAN WE BE FRIENDS?" Taiye asks Isabella in a quiet moment away from the celebratory din. She finds Isabella alone in the kitchen, peering into the fridge for something harder than zobo to drink.

Isabella cocks her head to the side and purses her burgundy-stained lips. "What do you mean? Aren't we already friends?"

Shaking her head, Taiye says, "I mean ... not really, we're not."

"Oh."

"I mean, we were fucking not that long ago."

"Fair." Isabella shrugs.

"I don't have a lot of friends," Taiye continues, "and I ... well, I would like to be friends, for real."

"Yes, I think we could be 'friends for real.'"

"Yeah?"

Isabella nods. "And if that fails, I could always introduce you to other potential friends." She giggles. "It's funny."

"What?"

"Just, you and your sister, you really didn't keep in touch with anyone from home, not even each other."

"Yeah, I guess it's kind of fucked."

"I wouldn't say fucked, just a bit sad that you thought you couldn't, maybe. I don't know your reasons, but it must be lonely."

"So, you and Toki sorted it out then?" Taiye changes the subject swiftly.

Unfazed, Isabella nods again. "Yes, we have." The smile she flashes is somewhere between a smirk and a sneer. Smug and sad all at once. "Will you come to my wedding?" she asks.

"If I'm invited, sure."

"Don't be daft. Of course you're invited."

"And are you happy?"

At this, Isabella roars in laughter, "Oh, girl, you don live abroad too long, abi person fit chop happiness?" Soberly, she sings a different tune than at her engagement party.

"I guess not." Taiye shrugs. "I still think it's important."

"Are you happy?"

"I'm tryi—"

Just then, Timi rushes into the kitchen, exclaiming, "Someone please explain to me how that Mukhtar bloke is so damn fine!"

Isabella laughs. "Star only fucks fine boys with money."

"Star needs to teach me something," Timi jokes.

LATE IN THE EVENING, all the guests save Isabella, Star, and Mukhtar have left. They are all happily overfed, lounging in the living room. Of the music streaming from Isabella's phone Timi asks, "Who's this?"

"It's Ikon."

"I love it," Kehinde says from where she is resting her head on Farouq's lap.

"What's that line?" Timi asks.

"'Some of us have angels, the rest of us have Yoruba,'" Mukhtar replies. At this, all but Farouq burst into laughter. Kehinde explains to him, "Young Yoruba men are ... fondly, referred to as Yoruba Demons when they're seductive fuckboys."

"Fondly?!" Isabella shrieks.

Star matches her tone. "Seductive fuckboy, I like am!"

"So," laughing, Kehinde continues, "basically, some of us have angels, the rest of us have demons."

"I like it."

Timi turns to Taiye and says, "So, what are you doing here?"

"What you mean?"

"For work?"

"I'm trying to figure that out."

"Why don't you start something?"

"Like my own business?"

"Yeah, like catering, or a food truck, or something." Timi yawns. "You're really good at it."

# Kehinde

I AM FIFTEEN WEEKS AND FOUR DAYS PREGNANT. My belly is swelling with purpose.

I've been accepted to an upcoming residency at a gallery in Newfoundland for next summer. I've waited almost two years for this opportunity, but I don't know if it will happen. My baby will likely be too young for that kind of separation, and I don't know if I'll be able to bring her along. I'll have to call and find out, but I've been sketching out some ideas to explore during the residency. I've also been trying to settle in and feel out how to be with Taiye and our mother, but God almighty, it's just all sorts of *somehow!*

For starters, Taiye just won't talk to me about her letters. Her friend Timi is in town. He flew in a few weeks ago, just before the wedding party, and he and Taiye cooked all the food. It was with a surprise twinge of jealousy that I watched them work together tirelessly in the kitchen, slicing, chopping, frying, steaming. They whipped up a feast of small chops—delicious finger foods like akara, puff-puff, mosa, asun, chin chin, peppered gizzards, and peppered snails—ofada rice and ayamase, fried plantains, and coleslaw. All laid out buffet-style on a plastic table draped in old white lace, dug up from the depths of our mother's closet. Alongside the hot food were large platters of sliced pineapples, mangoes, pawpaws, avocados, and sectioned tangerines. And as a centrepiece, a three-tiered honey vanilla cake, frosted in fluffy ivory buttercream and decorated with fondant, which Taiye painstakingly shaped into frangipani and hibiscus flowers.

It all tasted like old memories and good nostalgia. My nausea seemed to have taken a week-long break, because I devoured my way through the party and spent the following days picking away at the leftovers. I'm still feeling pretty ravenous.

Farouq's presence has been an antidote to some of the tension I feel with my mother, but he is leaving now. We are at the airport at three a.m. because the flight to Casablanca departs at 4:45, and it's best to allow sufficient time for any potential fuckery, which is highly likely in Lagos. Taiye drove us with Timi in the passenger seat (again with that twinge of jealousy). They are lingering at a crafts kiosk many feet behind us, fallen back after having said their farewells to Farouq. Taiye hugged him tight, and then, with a similar intensity to their first meeting, she said, "It's been so good to get to know you, Farouq." Looking at me, she added, "I'm thrilled that you get to be parents. Congratulations."

Farouq thanked her many times and planted a kiss on her cheek. Now he's telling me he's worried about leaving me pregnant while he goes to Tangier.

"It's too late now, baby," I joke. But when he frowns, I add, "The plan is the same. I'll meet you in two weeks."

"Yeah, okay," he says with hesitation. "Okay ..."

He is much browner than when he arrived, the freckles across his cheeks and nose have darkened and multiplied, and he is a bit fatter on account of Taiye's cooking.

"So, thoughts on Lagos?" I ask. He should be going through customs now; boarding is in a little over an hour.

"It's incredible." He relaxes into a smile. "I didn't get to see too much of it, though."

"Next time."

"I hope so." He nods. "Your sister is pretty cool."

"Yeah."

"And your mum."

I wave away the words I'm expecting him to say, but he says them anyway. "I really wish you would work through your issues with her."

I've told him about the sense of urgency fluctuating between my chest and my gut that seems to be growing as my baby does.

"Okay, baby boy," I say to him. "I'll miss you."

"I already miss you."

We kiss the way we do when we know we'll be apart for some time, a deep and desperate compensation for all the kisses that will be missed until we see each other again. I'm not concerned about the looks of discomfort we get from the sleepy travellers, but I am moved by the little girl in line ahead of Farouq. She looks to be about eight or nine years old, her eyes still crusty from sleep. She is crying loudly, looking at an old woman standing near the line but not in it. The woman is also crying, but silently. And she is trying to smile at the little girl despite the tears glistening on her face. The little girl is saying, "I don't want to go, I don't want to go" and shaking her head so that the pink plastic beads in her braids clack and clatter. I feel their sadness slide over my skin and envelop me as I embrace Farouq.

I HAVEN'T BEEN ABLE TO GO BACK TO SLEEP since we drove back from the airport. In Farouq's absence, my room is too big, and it makes me angry. Too many feelings in one body. I can't believe I'm only nearly four months pregnant—I feel close to bursting.

It's almost nine a.m., and the house is silent. Coca-Cola cat is curled up at the foot of my bed, asleep. Everyone in the world is asleep except me. Restlessly, I pull out Taiye's box of letters, finger through the many leaves of folded paper and envelopes and pull one out at random. It's a torn-out page with a ragged edge, and it's not dated.

*Letter no. 127*
*Africville Museum*
*5795 Africville Rd., Halifax*

*Kehinde,*
*The Africville Museum is a museum in the shape of a church. It's a replica of a church that the city of Halifax destroyed in the '60s. The whole town of Africville was destroyed because white people love destroying things, it's their*

*favourite thing. I'm kidding! Not really. Maybe. Yes, I'm stoned. I'm sitting in the grass outside the museum looking at the water, the Bedford Basin. The breeze is frigid, but I'm made of stone, so it's all good.*

*Let me tell you about Africville: In the 1800s, hundreds of Black folk settled here, and a majority of them owned their land (significant to note). Despite racist fuckery, the community was self-sustaining and thriving. It was poor, and the city refused to offer basic services like clean water and sewage removal. Instead, the city built a dump, a prison, and an infectious disease hospital right by the community. Lovely abi? The city eventually decided to relocate the residents without properly consulting them! Basically, the residents were moved, some forcefully, and their homes destroyed.*

*The church was the heart of the town; this replica stands to commemorate what happened. This is my second time here. I think it was built in 2012. I came here with Salomé around the time we first started seeing each other. She makes it a point to bring her first-year students, especially Black international students. She brought me here with her kid, Hachim.*

*Kehinde, I miss her desperately.*

*I am desperate.*

*That's the most accurate word I can think of to convey whatever is chewing me from the inside.*

*My apparition buddy tells me I'm not as worthless as I think I am. I don't even know why I fucked Salomé's TA. I know why I keep doing it, though, and it's pretty perverse. I'm pretty perverse.*

*There's this poem by Nayyirah Waheed that I keep thinking about. It's something about being in love looking like all the things you've lost finding you once more.*

*I want to be in love again. I want you to forgive me and come back to me and let us speak the same language again. I want Mami to be well and come back to us. I want Timi to remember me and come back to me. I want Salomé to forgive me and come back to me, to hold me again.*

*But don't they say wanty wanty no get?*

*Okay, I need to catch a bus back home. I haven't been able to sleep properly in a while, need to try today.*

*Mami is worried about you. Call her.*
*Always,*
*Me*

I've decided to force Taiye to talk to me, even if I have to read her letters out loud to get her attention. It's now 10:30 a.m. I find her lying on the grass outside by her hive. She is wearing yellow shorts and the same black T-shirt she wore when we dropped Farouq off at the airport, reading a book whose title I cannot make out, and smoking.

"Are you high?" I ask, startling her as I sit beside her.

"Yeah, hundred percent." She laughs.

"Where do you find weed?"

"This is from Star." She offers me the joint, and then pulls it back with a wince.

"Taiye, I want to talk about your letters."

She groans. "Oh, this girl, why do you just want to stress me?"

"I just want to talk."

"Okay." She sits up. "What do you want to talk about?"

"Well," I pull out the letter I've just read, "here you mention your apparition buddy. I'm just curious about it."

"You think I'm crazy."

"I'm not saying that."

"It's okay if you do." Shaking her head, she takes a drag from the joint.

"I don't. I'm just curious. You mentioned it a few times."

"Did I?"

"You did."

"How many letters have you read?"

"A lot."

"You think you have an idea of who I am from them?"

"I don't know."

"What do you really want to know, Kehinde?"

"Why did you send them so late?"

"I didn't."

"What do you mean?"

"I didn't send them. This girl I was sleeping with did."

"Salomé?"

Taiye winces again at the sound of that name. "No." She shakes her head. "Banke."

"Oh ..." The picture is taking shape now.

"Yeah, she went through my things one day, thought she was doing me a favour."

"So, you never intended for me to read them?"

"I mean ... at first, maybe." She exhales loudly. "I don't know."

"Why did you write me so many letters when—"

"When what?" she interrupts me.

"When you could have called?"

She throws her head back in joyless laughter that hurts to hear. "Are you delusional?"

"What?"

"How many letters are in that box?" She gestures at the box in my hands, and her joint goes out. She pulls out a lighter to reignite it. "You know how long I've been writing you? You know why?"

"Well, I'm asking you why!" I feel my body tense, and my tone grows defensive.

"Oh my God, Kehinde!" she exclaims. "Oh my God, you're so—" She shakes her head and chews her bottom lip. "I started writing them the year I went to live with Aunty Yemisi, after you refused to come with me. You refused to answer my calls, my texts, my emails, remember?" Her voice is low and hard, it comes out of her mouth with thick plumes of smoke that she blows away from me. "I wrote those letters because I was so fucking lonely, Kehinde." She stamps out her joint and gets up, saying, "Because you left me."

I try to scramble up with her, but my body is heavier, slower.

"Remember how you left me first?" I retort, after I manage to stand up. I feel myself growing ugly, the rage inside me swelling and licking flames into my throat. I sneer and say, "You were there, and you let that disgusting man touch me!" I swear I shed some weight as these words tumble out of me.

Taiye's face breaks open. She nods, as if something she always suspected has just been confirmed. She walks back toward me and, her voice softened, says, "I couldn't move, Kehinde. I tried, but I couldn't move."

"And how about all the other times?" This fury seems insatiable. I am standing behind it, weeping. "When you used to crawl into Mami's room at night, leaving me alone for that—that man to ... do you know how many times? You have no idea!"

Tears are glistening in streaks on Taiye's dark face. She sobs, "I'm sorry, Kehinde. Forgive me. I'm sorry."

She reaches for me, but I cannot bear it. I step away.

"If I could change it, I would let it happen to m—"

"But you can't! I'd never want it to happen to you, but why did it have to be me?"

# Kambirinachi

KAMBIRINACHI MAKES HER WAY INTO THE KITCHEN after awakening from a deep and dreamless sleep. She shoos the cat off the counter, where she stations herself to grate some ginger for tea, when she hears her daughters' raised voices coming from the backyard.

She knows.

She walks out slowly to join them. She wa—

*Let me—*

She wants to hold them close to herself. The—

*Let me speak for myse—*

The way she did when they were sma—

*I will speak for myself.*

*I want to keep them close to myself, to my chest, the way I did when they were small. When they believed in me and accepted my comfort.*

*My sweet Taiye looks at me when I come through the door, but my Kehinde's face is stone.*

*I look at my daughters, this split ball of light. It's painful what I've done to them, what I've allowed to be done to them. If I could undo it, if I must be honest—*

She wouldn't undo their birthing, no, but the rest of the pain, yes.

No child should ever suffer that. No child should have to eat that pain.

"What's going on, my loves?"

# Taiye

TAIYE'S BEES ARE RESTLESS IN THE HIVE, buzzing louder and louder.

*Will they swarm? Is the oyin, the queen, okay?*

Coca-Cola cat walks in lazy circles at Taiye's feet. Taiye wants to run. Every molecule in her body wants to escape this moment with her sister and their mother. There is a warm breeze rushing through the leaves above them.

Neither she nor Kehinde has answered Mami's question.

"What's going on?" Kambirinachi asks again.

Taiye starts to speak, but Kehinde's words are quicker.

"What's going on here is that my sister and I are revisiting the time when Uncle fucking Ernest repeatedly raped me. Night after night, while you two slept peacefully in the room down the hall!"

Kehinde's words are knives. Her face contorts in a vile sneer, but behind it is an echo of sadness, so much grief it will drown her.

Taiye reaches toward her sister's face to draw the sadness out, but Kehinde moves away. "Don't touch me!" she shouts.

Taiye tries her voice again. "Kehinde, I'm so sorry."

"You did nothing!"

"I'm so sorry."

"Stop saying that!"

"I can't. It's true, I failed you. And I'm sorry."

"Why didn't you stop it?" Kehinde demands of our mother.

"I didn't know until it was too late. I'm sorry." Kambirinachi says.

"And you?" Her blazing eyes turn to Taiye. "You didn't know either?"

# Kehinde

TAIYE SHAKES HER HEAD SLOWLY AT ME. She stammers, "No, Kehinde, of course ... I didn't ..."

"You can't tell me that!" I don't mean to scream the way I do, but these words are tearing their way out of me. "How, Taiye?! How could you not?!"

My breath is coming in short, rapid spurts. I inhale deeply in an attempt to regain control, but, but ... I point sharply at her. "*You* were supposed to *see* me!"

# Kambirinachi

MY KEHINDE IS A FRESH WOUND.

My Taiye is shaking her head slowly. Her eyes don't settle. They search and search for an answer, or a medicine.

Baby's song comes out of me in a hum, and Taiye's eyes grow wide. She looks at me in horror.

# Taiye

HOW CAN A MEMORY BLOOM OPEN WITH PRISTINE CLARITY where it never lived previously? Taiye believes that she might be going mad. She remembers it vividly now: the fury in her belly, the decision to slit the drunk man's throat, the hesitation, because—oh! It's such a hideous thing to do. She remembers her mami's hands guiding the knife away, then a sharp pain on her chin, and then a song—the same song that has haunted her for so long. Then the buoyant warmth and darkness of sleep.

"I think I tried to kill him." She rubs the scar on her chin. "Mami, *what* did you do?"

Kambirinachi shakes her head and shrugs. "I couldn't let you eat that darkness."

"And me?" Kehinde asks. She is crying freely, her body curved away from Taiye and her mother, one arm curled over her belly.

"I didn't know, Kehinde." Kambirinachi is still shaking her head.

"Mami, what song were you just humming?" Taiye's hands shake; her mind spins. "Mami," she raises her voice, "what is that song?"

"What song, Taiye?" Kehinde asks, confusion knotting her brows tight.

Surely, she didn't hallucinate it, did she? Is she so stoned that she hears music where there is none?

The screen door creaks open, and Timi's head pops through. "I'm sorry to interrupt. Is everyone okay?" he says, looking right at Taiye.

"Do you mind?" Kehinde snaps.

"Don't talk to him like that," Taiye retorts.

"Oh!" Kehinde scoffs. "Sorry to attack your precious Timi."

"Kehinde, why are yo—"

"It's all good, T," Timi says, cutting her off. He holds Taiye's gaze and gives her a small smile. "I'll be inside."

"I can't do this." Taiye backs away from her mother and sister. "I don't know ..." She shakes her head. "I'm too high for this."

"You're always too high," Kehinde says.

"Whatever." Taiye walks across the garden and back into the kitchen, leaving Kehinde alone with their mother.

# Kehinde

MY RAGE SUBSIDES SLOWLY.
   I don't want it to leave me yet.
   Underneath it ... underneath it, I don't know.
   I feel hollow ... lighter.

# Kambirinachi

TAIYE HAS GONE INTO THE HOUSE AND KEHI—

*Taiye has gone into the house and Kehinde will not look at me.*

*She stands with her body turned away from me, as if I am the enemy. As if she needs to protect the life growing in her body from me. Perhaps I am the enemy.*

*How can I fix this?*

*The thing that my child experienced is unbearable. And yet she bore it.*

*"How can I fix this?" I ask her.*

*But she only shakes her head and starts to walk away from me.*

*"Please, Kehinde," I plead her name. "Please, Kehinde. Talk to me. Tell me what I can do to mend this."*

*Her back is turned to me, yet I can see that she is shuddering. Her voice is ragged when she says, "I don't know, Mami. I want to forget."*

*I place a hand on her shoulder, and she does not flinch away from my touch. No, she turns around and rests her head against my chest. She lets me hold her.*

*There is no forgetting, but this—this holding, these tears, this closeness, the way my wounded child is letting me comfort her—it means something.*

# Taiye

"YOU OKAY?" Timi asks when Taiye walks into the guest room. He is packing his suitcase for his flight back to Amsterdam at the end of the week.

"Timz." She collapses onto his unmade bed. "I think I'm a little bit—" She taps her temple.

He chuckles, folds a light blue T-shirt in a tight square, and tucks it into his bag. "Aren't we all a little bit ...?"

"Perhaps."

"Oya, come and help me fold some of these."

"How did you even fit all these clothes in your bags?"

"Magic."

"Makes sense." She shrugs weakly.

"Okay, so why do you think you're crazy? What happened downstairs?"

"You know what?" Taiye sighs. "I don't actually know." Then she takes a ragged breath and starts to cry.

"Hey." Timi puts his clothes down and wraps his arms around her. "Hey, talk to me."

Taiye lets her tears run their course. It's a good and thorough cry, the kind that feels like a big stretch after a deep deep sleep.

Then she really tells him.

A WEEK LATER, Taiye drops Timi off to catch a 4:30 p.m. flight directly to Schiphol Airport. She kisses him softly on the lips and says, "Thank you, I love you, let's see each other more often."

He replies, "Bitch, I love you too." Then he adds, "Think about the food truck idea."

"Let's talk about it properly," she replies. "Call me when you land."

Taiye waits until Timi goes through customs and disappears through his gate. Then she heads back to the Island, stopping at the Falomo market. In the dirty shed behind the shop, where the chickens are kept, she points to a medium-sized brown hen with a large floppy comb and has it slaughtered and cleaned.

Back at home, she rubs the chicken generously with salt and yaji she bought from the suya guys on Bourdillon. She stuffs and trusses the bird before sticking it in the oven to roast. Then she starts to peel a small yam because when you need to make amends with your pregnant twin sister, it's best to have a meal prepared to accompany your apology.

Taiye slices the yam in small rectangular chunks and fries them in fragrant coconut oil. She rips apart lettuce leaves and quarters ripe tomatoes to make a salad with soft-boiled eggs and ribbons of carrot and radishes. For dessert, she mashes overripe plantains with eggs, flour, and yeast for mosa to serve alongside fresh juicy mangoes.

Then she searches for Kehinde.

# Kehinde

IT'S BEEN ABOUT A WEEK since my outburst in the garden, and Taiye has been steering clear of me since.

Mami and I, however, have spent some real time together. We went to Jakande Art Market to buy new waist beads, as I've rapidly outgrown my old ones. I picked five strands of translucent green, gold, and red beads long enough to encircle my expanding waistline twice, and Mami paid for them. She told me about my grandparents, about growing up in Abeokuta and Ife.

Now that we're home, she says, "I have to show you something!"

She leads me to the large closet by her bed and pulls out a big battered red suitcase with frayed seams and a broken metal zipper. She struggles to unzip it, so I squat beside her to help. Inside, preserved between sheets of wax paper, are stacks of iridescent paintings: bright and expressive renderings of greenery, trees, still lifes, and many many portraits of Papa, Taiye, and me.

I have no memories of her making art, but here they are, each piece with her sloppy signature: *Kambirinachi Adejide.*

"Mami, these are incredible."

She nods. "Thank you." She is beaming.

"The style—the quality of the brush strokes, the treatment, the way you use light and negative space, I do this too."

This is where I got it. From her.

She nods again. "I know."

"Thank you so much for showing these to me."

"You can keep some of them, if you want."

"Really?"

"Yes." She takes out one of Taiye and me asleep in each other's arms. We look to be about six years old. Our faces are identical. "Especially this one."

I look at the painting for a long time. "Thank you," I say again.

"I love you very much, Kehinde," she says. "Please remember this truth."

"I know," I say. "I wish you'd talked to me about it, about what happened."

"I should have." Kambirinachi shakes her head. "I failed. And I'm sorry, my dear. You didn't deserve it."

These words, my God ... "Thank you, Mami."


I AM STILL IN MAMI'S ROOM, poring over her paintings, when Taiye knocks at the door.

"Good evening, Mami," she says. "Kehinde, may I speak to you for a moment?" Her tone is formal, and she seems sober. When I am silent, she adds, "Please?"

Mami looks from me to her with a faint smile illuminating her face.

I follow Taiye slowly, past Coca-Cola cat curled up smack in the middle of the staircase, to the kitchen, where the delicious smell of yaji and chicken greets us.

And then I see the small feast that Taiye has prepared for us. A golden-brown roast chicken sits at the centre of the table, a bowl of salad, a platter of fried yams, a plate of mosa and thick mango slices.

"How's your tummy?" she asks. "I mean, does any of this make you want to vomit?"

"No, it makes me hungry."

"Okay, good." She arranges two place settings and says, "Please sit."

My mouth is watering.

"Thigh, breast?" she asks.

"All," I joke, but she doesn't smile. Instead, she carves a thigh, a large chunk of the breast, and a wing, and places them on my plate. After she serves herself, she sits, and I expect her to make the sign of the cross the way our father always did before meals, but she only looks at me with sad eyes.

"What's up, Taiye?" I ask.

"We haven't really spoken since the garden the other day."

"You've been avoiding me." I don't mean to be so short, yet the words jump out of me with sharpness.

"Yeah." She nods. "Kehinde, I want you to forgive me," she says. "You don't have to do it right now, but I really hope that you do eventually."

"I—"

"Please let me finish." She sniffs and spreads her palms open on either side of her plate. "I'm so sorry about what happened to you. I hate it, and it haunts me, and I wish it never happened."

She shakes her head, and then adds, "And it wasn't my fault."

Tears slide slowly down her cheeks. "I was a child, too. I wanted to stop him, but I froze, and I'm sorry. I didn't know, at least not entirely consciously, that he'd been doing that to you all along, and I'm sorry. I need you to forgive me."

Taiye doesn't wipe her tears away. She keeps her palms facing upward and looks me right in the eyes. "I understand that you blame me. I blamed myself for a long time, but I need you to forgive me ... I miss you *all* the time. You're all the good parts, and I don't want to continue like this," she gestures at the space between us, "with this emptiness. I don't want to write letters that I never send. I just want to be sisters again."

I hadn't noticed there was a tight ball in my chest until it starts to loosen. The urgency in my gut is satiated. I place each of my hands in Taiye's open palms, and I say, "I don't blame you. I'm just wounded."

"I know," she sobs.

"I'm sorry that I left you," I say, and I mean it. "All that time away, I didn't know how much it mattered to me ... and to you, too."

At this, Taiye pulls her hands away from mine. She covers her face and cries and cries. She's wiping her eyes and slowly breathes in and out. Through her tears, she chuckles and says, "I guess that's all it takes."

"Let's eat, Taiye," I tell her. "This smells incredible, and I'm starving."

# Kambirinachi

YEARNING TO HOLD THE ONES I LOVE—*my Kin calls that a farce. They tell me that I will forget, that this realm is all illusion, a passing breeze, water swirling down a drain, going going going gone, as though it was never there at all!*

*I owe so much time. It's the choice I made. The only viable payment is a return to We.*

*Come back and forget, they say.*

*But I don't want to forget.*

*They laugh at this, laugh at the notion of desire for anything outside of We.*

*Eyes opening backward, seeing frontward, beyond the beyond. On this side it looks like what some call madness, strangeness. I have been straddling two impossibilities for what seems like many lifetimes.*

*But my Kin, they say it's only been a moment. Come back and forget now, they say.*

*I will never forget. There are many ways. I choose the elegant path of remembering.*

*These days I see doorways everywhere. It seems my daughters have brought them to me. Ibeji can be like that sometimes, busy busy inadvertent bringers of fate. Though they will never understand. They will never understand because their blood flows only one way, on this side.*

*Perhaps on the next side their eyes will peel open. Perhaps.*

*I love my daughters in the language I know. The impossibility.*

*And I must go my way. I must owe no more.*

# Taiye

SENEGALESE BREAD, PITA, NAAN, Agege bread, baguette, brioche, soda bread, sourdough, molasses seed bread, sprouted grains, gluten-free, and many other variations of bread. Some of Taiye's attempts at these recipes were more successful than others. Her Agege bread, for example, failed to match the particularly dense and stretchy texture of the loaves she buys from the hawkers in Obalende. And her naan was just fine, nothing worth sharing, really. She has immersed herself in this task of perfecting her breadmaking skills in the three weeks following a tearful goodbye to Kehinde.

Their relationship did not transform drastically after that meal of roast chicken and fried yams, but it unlocked a door in both of them. They spent the remainder of Kehinde's time in Lagos tentatively peering through this new door, stepping in slowly, with questions and arguments, and quiet times together. Even after Kehinde flew to meet Farouq in Tangier, they spoke on the phone almost daily.

Taiye is shaping a large loaf of sourdough, her most consistently successful recipe, when her phone rings with a call from Kehinde.

She hears Kehinde sobbing on the other end of the line and asks, "What's wrong?"

"They won't let me travel!" Kehinde cries.

"Huh?"

"We're at the airport, and they won't let me fly back to Montreal." She hiccups. "They say I'm too pregnant and I can't fly."

"Can they do that?"

"Yes, but only if I'm more than thirty-six weeks pregnant."

"But you're not. Aren't you just nearly seven months now?"

"I know! I showed them the dated letter from the doctor, but they said I'm too big, and they can't risk it on such a long flight."

"Fuck."

"Yes, fuck is right!"

"What will you do?"

"I don't know. Farouq is trying to sort it out now, but Taiye, it's not looking good. Fuck, fuck, fuck!" Kehinde's breathing is laboured. "I'd rather have this baby in Lagos."

"Could you maybe fly back to Lagos?"

"I'm not sure yet," she says. "This is unbelievable!"

"Okay, try to just breathe a bit, yeah?"

"This is so frustrating." Kehinde is trying to calm her breathing. "You should have seen the way they were speaking to me, as if I'm an idiot. I'm pregnant, not stupid! Farouq is speaking with the check-in agent, and the woman is just shaking her head and saying it's their airline policy. I think they're just discriminating."

"How big have you gotten?" Taiye asks.

"I don't know, like, a bit bigger than I expected to be at seven months."

"Okay," Taiye inhales, "don't be angry, but is it even a little bit possible the doctor miscalculated?"

"Well, maybe, but why is that my problem?!"

Taiye cannot help but smile, only because she is happy that her sister called her in a crisis. She is grateful to share a moment of vulnerability with her again.

"Maybe," Taiye says slowly, "and don't be angry, but maybe you could try considering what having the baby there would look like? I mean, Mami and I would one hundred percent fly to meet you ..."

"Jesus." Kehinde sighs. "Fuck, I might have to ... oh God, Taiye, I can't believe how unprepared I am for this kid."

"Don't be hard on yourself, love. You didn't actually know you were pregnant for a bit."

"Actually, *you* knew I was pregnant before I did!"

"Stoned wisdom."

"Yeah, yeah." A muffled noise follows. "Taiye, hold on a sec."

Taiye waits for a long time with the phone cradled between her shoulder and her ear, hearing only the muffled din of Kehinde's conversation with Farouq and the check-in agent.

"I'm not happy about this," Kehinde finally says into the phone.

"No luck?"

"I need some kind of special medical certificate or something, oh God."

"Is this something you can get?"

"I don't know ... will you come here, please? Like if I can't get this thing and we have to stay?"

"For sure."

AFTER MUCH TRIAL AND ERROR, Taiye thinks she's discovered a trick to give her Agege bread that desired chewy texture: scalded flour. A simple combination of bread flour and boiling water creates a gelatinous dough that gives the bread that signature stretch without the need for potassium bromate, or any other dodgy preservatives. She sifts 350 grams of bread flour, seven grams of instant dry yeast, and a teaspoon of salt. After making a well in the centre of the flour mixture, she adds a gentle helping of honey, the cooled jelly-like scalded flour, and 140 millilitres of lukewarm water. Then, on a floured surface, she kneads the sticky dough for twenty minutes, stretching, slapping, and folding it. She massages in fifty grams of room temperature butter until the mixture transforms from sticky to soft and elastic. Next she lets the dough rise in a covered bowl for an hour.

While she waits, she swipes open her phone's blinking screen to find an email, not unlike one she's written and erased several times since she left Halifax, and not one she ever expected to receive:

Subject: Hello (i don't mean to intrude)
Salomé Colette <s.colette@sau.edu>
October 9, 2017, 1:07 AM
To <t.adejide@qmail.com>

Taiye,

I hope that you are well.

I don't mean to intrude. Forgive me if this is the case, and feel free to disregard this email.

I imagine you understand that I've written and deleted this email too many times in one sitting to not be considered, at least, a little bit desperate.

Today Hachim asked about you, and I lost my words in reply. I realize I don't really know where you are or what you're up to.

I've been thinking about (and missing) you. And thinking about (and missing) the casual magic of our time together. I imagine you've moved on entirely. I just thought I'd say hello.

Warmly,
Salomé

As she reads, Taiye laughs with something akin to relief. She returns to her bread dough, which has doubled in size. She pounds it down, divides and shapes it into four small loaves, and then leaves them for a second rise.

With her eyes closed and Our Lady's hands in her own, Taiye says a prayer for her sister in Tangier. She prays for the baby on its way through her. She prays for her mother asleep upstairs in her room, for her father on the other side, for Timi in Amsterdam, for Aiden wherever she is, for Bobby in New York, and finally, for Salomé in Halifax. She prays for their safe passage, whenever the time arises. And for each of them to know, however they must learn it, just how beloved they are.

By the time she glazes the twice-risen loaves with melted butter and sets them in the oven to bake, it is almost three a.m. She will have to sleep eventually, yes, but she will fall deep and heavy into rest, content in the knowledge that the woman who has dominated her thoughts is thinking about her, too. And perhaps there is forgiveness there as well.

LATE THE FOLLOWING MORNING, Taiye wakes up to find her mother standing by her beehive with a serene smile spread across her face and her eyes closed. She hums along to the buzzing of the hive.

"Morning, Mami," Taiye interrupts her humming. "How did you sleep?"

Kambirinachi's eyes flutter open, and her smile widens at the sight of her daughter. "Your bees are pleased."

"They are?"

"They are." She squeezes Taiye in a long hug. "How did you sleep, Baby Two?"

"You haven't called me that since I was small." Taiye kisses her mother's forehead. "I slept late."

"I thought I heard you puttering around in the kitchen last night."

"Yeah, I made bread." She takes her mother's hand and leads her inside to the kitchen. "Let's have some for breakfast."

Taiye boils three eggs until their yolks are the consistency of custard. She cuts thick slices of the bread and smears them with butter and shito.

As she serves her mother, she says, "I think I've come as close to making Agege bread as I can get."

"You've been trying for a while now." Kambirinachi takes a big bite. "I think you're right," she says, with her mouth full.

Satisfied, Taiye digs into her breakfast. "I booked our flights to join Kehinde. We'll get there around a week before her due date."

"Good, I'll have time for a quick trip to Abeokuta before then."

"What's in Abeokuta?" Taiye doesn't recall her mother ever expressing any desire to visit her childhood town.

"Just some old memories." Kambirinachi smiles. "And what about you, Baby Two?"

"What about me, Mami?" Taiye asks.

"Are you happy?"

Taiye considers the question as seriously as she can on a Saturday morning. "I think I'm closer to happy than I've been in some time, yeah."

"And are you going to take this cooking thing seriously?"

"What do you mean?"

"Well, I heard you and Timi talking," Kambirinachi says. "You want to open a restaurant?"

Taiye laughs, suddenly self-conscious. "Maybe," she says. "Or, like, a food truck, or catering." She shakes her head. "Something like that."

"I think you should do it."

"We'll see ..."

"No, we'll *do*," Kambirinachi says.

Mildly taken aback by her mother's sudden interest in her career, Taiye says, "Yes, Ma. We'll do."

THE SUN IS BLAZING HIGH ABOVE, and the sand almost burns Taiye's feet. She strips down to her underwear and stands on the shore, letting the cool seawater lick her feet. Our Lady nudges her farther into the ocean, and she steps in until she is waist deep and the water lifts and carries her forward. She floats face up, squinting against the sun and the sting of salt water.

*It could actually be okay after all your wahala,* Our Lady says, floating beside Taiye.

They are at White Sands, a private beach where Taiye pitched her idea of a food truck on the boardwalk to the manager, a university friend of Isabella's.

"I suppose it could," Taiye says. Then she laughs and laughs and laughs.

Subject: Re: Hello (i don't mean to intrude)
Taiye Adejide <t.adejide@qmail.com>
October 19, 2017, 11:49 PM
To <s.colette@sau.edu>

Salomé,

There are a lot of things I want to say, but I will start with the following:

I'm sorry I crossed that line.

I think of you and miss you all the time.

I'm in Lagos, at home, drawing up plans for a food truck and hanging out with my mother.

If you're open to it, I'd love to talk on the phone sometime.

No pressure.

My love to Hachim.

Always,
Taiye.

# Kehinde

TANGIER IS AN ANCIENT AND FASCINATING CITY, as beautiful as it is old. Those first few weeks, while Farouq spent his days interviewing scholars and activists, I happily explored the Kasbah, the Grande Mosquée, St. Andrew's Church. I saw as many films as I could at Cinéma Rif, I visited the American Legation, I walked along the stunning beach. I cried at the sparkling blue ocean and let the gentle waves lick my swollen feet. I ate everything I could imagine eating without promptly vomiting. I took pictures and smiled. I even started a glass bead collage of Farouq floating in a pool of orange juice—Morocco might very well have the best oranges in the world.

Then I was ready to go back to Montreal, to rest until this big baby pops out of my sore body, but no, apparently, I'm too big to fly.

And now I hate it here. My hatred is irrational and unreliable, of course; it only reared its silly head when I became trapped here.

It's been almost three weeks since that day at the airport, and Farouq is taking this forced stay as an opportunity to continue his research, and I swear, I might strangle his positive-thinking-make-the-best-of-an-inconvenient-situation neck! The good news is that we've found a private hospital that won't force us into bankruptcy, and Mami and Taiye will be joining us here a week before my due date.

Taiye and I have been talking almost every day. When she answers the phone today, her voice is sunny.

"Ugh," I say. "I don't want to ruin your day with my whining."

"Ruin away," she says.

And I intend to. I mean to tell her how frustrating it feels to feel so frustrated all the time, but just as I start to speak, I feel wetness pour out from between my legs onto the ugly bright orange carpet of the living room. At the same moment, Farouq comes through the front door, sweaty and sunburned.

"Fuck," I say to both of them.

"What's wrong?" they ask simultaneously.

"I think my water just broke."

# Kambirinachi

Oke oshimmiri anokataghi rie onye obula nke o na-ahughi ukwu ya anya.

*The ocean never swallows a person whose leg it does not touch.*

She willingly waded into the ocean of this human life and has thus been swallowed and devoured and devoured. But oh, she would do it again and again, if only to give her twins a taste of this life. And they *are* tasting it—feasting on it, in fact.

And she is ready to go home.

At this, her Kin rush forth in joy.

ON HER TRIP TO ABEOKUTA, she takes a cabu cabu to her childhood home. There she finds nothing but wild greenness covering the foundation where the house once stood. She walks through the green, paces through where she remembers each room used to be. Here the tiny living room, here the even tinier kitchen, here her parents' bedroom, her room, the bush of a backyard with the borehole. She thinks of her mother. She is sad to have driven the woman away with her very nature.

She doesn't regret this life, but it hurts, nonetheless.

Kambirinachi hails another cabu cabu and pays the old man driving a thick wad of cash to take her the hour and a half to the Ogun River. On the drive, she takes out a sandwich. Taiye made it for her to take on her trip, asking to join her mother as she piled lettuce, tomato, shredded chicken, and a dollop of shito on two thick buttered slices of her Agege bread. Kambirinachi told Taiye that she needed to go alone.

At the river, she polishes off the remainder of the snacks that Taiye packed her—

313

*I am full to bursting, but I eat the diced mangoes and the thick slice of buttery honey caramel cake. I step into the mouth of the brown river. I walk in until the ancient waters cover me, and then I leave my body empty and float into the vast sky. I float along a seam of light that leads me to my daughters so that I see Kehinde, crouched on the floor in the sparsely furnished flat in Tangier, a small pool of liquid between her bare and swollen feet. Farouq squats beside her, rubbing her back, trying to help her up. She is on the phone with her sister, crying, crying out. I see Taiye, standing in the kitchen of our home in Lagos, hands caked in thick globs of bread dough. She is on the phone with her sister, crying, listening.*

*"I can't do this!" Kehinde cries into the phone pressed hot against her ear. "I can't ..." Her voice strains from the pain of her contraction.*

*"You one hundred perce—" Taiye starts to say.*

*Kehinde shrieks, "You left me!"*

*"I'm right here." Taiye speaks gently, trying to bury the bubble of tears in her voice. "I never left you."*

*At the next contraction, Kehinde whimpers and collapses back into a crouch. Farouq goes down with her, holding her.*

*"Mami." The painful knot in Kehinde's abdomen tightens tightens, rigid muscles clenched painfully over many hard needles. Then they loosen. "Where is she?"*

*"She's on a trip to Abeokuta," Taiye answers. "But she's with us." Taiye isn't sure what she means by that, but she says it, and Kehinde hears it, and it means something to her, too.*

*Kehinde inhales and pushes. Inhales and pushes. Inhales and pushes. The conditions are ideal, and her body moves according to its design. The baby begins to slide out of her. Farouq frantically places pillows, sheets, and towels around her.*

*And I am here, above them. I recognize the life making its way through my daughter. I recognize Baby's song. I sigh, relieved that Baby has found a door through which to come. My girls will be all right. My girls will be all right.*

*I fly into the open arms of my Kin.*

*I rest.*

# Acknowledgments

I AM IMMENSELY GRATEFUL TO MY FAMILY—blood and chosen—for their unwavering love and support. Big love, and thank you, to my grandmother, who often seems to be writing something—letters, queries, etc., and always thought I would write a book one day. Big love to my brother Ike, a fellow storyteller who has always supported my weirdness and challenges me to eschew mediocrity. Big love to my aunties and uncles, and my cousins Chinedu, Ene, Kiki, and Ichukwu. Big love to my dear friends Hannah, Biyi, Monika, Carmel, Alanna, Frank, Wren, Marshall, Christine, Neil, Portia, Patricia, Arielle, Leanne, Adanna, and Seyi—thank you for witnessing, listening to, and encouraging me throughout the process of writing this book. Massive thank-yous to the incredibly supportive team at Arsenal Pulp: Brian, Jazmin, Cynara, Jaiden, and Doretta. Thank you, Shirarose, for your patient guidance throughout the editing process; I sincerely appreciate your support from beginning to end. Immense gratitude to the incredibly generous folks who read and blurbed this novel: Kai Cheng Thom, Zeba Blay, Canisia Lubrin, Tanaïs, and Catherine Hernandez. Thank you, Enrique Ferreol and Arts Nova Scotia, for the generous Arts Equity Funding Initiative Grant that allowed me to do some research required to make this book what it is. Thank you to GUTS *magazine*, the *Malahat Review*, *Winter Tangerine*, *Vol. 1 Brooklyn*, and *Transition Magazine* for publishing my short fiction over the last few years, thus giving me the confidence to carry on writing. And thank you to the baristas and bartenders at the many cafés and bars where I wrote portions of this book.